THE TRIAL

Robert Whitlow

WORD PUBLISHING
NASHVILLE
A Thomas Nelson Company

The Trial

Library of Congress Cataloging-in-Publication Data

Whitlow, Robert, 1954–

The trial / Robert Whitlow.

p. cm.

ISBN 0-8499-1642-9

I. Title

PS3573.H49837 T75 2001

813'.54—dc21 00-053397

CIP

Printed in the United States of America

3 4 5 6 PHX 9 8 7 6 5 4 3 2 1

To those who gather together in small groups and pray.
Be encouraged.

If two of you on earth agree about anything you ask for, it will be done for you by my Father in heaven.

—Matthew 18:19 (NIV)

Acknowledgments

A word aptly spoken is like apples of gold in settings of silver.
PROVERBS 25:11 (KJV)

THANKS TO MY WIFE, Kathy, who believes more than anyone I know in the beauty and value of the written word. And to my son, Jacob, who has a good eye for what rings true. I greatly appreciated the editorial help of Ami McConnell and Traci DePree—it was fun watching your minds work. Finally, special thanks for the assistance of Richard Murray, my friend and fellow lawyer.

And to those who prayed—you opened the windows of heaven.

Prologue

Truth will come to light; murder cannot be hid long.
THE MERCHANT OF VENICE, ACT 2, SCENE 2

CELESTE JAMISON TOSSED and turned but couldn't sleep. Afraid of waking her husband, she slipped out of bed and went downstairs to the kitchen. Her youngest son was a sophomore in college, so she and her husband had the big house to themselves—except, of course, when children or grandchildren invaded for a few days of happy, chaotic bedlam.

She filled a small glass with water from the tap and drank a few sips. Wide awake, she knew it was pointless to go back to bed. Opening the door to the sunroom, she switched on a small table lamp that cast its light against the potted plants and hanging baskets that filled the room. In the corner sat an old wooden chair that once graced the head of her grandmother's table in the farmhouse near Villanow. Celeste had painted it white to match the more modern porch furniture in the room, but it still looked a little out of place. When she sat down, the chair creaked slightly. Celeste closed her eyes, put her head in her hands, and waited.

"Over there! At the edge of the trees." The detective pointed to a spot where the beam of the patrol car's lights became tangled in the first few feet of the thick woods.

The deputy who was driving the patrol car slowed to a stop on the grassy shoulder.

Detective Mason unsnapped his pistol from its holster under his coat. "Shine the hand-held spotlight toward the woods. I saw some movement."

The light moved back and forth along the edge of the trees that lined the steep, mountain road. "There he is!" Deputy Gordon said.

Mason opened the car door. "Cover me," he ordered.

Gordon lifted the shotgun from its cradle in the middle of the front seat and rested it against the doorframe.

"Walk out with your hands over your head!" yelled the detective.

The large figure stepped from behind a tree and unsteadily lifted his right hand to shield his eyes from the bright light.

"Who are you?" the man called out. "I can't see."

"Echota County police. Hands up!"

The man raised his hands, took a step toward the light, and tripped over a large, dead tree limb. Raising himself to his knees, he shook his head from side to side.

Mason jumped across a narrow drainage ditch, stepped over the tree limb, and expertly handcuffed the suspect.

"Get up," he ordered.

With effort, the man rose to his feet and tripped again over the tree limb. As he fell, he grabbed the detective, who lost his balance and landed on top of him.

"Can you handle him?" Gordon called.

Mason stayed on the man's back and quickly frisked him for weapons. "He doesn't have a gun. Help me get him to the car."

The two officers lifted the man to his feet and half-carried, half-dragged him to the patrol car. Opening the rear door, they put him in the backseat, where he fell over to his side, unconscious.

"Does he have any ID?" Gordon asked.

"I felt a wallet when I frisked him." The detective took the man's wallet from the back pocket of his pants and flipped it open. "Here it is. Georgia driver's license. Peter L. Thomason, 316B Oakwood Apartments, Dennison Springs. Six feet two inches, two hundred twenty pounds, red hair, brown eyes."

Leaning into the patrol car, Officer Gordon reached across Thomason's still form. "I'll check his front pockets." He pulled out a few coins and a car key. "It's a Porsche. For the Hightower girl's car?"

"Let's take him in."

ONE

Each substance of a grief hath twenty shadows.
RICHARD II, ACT 2, SCENE 3

KENT "MAC" MCCLAIN checked the time on the grandfather clock that faced him impassively from the far corner of his walnut-paneled law office. The old clock was an antique inherited from his mother's side of the family and worked perfectly as long as the weights and chains were kept in proper tension. As a child, Mac would lie in bed and listen to the old clock's solemn announcement of each passing hour from its spot in the foyer of his parents' home. Many years later he cleared a place for it in the corner of his office; however, the clock's loud striking every quarter-hour disrupted meetings with clients, so Mac disabled the chiming mechanism. Now, except for a steady ticking, the ivory face with its large, black Roman numerals kept a silent, closed-lipped vigil.

It was almost 5:00 P.M. In a few minutes the office staff would pass through the reception room door and go home for the weekend. He would be alone.

His neatly combed brown hair was heavily streaked with gray, but Mac was in better than average physical shape for age fifty-six. Just under six feet, he only weighed twenty-five pounds more than when he graduated from law school at the University of Georgia, and he could still spend an afternoon hiking in the mountains east of Dennison Springs. But he couldn't take total credit for his good physical condition; it was genetic.

He'd also inherited his father's dry wit and his mother's compassionate brown eyes. Mac still maintained his wit, now a facade he hid behind, but it had been a long time since he felt compassion for another's pain. He hadn't blinked away tears for someone else's sorrow in years.

He heard the front door close and slowly poured a beer into the cold mug sitting on the corner of his desk. Except for Friday afternoons, he never drank at the office. Friday afternoons were different. On Fridays he didn't drink to mask the malaise he carefully concealed from the eyes of the world. Rather, he renewed a ritual from a happier time, a thirty-five-year-old tradition begun on crisp autumn Fridays during college days in Athens, Georgia. Mac lived in a fraternity house his senior year, and as soon as classes were finished for the week, he would take an iced mug from the refrigerator, carefully pour a beer, sit on the front porch in a rocking chair, and watch the traffic go by on Milledge Avenue. But today was different. Today was no celebration.

His heart beating a little faster than normal, he opened the bottom left drawer of his desk and took out the Colt .45 pistol issued to his father during World War II.

At the beginning of the war, the standard side arm for military officers was a six-shot Smith and Wesson .38 revolver, but the ferocity of the Japanese soldiers in the Pacific forced the American military to rethink its strategy. In close combat, a .38-caliber shell might wound a charging infantryman, but it did not have sufficient mass to knock him down. The arms makers answered with a more potent weapon, and when Mac's father made the shift from head of the trust department for a local bank to captain in the U.S. Army, he acquired the drab olive weapon that now rested on his son's desk.

Mac snapped out the clip. One by one, he extracted the bullets and lined them up like polished sentries on the edge of the dark wood. Bullets were small objects that could have devastating and deadly effect, especially when fired directly into the human skull at close range.

Opening the narrow middle drawer of the desk, he took out a bottle of prescription pain pills. In some ways, pills and bullets were remarkably similar. Of course, the pills were intended to relieve pain; bullets were designed to inflict it. But for Mac's purposes, bullets or pills would serve the same purpose—to end his suffering, once and for all. Mac shook the bottle. It was full.

How many of the potent pain relievers would it take? Half a bottle? Three-quarters? It wouldn't be that difficult to take them all. And then what would happen? Dizziness? Sleepiness? Nothingness?

Mac had not been able to decide which would be the best method of death—bullet or pill. Each had its advantages. There was something masculine about a bullet to the brain. Messy, but manly. Pills were more suitable for Hollywood starlets who discovered that bright lights and fame were just another path into the black hole of depression and despair. But pills were tidy; no hair need be disturbed, and whoever found him wouldn't have to deal with a horrific death scene. Mac's sense of decency and decorum argued for the pain relievers. His desire for swift certainty drew him toward one of the shiny metal sentinels. The issue remained undecided.

The phone on his desk buzzed. Startled, he set down the pill bottle, knocking over some of the bullets.

"Who is it?" he barked into the receiver.

"Judge Danielson on line one," his secretary answered.

Stepping back from the edge of the cliff, Mac brushed the bullets into his hand. "I'll take it, Judy. I thought you'd gone home."

"I wanted to finish the first draft of the Morgan brief. I'll be going in a few minutes. Have a good weekend."

"Uh, thanks. You, too."

Mac punched the phone button. "Hello, Judge."

"Glad I caught you before you started your weekend. Do you still have a cold one every Friday?"

"I'm looking at it as we speak." Mac held the phone to his ear with his shoulder, snapped the clip back into the gun, and returned it to its place in the desk drawer.

"Come over to the courthouse," the judge said. "I need to talk to you."

"What is it?" he asked. "I'm off duty."

"Just come. I'll explain when you get here."

"Can it wait until Monday?"

"No," the judge said simply.

Mac sighed. "Give me five minutes."

"Thanks. See you then."

Mac put the phone receiver back in its cradle. His hands slightly sweaty, he held the pill bottle up between his fingers. He resented the interruption of the judge's call. He was getting closer to a verdict in the hidden trial raging within the dark brooding of his soul. Life or death. Bullet or pill. He knew he didn't have to go to the courthouse; he could continue the secret trial interrupted by the judge's call. But the spell was broken; the jury deciding his fate would have to continue its deliberations at a later date.

Mac buttoned the top button on his shirt and straightened his silk tie. Grabbing a blank yellow legal pad, he locked the front door of the small, red-brick house he'd converted into an attractive law office and began the short walk to the courthouse. One of the advantages of practicing law in a town like Dennison Springs was convenience. The courthouse, the offices of the three major law firms, and two of the main banks were all close-by. Unless it was raining or bitter cold, he would often hand-deliver legal papers or go to the bank to make a deposit as an excuse to take a walk.

Mac knew every tree, stray blade of grass, and crack in the sidewalk along the way. He crossed the street and climbed the wide steps of the Echota County Courthouse. Built as a project of the Civilian Conservation Corps during the Depression, the large, square, red-brick building with its silver domed roof would not win any architectural awards, but it had a certain crude charm. Surrounded on three sides by long rows of crepe myrtles, it was wreathed in purple for a few glorious months in late summer.

The ground floor contained the office for the clerk of court, the probate judge, and a large vault where the deed records were stored. Except when he had to go to the clerk's office to file papers, Mac rarely stayed on the first level of the building. Climbing the worn steps, he went upstairs to the main courtroom with its high ceiling and tall windows that provided a spectacular view of the southern Appalachians. Mac didn't need to "See Rock City," the mountaintop tourist trap in Chattanooga. He could take in the panorama of the mountains free of charge every time he went to court. During the past thirty years, he had witnessed every nuance of the changing seasons on the distant hills from the courtroom vantage point. This afternoon, the pale yellows, oranges, and reds of mid-October dominated the view.

The courtroom was laid out like a miniamphitheater. The floor sloped gradually downward from the back of the room to a level area where the jury box directly faced the elevated judge's bench and witness stand. When trying a case, the lawyers sat on opposite sides of the jury, and everybody had a clear view of those called to testify.

Judge William L. Danielson was three years younger than Mac. Short and stocky, he was raised on a pecan farm in middle Georgia and moved to Dennison Springs after graduating from Mercer Law School in Macon. For the next fifteen years, he practiced corporate and commercial law as an associate and partner with one of the "big three," the law firms in town with more than five attorneys. During his years in private practice, Bill Danielson and Mac only squared off in court on one occasion. Mac won.

Judge Danielson's chambers were to the right of the bench where he presided. Mac walked into the office suite and knocked on the wooden frame of the open door.

"Come in and have a seat, Mac." The judge motioned toward a pair of wooden armchairs across from his light-colored oak desk. "I need your help."

Mac sat and waited.

Holding up a single sheet of paper, the judge said, "I'll get to the point. This is an order appointing you to represent Peter Thomason."

Mac's jaw dropped. "What! I haven't tried a major criminal case in years."

"I have a good reason—"

"Gene Nelson is public defender," Mac interrupted. "He handles these types of cases."

"Take it easy," the judge lifted his hand. "Gene called me an hour ago. He has a conflict. The pathologist from Atlanta who tested the defendant's blood for drugs is Gene's new brother-in-law. The man is certain to testify as an expert witness and will have to be cross-examined by Thomason's lawyer. If there is a conviction, I can't risk a habeas corpus from a smarty-pants lawyer down the road based on ineffective assistance of counsel."

"But why me?" Mac asked, slumping back in his chair.

"Because it involves the Hightower family," the judge said slowly. "Who else could do it?"

Mac didn't answer. Peter Thomason was charged with murder. But it wasn't a sordid domestic killing or the result of a botched drug deal. The victim was nineteen-year-old Angela Hightower, the only child of Alexander and Sarah Hightower, the most influential family in Dennison Springs.

A friend of Mac's once suggested that the Echota County Chamber of Commerce should sell bumper stickers that read, "Dennison Springs, Georgia. Owned and Operated by Hightower & Co." Alex Hightower's ancestors were among the first settlers in the area after Andrew Jackson ordered the U.S. Army to remove the Cherokee Indians from northwest Georgia and march them along the "Trail of Tears" to Oklahoma in the 1830s. By 1880, the Hightower family had built the first textile mill, chartered the first bank, and controlled the First Methodist Church. During the next hundred years, their economic interests expanded beyond the boundaries of Dennison Springs, and the family moved seventy-five miles south to Atlanta. But they kept strong ties to the area and spent a month each summer at the family estate on the edge of town. Hightower money was the backbone of several major business ventures in the area, and no local lawyer in his right mind did anything to antagonize them. No lawyer, that is, except Mac.

"I see," Mac said. "You don't know a young lawyer who would take the case without caring about the consequences?"

"Do you?" the judge responded.

Mac mentally ran down the list of possibilities and shook his head. "None with any criminal defense experience."

"I can't appoint someone who's handled a few nolo pleas in traffic court to a murder case."

Mac shrugged. "It's been awhile. The last major criminal case I handled was—"

"State versus Jefferson," the judge interrupted. "Three and a half years ago. You tried the case for three days to a hung jury. The D.A.'s office decided to nol-pros the charges and turn him loose."

Mac suppressed a slight smile. "You didn't think he was guilty, either, did you?"

"No comment. My point is that under the Sixth Amendment Thomason deserves quality representation."

"And you don't want to jeopardize another young lawyer's career by asking him to defend the man who may have murdered the Hightowers' daughter."

"Right." The judge leaned forward and picked up the order. "Even though you're an officer of the court, I'm not going to make you do this."

Mac raised his eyebrows. "I can refuse?"

"Yes. Consider it over the weekend and call me Monday morning."

"Does Thomason know about the conflict of interest?"

"Gene Nelson is going to talk to him this evening."

"Fair enough." Mac got up to leave. "I'll let you know first thing on Monday."

"One other matter," the judge said. "I understand Alex Hightower has hired Joe Whetstone from Atlanta to act as special prosecutor."

"Really? Bringing in the big guns for the execution."

"It will be a challenge."

"And you think I want a challenge?" Mac asked.

The judge shook his head. "You don't have to prove anything to me, Mac."

Mac stepped to the open door. "Will the county pay for an investigator and expert witnesses?"

"Anything within reason. I'll try to get it for you."

Mac walked down the steps of the courthouse. He'd read articles about the murder in the local newspaper. It would be a difficult case to handle. The Hightowers would spare no expense to obtain a conviction. Hiring Joe Whetstone as special prosecutor was just one step. The Atlanta lawyer would be supported by a cadre of associates, an army of paralegals, and the best investigators and expert witnesses money could buy.

Forgetting about the bullets, the pills, and his beer, he crossed the street. With each step, the secret, dark thoughts of his own death retreated. Thoughts about another man whose life hung in the balance before the eyes of everyone in Echota County took their place.

TWO

The best mirror is an old friend.
GEORGE HERBERT

AFTER THE AUTOMOBILE ACCIDENT that claimed the lives of his wife, Laura, and their two sons, Zach and Ben, Mac lived six months in the two-story, white-frame house where he and Laura raised their family. Only a couple of minutes from his law office, the house sat peacefully at the end of a tree-lined street in an older neighborhood behind the local high school.

The house with the green shutters was Laura's creation, an expression of her artistic ability and attention to detail. During construction, Mac worked long hours to pay the bills and left every major and minor decision to her. He didn't care what she did; he just wanted her to love it, and her delight was his reward.

For many years he came home for lunch on Wednesdays, a fringe benefit of practicing law only a few blocks away. The winter when Ben was four and Zach was two, Mac would wash Zach's hands, fix Ben a peanut butter and jelly sandwich, and together with Laura they would sit in the sunroom on the east side of the house eating soup and sandwiches for lunch. Later, when the boys were in school, Laura and Mac spent the time by themselves. They didn't say much. Mac talked all day at work and he needed silence, but quietly sitting in the same room with Laura yielded its own unspoken pleasure.

At other times Laura was his cheerleader, encouraging him during the lean years when he first started his law practice and occasionally kidnapping him to do something fun when his business prospered and work became too hectic. Whether he won or lost a case, her assessment never wavered. "You're a good lawyer," she told him matter-of-factly. Her words motivated Mac to make them come true.

After the funeral, a friend suggested that Mac ought to stay in the house and work through his grief, but after a few months of lonely evenings and restless nights, he put the house on the market. He couldn't continue walking into the kitchen and expecting to see Laura leaning against the counter drinking a cup of coffee.

He sold the house with green shutters and purchased fifteen wooded acres ten miles north of town. Picking the highest spot on the property, he hired a local contractor to build a spacious stone-and-cedar cabin that faced the mountains to the east and brought the outdoors inside through several large, plate-glass windows. The master bedroom was predominantly glass on two sides and came as close to sleeping outside as possible while still providing the comforts of home. His nearest neighbors were out of sight from his secluded vantage point, and he lived in scenic, if lonely, isolation.

As a boy, Mac had a male beagle named Buster who spent most of his time with Mac's grandfather in the country. Though small in size, purebred beagles make a lot of noise when they bay and bugle like silver-throated trumpets, so Mac's parents only let Buster inside the city limits for brief overnight visits. Mac enjoyed Buster so much that he always harbored the desire to own another beagle at some point in the future.

Now that he was in the country by himself, Mac indulged himself by purchasing two female beagles—Flo and Sue, and behind his new house, he built a large, chain-link dog run, where his pets stayed until he came home and released the brown-and-white sisters to roam and sniff in the woods each evening. Except during the coldest months of the year, Mac liked to sit on the long wooden deck that extended along the back of the house and listen with an experienced ear to the sound of the dogs as they chased rabbits or harassed an unfortunate opossum.

Turning onto the long asphalt driveway, he drove up the hill to the house and pulled into the garage. Flo and Sue barked wildly at the sound of his car, and he walked directly to the backyard to open the gate to the pen. The dogs jumped up to greet him for a few seconds then chased each other down the hill through the rustling leaves. Mac climbed the steps to the deck and looked toward the west. The sun was already below the tops of the trees, and the shadows cast by the branches reached out toward the house like long, black fingers along the ground beneath him.

The double doors to the deck opened into a combination living/dining room. The main living area of the house was a large open space with no dividing wall between the kitchen, dining room, and living room. A massive stone fireplace flanked by tall, clear windows provided a view of the mountains to the east. The master suite dominated the south end of the house; the sandstone-tiled kitchen and laundry room occupied the north end. Upstairs were two empty bedrooms and another bath.

Mac went into the kitchen and opened the refrigerator. He ate lunch at restaurants in town and rarely cooked anything more complicated than a scrambled egg at home. He fixed a roast beef sandwich and flipped on the evening news, which offered the usual spate of roped-off crime scenes. As he watched, he thought about the Thomason case. The change in lawyers wouldn't be on TV, but the trial itself might attract limited mass-media coverage. The final clip on the newscast was a story about a high-profile drug case in Atlanta. The defense lawyer, a man not much younger than Mac, sported a long, gray ponytail that would make a thoroughbred mare jealous. While talking to a TV reporter outside the federal courthouse, the lawyer slid in a pitch to the viewing audience for future business. Mac shook his head. He doubted an Echota County jury would be mesmerized by the man flipping his hair around the courtroom in Dennison Springs.

It wasn't cold enough to build a fire in the fireplace, but winter was on the way, and Mac's supply of firewood needed to be replenished. Pouring a whiskey, he watched a made-for-TV movie until his eyelids grew heavy and he dozed. Forcing himself awake, he went outside and found the dogs curled up on the deck. They scampered into their pen, and he gave them fresh food and water. He watched while they lapped out of the same dish. In a few minutes, they barked a good-night farewell and disappeared into the doghouse. Mac went to his bedroom and crawled into bed.

He woke up sweating and gasping for breath at 3:00 A.M. It was the usual nightmare. It began in different forms but always ended the same. Tonight it started in peace on a beautiful fall afternoon. Mac, Laura, and their two sons were walking around a lake. Mac looked at his boys and remembered another day, many years past, when they had taken off their shoes and waded into the cold water to catch tadpoles with paper cups. The dark mud squished under Mac's feet, and the tadpoles zigzagged crazily back and forth near the surface of the water. Laura sat on the grass and watched.

The scene shifted. Snow on the ground. The lake deserted. Mac in a hurry to get home. They were all in the four-wheel-drive vehicle. Even asleep, he knew what was coming, but in his unconscious state he could not stop the projector from flashing the scenes that came before his eyes. He looked at the boys sitting in the backseat. They were watching out the windows as flakes fell. He glanced at Laura, who smiled, reached out, and laid her hand on his shoulder. His heart beat faster, and he tried to turn his head away from the pictures that started coming more rapidly. The line between dream and reality blurred. Mac gripped the steering wheel and slammed his foot down on the brake pedal. Blackness descended. Mac didn't see the horror but felt its presence and knew what lay behind the veil. In the dream, he screamed. In his sleep he moaned and woke up. Immediately, his hand went to Laura's side of the bed and came up empty.

Splashing his face at the bathroom sink, he tried to wash away the guilt and grief neither water nor time could erase.

Several hours later, the morning sun flooded the bedroom with light. Mac rolled over for an extra few minutes of semiconsciousness before stumbling into the kitchen to fix a cup of black coffee. After a few sips the phone rang.

"Hello," he mumbled.

"Has the sun come up in the far north?" a deep voice asked.

"Barely," Mac answered. "I've not finished my first cup of coffee."

"I'm way ahead of you. Peggy fixed my favorite breakfast—I've already eaten three fried eggs, a couple of sausage patties, and several biscuits. I wanted to come out to see you this morning. How about breakfast in bed?"

"A single sausage patty on a flaky biscuit would be nice."

"The delivery truck will leave as soon as I put in a quart of oil."

Mac took a bigger gulp of coffee and came fully awake. "Ray, could you bring your chain saw and splitting maul? I was going to cut some firewood this morning."

"I'll wear my woodcutting overalls."

Mac and Ray Morrison had known each other since Mrs. Warlick's second grade class. They played next to each other on the offensive line for the high school football team and during the summers fished for rainbow trout in the cold water of mountain streams. After graduation, Ray married Peggy and joined the Marine Corps. After a few years in Korea and a tour of duty during the earliest days of the war in Vietnam, Ray returned home and moved to a neighboring county where he worked as a deputy for the local sheriff's department. He rose through the ranks and eventually ran for sheriff himself. He lost the election and moved back to Dennison Springs. Mac encouraged him to try his hand as a private detective, and within a few years, Ray was making plenty of money without the political hassles of being a county sheriff. Mac paid him a modest monthly retainer to ensure that no one on the opposing side of a case hired him before Mac could give him a call for help.

Wood splitting would go a lot quicker with Ray on the end of a maul. Mac put on his own work clothes and poured another cup of coffee. In a few minutes he heard the sound of Ray's truck coming up the driveway. Without knocking, the big man walked in the door from the garage.

"Here's your birthday present," he drawled, handing Mac a brown paper sack.

Mac held up the bag. "You know it's not my birthday. My birthday is in June."

"In case I forget, consider this your birthday present."

Mac took out four biscuits and sausage wrapped in wax paper. The pungent aroma filled the kitchen. "I thought I said one," he said.

"That's right. One for your birthday present. The other three are in case I get hungry while we're chopping wood. You never have much to eat around here. I bet you ate a sandwich for supper, didn't you?"

"Good guess. You should have gone to law school."

"And take a cut in pay?" Ray asked, wide-eyed. "Not me."

Mac bit into the biscuit. It was slightly crunchy on top, soft inside, with just the right baking-soda tingle. The sausage was crisp and cooked to perfection.

"Tell Peggy this biscuit was almost too good to eat. Do you want another cup of coffee?"

"Sure."

The two men sat in the living room, looking out the big windows for a few minutes until their cups were empty.

Mac got up and stretched. "Ready?"

"Let's do it," Ray responded. "One of my grandsons has a junior league football game at one-thirty, and I want to give you an honest day's work before I have to leave."

Mac drove his old brown International Harvester pickup truck around to the back of the house. The truck had a small winch on the front, which came in handy if the truck slid off the road into a ditch or got stuck in the mud. This morning the two men used the winch to drag dead trees out of the woods to a flat spot near the house where they could be sawed and split. Once they collected a half-dozen trees, Mac and Ray started cutting up the logs into twenty-four-inch sections with chain saws. Flo and Sue barked excitedly at the angry buzz of the saws and ran back and forth from the house to the woods. In an hour and a half, a respectable pile of cut wood lay on the ground.

Mac motioned to Ray, who flipped the kill switch on the saw. "Let's take a break before we split it."

They sat in rocking chairs on the deck and drank cold water. Ray popped an entire sausage biscuit in his mouth like a soda cracker.

"Are you feeling any older?" Mac asked, wiping his forehead with a red bandana.

Ray swallowed the biscuit and took another gulp of water. "Well, if I remember correctly, I'm about three months older than you are, but you don't have to rub it in."

"You look it on top," Mac said, eyeing the few stubborn strands of black hair clinging to the top of Ray's balding head.

"I've had my head in too many tight spots, that's for sure. But, to answer your question: When we all get together at Thanksgiving and Christmas and I see my kids and how old they look and my grandkids and how they've grown—" Ray stopped when he saw the look in Mac eyes.

"I'm sorry, Mac. That was stupid of me; I wasn't thinking."

Mac shook his head. "I asked, didn't I? I know what you meant. I've just been thinking recently."

"About what?"

"I'm tired."

"Of the legal wars?"

Mac paused, "Maybe."

Ray was silent for a moment. "You've been keeping to yourself for several months. That's one reason I called this morning. Peggy and I are worried about you."

"I'm not looking for sympathy."

"It's not that. It's being a friend."

A pair of bluebirds swooped down into the backyard and captured some insects stirred up by the woodcutting activity. Part of Mac wanted to tell Ray about the desperate debate that had been raging in his mind. About the loneliness, the nightmares, the bullets, and the pills. But entrenched masculinity kept his lips sealed. Even with a friend of fifty years, he couldn't bare his soul.

"Maybe I need a challenge," he said.

"What kind of challenge?" Ray asked.

"Something to get my adrenaline going."

They rocked in silence.

Ray broke in. "I have an idea."

"What?"

"Have you considered rock climbing?"

Mac sat up in his chair and laughed. "Only if we did it together."

Ray patted his ample stomach. "It will take a big rock. One with steps and handrails already cut into it."

"I have a better idea," Mac said. "I could quit practicing law and work for you as your bodyguard."

"You're not broad enough," Ray grinned. "You couldn't shield me from a bullet unless it was coming at me dead center."

"Well," Mac said slowly, "Maybe you could protect me."

"How?"

"From myself, by making me laugh. Come on, let's get to the wood."

Mac found splitting wood therapeutic. There was a swift finality to it. Stand the log up; take aim; swing the splitter over his head; strike with all his might; two pieces of wood fall apart. End of story. He was always amazed that a single, well-placed blow could split a substantial piece of wood in two. Mac used a twelve-pound maul with a fiberglass handle. Ray had a monster eighteen pounder with a steel handle that shook the earth and shattered logs as wide as thirty inches across with a single hit.

When they were in their twenties, Mac and Ray could split wood all morning with a couple of fifteen-minute breaks. Now they worked steadily for ten minutes and leaned on their mauls for five. Even so, by noon the light-colored inside of the split wood covered the clearing.

"That's enough," Mac said. "Do you want to throw a load on your truck?"

"Yeah. Sorry I don't have time to help you stack this under the deck."

"I'll do that another day. I'm beat."

Ray drove a shiny blue Ford pickup with a black vinyl bed liner and heavily tinted windows. They carefully stacked the wood until the rear of the truck sank to the frame under the heavy load. When they finished, Ray put his maul in the passenger seat.

"If my grandson makes the all-stars, I want you to come to a game with us."

"Just let me know. Thanks for helping."

"And I might bring him out one weekend to play with the dogs."

"Only if you bring more biscuits."

"Sure." Ray opened the door of his truck. "Oh, one thing."

"What?"

"About the job. You know, coming to work for me."

Mac grinned. "Give it to me straight."

"You're too old and weak."

Mac hit the side of the truck with the palm of his hand. "Just because you use a heavier maul than I do! That's discrimination."

Ray smiled and rubbed his hands against the sides of his overalls. "Maybe so. But, seriously, you're a good lawyer, Mac. You've got a gift, and God gives those gifts to be used, whether someone is a cop or an attorney. I'm sure there are challenges for you as a lawyer. Something you can do to help someone else."

"Thank you," Mac said, remembering the same words from Laura's lips many years before and his conversation with Judge Danielson the previous day. "Thank you very much."

THREE

Go Dawgs!

UNIVERSITY OF GEORGIA SPORTS SLOGAN

AFTER RAY'S TRUCK chugged down the driveway, Mac took a shower and positioned himself with a cold beer and a large bag of pretzels in front of the big-screen TV in the corner of the living room. Today was the annual bloodletting between the football teams from the University of Georgia and the University of Tennessee, and Mac didn't want to miss a minute of the battle. Knoxville, Tennessee, the home of the Tennessee Volunteers, was closer to Dennison Springs than Athens, Georgia, but Mac considered any talented young football player from northwest Georgia who accepted a scholarship to play for Tennessee a traitor of the highest order. This year's game between the two Southeastern Conference rivals was played before ninety thousand fans who filled Neyland Stadium in Knoxville with a sea of orange. The score was tied 7–7 at halftime, and Mac held on to hope for the second half. But two quick scores on long passes by the Tennessee quarterback in the third quarter buried the Bulldogs, and the Volunteers won 24–10.

Tired from his morning of woodcutting, Mac went to bed early and slept soundly. No dreams disturbed his rest. When he awoke Sunday morning, he winced at the stiffness in his right shoulder and left knee. But after releasing the dogs for a morning run, his joints loosened, and he decided to go to church.

Mac had attended Poplar Avenue Presbyterian Church since infancy, advancing through the ranks of nursery, kindergarten, confirmation classes, and Boy Scouts before his interest waned in his teenage years. When he returned to Dennison Springs and started his law practice, he successfully avoided all efforts to recruit him for leadership as a deacon or elder and slipped into the comfortable class of people known as nominal church members.

Mac's only religious commitment was to his Sunday school class, an all-male group officially listed in the church directory as the Westbrook Class. The class met in a sunny room on the second floor of the educational building named in honor of Horace Westbrook, a man who gave a generous donation to the church during the Depression. But the Westbrook class had, at best, a tenuous connection with the teachings of Jesus and virtually no interest in the meaning of true Christian discipleship. Instead, the group functioned as an unofficial chapter of the University of Georgia Bulldog Fan Club—Dennison Springs chapter.

Open to any Bulldog male from college age up, the Westbrook class did not discriminate against anyone except those who attended Georgia Tech, Tennessee, Auburn, Alabama, or Florida. A non-Georgia graduate might come once to the class, but few persons other than Bulldog faithful endured a full fifty-five minutes. From September 1 through December 1, Mac rarely missed a Sunday morning, and if the Georgia football team played in a postseason bowl game, he maintained perfect attendance through the first weekend of January.

Jim Lincolnton, the teacher of the class, bought two dozen donuts every Sunday morning and arrived at the church in time to turn on the coffeepot. As the members arrived, they drank coffee, ate donuts, and talked football. If Georgia won the previous day's game, many of the men wore red sport coats in celebration of victory, and the assembled group looked like a reunion of the Royal Canadian Mounted Police.

The class never discussed theology. No one knew or cared whether one, two, or three men wrote the Book of Isaiah. Instead, the Westbrook class saved its energy for down-to-earth issues—whether the coach of the Bulldogs should use one, two, or three wide receivers in a particular offensive formation or what was the best defense to employ against a talented running back for an opposing team. There was more enthusiasm about a hot linebacker prospect from Valdosta than interest in grappling with Paul's letter to the Ephesians.

After forty-five minutes of football talk, Jim told everybody to sit down. That took about five minutes. Then, he read a three- or four-paragraph devotional from a small magazine his wife received through the mail. When he finished, either Bill Dixon or Dr. Ben Swift volunteered to pray. No one else had to worry that they might be called on to speak to the Man Upstairs. The Sunday school dismissal bell rang about the time Bill or Ben said, "Amen."

Sometimes Mac stayed for the main church service. If Georgia won its game on Saturday, he took two coats: a red one for the Sunday school class and a blue or camel brown for the church service. The mood was somber this morning, the conversation subdued after the previous afternoon's defeat.

Dr. Swift stood next to Mac stirring his coffee. "I can't believe I paid three hundred dollars for four tickets to that game."

"It was tough to watch on TV," Mac responded. "I can imagine what it was like in person."

"All that Big Orange stuff; it hurt my eyes. And if I hear 'Rocky Top' on the radio in the next six months I may drive off a cliff."

"Did you know one of the Tennessee wide receivers who caught a touchdown pass in the third quarter was from Macon?" Mac asked.

"Yeah. Someone should call his high school coach and chew him out."

Toward the end of the class, the group pulled itself onto a happier plain and looked forward to an upcoming home game against Vanderbilt.

"Boys, have your red coats ready next week," Jim said as the men stood to leave the room. "And remember what Scarlett O'Hara said at the end of *Gone with the Wind*."

"What did she say?" Bill Dixon called out.

" 'Tomorrow is another day,' " Jim answered.

Mac didn't stay for the church service. He left the educational building and walked across the parking lot. Celeste Jamison pulled into an empty parking space beside Mac's car and got out.

"Good morning, Mac," the small, sandy-haired woman said, walking around to the front of Mac's car.

"Good morning," he answered. "Where's Bob?"

"At a sales meeting in Birmingham. He has a presentation in the morning and had to drive over early. How are you doing?"

"Still recovering from the ball game yesterday." he answered. Celeste didn't seem in a hurry, so he asked, "Are you still helping at the juvenile court?"

"Yes. I spend a couple of days a month serving as a guardian ad litem for deprived children. Did you hear Jeff's news?"

Celeste's son Jeff was the same age as Mac's older son, Ben. The two boys had been friends growing up, and Celeste had spent a lot of coffee time with Laura. Mac and Bob Jamison played a round of golf once a year in the Chamber of Commerce tournament, but the three of them didn't have much contact anymore. Sitting at a table for four with an empty chair was too awkward for Mac. After graduation from Georgia Tech, Jeff went to work for an architectural firm in Charleston that performed a lot of renovation of historic buildings.

"No."

"He and Sandi just found out she's pregnant. The baby is due next spring."

"Congratulations." Mac's most enduring image of Jeff was as the first baseman for the Westside Rockets, a Little League baseball team that had included Ben and a couple of their other friends. Jeff was a long, lanky boy with his mother's light-colored hair and his father's quiet demeanor. It was hard to picture him as a successful professional and soon-to-be parent. "I guess you'll be making a few trips to the coast." Mac put the key in the door of his car and unlocked it.

Celeste didn't move. "Mac?" she asked.

He turned toward her. "Yes?"

"If Georgia had beaten Tennessee, would you be doing okay?"

"Of course. Better than okay. We haven't beaten Tennessee in Knoxville in ages."

"And besides football?"

Mac gave her a puzzled look. "What do you mean?"

Celeste's eyes grew softer. "It will be nine years in December."

Mac leaned against the car door. He thought he was the only one who kept close track of the time.

"Don't worry about me. I'm—" He started to say "fine," but couldn't lie—"busy at work. I'm getting involved in a major case that will take a lot of time and keep me out of mischief."

"Would you be able to come for supper sometime soon? We never see you anymore."

"Maybe. Give me a call." Mac looked at his watch. "I won't hold you up any longer. The church service will start in a couple of minutes. You don't want to be late."

Celeste released him. "I'll be in touch."

Celeste glanced over her shoulder at Mac's car as she walked up the sidewalk to the front entrance to the sanctuary. She missed Laura. She grieved for Mac. He had been at the forefront of her prayers on several occasions during the past week. She hadn't known exactly why. But up close she saw that the spark of life Laura fanned into flame in Mac had died down to a black ember that no longer smoldered. What could she do about it?

She had asked Bob a few days earlier if he knew anything about Mac's current situation. He'd looked up from his book and shrugged. "I've seen him on the street several times recently, but he was in another world and didn't even speak to me. I don't think he was intentionally rude. His mind was someplace else."

"What do you think?" Celeste silently asked the blue October sky as she walked up the wide steps to the front door of the church and into the spacious sanctuary. Nothing came, and she sat down on the deep crimson cushion in her usual pew. She closed her eyes to prepare for the service when a still, small voice spoke clearly within her spirit: *"Hanging by a thread."*

The message was so distinct that Celeste involuntarily looked around to see if anyone else had heard it. People around her were finding places to sit, reading the morning bulletin, and whispering with their friends. The organist began playing softly. She repeated the phrase over and over in her mind. *Hanging by a thread. Hanging by a thread.* What did it mean? Mac's health? His sanity? His life?

FOUR

For such a time as this.
ESTHER 4:14 (NIV)

PRECISELY AT 9:00 A.M. on Monday morning, Mac buzzed Mindy Stockton, his receptionist. Mindy, a petite, strawberry-blonde twenty-year-old, started working for Mac the summer after she graduated from high school. She loved to talk, and the job as a receptionist seemed a perfect fit.

"Please get Judge Danielson on the phone."

Mac leaned back in his chair and waited for the call to go through. In a few seconds, Mindy's clear voice came through the speakerphone.

"The judge is on line two."

"Thanks." Mac picked up the receiver, took a deep breath, and dived in. "Good morning, Judge."

"Good morning." Danielson didn't waste time getting to the point. "What's the verdict?"

"I'll do it," Mac said simply.

"Great." The judge sealed the deal before Mac could change his mind. "Linda will fax you a copy of the order, but consider yourself on the case immediately."

"How long before it comes up on the trial calendar?"

"It was tentatively set for two weeks from now, but of course I'll postpone it because of the change in representation. Let me know if you need anything."

"Probably a continuance in the *Ketchem versus Trustmark Insurance* case. It's on the civil trial calendar next month."

"Who's on the other side?"

"Jerry Saylor."

"If Jerry has any problems agreeing to a continuance we can handle it on a conference call."

"Yes, sir."

"Try to file any additional paperwork on Thomason as soon as you can. Gene filed the standard motions."

"My next call is to him."

"All right. Thanks, Mac. After this is over, I'll buy you a very cold, Friday-afternoon beer."

Mac dialed the number himself. He respected Gene Nelson, the public defender who brought the uncompromising zeal of a Bolshevik revolutionary to his job defending people too poor to hire a private lawyer. More than 50 percent of the men and women charged with misdemeanors and felonies in Echota County met the financial guidelines for a free attorney. Crime in north Georgia didn't pay well or consistently. Most of Gene's clients were factually guilty and deserved punishment, but the pugnacious little lawyer had cultivated what Mac called "criminal defense lawyers' schizophrenia," a learned condition that allowed him to disregard guilt and focus exclusively on mounting a vigorous defense in the face of often-impossible odds. Fortunately, most of his clients pled guilty. Otherwise, Gene would have been more frantic than a hamster stuck on a wheel.

"Gene, Mac McClain. Do you have a minute?"

"Yeah. I'm getting ready to go to the jail. I have a sackful of new misdemeanor cases and need to interview my clients. What's up?"

"Judge Danielson told me about your conflict in the Thomason murder case."

Gene grunted. "Yeah. I can't believe my sister fell for a guy who works for the state crime lab. I guess it could have been worse."

"Worse?"

"He could be a prosecutor from New York City."

"What about future cases?" Mac asked. "Won't you have more conflicts?"

"No, the crime lab knows to flag Echota County cases and keep them away from my brother-in-law, but this one came up before the word went out."

Mac shifted in his chair. "Now that you're off the Thomason case, the judge wants me to represent him."

"You? Why not a younger lawyer?"

"That's a story in itself, but I called Judge Danielson this morning and agreed to take it. He's given me a continuance so I can get up to speed, but I need to come over and pick up the file as soon as possible."

"Come now. My new clients at the jail aren't going anywhere for an hour or so. I can give you a summary."

"Any good information in your file that will convince the judge to dismiss the case?"

Gene gave a gruff laugh. "I haven't had that type of evidence in months."

"Any confessions or eyewitnesses?"

"Zilch. Mostly circumstantial."

"What about your new brother-in-law? Do you think he'll be a good witness for the State?"

"He's carrying some baggage."

"What do you mean?" Mac asked.

"His name is George Doolittle III, but my sister calls him Skip. He's a chemist who has been on the job since January."

"The judge thought he was a pathologist. Is there a problem with his credentials or training?"

"No, but when he completes the requirements for his Ph.D. program next year he'll be—"

"Dr. Doolittle," Mac finished the sentence.

Gene chuckled. "Right."

After Mac hung up the phone he buzzed Judy Boyington, his secretary; Vicki Lorain, his paralegal; and Mindy and summoned them to his office.

Vicki walked in the door, sipping a cup of coffee. In her midthirties, the tall, thin, dark-haired legal assistant moved to Dennison Springs from Birmingham, where she had worked for a big law firm, Kilpatrick, Baker, and Hyatt. Highly competent, Vicki didn't have to be told twice how to do something. Judy and Mindy followed her into the walnut-paneled room.

A conference in Mac's office was not typical for a Monday morning. Leaning back in his chair, Mac quickly dispelled any hidden fears. "Nobody is in trouble. I have some news. Judge Danielson has appointed me to represent Peter Thomason, the young man charged with killing the Hightower girl."

Judy sat down in one of the brown leather chairs in front of the desk and sighed. Now gray-haired, she had worked as Mac's secretary since the first year of his law practice, and they had weathered countless legal wars together. "A murder case. Couldn't they find someone else to do it?"

"No. Given my history with the Hightowers, I was the logical choice."

"Any possibility of a plea bargain?" she asked.

"Don't rush to judgment. It's too soon to consider any plea. I haven't even picked up the file from Gene Nelson or talked with the defendant."

"I think it's exciting," Mindy piped in.

"It's not like a two-hour movie on TV," Vicki responded. "There's a lot of tedious work and pressure." Turning to Mac, she asked, "Is the State asking for the death penalty?"

"No, but the Hightower family has hired Joe Whetstone as special prosecutor to help the D.A."

"Isn't he the lawyer from Atlanta with the long ponytail?" Mindy asked. "He's cool."

"No," Mac said with a slight smile. "Joe Whitestone is the former assistant U.S. Attorney who sent Larry Fowler, the pornography kingpin, to prison for hiring someone to kill a competitor."

Mac tapped a legal pad on his desk with his pen. "I'm as sorry as anyone that the Hightower girl is dead. I wish she were still alive. I know what it's like to lose a child. Unless someone has been through something like this . . ." He paused. "But no lawyer in this town wants to be within a hundred miles of this case because of the taint that associating with the defendant is no doubt going to bring."

"And you're already tainted?" Vicki asked.

"Yes," Mac shrugged. "I took on the Hightowers many years ago, and even though I lost the case, it's never been forgotten."

"But your focus will be on representing the defendant, not defaming the Hightower family," Vicki said.

"Of course. But you can't underestimate the feelings of a parent who has lost a child. I wouldn't expect them to react rationally, and they won't. Alex Hightower may tell a newspaper reporter that the family wants justice, but I can assure you that he and his wife want revenge. And I can't blame them. My job is to provide justice—justice for Peter Thomason—and beginning today, my job puts me at war with their desire for revenge. I stand in the way of all the vengeance their money can buy, and the Hightower family will take my role in the process personally, very personally."

The three women were silent. Mindy's mouth was half-open.

"That was awesome," she said. "Did you think that up on the spur of the moment? I mean, the revenge and justice thing."

"Keep encouraging me, Mindy." Mac smiled. "I'll need it before this is over."

"Anything for me to do at this point?" Vicki asked.

"Not on the practical side, but I've not been involved in a major criminal trial since you and Mindy came to work here. Until this case is over, I may not be my usual, easygoing self."

"Which means?"

"I may act like a demanding jerk."

"I doubt you can be as bad as the lawyer I worked for in Birmingham." Vicki shrugged. "On a good day he made a grizzly bear look even-tempered."

"Perhaps. But I want to apologize in advance."

"In advance?"

"Yes. That way you can apply my apology to any problems or misunderstandings that come up later."

Vicki nodded slowly. "Interesting. Can I borrow your approach and use it with my husband?"

"Sure. I hope it works for you."

Fifteen minutes later, Mac sat down in Gene Nelson's simply furnished office. The public defender slid an expandable folder across his desk toward Mac. "I wish there were more to pass along. All the lab reports, coroner's report, Georgia Bureau of Investigation investigation, pictures, and local sheriff info is in here."

"Did Thomason give any kind of a statement?" Mac asked.

"Not really. He passed out in the patrol car at the time of his arrest." Gene picked up the folder and leafed through it. "Here's a copy of the incident report. I've flagged it in the file." He handed a single sheet of paper to Mac.

Slipping on his reading glasses from his shirt pocket, Mac read the document:

> 12:39 A.M. - August 2 - Norton Mountain Road - White male - 6'2" - 220 pounds, red hair, found in woods at mile marker 46, approximately 200 yards from the overlook, the site of the fatality involving Angela Hightower. Identified by GA driver's license no. 657398247 as Peter L. Thomason, 316B Oakwood Apts., Dennison Springs. Subject unable or unwilling to provide his name or any information about his conduct. He was placed in the patrol car and lay down on the seat. He appeared unconscious while we transported him to the ER at Gregory Memorial Hospital.
>
> Prepared by Kenneth Mason,
> Detective, Echota County Sheriff's Department

"Did they interview him later?"

"He spent the night passed out in the hospital. The next day Detective Mason read him his Miranda rights and asked him some questions. All Thomason said was that he couldn't remember anything."

"That's it?"

"Yeah."

Mac picked up the folder. "Give me your rundown on the case as it stands now."

"Okay, and I'm sorry this has been dumped on you."

"I know, I know." Mac waved off Gene's remark.

"You know the basic facts from the newspaper. Angela Hightower was staying with her parents at their big place on Summit Street. She had a few more weeks of summer vacation before going back to school at Hollins University in Virginia. Peter 'Pete' Thomason, a recent Auburn graduate, was working as a computer software design engineer for Aeromart Industries, a Hightower and Company research and development subsidiary. Boy meets girl at a cookout for employees at the Hightower residence, and they go to dinner a couple of times—once here and once in Chattanooga. Everything sweet and nice. I think the Hightowers liked young Thomason. August second was a Saturday, and the two youngsters left in the early afternoon to go to Atlanta. According to the Hightowers' statements, Angela wanted to take Pete to eat at an Italian place in north Atlanta, Buckhead area, I think. They left Dennison Springs in Angela's yellow Porsche. At 8:00 P.M. Angela called home from her car phone. Nobody answered the phone, but she left a message that something had come up, and it would be after midnight before they would get back to Dennison Springs. Her last words: 'I love you. Don't worry.'"

"I expect we'll hear that played for the jury."

"Several times. Sometime after midnight a guy from Morganton was driving his pickup on Norton Mountain Road and met a yellow Porsche traveling at a high rate of speed with its bright lights on. The Porsche swerved into his lane, and he hit the ditch."

"Was the Porsche going up the mountain?"

"Yeah. The pickup was on the way down. Otherwise, the man in the truck might have gone over the edge. Some of those curves have no guardrails."

"Did you interview this fellow?"

"Not yet, but it needs to be done. His name is McFarland." Gene pulled a list of witnesses from the file. "Rodney McFarland, age seventy-three, Route one, Box seventy-two, Morganton, no phone."

"Okay."

Gene continued. "Apparently, Mr. McFarland was hot. His truck was scratched, and he drove to the bottom of the mountain and called the sheriff's department from a convenience store. The dispatcher sent a patrol car to investigate and radioed another car coming from the opposite direction. One of the cars, let me see"—Gene flipped through some papers—"Yeah, Deputies Jefferson and Logan were in the car coming over the mountain. They spotted a damaged guardrail at the overlook and pulled over. Jefferson shone a light over the edge of the cliff, and they saw the Porsche at the bottom of the ravine. Logan scrambled down the rocks and found the girl in the vehicle, dead. Her purse was still in the car, and they identified her by her driver's license—Angela Hightower."

"It looked like an accident."

"Yeah, but Jefferson was suspicious because there was no sign of the driver and Angela was in the passenger seat."

"Where was Thomason?"

"That's where the other car comes in. Jefferson radioed Detective Mason and Officer Gordon and told them to be on the lookout for anyone leaving the area. On their way up the mountain, they spotted Thomason at the edge of the woods down the road."

"Running away?"

"I'm sure the State will argue that because he was a couple hundred yards from the overlook, but Pete was in no condition to make a serious effort at escape."

"Why was Detective Mason riding with a regular duty officer at the time of the call?" Mac asked.

"Just riding around. No specific reason."

"When they took Thomason to the patrol car, did Mason and Gordon know the Porsche had gone over the edge?"

"Yeah."

Mac ran his fingers through his hair. "If the girl died when the car went over the cliff, it wouldn't be murder. Vehicular homicide maybe, or reckless driving, but not murder."

"That's right. And I intended to argue a lesser-included offense to judge and jury. But there's a problem with that theory of the case. The autopsy shows she died of strangulation."

"The paper said her neck was broken."

"Correct. The broken neck may or may not have occurred when the car went over the edge, but according to the pathologist's report, asphxyiation was the cause of death."

"How was she strangled? What marks were left?"

"Bare hands or blunt object to the windpipe. Just a couple of small bruises."

Mac shook his head and looked past Gene's face at a spot on the wall behind him.

After a few moments of silence, Gene said, "I know what you're thinking. This one gets you in the gut. You know, I have a twelve-year-old daughter."

Still looking at the wall, Mac said, "Bad things happen to people who don't deserve it."

"And there aren't any answers."

"I haven't found any," Mac said, bringing his focus back to the public defender. "What was in Thomason's system?"

"He was a walking drugstore. He tested positive for barbiturates and amphetamines. Minimal alcohol."

"Any prior arrests?"

"No arrests. He's never jaywalked or chewed tobacco. One speeding ticket when he was in college three years ago."

"Any circumstantial evidence of recreational drug usage?"

"Negative. He claims he hasn't used anything since a little experimentation with pot in high school."

"How does Thomason explain the drugs in his system on August second?"

"That's hard to figure. You and I have both interviewed clients who were swimming in alcohol or saturated with dope but only admit to drinking a couple of beers or taking a few puffs from a joint. Not Pete. He claims he hasn't used any illegal drugs since high school and doesn't remember taking any drugs that day."

"Doesn't remember? That's pretty lame considering the lab report and the fact that he passed out in the police car."

"That's his story, and it looks like he's sticking with it."

"Family?"

"Mother dead. Father departed to parts unknown."

"What else?" Mac asked.

"Two things. Neither of which is good news."

Mac grimaced. "Go ahead."

"First, it's not come out in the papers—yet," Gene said grimly, "but the bloodwork on the girl was also positive."

"For what?"

"Rohypnol, known on the street as 'roofies.'"

"The date-rape drug?"

"Yes."

"Was she?"

"No. Nothing. But the drug was in her system."

"That's bad. What's number two?"

"There's an incident from Thomason's past that may come back to haunt him in the present."

Gene thumbed through a stack of papers until he found the sheet he was looking for. "I want to get this right because it is a bizarre tale. Thomason joined the Marine Corps as soon as he graduated from high school. My guess is that having grown up without a father he was looking for authority figures and male bonding. Anyway, he went through basic training at Parris Island, South Carolina. The night before graduation, he and two boot-camp buddies went out to celebrate and met two girls at a bar. Someone slipped a potent dose of Rohypnol in the girls' drinks."

"Was it Thomason?"

"He denies he knew anything about it until the next day."

"Sounds similar."

"Yeah. Thomason says he thought the girls were drunk when they left the bar with his two buddies. He returned to the base by himself. The next day he's ordered into the camp commandant's office and gets grilled by this old Marine general and a couple of his officers on his staff."

"What happened?"

"Thomason finds out that the girls woke up in their car near the beach and went to the ER at a local hospital, where a blood test showed the presence of the drug. They had not been assaulted, but one girl's father, a rich businessman, called the camp commandant. Pete's so-called friends had already been interviewed and blamed the whole thing on him. It was two against one, and Pete was given the choice of a dishonorable discharge on general, unspecified grounds or face a formal court martial. He decided to bail out of the military. Because the girls didn't really remember what happened and to avoid embarrassment to their families, no criminal charges were filed in South Carolina."

"Anybody able to back up Thomason's story?"

Gene shook his head. "Of course not. One of the guys involved is on Okinawa. The other is no longer in the Marine Corps and dropped out of sight. My guess is that they would hurt the defense more than help if this comes to light."

"The D.A.'s office doesn't know about this yet?" Mac asked.

"No. There is no criminal conviction, so it doesn't show up on any database. But if the State finds out about it and learns that Rohypnol was involved, they will parade this incident in front of the jury box and argue it as prior similar conduct that proves Thomason's criminal proclivity."

"That's what I'd do if I were the D.A." Mac ran his finger along the edge of Gene's desk. "Is Thomason any help at all?"

"If you don't mind listening to him deny doing anything wrong. He remembers everything about the Marine Corps incident that makes him seem innocent and draws a blank about this case, claiming total amnesia on the night of the murder until he came back to earth in the hospital with a sheriff's deputy standing over his bed. I talked to him the next day after he'd been transferred to the jail."

"What about his relationship with Angela?"

"According to Thomason, nothing beyond friendship at the time of her death."

Mac nodded. "So the State says in a drug-induced craze Thomason spiked Angela's drink and drove her someplace to take advantage of her. When she tried to fight him off, he killed her, took the body in the Porsche up the mountain, and rolled the car off the cliff to make it look like an accident."

Gene closed his folder. "And Joe Whetstone rests his case."

FIVE

I wonder men dare trust themselves with men.
TIMON OF ATHENS, ACT 1, SCENE 2

THE ECHOTA COUNTY JAIL was the same 1930s vintage as the courthouse. The ground floor of the red-brick building was occupied by offices for the sheriff's department and the county tax appraiser, and the second floor contained the cellblocks. A modern annex added in the 1980s housed the women's cellblock, two holding cells—a euphemism for drunk tanks—and three disciplinary lockup units for especially troublesome prisoners.

Most male prisoners were kept upstairs in six large cellblocks with eight prisoners in each cell. There was no need for surveillance cameras because everything occurred in full view of the four guards on duty in a central, open area called the "bull pen."

The county commissioners and the correctional system bureaucrats in Atlanta wanted to tear down the old jail and build a thoroughly modern facility with no natural lighting and solid steel doors, but the inmates opposed the plan and, in an odd attempt to exert influence on the correctional process, wrote crudely worded letters to prison officials in Atlanta and the local paper in an effort to save the old facility. The prisoners liked the fact that each cell had a barred window that gave them a constant view of the outside world. A man who can see freedom is not an absolute prisoner.

In good weather, the guards would open the windows a few inches for an hour or two in the late afternoon, and the prisoners could yell to wives, mothers, children, girlfriends, and relatives who congregated in small groups on the ground below. There were no secrets, and everyone's gossip was everyone's news.

For years Sheriff Leonard Bomar had successfully opposed efforts to demolish the old jail. Some accused him of being cheap and medieval in his ideas about incarceration, but the sheriff recognized that the inmates' limited contact with the outside world from the second-floor windows served as an incentive for some men to mend their ways.

—

"Can I help you?" a young deputy asked when Mac walked up.

The sergeant on duty looked up and growled, "Babcock, that's Mr. McClain. Who do you need to see this morning?"

"Peter Thomason."

Mac signed the registry sheet for attorneys visiting their clients.

The sergeant checked his list of inmates. "He's upstairs in four." Picking up a walkie-talkie from his desk, he said, "Attorney here to see Thomason. Bring him down."

"How've you been, Fred?" Mac asked the sergeant while they waited. Mac had represented the officer several years before in a land purchase.

"Busy."

"Are you still living south of town?"

"Yeah, I've fixed the place up and surveyed out a lot, which I'm planning to sell to pay off the balance of my mortgage. A neighbor called yesterday and made an offer. If I decide to accept it, do you have time to help with the sale?"

"Sure. Call Vicki at my office with the details, and I'll dictate a contract. The buyer will need to get his own attorney if he wants a title search."

"Thanks."

Mac heard the clang of a heavy metal door and saw a deputy escorting a prisoner dressed in an orange jailhouse jumpsuit down the freshly scrubbed hallway.

The tall young man had lost at least twenty pounds since he started eating jailhouse food and faced the stress of a murder charge. His red hair was cut short, and he shuffled along with his eyes on the floor until he was about ten feet from Mac.

"I'm Mac McClain."

Thomason's dark brown eyes narrowed, and he halfheartedly shook Mac's hand.

"Room one is open, Mr. McClain," Fred said.

Mac led the way down the hall and opened the solid steel door to the interview room, a ten-by-ten-foot cubicle devoid of furnishing except for a small metal table and three metal chairs. Thomason pulled out a chair and slouched down. Mac closed the door and sat opposite his new client. The young man's face was covered in freckles, and as a result he looked even younger than twenty-two. His nose and mouth were well proportioned, but his ears stuck out a little too far from his almost hairless head. He had broad shoulders and long arms; Mac guessed he played defensive end on his high school football team.

"I'm your new lawyer," Mac began. "I've been appointed by the judge because Mr. Nelson had a conflict with one of the witnesses."

"Yeah. He told me."

Mac looked for a sign that would reveal a young man intelligent enough to work in computer software design and gain the favor of a young woman like Angela Hightower. There was nothing there. Thomason sat slouched in the chair. Mac set a blank legal pad on the table.

"Do you go by Pete?"

"Yeah."

"I picked up your file, but I've not had time to read everything in it. Since there has been a change in lawyers, the judge is postponing your case so I can have time to prepare your defense."

"What defense?"

"I'm not sure about our strategy at this time. After I've reviewed everything, I'll come back and we can discuss things in more detail."

The angry eyes looked up. "Are you any good? The men in my cell say I'd be better off representing myself than having an appointed lawyer."

"I've won my share, but every case is different."

Thomason leaned across the table and brought his face close to Mac's. His dark eyes became intense. "I'm an innocent man, and I need a lawyer who will fight to prove it."

"That's my job," Mac responded.

"This is not right!" Thomason raised his right hand, and for a split second Mac thought he was going to have to fend off a blow. Instead, the young man slammed his fist onto the table.

"I hear you," Mac said, inching his chair away from the table.

Pete's loud voice echoed in the tiny chamber. "Do you? Will you listen to me? Tell me! Who will believe me? Who?"

Trying to bring calm into the room, Mac spoke softly, "Go ahead. I'll listen to you."

With less volume, the young man continued, "The other lawyer told me he couldn't help me unless I remembered what happened." He lowered his voice, almost to a whisper, "I don't remember. I dream, but I don't remember."

"Dream? Dream what?"

"About that night."

"What do you dream?"

Thomason put his head in his hands. "Last night was the worst ever."

Mac leaned forward. "Go ahead."

"It starts out happy. Angela and I are doing something fun. Different things. Eating pizza. Sitting on a bench in her backyard. Walking in a mall. That lasts for a while, then we are driving in her car. Once we are in the car, I have this feeling of dread because I know something horrible is about to happen. Then everything goes into a swirling blackness, and I have trouble breathing. I wake up sweating and can't go back to sleep for hours. I lie there trying to figure out what happened in the blackness, but I can't see into it. It's driving me crazy."

Mac knew exactly how the young man felt—his own dreams were much the same, but he didn't know what to say. He drummed his fingers on the table and decided to focus on the known, not the unknown. "When you're awake, you remember everything about August second until the time you and Angela were eating dinner at the restaurant in Atlanta?"

"That's right."

"Anything about the ride in the car back from Atlanta?"

"No."

"Nothing about what happened on the mountain?"

"No. Just like I told Mr. Nelson. I have a gap from the restaurant until the next day at the hospital. That's when I found out what happened."

Mac put his pen in his shirt pocket. "That's all for now. But I want you to know that your cellmates are wrong about appointed lawyers. I'm going to investigate every aspect of this case that I can. I will work as hard as I can to give you the best possible defense. If you think of anything, let me know—anything that comes to you, either awake or asleep. I'll track it down."

"Okay."

—

Outside the jail, Mac took an extra deep breath of the crisp fall air and exhaled. Gene Nelson had been right. Pete Thomason could not provide information for his own defense. No alibi. No explanation. No other angles. Mac would have to create a defense without the help of the only living person who knew what happened. It would be a difficult task.

Pete's dream wasn't admissible in court, but to Mac it was a clue. The blackness in Mac's own nightmare came at the point of his responsibility for the death of his family—some things are too horrible to witness, awake or asleep. He'd realized long ago that the darkness in his nightmare was a subconscious way of protecting himself from the horror of the truth—that he was guilty of killing his family. Was the darkness in Peter Thomason's nightmare any different?

At the office there was a stack of phone messages for Mac on Mindy's desk.

"The newspaper called," she said excitedly. "They want to interview you about the murder case."

"Was it Dennis Martin, the publisher?"

"No, a reporter named Barbara something."

"I don't care if it's Barbara Walters calling; I have no comment at this time. You handle it."

Mindy's eyes got bigger. "Me, talk to a reporter?"

"You can do it. All you have to say is that Mr. McClain has no comment at this time."

Mindy sat up straight in her chair. "Okay. Let me practice. 'Mr. McClain has no comment at this time.' How's that?"

"Perfect."

Mac took his messages into his office and buzzed Vicki.

When she walked through the door, he said, "I need a psychologist."

"What's wrong?" she asked, startled.

"Not me," Mac said. "Although it might help. I want a psychological evaluation of Pete Thomason. The judge said he would approve funding for experts."

"Local or national?"

"Better be local, say fifty miles. The judge probably won't pay airfare or significant travel time."

"Any other guidelines?"

Mac thought a moment. "Somebody with courtroom experience would be nice. Ask for attorney references we can contact before making a decision."

"Okay."

"And I need someone who can act fast. The judge has given me more time, but it's a rush job."

"How fast?"

"Someone who can do an evaluation within the next ten days to two weeks."

Mac leafed through his messages again and laid the stack on his desk.

"Anything else?"

"Yeah. Fred, uh, I can't remember his last name. One of the sergeants at the jail may call with information about a sales contract on some land."

"Okay."

"Thanks. That's it for now."

"I'll work on the psychologist ASAP."

Mac spent the remaining hour before lunch returning phone messages. He talked to Jerry Saylor, who agreed to a continuance in *Ketchem v. Trustmark Insurance Co.* The last thing Saylor's client wanted was his day in court against Mac's clients, a young couple who filed a claim on their homeowner's policy after their house burned to the ground. The insurance adjuster wrote a letter suggesting that the Ketchems may have burned the house themselves, then he delayed payment for months by hassling them over the value of the house and their personal belongings. Mac mailed a demand letter, and the insurance company sent a check, but there was enough evidence of bad faith to justify suing for punitive damages and attorney fees.

He spent the afternoon carefully going through Gene Nelson's file. There were a few tidbits from the investigative file. Fingerprint tests of the vehicle showed Pete's and Angela's prints all over the vehicle—except for the steering wheel. The report simply said, "No fingerprints were lifted from the steering wheel."

Fibers taken from the vehicle matched Angela's dress and Pete's shirt and slacks. But there were other fibers that did not match. Of course, many people could have been in and out of the car, but Mac wanted to know who those other people were and why they had been in Angela Hightower's car.

Late in the afternoon, there was a knock on Mac's door.

Without looking up from the report in his hand, Mac said, "Come in."

"I think I've found your psychologist," Vicki said. "Her name is Anna Wilkes, Ph.D. She has a practice in Chattanooga. Licensed in Tennessee, Georgia, and Virginia. Twelve years experience. B.A. from William and Mary, M.A. and Ph.D. from the University of Virginia."

Mac took off his reading glasses. "A woman?"

"Yes. You didn't say, 'Men only need apply.'"

"No I didn't, but Thomason is a big, intimidating guy. I'm not sure about sending a woman into the jail to evaluate him."

"Here's the rest of it. Dr. Wilkes has performed evaluations on both sides of the fence, prosecution and defense. I talked with Mike Bender in Rossville, and he said she has a good reputation with their judges and stands her ground in court."

"How soon is she available?"

"Her office said she had an open time slot this Thursday."

"That's good. Her fees?"

"Not out of line. They're faxing us a schedule of charges."

Mac mulled over the information for a moment. "Maybe a woman would be good. Show the jury that Thomason isn't too scary."

"How scary is he?" Vicki asked.

Mac remembered the reverberating sound of Thomason's powerful fist hitting the table. "Scary enough."

"What do you want me to do? Look for a male psychologist?"

"No, let's give Dr. Wilkes a try. If she doesn't work out, there's still time to bring in someone else."

"I'll call her office before I leave today."

"Also, prepare a motion requesting Judge Danielson's approval for the evaluation."

"Yes, sir."

Mac popped open his desktop phone directory. "While you're at it, include a request for Ray Morrison as private investigator."

"Anything else?"

"Phone Linda at the judge's office and ask if the judge can hear the motion in the morning." Mac turned over one of the pleadings filed by Gene Nelson. "It looks like Bert Langley is handling the file for the D.A.'s office. I'll give him a call."

District Attorney Langley was cordial. The middle-aged prosecutor had a thick Southern drawl and liked to tell out-of-town lawyers that he grew up in L.A. Then, after enjoying their puzzled expression for a few seconds, explained that L.A. was his abbreviation for "Lower Alabama." Bert had a sharp legal mind, and Mac respected him as a formidable adversary whose casual savvy carried a lot of weight with Echota County jurors.

"Just let me know what time you want to talk to the judge," Bert said. "I'll be in the office all morning."

"Any opposition to the motions?" Mac asked.

"Not unless you get out of line. I think the judge will approve your request."

Mac worked until eight o'clock. He rearranged Gene's file to his satisfaction and dictated the changes for Judy. In the process, he finished reading everything collected thus far. By the time the case came to trial, Mac would commit to memory much of the information in the case—

names, dates, technical data, and information about everyone related to the investigation. Unless calculated for dramatic effect, he never stopped questioning a witness to retreat to counsel's table to shuffle through a stack of papers in search of forgotten details. How could he expect the jury to adopt his theory of the case if he didn't know it himself? Juries appreciated rhythm, and he wanted them to go with his beat. But first, he had to find a stick and a drum.

SIX

And they did all eat, and were filled.
MATTHEW 14:20 (KJV)

THE NEXT MORNING, Mac came out of the judge's chambers into the main courtroom with an order approving payment for Dr. Wilkes and Ray Morrison.

"Mr. McClain!" someone called.

Turning, he saw a short, slender young man with brown hair and angular features walking rapidly toward him.

"Are you Mr. McClain?"

"Yes."

"I'm David Moreland, a new lawyer in town."

Mac didn't keep track of all the additions and subtractions to the local bar. He shook Moreland's hand. "Mac McClain."

"I've heard about you," the young lawyer said, "and wondered if we could get together for lunch?"

Mac inspected the earnest-looking young man more closely. David Moreland's khaki pants and blue sport coat were somewhat faded around the edges. Only his navy-striped tie looked fresh from the department store.

"Thanks, but I'm pretty busy. I've recently been appointed to a murder case."

"I know. That's what I want to talk to you about."

"Why?"

"I'd like to explain over lunch. Could we make it today?"

Surprised, Mac asked, "Today? Why so urgent?"

"I have an offer you can't refuse."

"Like Don Corleone in *The Godfather?*"

David grinned. "Not exactly."

"That's reassuring. Why don't you come by my office about noon."

"Thanks. I'll see you then."

Moreland retreated across the courtroom and began talking to a man sitting in the area reserved for clients.

Back at his office, Mac called Ray Morrison.

"How are you?" Mac asked when his friend answered the phone. "Sore from chopping wood?"

"No more than you are, I'd guess."

"It took me awhile to get moving on Sunday morning. Did you hear the latest courthouse news?"

"What?"

"I've been appointed to represent Peter Thomason."

"Whoa. Did you know about this on Saturday?"

"The judge talked to me on Friday and gave me the weekend to consider it. You said I needed a challenge, so I told him I'd do it."

"Don't blame me, but this is more up your alley than rock climbing. Let me know if I can help."

"It's too late to volunteer."

"What do you mean?"

"I already have an order from Judge Danielson authorizing me to utilize your services. I hope it's okay with you."

Mac heard Ray's chair squeak through the phone receiver as the big man sat up straight.

"You move fast once you make up your mind. Is there something we can sink our teeth into?"

"Too soon to tell. Can we get together on Wednesday?" Mac answered.

"Wednesday? How about ten o'clock?"

"Okay. Ten o'clock Wednesday morning at my office. Keep track of your minutes and hours. You're working for the taxpayers."

"That sounds good. It will be nice getting some of my money back into my own pocket."

Mac spent the rest of the morning catching up his other cases. Mindy buzzed him at noon.

"Yes."

"Mr. Moreland to see you."

"I'll be out in a minute." Mac finished dictating a letter, made one more phone call, and walked down the hall to the reception area.

Mindy was laughing with David when Mac rounded the corner.

"Sorry to keep you waiting."

"No problem. If you're ready to go, I'm parked out front."

Next to Mindy's Mustang in front of the office was a faded red 1970s era VW beetle. Mac saw the VW and asked, "Would you like me to drive my car?"

"Sure," Moreland said.

They got into Mac's car, a large, comfortable Buick with leather seats. Mac had owned Buicks for years.

"Where are we going?" Mac asked.

"You choose. I've not been eating out very much."

"Do you like homestyle food?" Mac asked as he turned the key in the ignition.

"Yes."

"Have you eaten at Josie's yet?"

"Never heard of it."

"It's unique. I think you'll like it."

Josie's Restaurant was four miles from the center of town on a two-lane country road. Josie and her husband, Frank, had transformed an ordinary farmhouse into the height of culinary delight for those who thought the best food on earth originated in the kitchens of the rural South. To Josie, the words *fat free* were synonymous with *tasteless,* and most people who frequented the restaurant believed that theories about cholesterol and diet were a left-wing conspiracy designed to deprive Americans of their constitutional right to eat fried chicken, creamed corn, and green beans seasoned with a touch of salted pork.

On the way to the restaurant, Mac and David engaged in another Southern tradition—unearthing any common roots or connections in family line or friends—by asking various permutations of the question, "Who are your people?"

"You're from Maryville, Tennessee?" Mac asked.

"All my life."

"Any other lawyers in your family?"

"A great-uncle in Sweetwater."

"What's his name? I referred a case to a lawyer there a few years ago."

"Stephen Bevins. He does a lot of wills and estates."

"I've talked to him on the phone several times," Mac said. "Seemed like a nice gentleman."

"He's one of the reasons I'm a lawyer," David replied. "He let me hang around his office when I was a kid. I used to pull down his case reports and look for something interesting to read."

The restaurant parking lot was full of an eclectic assortment of expensive cars and rusty pickup trucks.

"Broad clientele," David observed as Mac parked his car next to a truck filled with sawhorses and scrap lumber.

"Good food has a way of transcending all economic and social barriers," Mac replied.

Mac pushed open the front door. The noisy crowd of businessmen and laborers was lined up, waiting to pass down the self-serve buffet line. The interior of the house had been remodeled into two sections—a long kitchen to the rear and a much larger area in the front that served as the dining room. The activity in the back was open to view behind the steam table where the food was served. Josie was frying okra in two big black skillets, and Frank was sitting on a stool by the cash register. They both waved when they saw Mac.

"It's help yourself, all you can eat," Mac said to David. "No waiters or waitresses to bother you. The rolls are so-so, but the vegetables and fried chicken are the best in the area."

Mac always started out with the same assortment: creamed corn, green beans, pan-fried okra, fried chicken, and iced tea. The young lawyer followed Mac's lead, except he opted for mashed potatoes instead of okra.

They found a table in the corner of the busy restaurant and sat down.

"I want to hear about your offer, David," Mac said. "But not until you've had at least one plateful."

"Fair enough," David said. He briefly bowed his head before beginning to eat.

After his fork had made one round of everything on his plate, David wiped his mouth with a white paper napkin. "This is good. I've been eating my own cooking for four months."

"Myself for almost nine years," Mac said. "Without Josie I'd be skin and bones."

David took a folded sheet of paper from his pocket and handed it to Mac.

"Here's something I'd like you to look over while you eat."

It was a résumé. Mac quickly learned that David Moreland attended Vanderbilt University on an academic scholarship and graduated with honors from the University of Tennessee Law School, where he was notes editor for the *Law Review.* While in school, he clerked one summer for Fletchall, Hammontree, and Thames in Nashville.

Handing the paper back to David, he asked, "What in the world are you doing in Dennison Springs? With that résumé, you could land a job with some of the best firms in the southeast."

David took a sip of tea. "Let me ask you a question. Why are you in Dennison Springs?"

"I did fair in school but nothing like you."

"If you had been notes editor on the *Law Review,* would you still want to be sitting in Josie's today?"

Mac nodded. "Probably, yes. But I'm from here. This town is my home."

"Granted. Let me explain my own situation as best as I can." David captured the last bite of creamed corn with his fork. "I received a job offer from the Fletchall firm in Nashville. It's a forty-six-lawyer outfit that handles a lot of interesting stuff in the music industry. One of their clients is Shania Twain."

"Never heard of her. Any relation to Mark?"

"Different generation. It was a financially lucrative opportunity for a poor boy from east Tennessee, but when the time came to make a decision, I turned them down."

"Why?"

David hesitated. "For a variety of reasons I won't go into right now. Anyway, Vernon Moore called me last spring," David said, referring to an older lawyer in town. "He'd heard about me through a Christian legal network and phoned to find out if I was interested in a job. I drove down and liked him and the area. I love the mountains and didn't want to work in a concrete tower where the woods seemed as far away as the moon."

"That's something I can understand," Mac said.

"We came to an agreement, and I scheduled the bar exam for July. Then, as you know, Mr. Moore suffered a stroke and had to retire."

"Time-out," Mac said, looking across the room. "There are two bowls of peach cobbler with our names on them waiting at the dessert table."

Halfway through the cobbler, Mac said, "Back to your story."

"Okay. I took the bar exam and received my pass notice two months ago. Most of Mr. Moore's clients with pending cases couldn't wait for me to be licensed and hired other lawyers, but he was able to give me a little business, and I have enough money to buy your lunch today."

"We'll see about that in a few minutes. I want to hear your irresistible offer."

"Yes, sir. I would like to work with you on the Thomason case."

"I see." Mac paused. "You're not looking for a job as an associate at my office?"

"Not immediately, but I thought if we worked together on a big case it might lead to something more permanent. We could leave the possibility open."

Mac put down his spoon. "What is your experience in criminal cases?"

"Two DUI clients who pled nolo contendere and a shoplifting charge that was dismissed at preliminary hearing because the manager of the convenience store didn't show up."

"No public defender work while you were in law school?"

"No. Of course, I took a semester of criminal law and procedure."

"And made an A."

"No," David shook his head. "I made a B-minus. It was the lowest grade I received in law school."

"I can't remember what I made in criminal law and procedure," Mac said. "Most of what you need to know you learn by doing. That's why it's called 'law practice'."

David leaned forward in his seat. "Mr. McClain, I've heard you're one of the best lawyers in town, and I'm willing to do anything you need me to do."

Mac took a drink of tea. "Thanks for the compliment, and I appreciate your offer. But the answer is no. Two reasons. First, *State versus Thomason* is an appointed case, and Judge Danielson is not going to spend taxpayer money so two lawyers can ride around in the car and eat lunch at Josie's. If you were a pathologist or a chemist there would be no problem, but the judge knows I can handle the case without legal help. Second, you do not know the professional ramifications of involvement in this particular case. Angela Hightower's parents are not going to be favorably disposed toward the lawyer or lawyers who vigorously defend the man they believe killed their daughter. The Hightower family has significant influence in this community. Their opposition would make it much more difficult for you to establish your law practice, and you need help, not hindrances."

David couldn't hide his disappointment. "What about you? You don't strike me as an antiestablishment type."

Mac smiled. "I'm not a former hippie, but I burned my Hightower draft card a long time ago."

"How did that happen?"

"One of my first cases after I opened my law practice involved a riparian rights dispute with a Hightower company that operated a phosphate mine near a little town named Elon. The mine was polluting the water supply for the community."

"Sounds like a law school exam question."

"It was. This occurred years before the creation of the Environmental Protection Agency. After the company ignored several letters, I filed a suit for an injunction and damages in Echota Superior Court. A few days later, Cecil Hightower called and asked me to dismiss the lawsuit. He dropped a big hint that there might be a generous retainer in my future as a local counsel for Hightower and Company. When he couldn't bribe or cajole me into withdrawing from the case, he threatened to ruin my law practice. I hung up on him."

"Did you win the case?"

"No. But I learned that high-stakes litigation is take-no-prisoners warfare. I faced a battery of Hightower lawyers who filed motions I'd never heard of. They objected every time I opened my mouth and raised arguments I never anticipated. I lost on a technical motion at the conclusion of the case. I appealed to the Court of Appeals and Georgia Supreme Court but lost four to three. Years later, the mine closed rather than face federal scrutiny. But the damage to me was done. In thirty years of law practice, I've never represented any banks or businesses with

Hightower connections. A local lawyer told me not long ago about a memo from a Hightower executive in which I was mentioned as an 'opponent of our interests in the area.' "

"Is Cecil Hightower the father of the girl who died?"

"Grandfather. He's been dead for years. Angela's parents are Alex and Sarah Hightower. They live in a mansion somewhere in north Atlanta but spend a month here in the summer. I've never met them. They were staying at their Dennison Springs place when Angela died."

Mac looked at his watch, realizing that he needed to get back to the office.

"Lunch is on me," Mac said, picking up the bill and signing his name. "I have a monthly account here. It's been nice getting to know you, David. Maybe we can get together again after the Thomason case is over."

David was silent during the ride back to town, and Mac left him with his thoughts. When they pulled into Mac's office, David asked, "Can I make a closing argument?"

"Make it brief."

"I appreciate your concern for my professional future, but I didn't become a lawyer to run from challenges. I want to work on the case. If you change your mind, my offer is still open."

Mac looked at David's face and saw something vaguely familiar—a determined expression he'd seen when he looked in the mirror at himself as a young lawyer before going to court. "Argument noted," he said.

SEVEN

The face is the mirror of the mind,
and eyes without speaking confess the secrets of the heart.
ST. JEROME

TOOTHPICK RESTING CASUALLY between his teeth, Ray Morrison sauntered like a contented bear into Mac's office at 10:05 the next morning. The big man's greatest gift as an investigator was an ability to draw people into conversation. Ray never threatened, never raised his voice. He would simply start asking questions and, like an old-fashioned painless dentist, extract the relevant information from the mouth of the witness. Many times over the years Mac had hired Ray to interview a reluctant witness. Almost without fail, the detective would reappear at Mac's office a few days later with an affidavit or taperecorded statement containing everything the lawyer needed.

"Where do you want me to start?" Ray asked as soon as he settled comfortably in his seat.

"You know the basic facts from the newspaper?"

"Yeah."

"Let me supplement what you've read." Mac summarized his conversation with Gene Nelson and his initial review of the file.

"So I need to see Mr. McFarland in Morganton," Ray said when Mac finished.

"Yes. It's a couple hours' drive. He has no phone, and at his age I doubt he works a job."

"I know someone in the area I can call before I make the trip. He knows the back roads better than anybody else."

Mac continued, "Also, look over this list of law enforcement officers who may testify in the case." Mac handed him the D.A.'s witness sheet. "I can't make them talk to me, but there might be one or two who will answer a few questions voluntarily if the right person does the questioning."

Ray ran his large index finger down the list. "The GBI agents are out—no possibility of the detectives helping us. The only person I might have a chance with is one of the deputies who arrived at the accident scene on the mountain."

"Which one?"

"Tim Logan. His daddy worked with me years ago. Tim is the same age as my son, Larry, and his father and I used to take the boys to the Lake Winnepesoka amusement park when they were little. Tim was a good kid, and I bet he's a solid officer. He might talk to me."

"Give it some thought. No use wasting time on a rehash of what's already in the file. Anything else jump out at you?" Mac asked.

"Naw, but give me some time. It takes my brain longer to get in gear than it used to."

"Call me as soon as you talk to Mr. McFarland. We'll wait on Logan for the time being."

"Right."

Mac followed Ray into the reception area. "Thanks," he said.

"We'll chop this thing up and stack it neatly before we're done."

Mac checked his phone messages on Mindy's desk while Ray walked to the door and left.

Once he was gone, Mindy asked, "Does he carry a gun? I thought I saw a bulge under his coat."

Mac looked up. "That was probably a sausage biscuit. I don't think he carries a gun. He uses a lethal form of karate known as Koo Fu Mu. His hands and feet are registered with the FBI and the CIA."

Mindy's eyes widened. "Wow."

Mac walked back to his office, smiling. It wasn't fair. Mindy was too easy a target.

Mac phoned the psychologist's office and left a callback message.

Close to five o'clock, Mindy buzzed him.

"Dr. Anna Wilkes on line one."

Mac picked up the receiver and in his best professional manner said, "Hello, Dr. Wilkes, thanks for calling me back."

"Hold for Dr. Wilkes, please," a deep male voice responded.

Mac hated it when someone did that to him. He'd wasted his best hello on a guy who probably helped the psychologist put straight-jackets on people.

"Good afternoon, Mr. McClain," a pleasant female voice came on the line. "Sorry I didn't call earlier."

The psychologist's tone diffused Mac's irritation. "Oh, that's okay. Thanks for agreeing to evaluate my client."

"Glad to do it. Is everything arranged?"

"I've reserved an interview room at the Echota County Jail for Thursday afternoon beginning at one o'clock. Do you need directions?"

"I've been through Dennison Springs several times. The jail is near the courthouse, isn't it?"

"Next-door. Do you know anything about this case?"

"No. I'm sure it was mentioned in the Chattanooga paper, but I must have missed it."

Mac checked a sheet of paper on his desk. "I won't go into the facts, but I'd like you to determine the defendant's competency to stand trial, give your assessment of his mental capabilities, and provide an opinion of his psychological condition, including any mitigating factors in case of a conviction."

"Sounds like a standard evaluation. When will you need my report?"

"Within a week of the evaluation if possible."

"I could probably fax it by then and mail a copy to anyone else who needs it."

"That will be great. I'm going to talk to Thomason this evening about the evaluation. I'll prepare him then."

"Good."

"Your office should send your bill to me for submission to the court."

"I have a note to that effect from Ms. Lorain at your office."

"Do you have any other questions?"

"Is the case on the court docket for trial?"

"Pending. I was recently appointed to represent the defendant, and the judge is giving me time to prepare the case. It will definitely be tried before the end of the year."

"Please give me as much notice as possible of a trial date so I can adjust my schedule if my testimony is needed by either side."

"Of course. Anything else?"

"No. That's it for now."

Very efficient. He liked everything he heard except "if my testimony is needed by either side." The State had a long list of witnesses they could call. Mac needed a name to put on his side of the witness ledger.

Mindy buzzed him again.

"Yes?"

"You know the new karate center on Henderson Avenue?"

"Yeah, I've seen it."

"They offer Koo Fu Mu training."

"They do?"

"Yes. I'm thinking about taking it. You never know what kind of nut might come in the office. I need to be able to protect you."

"Uh, sure."

"I'm leaving now. I'll see you tomorrow."

Puzzled, Mac put the phone receiver back in the cradle.

Mac stopped by the jail to see Pete. Once again, his client followed him into the interview room and slumped down in a chair.

"I've arranged for a psychologist to interview you tomorrow afternoon," Mac began. "Her name is Dr. Anna Wilkes from Chattanooga. What you tell her is not confidential and will be included in a report sent to me, the district attorney, and the judge."

"Why a psychologist? I'm not crazy; I just don't remember anything."

"Maybe there's a reason you can't remember. She'll ask a lot of questions about your background and administer some psychological and mental aptitude tests. It's all right to tell her that you tried pot in high school, but don't mention the incident that led to your discharge from the Marines."

"I'm not an idiot, either."

"I didn't say you were. It's my job to give you advice whether you want it or not."

"How is this going to help my case?"

"We don't know. But it's worth the risk to find out what we can from a neutral professional."

Pete put his hands on the table. "Okay. Maybe I need to see a psychologist. I've wracked my brain trying to remember what happened that night, but whether I'm awake or asleep there's a black hole, and I can't see into it."

"You had a lot of drugs in your system."

"But I didn't take any drugs. I—"

"Wait a minute," Mac interrupted. "Let's stop there. How do you explain the results of the blood test, the amphetamines and barbiturates?"

"How do I know whose blood they tested? They could have used a blood sample from a drunk guy who stumbled into the hospital."

"Doubtful, and that doesn't explain the fact that you passed out in the back of the patrol car on the way to the hospital."

"Angela and I didn't have anything except a glass of wine with dinner."

"Are you sure that's all?"

Pete pushed away from the table and raised his voice a notch louder, "Would it help if I lied?"

"No, but it's my experience that even in unusual situations the truth makes sense. Remember, everything you tell me is confidential."

"I don't have any experience being charged with murder, and there's nothing else I can tell you."

"Okay. But if you remember anything, anything at all, I need to know." Mac stood to leave. "Oh, one other thing. I've hired the best private investigator in the area. He will be interviewing some of the people on the State's witness list."

"Witnesses? The other lawyer didn't tell me there were any witnesses."

"Not that kind of witness. Just people who may give testimony at the trial. Do you know anyone he should contact?"

"No. I wish I did."

"If you think of someone, let me know."

The following day, Mac spent the afternoon in his law library, but his thoughts often drifted to the evaluation Dr. Wilkes was performing or, he worried, attempting to perform. It was going to take someone with the skill of Anne Sullivan, the woman who unlocked the key to Helen Keller's dark, silent world, to unravel Pete Thomason's psyche.

At six o'clock the phone rang. Mac usually didn't answer the phone after hours, but he was tired of reading law books.

"Mac McClain's office," he said.

"Mr. McClain?"

"Speaking."

"This is Anna Wilkes. I'm on my car phone, and the reception is not very good."

"I can hear you."

"I just finished my evaluation and wondered if we could talk a few minutes before I go back to Chattanooga."

"Sure. My office is around the corner." Mac gave her directions.

—

Mac heard the bell on the front door ring and walked from the library, across the hall, to the reception area.

The psychologist was in her early to mid-forties, medium height, blue eyes with short, slightly curly dark hair. Professional, yet attractive. Mac extended his hand, "Mac McClain."

"Anna Wilkes." She put her hand in his.

"Would you like a cup of coffee?"

"Yes. I need a little boost."

"How do you drink it?"

"With everything."

Mac led her down the hall to his office. "Have a seat while I get your coffee."

He left Dr. Wilkes sitting in his office and went to the break room. When he returned, the psychologist was standing in front of a large, framed photograph of a mountain waterfall.

"Did you take this picture?" she asked.

"Yes."

Taking a sip of coffee, she asked, "Where is it?"

"Jacks River Falls in the Cohutta Wilderness. It's at the end of a four-mile trail along an abandoned roadbed. I've been there many times."

"It's beautiful," she said, sitting down and retrieving a white notepad from her briefcase. The psychologist sat very straight in her chair and propped some reading glasses on the end of her slightly upturned nose.

"I wanted to talk to you about Pete before I drove back to Chattanooga," she said.

"Did you have any problems?" Mac asked.

"Were you expecting any?"

"Uh, no, but I've seen a couple of outbursts of anger."

"He's angry, but the biggest hurdle I faced was establishing sufficient trust and rapport to conduct a valid interview and evaluation. It took more than two hours to begin testing, primarily because of his depression."

"How depressed?"

"Clinically depressed at a severe level. His depression, however, does not prevent him from understanding the nature of the charges against him. He is not delusional and has real, albeit detached at times, connection with reality."

"So he is competent from a mental standpoint to proceed to trial?"

"Yes. And although he's legally competent, he claims total amnesia for the eighteen- to twenty-four-hour period during which the crime apparently occurred. Thus, from a practical point of view, I don't see how he can assist you in preparing his defense."

"It's going to be a challenge. What do you make of the amnesia?"

"There are several recognized causes of amnesia. The best known is posttraumatic retrograde amnesia, the loss of memory following some physical trauma such as a blow to the head. That's what usually happens on TV."

"Okay."

"Pete said he had no signs of physical injury when he was arrested."

"Right. He was thoroughly checked at the hospital."

"A more common form of amnesia is alcohol- or drug-induced amnesia caused by habitual, long-term abuse of alcohol or mind-altering drugs."

"Did he tell you there were amphetamines and barbiturates in his system at the time of the arrest?"

"He mentioned the test but denied using any drugs."

Mac tapped the edge of his desk with his pen. "What do you think about the effect of the amphetamines and barbiturates? Could they have produced the amnesia he describes?"

"I would like to see the report on the amount of drugs in Pete's system, but in my opinion a one-night binge of those types of amphetamines and barbiturates would not produce the type of total inability to recall that he claims."

"Which means?"

"He may be faking."

Mac winced. "How can I determine if he's faking? I've been practicing law for thirty years, and nobody has perfected a 'truth-o-meter.' I don't trust lie-detector tests, and neither do the courts. They're not admissible in Georgia unless both sides agree, and I've seen cases where polygraph examiners looked at the same charts and came up with different conclusions."

"Could you arrange an evaluation with someone you think is reputable?"

"Possibly. If the results are favorable, I could show it to the district attorney and say, 'See. The boy is telling the truth.' On the other hand, if the evaluator found Pete deceptive, the prosecution couldn't use it against him because we didn't agree in advance that the findings would be admissible in court."

"What do you have to lose then?"

"Just a thousand dollars out of my own pocket. The judge won't authorize payment for an independent polygraph exam."

Dr. Wilkes ran her finger past the notes she had written in her notebook. "There is another possibility."

"What is it?"

"Are there still samples of Pete's blood from that night available for testing?"

"There should be. They draw at least two vials and retain one in case something comes up later."

"I think you need to have his blood retested for other drugs."

"I can do that, but I don't think the police sent someone else's blood to the lab, and I don't want more drugs to show up on Pete's rap sheet."

"That's not the reason. Once he settled down and started talking to me, Pete told me about the results of the blood test on Angela. He said there was Rohypnol in her system but no evidence of rape. Is that true?"

Mac hesitated. "Is this going in your report?"

"No. It has no bearing on Pete's psychological status."

"Okay. What he told you is true."

The psychologist continued, "Rohypnol has strong amnesiac properties; criminals use it because victims can't remember the crime. Labs don't normally check for Rohypnol unless they are specifically asked to do so."

"That's what I've heard."

"Who can't remember the crime in this case?"

Mac dropped his pen on his desk. "I need to have Pete's blood tested for Rohypnol."

"Yes, I think you do."

"Do you have any forensic training?" Mac asked.

"No specialized forensic training, and don't give me any premature accolades. I'm impartial. I just want to do a thorough job."

Mac looked out his office window as he considered the new defense raised by the psychologist's suggestion. "It's worth pursuing."

Dr. Wilkes continued, "My report will contain the results of my clinical interview, WAIS IQ testing, Rorschach, Beck's Depression Inventory, and General Achievement Testing. I can summarize by telling you that he is not psychotic, had an emotionally deprived upbringing, and is above average in intelligence. I'd like to do a full-scale MMPI, but I'm not sure the results would be valid given his current level of depression."

"Anything else?"

"No."

Mac walked the psychologist to the front door and shook her hand.

"Thanks for everything. Especially the suggestion about the blood test."

"Certainly," she said smiling.

Mac watched Dr. Wilkes walk to her car through the large picture window in the reception room.

That evening at home, Mac spent a few extra minutes on the deck throwing sticks for Flo and Sue to chase through the dry leaves. The dogs found a rabbit's scent and, baying at the top of their lungs, forgot about the dead sticks and raced up the next ridge. While he waited for their return, Mac looked up into the clear fall sky as stars made their evening debut. No city sounds or lights intruded into his thoughts or dimmed his vision of the heavens.

Dr. Anna Wilkes impressed him, and as he stared into the night, a vivid image of her face surfaced before his mind's eye. He blinked and shook his head. The image faded. Turning, he went into the house.

EIGHT

I have not yet begun to fight.
JOHN PAUL JONES

WHEN MAC RETURNED to the office after lunch the next day, Mindy pulled one of his phone messages from the stack on her desk and handed it to him.

"Bert Langley from the D.A.'s office phoned fifteen minutes ago. He asked you to call him back as soon as you came in."

Mac went into his office and dialed the number.

"Joe Whetstone is here from Atlanta," Bert said. "We have a couple of things to discuss with the judge on the Thomason case. Can you meet us in the big courtroom in a few minutes? They're bringing the defendant over from the jail."

"Why is Thomason going to be there?" Mac asked.

"Judge's orders."

"I'm on my way." Mac hung up the phone.

"I'll be at the courthouse," he told Mindy as he passed by her desk. "Don't know when I'll be back."

Mac pushed open the door at the rear of the courtroom. Everyone else was already present.

Joe Whetstone, his back to Mac, stood in front of the bench, talking with Judge Danielson. When the back door of the courtroom opened, Joe turned, glanced at Mac, and continued his conversation. Mac had never met Whetstone, but the Atlanta attorney had a well-earned reputation as a smooth trial lawyer. Rumor had it the tall, scholarly forty-year-old former assistant with the U.S. Attorney's office in Atlanta would run for Congress in the next election. Mac knew that close contacts with the Hightower family could prove valuable to Joe's financial and political future. Potential constituents would hear the name Whetstone and remember Joe as the champion of justice in Echota County.

Restrained by leg chains and handcuffs and clothed in his orange jumpsuit, Pete Thomason sat waiting at the defense counsel's table. A deputy with a pistol on his hip stood against the doorway where prisoners were brought into the courtroom.

As he walked down the gently sloping aisle to the front of the courtroom, Mac felt a few butterflies in his stomach. There was always nervousness before the first blows were landed in any fight, and Mac was very familiar with precase jitters.

He opened the waist-high wooden gate that separated the judge, jury, and lawyers from the general seating area, deposited his briefcase beside the defense table, and joined Joe Whetstone in front of the judge.

State v. Thomason officially began.

"Good afternoon, Judge," Mac said.

"Mac," the judge acknowledged Mac's greeting. "Do you know Joe Whetstone?"

"No, Your Honor," Mac and Joe Whetstone shook hands.

"We were just talking a little tennis," the judge said. "Joe plays in an ALTA league in north Atlanta and has a state ranking in his age classification."

"The judge is a dominant force in tennis in this neck of the woods," Mac said.

"Perhaps we can set up a time to play after the case is over," Whetstone said.

"I could use a lesson," the judge said. He opened a thick file folder and made the transition from the tennis court to the legal court. "I believe everyone is here. You may proceed, Mr. Whetstone."

Mac returned to the defense table and sat down.

Pete leaned over. "What's going on?"

"I don't know. We're about to find out."

When Joe stood to begin his presentation, the back door of the courtroom opened, and a petite, somewhat breathless young woman, dressed in blue jeans, dark green shirt, and cowboy boots, slipped into the room and sat down on one of the back benches.

Holding up his hand to stop the prosecutor, the judge said, "Please come forward."

The woman looked around and asked, "Me?"

"Yes," the judge said. "Come forward and tell me your interest in this case."

Her boots clicking on the wood floor, the woman walked quickly down the aisle. "I'm Barbara Williams, a reporter from the *Echota Express.* I'm covering the Thomason case."

"Have a seat in the front row, Ms. Williams, while I handle something with the lawyers."

Mac stood.

"At this time I am imposing a media blackout in this case and instruct all parties and their counsel not to discuss this matter with any media source until the jury is selected and the trial begins."

Whetstone spoke, "But—"

"No, sir," the judge said. "I do not want any pretrial publicity to taint the jury pool. I don't want to move this case to another county and inconvenience all the witnesses who live and work in this area."

"Do you have any objection, Mr. McClain?"

"No, sir."

"Mr. Whetstone and Mr. Langley?"

"No, sir," Joe Whetstone and Bert Langley said together.

Turning to Ms. Williams, the judge said, "Do you understand my instructions? The lawyers and parties cannot talk to the media about this case until a jury is selected."

Mac could see the flush in the reporter's face, but she bit her lip and said, "Yes, sir."

"Thank you. You may now leave the courtroom."

They waited until the fading tip-tap of the reporter's boots signaled she'd left the room. "All right, Mr. Whetstone, proceed."

Joe began, "Two things, Your Honor. First, we are filing a Supplemental Notice of Compliance under *Brady versus Maryland* and the Georgia criminal discovery statute. You have a copy of the notice, and I am handing one to Mr. McClain." He placed several sheets of paper on the table in front of Mac and Pete. "The State has located several witnesses who will testify about prior similar conduct by the defendant in which he utilized the date-rape drug Rohypnol in an incident involving two young women several years ago in South Carolina. No criminal charges were filed, but as a result of the incident, the defendant was dishonorably discharged from the Marine Corps."

"Are statements from the witnesses attached to your notice?" the judge asked.

"Yes, Your Honor. Some of the individuals were interviewed on tape and I am furnishing a transcript to you and Mr. McClain. Copies of the original tape recordings will be delivered to Mr. McClain by the first of next week."

"Go ahead."

"I am also delivering to Mr. McClain pictures of Angela Hightower while she was alive and then after her death." He handed Mac a large brown envelope.

It was standard practice for prosecutors to show the jury studio-type pictures taken of murder victims before their death. The jury would contrast the face of the deceased while alive with the gruesome photos taken at the crime scene or the morgue.

Mac remembered a case handled by Gene Nelson in which a young mother shot and killed her alcoholic husband, who frequently beat her senseless. The grand jury charged her with murder. The district attorney waved a glossy photo of the husband dressed in a suit and looking sedately into the camera in front of the jury and told them this was how the victim appeared when he was alive. Gene countered with a blown-up picture of the man in an obvious state of intoxication with a bottle of whisky in one hand and the baseball bat he used to batter his wife in the other. The defense lawyer argued that the photograph was a more accurate depiction of the way the husband portrayed himself to his unfortunate wife. The jury returned a verdict of involuntary manslaughter, and the judge released the woman on probation.

Of course, Mac's case was completely different. The pictures of Angela would be one of the most emotionally damaging parts of the State's case against Pete. Mac left the envelope unopened on the table and slid it away from Pete's manacled right hand.

Pausing to look at Pete, Whetstone continued, "After consulting with Mr. Langley and based on our review of the facts and circumstances surrounding the murder of Angela Hightower, the State has authorized me to inform Your Honor of its intention to seek the death penalty upon conviction of the defendant."

Mac jumped to his feet. "Your Honor, there is no evidence of aggravating—"

The judge held up his hand. "I want to ask that myself, Mr. McClain." Turning to Joe he asked, "What are the aggravating circumstances supporting imposition of a death sentence? It's my understanding there was no sexual assault of the victim."

"That's true, but we believe the evidence will show two other grounds which support a sentence of death. First, the defendant is guilty of a murder committed in conjunction with the crime of kidnapping. Although Angela Hightower initially consented to accompany the defendant to Atlanta, there was a change which rendered her continued presence with him to be against her will. Second, this murder was 'outrageously or wantonly vile, horrible, or inhuman' and involved an aggravated battery against Ms. Hightower. The manner in which the defendant sought to dispose of the body of the victim and the degree of trauma in her preceding death were particularly brutal."

The judge took off his glasses. "Mr. Whetstone, kidnapping may be an aggravating circumstance, but I do not think what happened to the victim's body after her death would satisfy the legal requirement for the death penalty. Every murder involves some form of injury prior to the person's death."

"I understand, Your Honor. But it only takes one aggravating circumstance to support the imposition of the death penalty. The facts prior to death are still being developed by the GBI and Mr. Hightower's private investigators."

"Anything else?"

"Not today."

The judge turned to Mac, who was still struggling to come to terms with the shift in the magnitude of the case. "Mr. McClain, do you have anything to bring before the Court?"

"Uh, yes, Your Honor. I request authorization to have Mr. Thomason's blood retested by an independent lab."

"Granted."

The judge looked closely at Mac. "Mr. McClain, given the State's announcement regarding the death penalty, it will be necessary to appoint additional counsel to assist you in the matter. Perhaps Mr. Walker would be an appropriate choice."

Bob Walker was the best young trial lawyer in the circuit. Very busy, he would privately scream in protest at such a major disruption of his life, but in public he would do his duty in a zealous manner.

"Thank you, Your Honor. Mr. Walker would be an excellent choice." Mac paused. "However, if I could make a request?"

"Go ahead."

"Would you consider appointing David Moreland as co-counsel?"

"Who?" Bert Langley asked in a stage whisper to his paralegal from the prosecution table.

"The young man from Tennessee who was admitted last month?" the judge asked.

"Yes, sir. I have already spoken to him, and he is willing to assist me."

"Very well. Consider it done. I'll have an order signed Monday."

"Anything else, gentlemen?"

"I would like to talk to Mr. Thomason in private before he is returned to the jail," Mac said.

The judge nodded. "Deputy, please take the defendant into the jury room so Mr. McClain can speak with him."

The judge rose from the bench, and everyone else cleared out of the courtroom in less than a minute. It was, after all, Friday afternoon.

Pete was sniffling and wiping away tears with the back of his hand when Mac came in, closed the door, and sat down next to him. There had only been three death penalty cases in Echota County since the U.S. Supreme Court ruled that each state could decide whether a murderer could be sentenced to death. Mac had not been involved in any of the previous Echota County trials, all of which resulted in guilty verdicts and death sentences. The most recent case, in which a man was convicted in a brutal, execution-style killing of a bank teller during a robbery, had completed its eight-year journey through the appellate court system. The man had been executed shortly before Pete's arrest. Mac was not philosophically opposed to the death penalty, but debating the theoretical appropriateness of society's decisions on crime and punishment was not the issue for the young man sitting beside him. Pete was facing his own death, and Mac was his primary line of defense.

Acutely aware of the inadequacy of any words in his vocabulary at that moment, Mac began, "I know you're upset. But I need to tell you a few things." He handed his handkerchief to Pete, who blew his nose.

"I had a good meeting with Dr. Wilkes, the psychologist. She suggested you may have had Rohypnol in your system and that's the reason you can't remember what happened. If so, it could give us a defense based on lack of mental capacity to form the intent necessary to commit a crime."

"What?" Pete asked, coming out of his fog.

"You were too out of it to choose to hurt Angela."

"Also, why would you take a drug that would knock you out if you wanted to harm Angela?"

"But I didn't take anything. I didn't hurt Angela. I didn't hurt those girls in South Carolina." Pete raised his voice. "But who is going to believe me?"

"That's my job—to present a believable case. This blood test is a first step."

"What was all that about vile and inhuman?" Pete asked.

"I don't know any evidence that supports Whetstone's contention, but I'm more concerned about the kidnapping allegation. We'll have to check it out legally. In the meantime, I suggest you do what I do. Adopt a mind-set that does not automatically accept what the prosecution says as true. They have to prove it to the jury. Try to resist the pressure to give up."

"Who is the lawyer from Atlanta, and why is he involved?"

"He's someone Mr. Hightower hired as a special prosecutor. He's paid to do the same thing the district attorney would have done anyway."

"And the new lawyer who's going to help you? Is he any good?"

"David Moreland. He's very intelligent and, importantly, he wants to help. He may come by to see you. The same confidentiality rules apply to him as me. You can tell him anything."

Pete shook his head. "Do I have a chance?"

Mac didn't answer until Pete raised his head and made eye contact with him. "Oh yes, you've got a chance. We've just begun to fight."

NINE

One finds many companions for food and drink, but in a serious business a man's companions are few.
THEOGNIS

THE JAIL WAS so close to the courthouse that deputies often walked prisoners back along the narrow sidewalk that connected the two buildings. Following a guard, Pete shuffled outside, his gait restricted by the chains around his ankles. Glancing sideways at the cars passing by the courthouse on the street, he saw a couple of boys in the back of a pickup truck lean forward and point in his direction at the sight of his orange jumpsuit.

When he reached his cell, Pete didn't mention what had happened in court to his cellmates. The news would spread fast enough on its own. No one talked to him much anyway. Prisoners charged with murder were treated differently by everyone—guards, other prisoners, jailhouse administrators. There was something about a murder charge. No one could pretend it was a petty problem. No one could joke about it. Someone had died. And now, the accused faced the possibility of death or the rest of his life in prison.

He lay in his bunk the rest of the afternoon. Kitchen workers slid supper trays into the cells. Tonight's fare was a small square of gray meat, mashed potatoes, carrots, and a scoop of brown pudding. Pete's meal sat untouched beside his bunk. He turned away from the other men in his cell, who were playing cards. Silent tears coursed down his cheeks until the edge of the thin pillow under his head was wet with sorrow.

During his own brief walk from the courthouse to his office, Mac began the process of regaining his equilibrium under the responsibilities that now rested on his shoulders. There was an emotional burden associated with any legal case no matter how minor, but different types created various levels of stress.

On Mac's grading scale, disputes between prosperous businesses or wealthy individuals were the least burdensome. The parties might become red in the face during the course of the litigation, but regardless of the outcome, nobody would miss his next tee time at the golf club or forgo a planned fishing vacation on the coast.

Pressure increased when he represented an individual who was severely injured. The outcome of those cases would have a significant effect on the client and his or her family for many years.

Mac rarely handled divorce cases. The issues surrounding marital breakup and custody of children were gut-wrenching. Mac hadn't entered the domestic relations wrestling ring in years.

Four times in thirty years of law practice Mac had served as defense lawyer in a murder case. Two times he stood solemnly beside a man and heard the judge sentence his client to life in the Georgia State Penitentiary. Twice his clients walked out of the courtroom free men after a jury found them not guilty. Murder trials were unique, and the stress caused by the responsibility of one human being for another had few parallels. Only doctors and nurses who treated patients with serious medical problems knew a greater responsibility. *State v. Thomason* would be Mac's first death penalty case in more than thirty years of law practice. He could only imagine what it would be like to hear the judge sentence Pete to death. He didn't want to find out.

Seated behind his desk, Mac summoned the troops into his office. His three employees once again gathered before him.

"The State is seeking the death penalty in Thomason," he said.

Judy sank down in a chair.

"Are they serious or just trying to pressure you into a guilty plea for a life sentence?" Vicki asked.

"Possibly, but based on my conversations with Thomason, a guilty plea is not an option."

"How do you feel?" Vicki asked.

"Shaken, but recovering. It's time to get busy."

"What next?"

Mac shifted in his chair. "The judge approved an independent blood test. Vicki, locate a private lab and make arrangements for proper transfer of the sample from the state crime lab. I want a specific test for Rohypnol in Pete's blood."

"Yes, sir."

"Also, the judge has appointed another lawyer to help me."

"Who?" Judy asked.

"David Moreland. He's very green but, according to his résumé, very smart."

"He's funny, too," Mindy added.

"Yes, I forgot," Mac said. "He's very funny."

Judy and Vicki exchanged a puzzled look.

"Mindy, please copy everything in the Thomason file for Mr. Moreland. I'm going to call him in a few minutes and ask him to come over so we can go over the case."

"Yes, sir."

"I guess that's all."

As the women turned to leave, Mac said, "Vicki. Good job finding a psychologist. She has already been a help."

Mac called David Moreland's office. Not surprisingly, the young lawyer answered the phone himself.

"David Moreland's office."

"David, Mac McClain. I thought some more about your closing

argument the other day and have some news for you. Judge Danielson has appointed you as my co-counsel in the Thomason case. An order will be issued Monday."

"Great. Thanks for reconsidering my offer."

"That's not exactly how it happened. The State intends to seek the death penalty and under the local court rules that means another lawyer is automatically assigned to the case."

"The death penalty?"

"That's right. And this is not a law school trial practice course."

"Have you ever handled a death penalty case?" David asked.

"No. We'll learn together."

Mac listened to several seconds of silence.

"Okay. What do you want me to do?"

"Come over in about forty-five minutes. My receptionist is copying the file for you."

"I'll be there."

—

Mac read the witness statements Joe Whetstone had given him. He wasn't too surprised that the State's investigators had discovered the dark blot on Pete's record. Staff Sergeant Walter Monroe, currently stationed in Okinawa, gave a detailed account that made Pete sound like an apprentice to the Boston Strangler. There was nothing in the file from the other Marine involved in the incident, Harry O'Ryan, "address unknown." One of the girls, Sally Tompkins, told investigators that Pete bought her a drink at the nightclub where they met, but neither girl remembered leaving the bar nor any events thereafter.

The pictures of Angela were tough to look at. The contrast between the girl's high school graduation picture and the scratched and bruised face at the bottom of the cliff was tragic beyond words. Thinking about the pain Alex and Sarah Hightower were experiencing, Mac carefully put the pictures back in the envelope. Others might not sympathize, but Mac was no stranger to their painful brand of sorrow. He'd seen death up close.

A law book propped open on his desk, Mac was making notes when Mindy buzzed him.

"David Moreland is here."

"Okay. I'll be right out."

"Also, Dr. Wilkes is on line one."

"I'd better talk to her," Mac said. "Give David the file you copied and tell him I'll be with him in a minute. He can wait in the library."

Mac wasn't going to waste his best hello a second time on Dr. Wilkes's male straight-jacket assistant.

"Hello," he said gruffly.

"Mr. McClain?" Anna Wilkes's voice came through the receiver.

"Oh, yes. Dr. Wilkes. How are you?"

"Fine. Did I call at a bad time?"

"I found out earlier today that the State is seeking the death penalty in the Thomason case."

"Does Pete know?"

"Yes. He was in court when the special prosecutor announced his intentions."

"How is he?"

"Devastated."

"Have you made arrangements to have Pete's blood retested?"

"Yes. The judge approved it, and my paralegal is working on it. I hope your hunch is right. I need something to back them down."

"Let me know. But actually, the real reason for my call is personal. I'm taking my son to the mountains east of Dennison Springs on Sunday afternoon and wanted your advice about places to visit. I remembered the photograph on the wall in your office and thought you might have some suggestions."

The psychologist's request reminded Mac that the world continued to turn regardless of *State v. Thomason.*

"I checked the weather forecast, and it's supposed to be sunny and mild," she said.

"Most places worth seeing are somewhat hard to find if you don't know the area. I'll be working Sunday afternoon. Why don't you stop by the office—I'll draw a map and give you directions."

"Are you sure? I don't want to impose."

"It will be easier than trying to tell you over the phone. What time?"

"We'll be leaving Chattanooga after church and should get to your office by one-thirty."

"I'll be here. Just ring the bell if the front door is locked."

Mac hung up the phone and daydreamed about one of his favorite spots in the mountains. It was a place called Bob Stratton Bald, a grassy meadow on top of a five-thousand-foot-high mountain in western North Carolina. On one side of the open clearing was a tiny spring that bubbled out of the ground and began its long descent across smooth stones into the valley below. On the other was a place where Mac liked to camp underneath some small trees and, after his campfire died down, gaze at the thousands of stars that couldn't be seen on the clearest night within fifty miles of city lights. It was a unique place. Then he remembered David Moreland.

Mac looked in the library, but the young lawyer wasn't there. He heard the sound of Mindy's laugh from the reception room and stuck his head around the corner. David was sitting in a chair next to Mindy's desk.

"Sorry to keep you waiting, David. This is a law office, not a doctor's waiting room."

"That's okay."

"Mindy, it's after five. You can go on home."

"I didn't mind staying a few minutes extra," Mindy said, smiling at David.

Carrying his freshly copied paperwork from the Thomason case, David followed Mac down the hall.

"I was reviewing additional information served on us this afternoon," Mac said. "I'll make a copy of the statements for you before you leave."

It was Friday afternoon, and Mac felt the tug of his weekly ritual. "Before we get to work, let me ask you a question."

"What?"

"Were you in a social fraternity at Vanderbilt?" he asked.

"No," David said, a surprised expression on his face. "Will Phi Beta Kappa do?"

Mac shook his head. "Probably not. I was going to have my Friday afternoon beer. It's a collegiate thing. You can have one, too, but I'm not sure what a Phi Beta Kappa from Maryville, Tennessee, drinks to unwind on Friday afternoons."

David laughed. "Spring water is my beverage of choice."

"I think my bar stocks that. I'll be right back."

Mac returned with a beer, a plastic bottle of spring water, and two frosty mugs. He set the mugs and drinks on a small, glass-covered table and poured their drinks.

"I want to propose a toast," Mac said. "A prayer might be more effective, but I'm a better toastmaster than prayer-maker." Raising his glass, he said, "To our cooperative efforts on behalf of Pete Thomason. May we conduct ourselves with skill and integrity."

"Amen," David said as they clinked glasses.

"If you'll bear with me, I don't want to do anything serious right now except enjoy my beer."

"Okay. I'll pretend I'm sitting with my feet in a cool mountain stream on a hot summer day," David said.

"That's the idea."

So the two men sat silently in their chairs, sipping their drinks, and taking journeys down imaginary paths. Reality would draw them back soon enough.

In a few minutes, Mac drained the last drops of his brew and set his mug down on the table. "I've enjoyed drinking with you, David. I'd be honored if you would join me about this time one Friday afternoon in the future."

"Thanks."

"Now to the task at hand. Except for our little interlude, keep track of your time spent on the case so we give an accurate bill to the county. The hourly rate is low, but at least you will get something."

"I've already adopted one rule for my law practice," David said.

"What's that?"

"It's better to be working for something than doing nothing for nothing."

"That's true."

"Yes, sir."

"Oh. You may continue to say 'yes, sir,' but now that we have had our frosted-mug, male-bonding experience you may, if you choose, call me Mac."

"Thanks. I'll probably ease into that."

"I know I must look old to you."

"Yes, sir."

Mac chuckled. "Mindy was right about you."

"In what way?"

"She said you were funny."

Mac gave David a summary of the case and brought him up to date regarding his conversation with Dr. Wilkes and the supplemental information received from the State. "At some point you can look at the pictures of Angela the State intends to use at trial." Mac put his hand on the envelope resting on his desk. "Do you know the law on their admissibility?"

"Usually admissible as demonstrative evidence according to the Court of Appeals in *Kirkland versus State,*" David responded.

"Correct."

"I may as well get it over with."

Mac handed the envelope to David, who silently looked at each one then put them back in the envelope.

"Do you still want to defend Thomason?"

"I'm hoping he didn't do this."

"What if he did?"

"Has he told you that?"

"No. So far, he consistently says he doesn't remember anything."

"Then he needs lawyers to represent him through the process."

"Good enough. Here is a key to my office so you can come and go to do research as you please. What kind of secretarial support do you have?"

David held up his hands and wiggled his fingers. "Forty-eight words a minute with only two errors."

Mac shook his head. "No. Judy Boyington, my secretary, can handle all the typing. Here's a tape recorder and a pack of blank tapes."

David put the recorder and tapes in his coat pocket.

"My paralegal is Vicki Lorain. She can do most everything we do except sign pleadings and appear in court. Of course, you've met Mindy."

"Yes."

"This weekend I want you to do your own review of the file and prepare a detailed memo identifying every legal and factual issue that you think is important and relevant. At this point I'm not as interested in answers as making sure we know all the questions."

TEN

I have set watchmen upon thy walls, O Jerusalem.
ISAIAH 62:6 (KJV)

MAC SPENT ALL DAY Saturday at the office working on his "other business," the term that now applied to everything except the murder case. David didn't show up, and Mac concluded the young lawyer probably decided to spread the Thomason case papers across the floor of his apartment.

While he worked, Mac listened to the Georgia football game on a small radio he kept in his office. In Mac's opinion, listening to the game on the radio was better than watching it on television. Larry Munson, the "legendary voice of the Georgia Bulldogs," could create a scene with words that was more graphic in the imagination than what could be seen with the natural eye. Mac could still replay Munson's description of the hysteria of the crowd after a final score by the Georgia team against the University of Florida many years before.

Today, Georgia easily won its game against a weaker opponent, and that settled Mac's plans for the following morning. He would put on his red sport coat and go to church.

When Laura and the boys had been alive, the McClain family's commitment to church was not linked to the fate of a football team. Laura McClain—together with Celeste Jamison and a few other women—was a member of the Mable Ray Circle.

Since time immemorial, Presbyterian women have met together in small groups called "circles," so named because the ladies often placed their chairs in a circle. There were morning circles, luncheon circles, afternoon circles, and evening circles. Some of the circles were the female counterparts to Mac's Sunday school class, and the women who attended had more interest in gardening than God. But for ten years before her death, Laura belonged to the Mable Ray Circle, a gathering of five to seven women who met in a small study adjacent to the main sanctuary every Tuesday morning from 9:00 until 11:00.

The Mable Ray Circle began in 1942. Mrs. Ray and four other women met together once a week for one purpose—prayer. No donuts, no coffee. Just prayer. It was a serious time; the world was at war, and the women focused their intercession on behalf of the men and women from Dennison Springs serving in the armed forces during World War II. For three years they prayed diligently on behalf of those in harm's way. It didn't matter whether the soldier, sailor, or airman was Presbyterian, Methodist, Baptist, Pentecostal, white, black, brown, rich, or poor—the women prayed. At Mrs. Ray's suggestion, they recorded in notebooks the prayers offered for each person. After the war ended, the answers to their prayers came to light. Men and women returned to Echota County and told about their wartime experiences. Time and time again the prayer journals revealed precise prayers for specific individuals at crucial times—undeniable proof of the involvement of the Holy Spirit in the prayers of God's children. Mrs. Ray died in 1948, but the prayer group did not die with her, and the women voted to name the circle in her honor and memory.

Other leaders arose, but the focus of the circle remained true to Holy Spirit—inspired, specific prayer. In the 1950s, the group interceded for those who served in the Korean War. In the 1960s, they prayed Dennison Springs through the racial tensions surrounding integration of the schools and societal recognition of equality between the races. In the 1970s, the group prayed earnestly for the children and teenagers who faced the advent of drugs to the area. Many young people's lives were spared, saved, and changed because of the prayers of a small group of women in a Presbyterian church. Occasionally the circle touched on national or international issues, but the bread and butter of their activity remained prayer for the Dennison Springs area. The prayer notebooks, neatly organized and indexed, stood as witnesses to their faithfulness on shelves in the room where they met.

Mac had been aware of the Mable Ray Circle before Laura became involved. As a boy, he'd heard some of the wartime prayer stories, but the notion of prayer as an active force in the affairs of men and women did not fit within his outlook on life. Laura's involvement puzzled him, and after she started going to the meetings, Mac noticed that she talked about Jesus in a different way, as if he lived two houses down the street.

After a joyous time celebrating Georgia's victory in Sunday school, Mac stopped for a drink at the water fountain in the hallway. When he raised his head, he saw Celeste Jamison exiting her Sunday school class. Celeste's eye caught his, and she waved her hand.

"Mac! Do you have a minute?" she called out.

Mac waited until she made her way to him through the crowded hallway.

"I read in the paper that you're representing the man charged with killing the Hightower girl."

"Yes. You won't read much more because the judge has ordered a media blackout. Of course, I can't say anything about it anyway."

"Oh, I didn't want to ask you questions about the case," Celeste replied. "I wanted you to know that we are praying about the situation on Tuesday mornings."

"You are?"

"Yes, we discussed it at our meeting and everyone believes the situation needs our prayers."

Mac's mind raced in a couple of directions at once. What would the women pray? For Pete's acquittal? For his conviction? For Joe Whetstone?

Did they really believe their little group could make a difference? If they could, did he want them meddling in the situation?

He settled on the most noncommittal response that came to mind and said, "That's interesting."

Celeste continued, "If there is something specific you want to pass along to us for prayer without violating the rules, give me a call."

Clueless about what that might be, Mac said, "I'll do that."

"Don't forget," she said, turning toward the stairwell that led to the sanctuary.

Mac left the building and between the exit and his car promptly forgot what Celeste Jamison had said.

Mac drove directly to his office. Several hours later he was finishing a memo to Ray Morrison when the doorbell rang. He looked out the window. On his front step stood Anna Wilkes, dressed casually in a University of Virginia sweatshirt and jeans, accompanied by a dark-haired boy of ten or eleven with his mother's eyes and nose. Mac opened the door.

"Come in. I meant to unlock the door."

Anna greeted him with a smile and introduced her son. "Mr. McClain, this is Hunter."

Mac shook the boy's hand. "Have a seat in the library," he said, leading them into the former dining room now lined with bookcases. A computer terminal nestled in the corner. "Would you like something to drink?" he asked.

"We're going to eat lunch as soon as we leave here," Anna said.

"I'm thirsty," Hunter said. "Could I have something?"

"Do you have any spring water?" Anna asked.

"In the refrigerator," Mac answered, wondering if he ought to buy stock in the bottled water company.

While Hunter drank his water, Mac asked Anna, "Where do you want to go?"

"Are apples in season?"

"They should be."

"Where are the best orchards?"

"About an hour from here." Mac spread a map out on the table.

"I'd like to take Hunter to a big orchard. Maybe someplace where we could pick our own."

"That should be easy enough to find." Mac put his finger on the map. "We're here. You will take Highway 53 east until it intersects U.S. 411 south. Go south several miles until you pass a lumberyard. There is an intersection with a convenience store on the left and a place where a man in old, blue overalls boils peanuts in a big iron pot over an open fire beside the road. Buy some peanuts to eat in the car."

"Boiled peanuts? I'm not sure about that."

"You want Hunter to have a comprehensive, north Georgia mountains cultural experience, don't you?"

"I've never eaten a boiled peanut," Hunter said. "What do they taste like?"

Mac rolled his tongue in his mouth. "A good boiled peanut is hot and salty on the outside with a little bit of crunch left in it when you bite down to chew. Once you start eating them it's hard to stop until the bag is empty."

Anna smiled. "I'm still not sure about boiled peanuts."

"Just something to consider. Turn left at the peanut pot and go a few hundred yards to an intersection. You will see a historic marker on the right. Turn right. You are now on a road that follows one of the original Indian trails across this region. After passing the marker you will drive under a very low railroad bridge. The bridge is old, and I would not want to be under it when a train passed over."

"Okay. Stop before the bridge if there is a train in view."

"You will come to Highway 282."

"Where are we going to eat lunch?" Hunter interrupted.

"That's easy," Mac said. "There is a great restaurant on the way. It's before you reach the boiled peanut spot, so you can have the peanuts for dessert."

"Is that where you ate lunch?" Hunter asked.

"Uh, no. I've been working. I haven't eaten lunch today."

"Why don't you have lunch with us?" Hunter asked. "You could make sure we find the man who sells the boiled peanuts."

"Well—"

"That's a good idea," Anna said.

Mac hesitated. "I'm not trying to intrude on your time together."

"Not at all. I know you're busy, but it would do you good to take a break for an hour or so."

Mac smiled. "Is that your advice as a psychologist licensed in the state of Georgia?"

"If that's what you need to hear—yes."

Mac stretched. "Okay. Talking about boiled peanuts has made me hungry."

Mac locked the front door. "The after-church crowd should be clearing out of the restaurant by now. You and Hunter can follow me in your car."

Josie's Restaurant didn't serve lunch on Sunday in the fall and winter, but Mac had more than one restaurant on his fine-dining menu.

The Rock Springs Restaurant sat comfortably beside the main route from Dennison Springs to the mountains in the east. Unlike Josie's, which featured a self-service buffet line, the Rock Springs Restaurant employed waitresses who took orders and brought customers generous plates of food. The owner of the eating establishment—a large, older woman with a gray, beehive hairdo—always sat at the cash register surveying her domain.

"Hey, Mac," several employees called out as the threesome made their way to a table for four.

"You're something of a celebrity," Anna commented.

"Not really. Watch what happens to the older couple that followed us in from the parking lot."

In a few seconds, an elderly man and a woman with a cane walked in and were welcomed by name with a similar chorus of hellos.

The menu was a single sheet of paper with the meat items listed at the top, the vegetables underneath, and desserts at the bottom.

"What do you recommend?" Anna asked.

Mac put on his glasses and reviewed the day's offerings. "The meat loaf is tasty. The broiled fish is consistently good. But the fried chicken livers are outstanding. Crisp, not too greasy, with a light brown crust. They melt in your mouth after a few seconds even if you decide not to chew them."

"Is that what you're going to order?" Hunter asked.

"Have you ever eaten a chicken liver, Hunter?"

"No, sir. I don't even know what it looks like."

Mac looked at Anna. "What have you been feeding this boy? He's never eaten a boiled peanut or seen a chicken liver."

Anna laughed. "I didn't realize he was deprived."

Mac turned to Hunter. "I can tell you with confidence that the first man who ate a chicken liver did not make his decision based on appearance."

"It was a brave man who first ate an oyster, too," Anna added.

Mac nodded. "Different region, same principle. People in the South started eating chicken livers because they could not afford to waste any part of the chicken. It's the same with gizzards and necks, although that is another story. Food was scarce and no matter how they smell or taste, livers are edible."

"If you order them, I'll try one," Hunter said.

"It's a deal." Mac looked at Anna and raised his eyebrows. "Chicken livers for two?"

She shook her head. "I'll pass today."

Mac ordered the livers, Anna selected the fish, and Hunter chose a fried chicken breast. Hunter declined the carrots that came with the meal and instead selected mashed potatoes with no gravy and green beans.

When their waitress set the platters of food on the table, Anna asked, "Do you mind if I pray?"

"Go ahead."

"Father, thank you for this day and this food. Bless Mac in every aspect of his life and work. In Jesus' name, amen."

While Anna prayed, Mac stole a peek at Hunter, who sat with his eyes squeezed tightly shut.

As soon as Anna said, "Amen," a very hungry Hunter dove into his plate.

"Are you ready for a chicken liver?" Mac asked in a couple of minutes.

"Okay."

"You might want to put ketchup on it," Mac suggested. "Here's a small one." He scooped up the liver with his spoon and held it out for Hunter to spear with his fork.

Hunter held up the dark morsel and looked it over thoroughly. "Does it have any fat on it?" he asked.

"No; it's pure, nutritious meat."

Hunter dipped it in ketchup. Mac and Anna watched as the bite disappeared in the young man's mouth. He chewed for a few seconds and swallowed.

"How was it?" Mac asked.

"Not bad. I don't think I'd want to eat it every day."

Mac patted him on the back. "That's fine. In time you'll enjoy a plateful and wish you had more."

They concluded the meal with pie. Coconut cream for Mac and Anna—peanut butter for Hunter.

"This was good," Hunter said. "I'd like to come back."

"We might do that," his mother said.

"If you come with us, Mr. McClain, we can both order the livers."

"It's a deal," Mac said.

Mac pushed back his plate and drew a map, complete with a small black pot, on a paper napkin. "Is this clear enough?" he asked when he finished.

"It's great. I don't think we'll have any problems."

Mac picked up the check. "Lunch is on me."

"No, I'll pay our part," Anna said.

"Let me," Mac insisted. "It was worth it to watch Hunter eat his first chicken liver."

Anna and Hunter turned left from the parking lot. Mac turned right. He looked in the rearview mirror at the quickly receding car and smiled. Hunter reminded him of his younger son, Zach, at that age. Zach was always willing to try something new to eat, while his brother, Ben, stuck to a steady diet of hot dogs and hamburgers. When Zach was twelve, he ate black caviar on a cracker at a political fund-raiser in Atlanta. Mac smiled, remembering again the look on Zach's face when the caviar hit his taste buds.

It had been fun being around a boy again and nice to get out of the office. Mac wondered where Hunter's father lived. Anna Wilkes didn't wear a wedding ring.

ELEVEN

My heart's in the Highlands.
ROBERT BURNS

MAC ARRIVED AT the office Monday morning and found David Moreland working in the library.

"How was your weekend?" David asked.

"Better than usual."

"I just finished dictating the memo you wanted," he said.

Vicki stuck her head into the library.

"Vicki, this is David Moreland."

David stood. "Pleased to meet you. Mr. McClain speaks highly of you."

"That's good to know," she said, smiling.

"Have you found a lab to retest Thomason's blood?" Mac asked.

"Yes," she answered. "I talked with Peachtree Forensic and Chemical Services on Friday. I'm going to fax them the information this morning."

"How soon will they be able to run the test?"

"I told them what you were looking for, and they can provide results within two to three days after receiving the blood sample."

"I'll call Bert Langley at the D.A.'s office to arrange transfer of the blood from the state crime lab."

"Okay. I'll let the lab know it's coming."

Turning to David, he said, "I'll ask Judy to type your report first thing this morning. Have you two met?"

"No."

"Come with me." Mac led the way down the hall and introduced them.

"Thanks for helping," David said, handing her the tape. "Let me know how to improve the clarity of my dictation."

Obviously surprised, Judy said, "Uh, sure."

"Do you want to stay here today or go to your office?" Mac asked David.

"My office. My answering machine is on, but I'd rather be there. I don't want to miss my million-dollar case."

"I know. I'm still waiting for that call myself."

After David left, Judy turned to Mac. "Do you want me to tell you how to improve your dictation?"

Mac scowled. "No, just be glad I'm not calling you into my office every five minutes to take shorthand."

At ten o'clock, a man who had suffered a broken leg in an automobile accident, called Mac. The other driver had run a stop sign and caused the wreck, so there was no question of liability. It would not be a complicated case. Mac prepared to schedule the man for a quick appointment but suddenly changed his mind.

"I'm involved in a murder case right now, but I can refer you to another lawyer."

"Who is it?"

"David Moreland. I'm sure he will do a good job." Mac gave him David's number.

"I'll call him right now."

Two hours later, Judy brought David's memo into Mac's office. "The boy has a brain, doesn't he?" she said.

"Why?"

"He didn't see your summary of the case?"

"No, I had it in my briefcase. I wanted him to take a fresh look."

"He mentioned almost everything you did and added a few other items that made some sense to me."

Mac read the synopsis and called David.

"Thorough job on the memo," Mac said. "But are you sure you think a polygraph exam is a good idea?"

"It would be nonstipulated so it wouldn't be admissible at trial, but if it goes our way, we could show it to the State and ask them to back off the death penalty."

"I've had some bad experiences with polygraphs in the past, but I think you're probably right."

"Do you know an examiner you trust?"

"No."

"I could try to locate someone."

"I'll ask Vicki to work on it. I have another job for you."

"What is it?"

"You know that the trial will have two parts: a guilt-or-innocence phase and a sentencing phase."

"Yes, sir. We'll have a chance to put up additional evidence if the defendant is found guilty."

"Correct. I want you to start developing a plan for the sentencing phase of the trial." There was a long silence on the other end. "Are you still there?" Mac asked.

"Yes," David said. "You're not going to ask me to handle the death penalty phase, are you?"

"We're working together. Remember—you don't run from challenges."

"Did I say that?"

"It was in your closing argument when you were trying to convince me to bring you into the case."

"Yes, but—"

"Relax. I'm just asking you to do the bulk of the preparation. Call lawyers who have handled death penalty cases and ask them questions, read articles, collect good ideas."

"Yes, sir," David said.

"That's it. We'll see what develops."

"Oh, I had something else to mention to you," David said. "I'm meeting with a prospective client this afternoon. He was hurt in a car wreck and has a good claim. After I interview him, I'd like to discuss the case with you."

"I'll be glad to help." Mac rewarded himself with an internal pat on the back. "We'll talk after you meet with him."

Mac dialed the district attorney's office.

"Bert, you really laid one on me Friday when Whetstone asked for the death penalty."

"Joe Whetstone believes he can make it happen."

"What's your role going to be?"

"Joe and his staff will try the case, but any plea negotiations will go through my office."

"That's what I thought."

"Do you want to talk about a plea?"

Mac decided it wouldn't hurt to find out the D.A.'s perspective. "What did you have in mind?"

"If your client wants to fold his tents and plead guilty prior to trial I would recommend life without parole. Do you want me to put that in a letter to you?"

"Not now."

"Think about it and let me know soon. Closer to trial, there may not be an offer on the table."

"What if Thomason passed a polygraph test?"

"That depends. Do you want me to set one up with the GBI examiner?"

"Is there a private examiner you trust?"

"Not really. If Thomason passed a nonstipulated test, it wouldn't make the charges go away, but it might affect a plea offer."

When he hung up, Mac said to Vicki, "It may not do any good, but let's set up a polygraph exam with someone who has good credentials. You know, former police examiner, twenty years' experience."

"What's my budget?"

"Since it won't be used at trial, I have to pay for this out of my pocket."

Vicki raised her eyebrows. "So, money is no problem?"

"I didn't say that. Do your best to find someone good and reasonable," Mac said. "We need someone willing to travel to Dennison Springs. I can't check Pete out of the jail, swing by McDonald's for a cheeseburger, and drop him off at the polygraph examiner's office for a few hours."

Ray Morrison's truck steadily zigzagged up a dirt road until he saw the large poplar tree that the owner of the bait-and-tackle store told him marked the entrance to Rodney McFarland's driveway. Sure enough, just past the tree, a narrow gravel road angled sharply up the mountain on the left. At this elevation some of the leaves had already fallen from the trees, and the rest were in a full explosion of color. Mr. McFarland obviously preferred his mornings brisk and his neighbors distant. Ray began honking his horn as soon as he started up the drive. Mountain people didn't like to be surprised by a stranger's approach, and the last thing Ray wanted was a nearsighted old man pointing a shotgun in his direction.

Ray pulled to a stop in front of a faded, gray, single-story wooden cabin. The newest structure on the property was a freshly painted outhouse with a half-moon cut in the door. A hand pump for water stood in the front yard.

A skinny, white-haired man with a scruffy beard opened a screen door and stepped to the edge of the front porch.

"Howdy," Ray called as soon as he got out.

"You from the government?" the old man asked with a slight quiver in his voice.

"No, sir. Are you Mr. Rodney McFarland?"

"I be."

"My name is Ray Morrison. I'm doing some investigation about the night your truck was run off the road near Dennison Springs. I was wondering if I could talk to you a minute."

"Well, I guess if you drove all the way up here to see me, it wouldn't be right of me to send you on your way without having a talk."

"Do you still have the truck?"

"I wouldn't trade her for a brand-new one."

"Could I see it?"

"I reckon you could if you come on around to the side of the house."

The old man came down the steps with surprising speed and led Ray around the corner of the house. Under a large oak tree was a truck covered with a brown plastic tarpaulin.

"Here she is," Mr. McFarland said, pulling off the cover to reveal a 1968 white Ford pickup in very good condition. The front bumper was slightly bent on the passenger side of the vehicle.

"Nice truck," Ray said sincerely.

"She's my baby."

"How long have you had it?"

"Bought it new off the lot in Blue Ridge."

"Would you mind telling me how it was damaged?"

"Nope."

The old man reached in his back pocket and pulled out a foil pouch of chewing tobacco. He deposited a generous wad in the right side of his mouth. Ray figured the story wouldn't really get going until Mr. McFarland was ready to start spitting.

"Well, it was in the summer, you know. Either Friday or Saturday night. I'd gotten word late in the evening that my granddaughter was fixin' to have her baby, and I wanted to be there at the hospital if I could make it in time. She had a boy, my first great-grandson. Guess what they named him?"

"Rodney?"

"That's a good guess. Rodney Keith Hornbuckle is the little fella's name. My granddaughter married a Hornbuckle. You might know them. They live on the north side of Echota County."

"I know a Leroy Hornbuckle."

Mr. McFarland slapped his leg. "That's her husband's uncle. How do you know Leroy?"

"Just met him once or twice. What happened next?"

"Oh yeah. It was already dark when I left out of here. I was making good time. You know, that truck will do sixty-five on a straight stretch of road without any vibration in the front end."

"I can tell you have good tires on it."

"I never buy foreign tires. I buy American. Everything on this hill was made in the U.S.A. except my radio. I bought a General Electric thinking it was made in Pennsylvania or someplace like that, but when I got it home it said, 'Made in Taiwan' on the bottom."

"You were making good time to see your granddaughter."

"I'm gettin' to that. I came over the mountain about midnight. There was no traffic on the road when these two cars came around the corner."

"Two cars?" Ray asked.

"Yeah, a yellow one and a dark purple one."

"Purple?"

"Here, let me show you."

Mr. McFarland went to the rear of the truck on the driver's side of the vehicle.

"Here is where he nicked me."

Ray leaned over and rubbed a narrow twelve-inch streak of dark paint. "Was it burgundy?"

"That's it. Help me remember that. Ask me that color again before you leave. Burgundy. It was a burgundy four-door. Can't tell you if it was a Lincoln, Cadillac, Buick, or what. But it was a big one."

"Tell me again what happened."

"These two cars, the yellow and the, uh, burgundy one was tearing up that road like they owned both lanes. The yellow one almost hit me, and I was aheading for the ditch when the other one must have barely sideswiped me."

"Did you tell the police about the burgundy car?"

"No, I didn't know it had hit me until I looked the truck over real good the next day. It was the yellow car that ran me off the road. I told the police about it, and I heard later the girl driving it went off the side of the mountain and was killed. I was mad at first, but when I found out about the girl I felt sorry for her family."

"Could you see who was driving the yellow car?"

"I couldn't tell about either car. I guess they had their bright lights on. It happened pretty quick."

"It always does. Has the insurance company settled with you?"

"Are you kidding? I'm still waiting for one of those adjustment fellows to come up and look at my truck."

"Could I take some pictures?" Ray asked. He doubted any insurance adjuster would go to the trouble of locating Mr. McFarland.

"Sure."

Ray took shots of the bumper and the streak along the side. "I'd like to scrape off a little of the burgundy paint and see if I can find the car that hit you."

"Would you do that?"

"It's pretty important."

"That would be right nice of you."

Ray carefully shaved several flecks of the paint into an empty pill bottle. Showing it to Mr. McFarland, he said, "You saw me put the pieces of paint into the bottle, didn't you, Mr. McFarland?"

"I reckon I did. I'm close enough to spit on your shoe."

"Thanks for not doing that."

As they walked across the front yard, Mr. McFarland grabbed Ray's arm. "Do you want a drink of water before you leave?"

"Yeah, I'm kind of thirsty."

The old man picked up a battered tin cup from the top of a tree stump, grabbed the handle of the pump, and after a few vigorous strokes, filled the cup.

"Here, you go first," he said handing the cup to Ray who, making sure there wasn't anything alive or dead in the bottom, took a long cool drink.

"Good water," he said.

"Better than any city water," the old man refilled the cup, spit, and took a swallow himself.

"Thanks, Mr. McFarland. I'll be in touch."

"Come back anytime. I don't stray far from home."

"Oh." Ray stopped at his car door. "Tell me that color?"

A toothless smile split the old man's face. "Burgundy. I can't say I didn't learn something today. Burgundy. That's a fancy word." Mr. McFarland hopped up on his porch and waved good-bye.

Several hours later, Ray put the pill bottle on the edge of Mac's desk.

"You don't think he picked up the scrape in the parking lot of the Piggly Wiggly grocery store?" Mac asked.

"The old guy probably never goes to the grocery store. There are enough squirrels and rabbits on his hilltop to satisfy his taste for meat. The truck was in mint condition. I believe he knows where his four-wheeled baby suffered every dent and ding."

"You believed him?"

"Mac, we shared water out of the same tin cup from the pump in his front yard. We are almost kinfolk."

Mac chuckled. "I'll see if the forensic lab Vicki contacted in Atlanta can do an analysis on the paint sample."

"Let me know," Ray said. "And if Mr. McFarland is right, I sure would like to talk to the driver of a certain burgundy car."

TWELVE

Am I my brother's keeper?
GENESIS 4:9 (KJV)

ALEX HIGHTOWER TURNED forty-four on Labor Day following Angela's death. He and his wife, Sarah, lived exactly eight-tenths of a mile from the governor's mansion in the exclusive area of northwest Atlanta known as Buckhead. Whether the Hightowers' home or the governor's residence had more square feet of heated living space had never been definitely settled. However, the governor lived four to eight years in the state-owned residence; the Hightower family had occupied their Buckhead mansion for more than forty years.

The first eighteen years of his life, Alex had been the only child who ran up and down the long halls of the Hightower residence, climbed the old trees in the large wooded area on the estate called "The Forest," or drove one of his father's antique sports cars down the long driveway to West Paces Ferry Road. Then Cecil and Maureen Hightower were surprised by an unexpected pregnancy. Spencer Hitchcock Hightower arrived nine months later.

Spencer bore the distinguishing marks of all the Hightower males: reddish-brown hair, fair skin, and a sharp, analytical mind. But from the beginning, Cecil viewed his second son as an intrusion, a complicating factor in the elder Hightower's efforts to ensure an orderly transfer of power from one generation to another. Spencer's existence spoiled his plans, and when the new arrival proved to be a cranky, difficult baby and a demanding toddler, Cecil shut him out of his life as much as possible. To compensate, Maureen pampered Spencer, and by the time he celebrated his fifth birthday, the younger Hightower was an incorrigible brat.

When he was old enough for school, Spencer's attitude and conduct led to his dismissal from one learning institution after another, until his parents gave up on outside education and hired private tutors to teach him at home.

Alex graduated from Westminster Schools shortly after Spencer's birth and left Atlanta to attend college at Dartmouth. After receiving a degree in finance and economics from Dartmouth, Alex worked for two years with First Illinois Corporation in Chicago, where he met and married Sarah Smithton, the youngest daughter of the admiral-in-command of the Great Lakes Naval Training Center. A year later, Cecil summoned the newlyweds to Atlanta, and Alex began the process of assuming control of Hightower & Co. Initially, the young couple opted not to buy a house but purchased a Buckhead condominium for six thousand dollars cash and set up housekeeping. A big house would come later.

Maureen Hightower died of cancer when Spencer was in his early teens. Afterward, Cecil and his younger son lived in opposite ends of the big house and by mutual agreement kept away from each other as much as possible. When Spencer finally graduated from a local community college, his father bought him a house in a nearby Buckhead neighborhood, more for Cecil's peace and quiet than as a reward to his son. Spencer didn't want to work, and with his father's money, he didn't have to. Every penny of the "income" he received by serving as a token member of the boards of directors for several Hightower & Co. subsidiaries fueled a self-centered, hedonistic lifestyle. The real family power had been vested in Alex, and after Cecil's death, Alex moved into the family mansion and assumed day-to-day control of the Hightower holdings. Left to themselves, the two brothers maintained an uneasy truce occasionally broken by open conflict and harsh words.

Cecil established long-term trusts for both sons in his last will and testament, and even at age forty-four, Alex only had absolute control over half the corpus of his portion of the estate. Spencer's trust restricted access to any significant funds until he reached age thirty, and at twenty-six, he had four more years to wait before tapping into the main vein of his inheritance. In the interim, Alex served as cotrustee of Spencer's affairs with Dr. Lewis Newborn, a psychiatrist and family friend who, for years, had been the only person able to communicate effectively with Spencer. To relieve himself of the pressure of dealing with Spencer, Alex let Dr. Newborn oversee Spencer on a month-to-month basis; Alex reviewed the accounts at the end of the year.

From his desk, Alex had a panoramic vista of the Atlanta skyline that swept across the windows of his large corner office on the thirty-sixth floor. One sign of wealth and power was the ability to summon people into his presence, and in obedience to a phone call the day before, Joe Whetstone waited outside for his audience with Mr. Hightower.

"You may go in now," an expensively dressed receptionist said.

Joe opened the heavy, wooden door. Alex looked up from his desk and motioned for Joe to sit down. "Bring me up to date," he said curtly.

"Do you know about the change in defense lawyers?"

"Yes. McClain, isn't it?"

"Right. He's in his midfifties. A sole practitioner without a lot of technical support."

"My father mentioned him years ago. He's been a problem to us in the past."

"It appears he has an ax to grind," Joe agreed. "I heard from the local D.A. that the judge gave McClain a chance to refuse the case, but he said he was the only lawyer who could successfully defend Thomason."

Alex shook his head. "I hope he regrets his decision. Regrets it very, very much."

While Joe Whetstone was briefing Alex Hightower, the women of the Mable Ray Circle gathered on Tuesday morning in the small, windowless room adjacent to the narthex of the Poplar Avenue Presbyterian Church. Originally designed as a meeting place for the board of elders who governed the affairs of the church, the prayer room contained a polished walnut table surrounded by ten chairs. A thick red carpet covered the floor, and a dark wooden bookcase lined one wall. In the corner rested a smaller bookcase with a locking glass front. An oil painting of the crudely built first sanctuary of the church hung on the wall opposite the door.

Seven women, ranging in age from twenty-four-year-old Kelli Baker to seventy-six-year-old Naomi Morgan, took their seats around the table. Kathy Howell, a longtime member of the group, served as recording secretary, an important function since the prayer journals that filled several shelves of the smaller bookcase fueled the faith and hope for the women's intercessory prayers. Kathy possessed the two qualities needed by the group's scribe—an ability to crystallize the essence of a person's prayer in concise form and good handwriting. She always stayed after the meeting to index the prayers based on subject and substance.

Once everyone was seated, Naomi opened the meeting with a simple request. "Father, help us pray today in harmony with your son, Jesus. Cleanse us from anything that would hinder our agreement with your will and unity with one another. Let us pray for others with the love that you have for them. We adore you; we worship you. In Jesus' name, amen."

Then it happened.

There was not always a tangible awareness of God's presence when the women met. Sometimes they prayed with no assurance that their prayers traveled an inch beyond their lips or that the yearnings of their hearts reached within a million miles of heaven. But today was not one of the dry times that tested their perseverance and commitment.

No one moved. No one spoke.

Outside the room, the world's inhabitants scurried about in frantic frenzy. Inside the chamber, seven women waited quietly in hushed stillness. Celeste remembered a Bible verse. "God is in his holy temple, let all the earth be silent before him." Over and over the verse echoed in her spirit, and with each majestic refrain, she saw a new aspect of its truth, a glimpse of God's glory that would be over the earth when it reached its literal fulfillment. To be with him in the midst of his glory would be enough. Forever.

Time passed. The women waited.

Then, in a strong, steady voice, Naomi repeated the call of the mysterious heavenly creatures who never ceased expressing one of God's most unfathomable qualities. "Holy, holy, holy," she said. Several women bowed low, their faces in their hands. Kelli slipped from her seat and knelt on the carpet.

The women worshiped.

There are many ways to worship God. A song, a prayer, a word, a poem, a phrase, an emotion, a physical act, an intention of the heart, and countless other expressions can fit within the framework of accepted adoration. But this day, the women worshiped in the beauty of quiet holiness. It was the activity of heaven brought to earth.

And the gates of heaven opened.

Evil exists in the world; good lives in the spirits of God's children. And from the reservoir of redeemed hearts, prevailing prayer can issue forth even when no words are spoken. Celeste remembered another verse, "Your father knows what you need before you ask him." There was a time to speak and a time to be silent, and because of the Lord's omniscience, either could be the method of the moment. On this day, the unspoken thoughts and petitions of the women's hearts began to ascend from the room like incense that could be seen and smelled, but once it was released, could not be contained or defined. Obedience to the Holy Spirit, not commitment to religious formalities, brought vitality to their communication with heaven.

Names, faces, problems, and difficult circumstances came to mind—sometimes matched to an intercessory thought, sometimes joined to a deeply felt emotion, sometimes without any insight. No one prayed aloud; each knelt at her own altar. But for each person and situation, a suitable petition issued forth to the King of kings and Lord of lords, the One who holds all things in the hollow of his hand.

More than an hour and a half passed before release came. Then, within a few minutes, each woman raised her head, opened her eyes, and returned to the familiar feel of contact with this world. Several eyes glistened. Others beamed with joy.

"Wow," Kelli said.

"Yes," Kathy said. "Wow."

"Don't worry," Kelli added quickly. "I'm not going to try to analyze what happened. I realized that silence can be more powerful than words."

Celeste nodded then looked to Naomi. "Will you complete it?"

The old woman leaned back in her chair, looked toward heaven, and prayed with open eyes, "Father, we say, 'thank you, thank you, thank you.' For Jesus' sake, amen."

THIRTEEN

No hinge nor loop to hang doubt on.
OTHELLO, ACT 3, SCENE 3

AFTER RUNNING INTO several dead-ends, Vicki found a polygraph examiner with good credentials. Larry Davenport had worked twelve years for the Marietta, Georgia, Police Department before starting a private agency that specialized in employment-related testing. He had credibility, even if some of the people he tested did not.

Mac visited Pete at the jail to prepare him for the exam.

"Have you ever taken a lie-detector test?"

"When I went to work for Aeromart."

"Any problems?"

"I got the job."

"Good. If the results of this test are favorable, I will show it to the D.A.; if not, it will never leave my file."

"It will show I'm telling the truth," Pete said emphatically.

"I hope so."

"What about the blood test you mentioned?"

"The results aren't in."

Mac checked the notes on his legal pad. "One other thing. Ray Morrison, our investigator, uncovered an interesting piece of information."

"What?"

"Do you remember anything about driving up the mountain?"

"No, but I keep trying. Saturday night I had the worst nightmare yet. Even in my sleep, I tried to remember what happened, but it ended in the same blackness. Like I told you, that whole time period is a hole. A total blank."

"Maybe this will bring something to mind. The investigator interviewed an elderly man named Rodney McFarland, who was driving his pickup down the mountain. He met the yellow Porsche on the way up to the overlook. The Porsche came across the center line into his lane, and Mr. McFarland swerved toward the ditch. He told Ray there was a large, dark, burgundy car keeping pace with the Porsche. The second car sideswiped Mr. McFarland's truck. The police report did not mention any other vehicles. Ray took a paint sample, and we are going to have it analyzed."

Pete shook his head. "I don't know anyone who owns a car like that. How does that help?"

"I'm not sure, but whoever was in that car may know something about what happened at the overlook. The whole thing raises questions. And questions about what happened that night can create a reasonable doubt about your role in Angela's death. A reasonable doubt is what we need to convince a jury to set you free."

Larry Davenport arrived at the jail the following morning. He explained to Pete that the typical polygraph examination in a criminal case lasted about an hour and a half, the longest part devoted to the pretest interview because it laid the foundation for the validity of the actual questions to follow. Davenport gave Pete detailed instructions about polygraph procedures, made sure he understood how the equipment worked, talked at length about the issues for questioning, and reviewed the wording of the questions to be asked during the test.

Then Davenport placed rubber tubes across Pete's upper chest and abdomen, slipped two metal finger plates onto his ring and index fingers, and wrapped a blood pressure cuff around his upper arm. These devices would enable Davenport to measure respiration and movement, changes in the skin, and relative blood pressure and pulse rate. In theory, a lie is detected by physiological changes in more than one of the three indicators—increase or decrease in blood pressure, increase or decrease in heart rate, and change in blood volume. Jailhouse lore held that a polygraph could be fooled by "countermeasures," such as putting a tack in a shoe and pressing down on it when asked both control and relevant questions so that the measurements would be the same. But experienced examiners can usually spot countermeasures, and they argue that the only people who can fool a polygraph are the tiny sociopathic segment of the population who can tell a lie and honestly believe it to be true.

Once he finished the interview and hooked Pete up to the machine, Davenport began his questioning.

"Is your name Peter Thomason?"

"Yes," Pete said in a monotone.

"Do some people call you Pete?"

"Yes."

"Did you graduate from Auburn University?"

"Yes."

"Are you taking this polygraph test at the Echota County Jail?"

"Yes."

"Are you taking this test voluntarily?"

"Yes."

A chart rolled out of the machine documenting the physiological changes that occurred as Pete answered each question. Then Larry began asking the "relevant" questions, the questions that could be the difference between life and death, freedom or the electric chair. Pete sat rock still.

"Were you with Angela Hightower on August second?"

"Yes."

"Did you give Angela Hightower any drugs on August second?"

"No."

"Did you physically harm Angela Hightower?"

"No."

"Did you murder Angela Hightower?"

"No."

The chart discharged its findings. With an experienced eye, Larry watched the tracings the machine produced. When he completed a cycle of all relevant questions, he asked, "Are you ready to go through them again?"

"Yes. How did I do?" Pete asked.

"That will be in my report to your lawyer. Is your name . . ."

Friday afternoon, Vicki brought a fax into Mac's office and handed it to him.

"This just came in from the polygraph examiner."

Mac quickly read the results of the test.

Dear Mr. McClain,

Per your request, Mr. Peter Thomason was administered a MGQT polygraph examination at the Echota County Jail. The examination technique used is routinely employed by the federal government because it permits independent review, evaluation, and verification of data by other examiners who are not present during the examination.

During the pretest interview, relevant questions were developed with regard to the issue of Mr. Thomason's activities on August second. These questions were reduced to writing and reviewed one by one with Mr. Thomason. The relevant questions were administered to him together with various control and irrelevant questions.

When asked whether he gave any drugs to Angela Hightower, Mr. Thomason responded, "No." In my opinion, his response to this question was truthful. When asked whether he physically harmed Angela Hightower, Mr. Thomason responded, "No." In my opinion his response to this question was truthful. When asked if he murdered Angela

Hightower, Mr. Thomason responded, "No." In my opinion his response to this question produced equivocal results in the readings, thus raising the possibility that he was not truthful, but not conclusively demonstrating deception.

If I can be of further assistance, please call upon me.

Sincerely,
Larry Davenport
Polygraph Examiner
Ga. License #439

When he finished, Mac looked up at Vicki. "Did you read this?"

"No. I brought it directly to you."

"Take a look," he said.

In a few seconds, she said, "Huh?"

"Good answer," Mac said. "You should go to polygraph examiner school."

Mac telephoned David Moreland.

"I have the results of the polygraph. He made B-minus or C, depending on how you interpret it." Mac read the brief report over the phone.

"It's mostly good. I mean we couldn't ask for more on the issue of the drugs or physically harming Angela. But it's inconclusive on the ultimate question."

"Correct."

"Would it do any good to call Davenport and ask him about it?" David asked.

"Considering his conclusions, I doubt there's anything definite he can say."

"What do you make of it?"

"Use logic."

There was silence on the line for a few seconds. "Pete didn't harm Angela, but he possibly played a part in helping the person who did."

"Exactly."

"Have you talked with Pete?"

"I will in thirty minutes at the jail. I also have a copy of Dr. Wilkes's report."

"Any surprises?"

"No. It's consistent with her verbal summary. There are some points we can use at an appropriate time. I do have one other bit of information."

"What is it?"

"Meet me at the jail. We'll go over it then. Anyway, it's time you met our client face to face."

David was pacing back and forth on the short sidewalk between the jail and the parking lot when Mac arrived and handed him the packet of papers. They stood outside on the grass and talked.

"Mindy made copies of the report from the psychologist and"—Mac picked a sheet out of the stack—"the results from the lab that tested Pete's blood for Rohypnol. Look them over before we go inside."

After scanning the pages, David asked, "Does Pete know the results of the blood test?"

"Not yet."

"What do you want me to do when we talk with him today?" David asked.

"Nothing. Shake his hand, sit quietly, and I'll handle everything. If you have any questions, ask me later."

"Okay."

Entering the lobby, Mac asked David, "Have you been inside the jail yet?"

"No."

They waited for the buzzing sound, which signaled the release of the electric lock on the solid metal door that separated the public waiting area from the cellblocks.

"One of the worst parts of jail for the prisoners is the boredom," Mac said as they walked down a narrow corridor to another metal door.

"Some inmates sleep twelve to fourteen hours a day. It's called 'bunking your time.'"

Mac and David waited in the hallway while a deputy brought Pete down from the cellblock.

"Pete, this is David Moreland, the other lawyer who will be working on your case."

David looked small beside the much bigger defendant. They went into the interview room and sat down. Mac pulled out the letter from the polygraph examiner and slid it across the table.

"Here are the results of the polygraph test."

After reading the brief report, Pete hung his head. "I can't believe it. I thought I passed it. I mean—"

"You didn't fail," Mac said. "It supports what you've said about not giving Angela any drugs or physically harming her. On the rest, it's inconclusive."

"Which means it doesn't help."

"But it doesn't hurt you, either. This test is not admissible in court. We could agree to a stipulated test that would be performed by a GBI examiner, but based on this test it would be a risk, a big risk."

"Do you know the GBI examiner?"

"No, he's been here less than a year. Most defense lawyers don't have much confidence in lie detectors, because their clients are not telling the truth, and the polygraph shows it."

"I'm not lying!" Pete's voice grew louder, and he pushed the report across the table. "I didn't kill Angela. I don't care what this report says."

"I didn't say you were, and the test doesn't indicate conscious deception."

Pete set his jaw and clenched his teeth. "I want another test."

Mac wasn't expecting this. "I had to pay for this test. I'm not sure it would be worth it to—"

"No, I want a test with the GBI examiner. Maybe he knows what he's doing."

"But that would be a stipulated test. If you failed, it could be used against you in court."

"What have I got to lose?"

Mac leaned forward. "A lot."

Pete scowled. "I'm already being railroaded."

"Listen." Mac waited until Pete looked him in the eye. "If you fail a GBI test, it would be like lying down in front of a train and waiting for it to cut you in two. The case against you is circumstantial. That means there is nothing directly connecting you with Angela's death. No confession. No eyewitnesses. Nothing specifically pointing to you. A failed polygraph would be devastating. Here's my advice as your lawyer who is responsible to look out for your best interests—no stipulated polygraph."

Pete hesitated. "I still think it could be my only ticket out of here. There's no way the D.A. would try me for a murder if their own expert said I'm telling the truth."

"We don't have a promise from the D.A.'s office to do or not do anything. Polygraph or no polygraph. "

"But what can I do?" Pete said bitterly. "I'm innocent."

Before Mac could answer, David blurted out, "Pray."

Startled, Mac and Pete both looked at David, who said, "Uh, that just popped out."

"I guess it couldn't hurt anything to pray," Mac said. "We need every source of help available."

Pete shrugged. "I've been praying. What else can I do lying in my bunk night after night? But it hasn't done any good."

Mac slid a stack of papers across the table. "Here is the report from Dr. Wilkes, the psychologist. Don't try to read it now, but some of her findings are helpful. You're not a psychopath, and she says you're unable to offer proper assistance to us as your lawyers because you can't remember anything that happened the night Angela died."

"That makes sense."

"It does, but it probably won't convince the judge to rule that you are incompetent to stand trial. I'm sure the State will schedule another evaluation with a psychologist or psychiatrist of their choosing. I'll let you know."

"What about the blood test?" Pete asked. "Do you have the results?"

Mac steadied himself for an explosion. "The blood test came back from the lab in Atlanta. There was no sign of Rohypnol in your bloodstream."

Pete didn't explode. Instead, he deflated, and in a subdued tone asked, "Why can't I remember, then?"

Mac pushed back his chair and rubbed his temples. "Nobody knows. Nobody."

FOURTEEN

Your ears will hear a voice behind you saying,
"This is the way, walk in it."
ISAIAH 30:21 (NIV)

AS THEY WALKED across the parking lot away from the jail, Mac asked, "What do you think of our client?"

"I guess I agree with Mr. Davenport," David said.

"Inconclusive?"

"Yes."

"He's not the easiest guy to help," Mac said. "Sometimes a defendant will concoct a story about the charges against him that lets him off the hook. Then, while he's locked up, he goes over it in his mind until he actually believes it himself and repeats it in convincing fashion to his lawyer. Pete's approach is different. He claims he's not guilty, but he has no story—true or otherwise."

They reached their cars. "Let's go back to my office for a few minutes," Mac suggested. "It's Friday afternoon."

"Okay."

They went into the library. During a major trial, the normally peaceful library became the war room. In a few weeks, the room's dark-hued wooden table and crimson oriental rug would be covered with pleadings, reports, and exhibits.

Mac paced back and forth. He told David about Ray's interview with Rodney McFarland.

"That's a tidbit," David said.

"But we need something the jury can sink its teeth into. If Pete is unable or unwilling to provide a plausible story about the night of August second, we need to do it for him. A story that will explain the drugs in his and Angela's system and why she died."

"Did you read my suggestion that someone should interview Angela's college friends? Maybe they could give us some insight into Angela's relationships. You know, maybe uncover another angle of attack against the State's case."

"Yes, and I think it's a good idea."

Mac buzzed Vicki and summoned her to the library.

"Vicki, I want to send Ray Morrison to Hollins University in Roanoke."

"The girls' school?"

"He'll fit right in. Angela Hightower was a student there. Check flights from Chattanooga to Roanoke. I'll call Ray before I go home or first thing Monday morning."

When Vicki left the rom, Mac asked David, "What else?"

David thought a moment. "Nothing comes to mind."

Mac stopped pacing and looked at his watch. "It's almost five o'clock. Would you like a cold one?"

"Sure."

"Still spring water?"

"Yes."

Mac returned with two cold mugs, a beer, David's water, and a bowl of pretzels. He set the pretzels in the middle of the table and said, "Spring water and pretzels. That's a new combination."

Mindy peeked into the library and smiled at David. "Is there anything I can do for you before I leave?"

Mac turned the beer bottle up and poured the last drops into the white foam that touched the top rim of his mug. "No, thanks. Have a good weekend."

Mindy gave David one last look and retreated.

"Today, I'd like to talk while we drink," Mac said.

David took a sip of water. "What do we talk about?"

Before answering, Mac took a long drink and released a satisfied sigh. "Let's see. We can't talk about the respective merits of lager and Pilsner beers. And one spring water is the same as another. Are you a college football fan?"

"Not really. Remember, I went to Vanderbilt. 'Go Commodores.'"

Mac nodded. "Of course. That makes football a painful subject. Did you have a favorite team growing up?"

"I was a baseball player as a kid, always played second base. I grew up splitting my allegiance as a fan between the Braves and the Reds, but mostly went to see the Smokies, the double-A team in Knoxville. I never got too excited about football and only went to a few games when I was in law school at Tennessee. I saw the Georgia-Tennessee game two years ago."

Mac remembered the result. It was worse than the most recent Georgia loss. "No, let's not talk about that game." He took another drink before continuing. "Do you remember telling me at lunch the other day that there were other reasons why you turned down the job with the big law firm in Nashville?"

"Yes."

"I'm curious what they were. I'd think it would have been a great opportunity."

It was David's turn to take a long drink. "Okay," he said. "But it may be hard for you to accept."

"Try me. This is my most receptive thirty minutes of the week."

David picked up a pretzel. "God told me."

"God?"

"Yes, God."

"All right," Mac said slowly. "God told you not to go to Nashville, Tennessee, and work for a prestigious law firm."

David popped the pretzel in his mouth. "Not audibly, like in *The Ten*

Commandments. He spoke to me through a verse in the Bible. That's how I knew not to take the job."

Mac put his mug down on a glass coaster. "As far as I know, the Bible we use in the Presbyterian church doesn't mention the Fletchall law firm; Nashville, Tennessee; or Dennison Springs."

"Right. But it's similar to applying a legal precedent from an old case to a new set of facts. Here's what I did. First, I prayed and asked God to direct my steps according to Proverbs 3:5–6."

"Which says?"

"'*Trust in the Lord with all your heart and lean not on your own understanding. In all your ways acknowledge him and he will direct your paths.*' That put me in a place of dependence on the Lord to guide me. Then, I waited and continued praying."

"What happened?"

"Do you have a Bible?"

"Uh, I think Judy has one on her desk." Mac got up and returned in a moment with a small brown Bible. "Will this do?"

"Yes." David continued, "A couple of weeks later, I was reading in Genesis about Abraham's son Isaac. There was a famine in the land of Canaan, and Isaac considered a move to Egypt. His plan made perfectly good sense because with the Nile River as a reliable water source Egypt would be the best place to find food when times got tough." David opened the Bible, flipped to a passage, and continued. "But it says in Genesis 26:2 that 'The Lord appeared to Isaac and said, "Do not go down to Egypt; live in the land I tell you to live."' When I read those words, I thought about my decision whether or not to move to Nashville. An old precedent, a new set of facts. Without a doubt I was living in a land of famine. You saw my car. When I leave your office, there will be a small spot of oil on the pavement because of a leak in my crankcase. And just like Egypt and the Nile to Isaac, Nashville represented security to me, a steady source of money and a way out of poverty. Over the next few days, I continued to mull the whole thing over and became more confident that the Lord was directing me through the verses in Genesis not to go to Nashville. I called the hiring partner at the law firm and turned down the job."

"Did you tell him this story about Isaac and Egypt?"

"No, I gave him a sanitized version. Basically, 'Thank you for you offer, but I'm exploring other options.'"

Mac sat back in his chair. "Interesting. Do you know the problem I have with what you've told me?"

"That it's too subjective."

"Right."

"That I could find a Bible verse to support any decision or plan that suited my fancy," David said.

Mac smiled. "Counselor, you're doing a good job anticipating the judge's response to your position."

"I can't deny the subjective component of receiving direction from God. However, even though we like to think we're completely rational, reason-oriented creatures, a lot of what we think and do is not based on objective assessment of facts and data. I've never been in love, but I don't expect it's a completely rational experience."

Mac stared past David's shoulder at the bookcase behind him. "I have. It isn't."

"And I've been told there are levels of communication that only a man and woman who love each other can experience. It's the same between a Christian and Jesus. My personal relationship with the Lord is the doorway to communication with him."

"Every woman on the jury is eating out of your hand."

"Thanks," David said with a grin. "This communication thing involves risk, but I've decided to take my chances. I mean, if I'd gone to Nashville, I wouldn't be here to help you."

"And I hope you've just begun to help." Mac drained the last drops of his beer. "Interesting. I don't ever remember a conversation quite like this on the porch of my college fraternity house on Friday afternoons. How to talk with God didn't come up on a regular basis."

After David left, Mac called Ray's office but couldn't reach him and decided not to bother his friend at home. Vicki left a memo about airplane flights to Roanoke on Mac's desk—the earliest available flight didn't leave until Tuesday morning. Monday would be soon enough to talk to Ray. Mac took the two empty mugs to the kitchen and thought about David Moreland. The young pilgrim was a piece of work. A high IQ, but some strange ideas.

—

Mac spent a quiet weekend at home. There was no football game on Saturday afternoon to occupy his time, so he stacked wood and made a valiant effort to rake most of the leaves that covered the small patches of grass in the front and rear of his house. Flo and Sue loved leaf-raking time. For them, every pile was an open invitation to hidden adventure. They waited until Mac accumulated a large mound, then they dove in, burrowed down, and stayed completely still for about ten seconds before exploding out to chase each other around the house. A houseful of ten-year-old boys couldn't have caused more mischief. Mac let them play until their tongues hung out. Then he put them in their pen and finished his work.

Mac sat on the deck for an hour or two in the evening. At first, he thought about the Thomason case, but then his thoughts shifted to his lunch with Anna and Hunter Wilkes. He had enjoyed Hunter and appreciated a boy that was not so bound by fear, shyness, or the effects of MTV that he couldn't talk to an adult or consider trying something new. Mac had served as a Boy Scout troop leader when his sons were coming through the ranks, and he'd forgotten how much he enjoyed the company of youngsters.

When Mac went to bed, no nightmares disturbed his rest, and he slept later than usual. Because there was no football game to discuss in Sunday school, Mac didn't go to church.

—

It was midafternoon on Monday before Ray Morrison appeared at Mac's door.

"Do you have your bags packed?" Mac asked.

"I travel light. I have enough stored in here"—Ray patted his stomach— "to last three or four days."

"More like three or four hours. Can you make a quick trip to Hollins University in Roanoke, Virginia, and interview Angela's college roommate or anyone else you turn up? Vicki has checked on flights. You leave Chattanooga at eight-fifteen tomorrow morning, be in Roanoke by nine-ten, snoop around all day, and catch an afternoon flight at six-thirty. You'll be home for a late supper."

Ray looked down at the floor. "Tomorrow is fine, but what if the plane crashes and I'm killed?"

"What? You don't want to fly? You flew in the military, didn't you?"

"Uncle Sam didn't give me a choice, but as a civilian I'd rather ride backward on a mule to Virginia than crawl into a twin prop from Chattanooga to Roanoke."

Mac chuckled. "Suit yourself, and I promise not to tell anyone you're human. You can drive to Bristol then cut over through southwest Virginia."

"Don't worry about the navigation. My Ford mule and I will get there."

"Okay. Here's the plan. I want to know anyone who may have had a serious grudge against Angela: jilted boyfriend, groundskeeper who stalked her, professor who tried to proposition her, jealous classmate. Who knows? Just put your nose to the earth and see where it leads."

"Do you know her roommate's name?"

"Yes, the State has her on their witness list for the sentencing phase of the trial." Mac tore off a sheet of yellow legal-size paper and handed it to him. "Joan Brinkley from Fayetteville, North Carolina. Vicki checked, and she's enrolled again this year. Lives on campus in a dorm."

"I think I'll drive up tonight and go to the school early in the morning before classes start for the day."

"Fine. Call me if you need anything."

Joan Brinkley's campus address in hand, Ray left Mac's office, stopped by his house to kiss Peggy good-bye and drove through the night to Roanoke. Arriving at 2:00 A.M., he checked into a motel near the Hollins campus for a few hours' sleep, and by seven o'clock the next morning was sitting outside the door of the dean of students, waiting for the office to open.

Nestled in the mountains of southwestern Virginia, Hollins had survived the Civil War of the 1860s and the feminist movement of the 1960s. The later period had been a bigger threat, and at the time some educators predicted that women's liberal arts colleges would go the way of the hoop skirt. The experts, as usual, proved wrong.

The central campus area, known as the Quad, was classic, small Southern college—old brick buildings positioned around a grassy rectangle and a handful of enormous oak trees. The administration building was surrounded by a fifteen-foot-wide wooden porch perfect for lazy strolls and casual conversations.

Dr. Marjorie Plant, dean of the thousand young women enrolled at the school, arrived at her office promptly at 7:59 A.M. She found a sleepy-eyed Ray Morrison slouched down on the narrow bench beside the door.

"May I help you?" she asked.

"Yes, ma'am. My name is Ray Morrison, and I'm a private detective from Georgia, working on the Angela Hightower murder case. Could I talk to you for a minute?"

"Yes, of course." Dr. Plant unlocked the door and led Ray through the secretarial area into her own office, a large, book-lined room that overlooked the Quad. "Have a seat. I thought they caught the man who murdered Angela."

"They have arrested a young man, but he's not gone to trial. I'm working for the lawyer representing him."

"I see," the dean said crisply. "Then I'm not interested in talking to you. We want justice in this horrible matter, not someone escaping punishment." She got up from her seat, signaling the end of their brief conference. Ray didn't move his large frame. He had not driven most of the night and sat on a hard wooden bench for an hour to give up easily. He kept talking.

"Dr. Plant, when a complaint is brought against a student, do you immediately decide to punish her by suspension or dismissal from the school?" he asked.

"No," Dr. Plant said, standing beside her desk. "But this is murder, not pulling a fire alarm as a prank in a dormitory."

"Exactly my point, ma'am. How much more the need to thoroughly investigate the situation before rushing to judgment. If the boy's guilty, so be it, but I've been a police officer for many years and the initial evidence doesn't always point to the guilty party. You can't jump to conclusions."

Still standing, the dean hesitated. "What do you want?"

"Not much really. I would like to talk to Joan Brinkley, Angela's roommate last year. Perhaps Joan knows other girls who could provide information."

"About what?"

"Nothing complicated. Do the girls know anyone in the area who may have had a negative relationship with Angela? Things like that."

Dr. Plant tapped the corner of her desk. "All right. You can talk to Joan, but only here at the administration building and only if she wants to meet with you."

"That will be fine. Thank you."

Dr. Plant took Ray across the hall to the boardroom. While he waited, Ray looked at the portraits of former presidents of the school that lined the walls. One of the early leaders was a serious-looking fellow named Horace R. Morrison, Ph.D. *Probably a relative of mine,* Ray yawned. In a few minutes, the door opened and in walked a slender, blue-eyed young brunette carrying a red backpack loaded to capacity with heavy books.

"I caught her on the way to an early class," said Dr. Plant. "Joan, this is Mr. Morrison, a private detective. I have given him permission to ask you some questions about Angela, but if something comes up that makes you uncomfortable you do not have to talk any further with him. Just let me know. I'll be in my office."

"Thank you, Dr. Plant," Ray said.

When the door closed, Ray sat down at the long conference table that stretched the length of the room.

"Hi," he said. "Why don't you lighten your load for a few minutes?"

"Okay," the girl said with a nervous laugh, slipping off her backpack. "I wasn't expecting you to come. Actually I wasn't sure anyone would come. You know, I didn't know if it was important or not about the letters. I don't have them, the letters she got. But I know Angela wrote to her parents after the third one. I didn't know if it was a big deal, but then she was killed, and I didn't know if it was important or not." A tear escaped from Joan's eye and ran down her cheek. "Here, I'll show you."

Completely clueless, Ray said, "I'm sorry. I know you're upset."

Joan zipped open her backpack and took out a gray laptop computer. Flipping it open, she turned it on. While they waited for it to boot up, she said, "I know you'll want copies. Maybe Dr. Plant has an extra floppy disk in her office."

"We'll check in a minute," Ray said. "Let me read the letters first."

"There may be more, but Angela only wrote two on my computer. We were talking about the situation at the library, and she was so mad. She asked if she could use my machine to write her dad's younger brother. Of course, I said yes."

The main menu screen popped into view. Joan went into the word processing program and in a moment pushed the machine across the table to Ray. "Here's the letter she wrote to her uncle."

1 APRIL

SPENCER,

DO NOT CALL OR WRITE AGAIN!! I DO NOT WANT TO SEE YOU OR TALK TO YOU. IF I HEAR ONE MORE WORD FROM YOU, I WILL TELL MY PARENTS. I MEAN IT. GET SOME HELP!

ANGELA

A very awake Ray pushed the computer back to Joan. "Okay. I guess I do need that on a disk. You said there was another letter, one to her parents?"

"Yes. I thought about erasing both of them, you know, because it was Angela's personal business, not mine. I didn't know what to do. Who to call or anything. Did I do the wrong thing, keeping it?"

"No, you did the right thing. Can you bring up the other letter?"

"Oh yeah."

In a couple of seconds, Ray was reading again.

1 April

Dear Mom and Dad,

I don't know how to tell you this except to just come out and say it. Spencer has been bothering me. Last fall at the steeplechase in Dunwoody, he followed me around all day, stood too close to me, and said some things he shouldn't have said.

Then he started writing me letters telling me how much he cared for me and saying he wanted to come see me here at school. I called and told him to stop, and he left me alone until I was home for Christmas. Then he started back, only worse. One night, he made a pass at me in the downstairs hallway and I slapped him—hard. He got mad, and I hoped that was the end of it.

Now I have started getting more letters, and he has left three phone messages for me in the past week! This has got to stop. Can't his psychiatrist do something for him? Do his doctors know what he's doing?

I'm mad, frustrated, and scared. I don't want him showing up on campus and embarrassing me in front of my friends. Dad, please take care of this. I'm sorry, but it's not my fault, and I want it to stop.

Love,
Angela

When he finished reading, Ray asked, "Do you know if she sent these letters?"

"I know she sent the one to her uncle because I mailed it for her. I don't know about the one to her parents."

"Do you know if Spencer ever threatened her physically? Did she have a reason to be scared?"

"I don't know. Angela never told me exactly what happened over Christmas break. It was just kind of creepy."

"After this letter was sent to Spencer, did he call or send her any more letters?"

"Yeah, I think she did get a couple more. I know she threw one away without opening it. We got out of school the third week of May, so it wasn't that long until summer vacation."

"Did he ever show up on campus?"

"No. I would have known if he had done that."

"Did Angela tell any of the other girls about this?"

"I doubt it. She made me promise not to mention it. You know, like she said, it was kind of embarrassing."

"Anything else?"

"No," Joan sighed. "I sure am glad to get this off my chest."

"I bet you are. Go ahead and ask Dr. Plant for a disk. I would like copies of these letters, and you should keep them on your machine, too."

While Joan was across the hall, Ray sat back in the leather chair, looked at Dr. Morrison's portrait, and thought about Joan's revelation.

No. Angela never sent the letter to her parents. If she had, she might still be alive.

FIFTEEN

Behold, and see if there be any sorrow like unto my sorrow.
LAMENTATIONS 1:12 (KJV)

I'LL FILE THE motions at the courthouse myself," Mac told Judy. "I need to get out of the office for a few minutes and stretch my legs."

It was almost noon on Tuesday morning when Mac walked out the door for the short jaunt to the courthouse. It was getting cooler. Even at midday, the air held a hint of morning crispness. Without the haze of summer, the mountains to the east stood out so clearly that it was almost possible to pick out specific trees.

Crossing the street in front of the courthouse, he noticed a white car that looked vaguely familiar. It had a Tennessee license plate, but he couldn't connect the owner and vehicle until he had walked several feet past it along the sidewalk. He stopped. It was Dr. Anna Wilkes's car. He wondered if the psychologist was meeting privately with the D.A.'s office.

Mac's face grew grim and he set his jaw. There wasn't any prohibition against communication between Anna Wilkes and the prosecution. But Mac had viewed Dr. Wilkes as an ally, not a potential adversary. Expert witnesses always made Mac nervous. By definition they possessed specialized knowledge and with that knowledge came the power to affect the direction of a legal proceeding. Mac didn't want anyone helping to steer *State v. Thomason* toward the electric chair. He filed his paperwork in the clerk's office, but instead of returning to the office, he decided to find and confront Dr. Wilkes. He didn't have a long search.

Coming down the steps from the upstairs courtroom, Dr. Anna Wilkes was smiling and talking with D.A. Bert Langley. She saw Mac and nodded in his direction. Mac didn't respond but positioned himself at the bottom of the stairs and waited.

Bert spoke first. "Mac, how are you?"

"Not bad," Mac answered. "Who's your friend?"

"Dr. Anna Wilkes, a psychologist from Chattanooga. Dr. Wilkes, this is Mac McClain, a local lawyer."

Anna was dressed professionally—blue skirt, matching jacket, and white blouse. She gave Mac a strange look.

"Bert!" a voice called from the top of the stairs. "The judge has something else to ask you."

"Excuse me," Langley said as he turned and walked back up the stairs.

When they were alone, Anna asked, "What was that about?"

"It's fairly obvious. I'd hoped you wouldn't be playing both sides of the case so aggressively."

Anna looked confused for a second then laughed. "You've eaten a bad plate of chicken livers, Mr. McClain. I wasn't fraternizing with your enemies. I've been testifying in a juvenile court case involving a young girl I've seen in my practice. This hearing was scheduled weeks ago, long before you asked me to evaluate Pete Thomason."

"You didn't talk to Bert Langley?"

"Not about Pete. He didn't see me until I took my seat in the witness chair. And the report I faxed you wasn't mailed until yesterday. I doubt he's received his copy." Anna smiled. "You should have seen your face. You looked like you were going to bite my head off. Is that the way you always glare when you're about to cross-examine someone?"

Mac relaxed. "Sorry. I mean there's nothing that prevents you from talking to the State. It's just that I—"

"Want to know that I'm not going to waffle in my evaluation. I won't."

"Yeah, that's it. I've been doublecrossed by expert witnesses in the past."

"I understand."

Mac put his hand on the stair railing. "Are you finished with your testimony for today?"

"I'm not sure. The judge wanted to take a break and told me to come back at one-thirty."

"Could I buy your lunch? I mean, unless you were going with Bert."

"No, Mr. Langley didn't offer to buy my lunch, either. I'd be glad to accept your offer as long as you promise me one thing."

"No chicken livers?"

"That, too. Promise you won't give me that look if you ever question me in court."

Mac held up his hand. "I promise."

They walked out of the courthouse together.

"Do we walk or drive?" Anna asked.

"Drive. The place I have in mind is a few miles out of town."

They got in Anna's car and Mac gave her directions to Josie's Restaurant. On the way, he told her the results of Pete's drug test.

"Hm," she said. "I'll give it some more thought."

"It looks like a dead end, but I appreciate the suggestion."

The parking lot was full, and the restaurant was bustling with its eclectic noonday crowd.

They went through the buffet line. Mac selected the usual—fried chicken, green beans, creamed corn, and okra. Anna opted for vegetables, in smaller portions than Mac. After they found a table and sat down, she said, "This is like eating at my grandmother's house when I was a girl."

"You must have had a lot of relatives."

"A large family, but not this many." Before Mac started eating, Anna bowed her head and prayed, "Father, thank you. You are a good God who takes care of his children. Bless this food. Amen." The psychologist was professional and articulate in regular conversation, but when she prayed she became almost childlike.

"Where is home?" Mac asked, as he cut a bite of chicken.

"Southwestern Virginia. A little place in the mountains called Lebanon. It used to be coal country."

"You don't look like a coal miner's daughter."

"I'm not. Baptist minister."

They ate in silence for a couple of minutes while Mac absorbed Anna's comment about her background and wondered how a Baptist minister's daughter became a clinical psychologist. He decided not to explore the topic and settled on something safer. "How is the food?" he asked.

"Good. Just like my granny's house."

"Did you call her Granny?"

"Yes. It fit her. She was a little woman who wore her hair in a bun and lived in a small white farmhouse with big trees in the front yard. Every summer I spent a week with her. It was only a few miles away from our home, but it was like a big vacation to me. In the afternoons we'd walk hand in hand to a nearby country store and buy something cold to drink. She'd cook my favorite foods for supper and let me stay up late at night reading in bed."

"Keep going."

"About what?"

"Your life story."

Anna raised her dark eyebrows. "My life story? Do you want to cross-examine me, or should I give it in narrative form?"

"Remember, I promised no cross-examination. Pretend you are writing a psychological report on yourself. Begin with your background and bring it up to the present."

"That's pretty personal."

"I'm a lawyer. Everything you tell me is confidential."

Anna took a sip of tea. "I'll be selective. You've read about my educational and professional training. I'm the eldest of five girls. My father served the same church for thirty years and is one of the greatest men I've ever met. I have an eleven-year-old son named Hunter. My parents still live in Virginia, and my siblings are scattered across the eastern part of the country from Connecticut to Georgia."

"What about your grandmother?"

"She died about fifteen years ago."

Anna nibbled on a piece of cornbread. "What about your life story?"

Mac put down his fork. "Well, I'm from Dennison Springs. Lived here all my life except for the time I was in school at the University of Georgia. How did you get to this area?"

"My husband, Jack, was a Washington and Lee graduate. After we married, he worked ten years in a management position with a utility company in Virginia. I completed my education, and we tried to start a family. Jack was not happy in his job and placed his résumé with a headhunting firm that found a position for him with TVA. I finally got pregnant, and we moved to Chattanooga to start a new life. We hoped Jack would enjoy his new job, and I wanted to do some part-time psychological testing and raise a family. I guess there was enough of my mother and granny in me to want a house full of kids, friends, and pets."

Mac again checked for a wedding ring, but Anna's finger was bare. "Is your husband still with TVA?"

"No, I'm a widow. Jack committed suicide several weeks before Hunter's birth. I'm a psychologist, but I was unable to help my own husband."

At the mention of suicide, Mac had trouble swallowing. "I'm sorry. I wasn't trying to pry."

"That's okay. I've talked about it many times during the past ten years. I guess it lets people know that even though I'm a professional counselor my own life hasn't been trouble-free. I know what pain feels like."

Mac's hands became clammy.

Anna continued, "Whatever was bothering Jack became worse after the move to Chattanooga. Eight months into my pregnancy, I came home after shopping for baby things and found him unconscious on the living room sofa. A first I thought he'd had a heart attack or stroke."

"Did he, uh, use pills?" Mac asked in a quiet voice.

"Yes, he swallowed a bottle of sleeping pills. They rushed him to Erlanger Hospital, but it was too late. He slipped into a coma and died two days later. No note, no explanation, no reason."

"Do you wish it had been quicker?"

"His death?" Anna asked, puzzled.

"Uh, yeah."

Anna studied Mac for a second. "I never thought about it like that. It was terrible during the two days he lingered in a coma, but it was a horrible shock no matter what."

Mac shook his head to dispel the fog that had settled on his brain. "I'm really sorry. You don't have to go into all this."

"It's been a long time ago; I've had to go on with my life."

Mac tried to eat, but he had completely lost his appetite. "How has Hunter handled everything?"

"He has his ups and downs. He was born three weeks after I buried my husband. There was no money from life insurance policies because of the suicide, so I invited my Aunt Jean to move to Chattanooga from Virginia to help take care of Hunter. I found a job working as a staff psychologist with a large clinic for two years. About eight years ago, I opened my own office."

Mac looked at his watch. "You need to get back to the courthouse."

In the car, Mac was lost in his own thoughts, staring out the window at the passing countryside.

Anna broke the silence. "I'm sorry we didn't have a lighthearted lunch. I probably should have talked about Hunter's soccer team."

"No, no. That's okay. It's just so, uh, so—" Mac paused.

"Sad. I know. But it's not the end of the story. There's more; it gets better. Sometime I'd like to tell you the good parts."

"Okay."

They pulled into a parking space in front of the courthouse. "I did all the talking," Anna said. "You didn't tell me about your family."

"No," Mac responded. "I didn't."

He opened the car door and got out before she could ask another question.

"I'm going back to the office," he said. "I have a busy afternoon."

"Thanks for lunch. I'll call if I have any ideas about Pete."

Mac turned away and crossed the street. Anna watched him for a few steps. He'd certainly closed down tight when she asked about his family. Maybe it was her imagination, but it almost looked as though he was stooped over, laboring under a heavy load.

Earlier in the day, the Mable Ray Circle gathered in the prayer room at the Poplar Avenue church. This week was different from the previous one. No overwhelming sense of the awesome presence of a holy God bowed them down in silent worship and intercession. Today, there was a lightness, a sweetness in the air, more like spring than fall, and they prayed openly with hopeful expectation.

One topic on the agenda was the local school system—students, teachers, administrators. Another was the spiritual vitality of various churches in the community, not just their own church or denomination but others with different signs in front of their places of worship. After an hour, they directed their focus to the Thomason murder case. They prayed for the Hightower family, Peter Thomason, the prosecutors, Mac, Judge Danielson, and the jurors who would eventually decide the case.

Celeste prayed for Mac. "Father, strengthen every thread of your love and grace for Mac. Please Lord, send people across his path to speak the truth in love."

After the prayer meeting ended, Celeste went home and ate a salad for lunch. She was scheduled to assist as a volunteer at the juvenile court in the afternoon, and she drove up at the same time Mac and Anna arrived back from lunch at Josie's. Mac had a grim look on his face as he left the car, and Celeste saw Anna Wilkes stare after him for several seconds. She got out and caught up with Anna, who was walking slowly up the sidewalk.

"Hello," she said. "I'm Celeste Jamison."

Anna stopped and faced her. "Anna Wilkes. Have we met before?"

"I don't think so. I saw you with Mac McClain."

"He recently hired me to help with a case, and we had lunch together."

"Are you a lawyer?"

"No, a psychologist from Chattanooga. How do you know each other?"

"We go to the same church, and before her death, Mac's wife was one of my best friends."

Anna's face grew serious. "Oh, I asked him about his family right before we got out of the car, and he left in a hurry. It puzzled me. I didn't know I'd hit a nerve."

"It's not just his wife. He also lost both of his sons at the same time. The whole family was in a horrible wreck about nine years ago. Only Mac survived."

As the force of Celeste's words hit her, Anna's eyes suddenly blurred with tears. She reached in her pocketbook for a tissue. "Sorry. I barely know him. I lost my husband, too, but the pain he carries, I feel—" she stopped. A strong wave of sorrow washed over her. "What's happening to me?"

Celeste looked intently into her face. “Are you a Christian?”

Anna nodded through tears that pooled at the base of her eyes and threatened to cascade down her cheeks.

Celeste lightly touched Anna’s shoulder. “I’d say it’s a burden from the Lord.”

SIXTEEN

For a moment the lie becomes truth.
DOSTOEVSKI

RETURNING TO THE OFFICE, Mac walked through the door as Mindy put a caller on hold.

"It's Pete Thomason," she said. "He's out for his exercise time."

Mac took the call in the library.

"I've thought a lot about the stipulated lie-detector test," Pete began. "I want to go ahead with another test. One that we can use in court. I'm sure I'll pass it and get this thing over with."

"I can't recommend—"

"I know what you told me," Pete interrupted.

Mac continued. "There's no guarantee the State will dismiss the charges even if you pass."

"But you said the case is circumstantial, and a test would prove I'm innocent."

Mac started to argue, but stopped. "I'll come by to see you later today."

Bert Langley phoned a few minutes before five o'clock. The D.A. had an edge to his voice. "I just received the psychological report in the Thomason case from a Dr. Anna Wilkes in Chattanooga. What's the deal playing dumb with me earlier today?"

Mac considered lying and claiming he'd never met Anna Wilkes in person before but said, "It was a misunderstanding. Sorry."

"I'm not laughing, and I don't think the judge is going to buy her theory that Thomason isn't competent because he claims he can't remember the night of the murder."

"It would be a stretch," Mac admitted.

"I faxed the report to Joe Whetstone, and he's going to schedule another psychiatric evaluation for the defendant."

"I thought that might happen. Do you know when?"

"Joe is aiming for this week, but I'll give you at least twenty-four hours' notice."

"All right."

Bert paused and continued in a calmer tone, "Okay, Mac. No more stonewalling. I can hear it in your voice. What else do you have? You have to tell me under the criminal discovery rules."

"Nothing, except that your evidence is circumstantial and doesn't fit the profile for a death penalty case. Withdraw the death penalty request."

"Our case may be circumstantial, but we've got the guy at the scene of the crime with an opportunity to kill and a dead girl with Rohypnol in her system. You'd have to give me a good reason, a very good reason."

"I'm working on it, but I don't have anything yet."

"What's Ray Morrison uncovered?"

"Nothing that would convince you. "

Bert shifted gears. "One other thing. Does Thomason want to submit to a stipulated polygraph with the GBI examiner?"

Mac wondered if someone at the jail had overheard Pete's earlier call and tipped off the D.A. "If he passes it, would you dismiss the case?" he asked.

"I've already talked it over with some of the others here at the office. The Hightower family would be hard to convince. They're sure Thomason is the man who killed their daughter. But if he passes a GBI test, it's a different situation."

"But you didn't answer my question. If he passes a stipulated test, will you dismiss?"

"No promises. But I think Joe Whetstone would have a hard time trying to convince a jury that Thomason is the killer."

"Okay."

"And," Bert added, "if Thomason fails the test, life without parole might look like a sweet deal compared to the only other alternative."

The Beulah Land Christian Bookstore was located on the main street through Dennison Springs. The owner of the building rented space on the second floor to a small insurance agency, a telephone marketing outfit, and attorney David Moreland. The entrance to the upstairs offices was located on a side street near the rear of the building. Mac opened a glass door that screeched when it scraped across the tile floor. A small signboard listed David's office as Suite 202.

Mac climbed the stairs and walked down the hallway to an opaque glass door on which was stenciled in gold paint, "David Moreland, Attorney at Law." He opened the door and stepped into a tiny waiting room that contained three metal chairs and a small coffee table with an out-of-date issue of *Newsweek* on it.

"David, are you in there?" he called.

David peered around the corner. "Sorry I didn't hear you. Welcome to my humble work quarters."

Mac walked into David's office. Two imitation-leather chairs served the needs of clients. The young lawyer's desk looked suspiciously similar to the one used by Mac's tenth-grade chemistry teacher, and he wondered if a close inspection might reveal a few pieces of dried chewing gum under the desk's top. David's diplomas hung in plain, black frames on the light green walls. A picture of David with a happy-looking beagle sat on the corner of the desk.

Mac picked up the picture. "Do you still have the dog?"

"Yes, that's Bozo. He's with my parents until I have a place to keep him."

"Bozo?"

"He was a clown when he was little."

"Nice-looking pup," Mac said. "Is he AKC registered?"

"Yes. Championship bloodlines. His registered name is Reginald Balfour Carpathian, but he won't answer to that. He likes Bozo."

"I have two nice females and there is a big demand for good beagles around here. Maybe we could go into business on some pups."

"Let me know and I'll talk it over with Bozo."

Mac loosened his tie. "So how's the law business?"

"You know about the car wreck case, and I've taken in a couple of adoptions and a name change. I also have an invoice ready for submission to the county in the Thomason case."

"Good. Give it to me and I'll take it to the judge tomorrow for approval. Speaking of our client, I talked to Bert Langley at the D.A.'s office a few minutes ago."

"And?"

"He's probably willing to back off the death penalty request if we can show him something that shakes the State's case."

"Did you tell him about the other car?"

"No, not yet. But he suggested a GBI polygraph."

"What did you say?"

"Nothing, but Pete called earlier today and demanded another test."

"You're kidding. I thought you talked him out of it the other day."

"Apparently not."

—

David drove his VW and followed Mac the four blocks from the bookstore to the jail. Looking in his rearview mirror, Mac smiled. Someday the young lawyer would have a decent office and drive a BMW.

They parked next to each other in front of the jail.

"How is the oil leak?" Mac asked.

"Manageable. Still a quart a week." David stopped at the edge of the parking lot. "Before we meet with Pete, I need to ask you something."

"Okay."

"I'm uneasy about him submitting to a State-administered polygraph."

"Spoken like a true defense lawyer. I'm going to oppose it as vigorously as I can."

"Well, it's more than that." David stopped. "I don't trust the GBI examiner."

"I don't know him. But it's not likely he wants to win the defense lawyer's best-friend award."

"Actually," David said slowly. "I prayed about this possibility over the weekend."

Mac bit his lip. "Go ahead."

David pulled a New Testament with Psalms and Proverbs from his shirt pocket and began to talk more rapidly. "I believe Psalm 35 describes Pete's case, especially verses 11 and 20: 'Ruthless witnesses come forward; they question me on things I know nothing about. . . . They do not speak peaceably, but devise false accusations.'"

"Most defense lawyers would agree."

"Yes, but I think it's a warning for us in this particular case, and I'd like to mention it to Pete."

"As a reason not to take a polygraph?"

"Yes."

Mac hesitated. "I think it's Russian roulette with four bullets in the gun for Pete to insist on another polygraph test, but it's unprofessional to drag your intuition about the Bible into this case. It's one thing for you to personalize biblical interpretation and rely on it yourself; it's another to impose it on others, especially someone who is dependent on us for legal advice that affects whether he may live or die."

David held his ground. "It's not intuition, and I'm not trying to impose my will, but if he wants to take a polygraph test, I want to counsel him from every perspective."

"Can you name a section in the Code of Professional Responsibility that covers legal advice based on the Bible?" Mac asked.

"A lawyer shall zealously represent the client?"

"Not good enough. Only if a client requested the type of counsel you want to give would I consider it a possibility, and then it would need to be clear that your comments were not offered as 'legal' advice."

"Okay," David backed off. "You're the boss."

"No, I'm the lawyer. The client is the boss."

Forty-five minutes later they came out of the jail. Despite all Mac's efforts to warn Pete of the dangers of a stipulated polygraph, the "boss" had made his demands clear.

"I hope I do a better job convincing the jury than I did our client," Mac sighed. "I'll call Bert Langley in the morning so he can set up the GBI test. Do you want to attend? You can't be in the room, but you could get a feel for how the process works."

"Yes. I'd like to be there, for better or for worse."

The following morning Mac phoned Bert Langley and asked him to schedule the polygraph exam. In less than fifteen minutes Mindy buzzed him. "Bert Langley on line two."

"Mac, the GBI polygraph is set for this afternoon at one o'clock at the Georgia Bureau of Investigation District Office in Cartersville. It's about an hour's drive, so Thomason will leave the jail at eleven-thirty if you want to talk to him before the test."

"No. David Moreland is planning on coming."

"Do you want him to sign the stipulation on admissibility?"

Mac started to agree, then remembered David's reservations. "I'll swing by your office and do it myself. David's not familiar with the form. Anything else?"

"Joe Whetstone has scheduled an independent mental evaluation with a psychiatrist from Atlanta on Friday. You need to tell your client to cooperate."

"Do you have the psychiatrist's name and professional qualifications?"

"Joe is faxing it to us, and I'll send it over as soon as I receive it."

Ray Morrison arrived back in Dennison Springs about the same time Pete Thomason, in handcuffs and leg chains, entered the Georgia Bureau of Investigation District Office for northwest Georgia. David Moreland and the GBI examiner, Sergeant Tom Laird, a clean-cut officer in his early thirties, were waiting for him.

"I need to speak to my client for a minute," David said.

The officer nodded. "There is a conference room down the hall on the left."

Shuffling along, Pete followed David into the room, and they sat down. "You can still back out of this test," David said.

"I told you yesterday that I've made up my mind. If you were in my shoes, you'd be looking for a way out of this mess. Waiting for something to turn up just won't get it."

"Okay. You need to pay attention to everything that happens during the test, and if it's any different than the one you had at the jail I want to know about it."

"I'll pay attention. Will they tell me the results today?"

"I doubt it, but as soon as we know anything Mr. McClain or I will come by the jail and let you know."

"Anything else?"

"No, just tell the truth."

"I always have."

David sat in the waiting area. And prayed.

While David waited, Mac received a fax with the results from Peachtree Lab on the burgundy paint sample lifted from Rodney McFarland's truck.

His phone buzzed. "Ray Morrison is here to see you," Mindy said.

"Good timing. Send him back."

The private detective strolled into Mac's office, sat down, and yawned.

"How was your trip?" Mac asked.

"Productive. I didn't get back until late last night or I would have been by earlier today. I've written a report, but there are some things I wanted you to know right away."

"Before you tell me, I have the results of the test on the paint sample from Mr. McFarland's truck." He handed the sheet to Ray.

The detective read aloud, "Lincoln Town Car, paint number 4659-3, marketed as 'midnight purple.' I owe Mr. McFarland an apology—he told me it was a purple car."

"The chemist says it's a specialty color, not very common. Vicki is checking with Ford to find out the number of midnight purple cars that were manufactured and how many were shipped and sold in the southeast region."

"I have something for you to read," Ray said. "Remember Joan Brinkley, Angela Hightower's roommate?"

"Yes. Did you talk to her?"

"Yeah, and she gave me copies of two letters Angela wrote on Joan's computer toward the end of the school year." He handed two sheets of paper to Mac. "Read the short one first."

Mac let out a sharp breath. He looked at the old grandfather clock, picked up the phone, and buzzed Vicki. "Call the GBI district office in Cartersville and get David Moreland on the phone as soon as possible." While he waited, Mac read the letter to Angela's parents. "This is incredible."

Ray spoke, "The roommate says she mailed the letter to Spencer Hightower for Angela but doesn't know if the other one was ever sent."

"Did Spencer come to Hollins?"

"Not that I could find out. I talked to several other students and Angela's faculty advisor but didn't turn up anything else."

Mac checked the clock again. It was one forty-five. He hoped that typical governmental inefficiency would have delayed the start of the test. He shifted nervously in his seat. "I can do something with these letters if Thomason hasn't already sunk the case by failing a stipulated polygraph."

"A polygraph? Why would you let him do that?"

Before Mac could answer, the phone buzzed and Vicki said, "David Moreland's on line two."

Mac punched the speakerphone button. "Have they started the test?"

"They took him in about an hour ago. What's happened?"

"I don't have time to explain. Knock on the door and stop the test. I mean immediately."

David put down the phone without hanging up and started quickly toward the examination room. Before he reached it, the door opened and one of the deputies who drove Pete to the GBI office stepped out. Pete followed him. A second deputy emerged, then Sergeant Laird appeared.

"Are you the accused's attorney?" he asked.

"Yes."

"I found your client significantly deceptive on every relevant question. My written report will be ready in a couple of days."

"No!" Pete yelled out. "That's not right!" He jerked around and started toward the polygraph examiner.

"Get him out of here," Laird told the deputies.

The deputies grabbed Pete's arms and turned him toward the door. "Do something!" Pete called out as the deputies half-led, half-dragged him out the front door.

"I want copies of the charts," David demanded.

"You'll have to talk to the D.A. about it," Laird shot back. "Unless I hear from him, the charts stay with me." Turning on his heel, he went back in the examining room and shut the door.

David walked slowly back to the phone. "It's too late," he told Mac.

"He's already finished the test?"

"Yeah. He failed. Totally. The examiner found him deceptive on every relevant question."

Mac swore. “That idiot! I’m holding two pieces of paper that could have been his tickets to reasonable doubt. What a stupid idiot!”

Mac’s face turned redder and redder. He sputtered for a few seconds and then said, “Come to my office. We’ll talk then.”

David said, “Yes, sir,” to a dead receiver.

At the news of the failed polygraph, Mac’s ten-second fantasy of hope for the Thomason case evaporated like a morning mist in July, but by the time David arrived at the office, he’d already started channeling his frustration into developing a new theory of defense. He met David in the library and laid Angela’s letters on the table. “Read these. You’ll see why I called.”

David picked up the sheets and quickly scanned them.

“Wow. Who is Spencer Hightower?” he asked.

“Alexander’s younger brother. I’d guess he’s in his midtwenties by now.”

“What do you know about him?”

Mac began pacing. “There’s been gossip about him for years. All I remember is that Spencer is a lot younger than Alex and a bad egg. From the looks of what you have in your hand, he’s a thoroughly rotten egg. The kind of person a jury would love to hate.”

“But even with these letters there’s no real connection between him and Angela’s death.”

“I don’t have to prove that Spencer personally killed Angela. He could have hired someone to do it. All I have to do is convince the jury that Spencer *might* have been behind the murder. That’s enough for a reasonable doubt about Pete’s guilt. I could argue two motives. First, he’s insanely angry in a twisted way because she rejected him. Second, he wanted her dead so he could control more of the Hightower money.”

“Your second point isn’t mentioned in the letters.”

“Right. But everyone knows that the prospect of lots of money can drive people to do crazy things, even people who already have more money than the rest of us. Old Cecil Hightower may have tied up Spencer's inheritance in all kinds of trusts, and the only way Spencer can get to it is to kill everyone else in the family. He started with the weakest member—Angela."

"That's far-fetched."

"Probably so. But if I can show that Spencer is mentally unstable, introduce the letters, and mention the Hightower wealth, and the jury's imagination can take them the rest of the way. I guarantee you that one juror who believes this case is a big, mysterious conspiracy will carry a lot of weight when it comes time to deliberate a verdict."

"What do we do now?" David asked.

"Tie Pete to a post and give him a whipping. If he hadn't insisted on the polygraph test, we'd have the upper hand. Those letters from Angela don't *prove* anything, but they raise the kind of questions that could sway a jury or influence Bert Langley to back away from the death penalty. You were right about the polygraph—I should have let you hit Pete over the head with the biggest, blackest Bible you could find."

"There's one other thing we haven't considered," David said.

"What?"

"That the results of the GBI polygraph are correct. If they are, Pete Thomason deserves to die."

SEVENTEEN

The unfeigned faith that is in thee, which dwelt first in thy grandmother Lois, and thy mother Eunice.
2 TIMOTHY 1:5 (KJV)

MAC AND DAVID worked quietly in the library as the hands of the clock in Mac's office crept toward midnight. After several hours of legal research, their brains grew a little foggy. Mac closed a reference book and put down his pen.

"I'm done. This day has stressed me out," he said.

"Me, too." David logged off the computer he was using.

"I've been thinking about what you said about the polygraph test," Mac leaned back in his chair and stretched. "You know, the fact that Pete may be guilty and deserves the electric chair."

"It hit me today as they dragged him out of the GBI office. It was like the scene shifted, and I saw him being led to the electric chair."

"You're not claiming divine revelation of his future, are you?"

"No. It was probably my imagination."

"Do you want out of the case?"

David hesitated. "No. I think I'm supposed to help."

"Are you still sure?"

"Yes."

"Good. I need it." Mac stood up and stretched. "I'm going home and hope I don't have nightmares about polygraph exams."

"Is there any restriction on my access to Pete?" David asked. "I think one of us should see him tonight."

"You can see Pete at three in the morning if you want to. Effective assistance of counsel is a twenty-four/seven proposition."

It was 12:15 A.M. when David pulled into the jailhouse parking lot. He turned off the engine, put his head down on the steering wheel, and prayed.

Jesus had been a part of David's life for as long as he could remember. As a youngster growing up in the shadow of the Smoky Mountains, he spent many an east Tennessee night with his head on his mother's lap during revival meetings at the Mount Gilead Pentecostal Church. On a hot July night when he was eleven, he knelt on the floor and "prayed through" to an assurance of salvation.

David's great-grandfather was a Pentecostal pioneer, part of a zealous band of men and women who burst out of the mountains of eastern Tennessee and western North Carolina in the early 1900s "full of fire and the Holy Ghost." Wesleyan in theology without knowing much about John Wesley, and bold in evangelism without apology for their emotional appeals, the early Pentecostals jumped feetfirst into the rural communities where they lived. Jobs were lost and families divided, but many souls saved and lives transformed. By the time David's grandfather began his ministry, the Pentecostal movement was no longer a wild, untamed river always threatening to overflow its banks. It still provided an exciting ride in spots, but it had begun to cut a deeper, wider channel.

David's grandparents spent the first fifteen years of their marriage as missionaries to Argentina. The seeds that they, and others like them, planted in the hearts of the Argentinean people grew rapidly, and now there were more members of his grandparents' denomination in Argentina than in the United States. David could sit for hours and listen to his grandmother tell stories about the salvations, healings, and miracles that flowed unchecked in the early years of their ministry in South America.

By the time David's father and mother married in the early 1970s, the Pentecostals had finally achieved something that was unthinkable in the days of David's great-grandfather or grandfather—respectability. The Mount Gilead Pentecostal Church had padded pews, a new Hammond organ, and an air-conditioned Sunday school wing. Except when an old-timer "got happy" and ran up the aisle or made a quick lap around the sanctuary, the worship services at Mount Gilead were not much different from other churches down the road. They even had a Sunday morning bulletin.

—

The deputy on duty didn't raise any objections when David asked if he could see Pete, and in a couple of minutes, the young lawyer and his client were sitting in the interview room.

"Were you asleep?" David asked.

"No, there were some guys making a lot of noise in my cell, and I was still upset about today."

"I'm sorry about the results of the test. Anything different about the procedure?"

Pete rubbed the top of his close-cropped head. "He asked the same kinds of questions, but the interview before the test was different."

"How?"

"The way he talked to me was more like an interrogation than an interview. He told me it was impossible for the machine to be wrong and that he had caught tons of people in lies who had passed other polygraph tests. By the time he hooked me up and turned on the machine, I was so upset there was no telling what the needles were doing."

"We can find out about the effect that kind of interview could have on the validity of the results."

Pete slumped down. "I had my hopes up today. This has been tough."

"I know. But there is another reason I came by."

"What?"

"Did Angela ever talk to you about her Uncle Spencer?" David said.

"Who?"

"Her father's younger brother. He's not much older than you are."

"Oh yeah. I remember him. He was at the cookout when Angela and I first met. He kept to himself, and I wouldn't have known who he was if someone hadn't mentioned that he was Mr. Hightower's brother. What does he have to do with my case?"

David told him about the letters. He finished by saying, "Mr. McClain was telling me about them when they brought you out of the examination room. We were going to stop the test. But it was too late."

Pete hung his head. "I've totally messed up. I ought to be mad, but I don't feel anything."

"It's done. We have to go on."

"That's easy to say. Hard to do."

"So, did Angela ever mention Spencer?"

"Not that I remember. She didn't tell me about him bothering her."

"Did she ever mention any problems with other men?"

"No."

"How many times did you date Angela?"

"Three or four. We were more friends than anything else."

"No romance?"

"It might have led to that eventually, but we just hit it off as friends and did some things together. She didn't have a boyfriend, and I wasn't dating anybody."

"What did you talk about?"

"Different things. Her school, my work. Religion."

"Religion?"

"Yeah, she'd worked at a Christian camp for kids during the first part of the summer and had a religious experience. We talked about God several times. I thought about it the other day when you said I should be praying."

Maybe Pete was guilty; maybe not, but his comment about prayer was enough of an open door that David decided to see if he could squeeze through. "Could I pray something now?" he asked.

Pete hesitated, then he said, "Okay."

David began, "Father God . . ."

After a call from Mac the next morning, Ray Morrison tracked down Deputy Tim Logan at Bodybuilder's Inc., a health spa with a male clientele.

"Hey, Mr. Morrison," Tim said.

"Good to see you, Tim. Still on third shift?"

"Yeah. I come here to work out before I go home and sleep."

"What are you bench-pressing?"

"I work out with 200 to 225."

Short and stocky, Tim lifted weights for strength and bulk. He had no interest in trying to mimic the well-oiled specimens who adorned the covers of magazines at the grocery store.

"Will you spot me?"

"Okay. Show me your max."

Tim popped 275 pounds in the air, moved up to 300, and slowly raised 325 before getting up from the bench.

"I've gotten 340 up a couple of times, but I don't want to bust a gut showing off and have to stay out of work for six months."

"That's good. Are you finished?"

"Yes, sir."

The men sat down at a table in the spa's refreshment area, and Tim took a few swallows of Gatorade. "I heard you were working on the Thomason case," Tim said.

"That's why I stopped by. Can I ask you a few questions?"

"Between you and me?"

"Yes. I won't pass anything along without your permission."

Tim wiped his head with a towel. "Ask me."

"Why were you and Jefferson on the mountain?"

"We received a complaint about some rowdy teenagers camped on top and drove up to settle them down. After we finished tucking the kids in their tents, we got back in our patrol car and started back to town. That's when the call came in about someone running a truck off the road."

"Who was driving the patrol car?"

"I was. Jefferson was writing up a report about the campers."

"After you received the call, did you meet any other cars coming up the mountain?"

"There wasn't any traffic. It was after midnight."

"Did you meet any cars at all?"

Tim paused. "You know, we did. I remember Jefferson was trying to drink a cup of coffee while writing his report about the campers when a dark car came around a corner a little too fast and came over in my lane. I jerked the wheel, and Jefferson's coffee spilled on him and his report."

"If you hadn't been responding to the other call, would you have turned around and followed the car?"

"I doubt it. It wasn't that bad."

"Any idea on type of vehicle, color?"

"Nothing except that it was a dark color. Maybe black or dark blue."

"Midnight purple?"

"I'm not sure what that looks like."

"That's okay, neither do I."

"We slowed down at the overlook and spotted a bent guardrail. We thought it might have something to do with the call and stopped. I shined a light over the edge and saw the yellow Porsche. I scrambled down to the car. The Hightower girl was dead in the passenger seat."

"Is there anything about the crime scene that's not in your report?"

"No. We thought the girl died going over the edge of the cliff, but the autopsy showed otherwise."

"I know that." Ray paused. "Can this go on the record?"

"You think this other car may have been linked to the murder?"

"Possibly."

Tim took another swig of Gatorade. "Yes, sir. It's on the record."

After talking with David about the way Sergeant Laird administered the stipulated polygraph examination, Mac steeled his nerve and called Bert Langley.

"Is your client ready to cave in?" Bert asked. "I can't keep a life without parole deal on the table indefinitely."

"No. I want to have an independent expert look at the charts from the exam."

"I can get it to you, but your client is fried."

After Mac hung up the phone, Ray lumbered through the door, sat down, and reported on his interview with Tim Logan.

"That's a tie-in," Mac said. He picked up a slip of paper from his desk. "Vicki located the information about midnight purple Lincolns. There were 1,689 manufactured during that particular model year and 478 of them were shipped to the southeast region."

"That's a lot of cars."

"The southeast region includes eight states."

"Where are we going to focus the search?"

"Chattanooga, Atlanta, and Spencer Hightower's driveway," Mac said. "Vicki will handle the car dealers in Chattanooga and Atlanta; you will check out young Mr. Hightower."

"Is it in the big city?"

"Yeah. I know you don't like Atlanta, but at least you don't have to fly. He lives in a ritzy neighborhood near Lenox Square."

"I can handle it. What else do you want me to find out?"

"Everything. I want to know how he likes his eggs Benedict."

"Huh?"

"Find out if he eats grits for breakfast."

After Ray left, Mindy buzzed Mac.

"Anna Wilkes on line one."

"Is it her or the guy who works for her?"

"It's her. She sounds nice."

Mac kept it to a simple, "Hello."

"How's Pete doing?" Anna asked.

"Not too good. I'd better not go into any details, except that the State's scheduled another psychiatric exam. For tomorrow afternoon."

"Can you tell me who it is?"

"Yeah. I have the psychiatrist's name and qualifications somewhere on my desk." Mac shuffled through his papers. "Here it is. Dr. Louis Newburn. B.S. from University of Florida, medical and psychiatric training at Emory in Atlanta, Diplomate of American College of Psychiatry. Ever heard of him?"

"No."

"Probably someone Joe Whetstone knows. I don't expect much from him except to contradict your report."

Anna was silent for a few seconds and Mac asked, "Are you still there?"

"Yes," she said, then added quickly, "I'd like to pay you back for the two lunches by inviting you to supper with Hunter, my Aunt Jean, and me at my house tomorrow night."

Mac almost dropped the phone. "Uh, tomorrow?"

"Yes. Since it's Friday evening, I thought you might want a break."

"I don't know if I can. I'm working most nights keeping the rest of my practice afloat while pedaling as hard as I can in Pete's case."

"I know you're busy, but everyone needs a break. Hunter has talked about you several times."

The mention of Hunter stopped Mac's racing thoughts. "Really?"

"Yes. He wants to show you his baseball card collection. Something about a few old cards he wants to ask you about."

Mac chuckled. "Probably players younger than me. What time?"

"Would seven o'clock be too early? It's a forty-five minute drive from Dennison Springs to my house."

Mac decided to take the plunge. If things got too uncomfortable with the adults, he could sneak away with Hunter and look at baseball cards. "Seven would be fine. Where do you live?"

EIGHTEEN

The sorrows of death compassed me.
PSALM 18:4 (KJV)

THE NEXT MORNING Mac had a lightness in his step. He took a deposit to the bank and on the way back bought a cup of flavored coffee at a new coffee shop that had opened around the corner from his office. When he opened the door to the office, he greeted Mindy cheerfully and walked past Judy's desk, whistling.

In a few minutes, Mindy came down the hall to see Judy.

"What's going on?" she asked. "I thought I heard the boss whistling."

"You did. He sailed past here with a cup of coffee and a smile on his face."

"It's a woman," Mindy said confidently.

"No way," Judy said, taking off her glasses. "He shut down after his wife's death. Laura was a saint, and the field of eligible candidates in town is pretty slim."

"It's a woman," Mindy repeated. "I can tell about these things."

"If your womanly intuition is so accurate, who is it?"

"The psychologist from Chattanooga. Dr. Anna Wilkes. She is really nice on the phone."

Judy shook her head. "All he's done is talk to her on the phone a few times about a murder case. She's probably married."

"We don't know that. They could be meeting on the side. I think it would be hard for a psychologist to find the right person. You know, they would analyze everyone they met and find out what was wrong with them."

Mac came out of his office and gave Judy a dictation tape. In spite of her doubts, Judy couldn't resist. "Mac, have you personally met the psychologist you hired in the Thomason case? Dr. Wilkes, isn't it?"

"Yeah, several times. In fact, we ran into each other recently at the courthouse."

"What's she like?"

"Very competent and professional. I think she'll make a good witness if we have to use her in the case."

Mac turned away and went back to his office.

"See!" Mindy said. "I told you."

Judy put the dictation tape in her transcriber. "Don't jump to conclusions. He said she was competent and professional, not charming and attractive."

—

Mac spent the rest of the afternoon on the phone and reviewing medical records in some of his other cases. He wondered several times how Pete was doing with the State's psychiatrist. He thought about stopping by the jail after work but decided to wait until Saturday. He didn't want to get tied up at the jail and be late for supper in Chattanooga.

At 4:45 P.M. he called David Moreland.

"Are you coming over for our weekly ritual?" he asked.

"If you want me to. I thought maybe I wore out my welcome last week talking about Egypt and the Fletchall law firm."

"As I recall, I asked the question and violated the cardinal rule of cross-examination."

"Never ask a question for which you don't know the answer?"

"Correct. Ten minutes?"

"I'll be there."

Mac stayed in his office. He heard the front door open, but Mindy didn't buzz him. Judy and Vicki left to go home, and after a few minutes, he walked to the reception area to see if David had arrived. He found the young lawyer standing by Mindy's desk with a sealed plastic container in his hand.

"Ready?" Mac asked.

"Sure. I'll be in the library in a minute."

Mac went to the kitchen. He decided to pop some popcorn in the microwave and waited while the bag slowly turned around on a paper plate. He put the popcorn in a bowl and took it to the library. David still wasn't there. He returned to the kitchen for the mugs and drinks and set them up on the library table. After waiting another minute, he was about to go back to the reception area when David came in with the plastic container under his arm.

"What do you have in there?" Mac asked, as he poured his beer into the mug.

"Chocolate-chip cookies. Mindy made them for me. Do you want a cookie with your beer?"

"No, but I know what we need to talk about today."

"What?"

"The ways of women."

David put the cookies on the table and tipped his water bottle into his mug. "All she did was give me some cookies."

"You're smarter than that. First it's cookies. Then she'll move up to something more serious."

"Like what?"

Mac took a drink. "Cookies are a reliable indicator of a woman's feelings, but they're still kindergarten stuff. There's only one foolproof way to know if you've met the right woman. If she cooks this for you she's the right one, and you should never let her go. It's proven to be one hundred percent accurate."

David waited. Mac ate some popcorn and took another drink. Finally, David said, "Come on. Give me the benefits of your wisdom and experience."

"You have to really want to know."

David chuckled. "Please, tell me. How's that for pleading?"

"Are you listening?"

"Yes, sir."

Mac took another drink and leaned forward. "You know you've met the right woman if she invites you over for a big plate of hot, juicy, fried chicken livers. Any woman who will do that for a man understands the meaning of true love."

Anna Wilkes lived in an older area of Chattanooga named after David Brainerd, the New England missionary of the early 1700s who spent his short life preaching the gospel to native Americans in New Jersey and Pennsylvania. Hundreds and hundreds of Cherokees were educated and converted to Christianity through the efforts of the missionaries inspired by Brainerd's efforts, and many forced to relocate to Oklahoma along the infamous "Trail of Tears" sang hymns as they walked and died along the route west. All that remained of the original 1800s mission was a small cemetery at the edge of a shopping mall parking lot.

Mac turned onto a short street that ended in a cul-de-sac. Anna's house was an old brick split-level with well manicured bushes and flower beds. A basketball goal stood beside the driveway near the two-car garage.

Hunter opened the front door before Mac could ring the doorbell. "I saw you pull up," he said. The young boy led Mac into the kitchen where Anna was standing at the stove, wearing a blue sweater, jeans, and a white apron decorated with strawberries. Mac could smell an apple pie in the oven.

"Welcome," she said with a smile. "Supper is behind schedule but in process."

Mac looked down at his tie. "I should have gone home and changed."

"Don't worry about it. Have you met Jean?"

At that moment an older woman about Anna's size but with short white hair and thick round glasses came into the kitchen. "Jean Simmons, this is Mac McClain."

Jean extended a wrinkled hand and gave Mac a surprisingly firm handshake.

"Do you want to see my room?" Hunter asked.

"Go ahead," Anna suggested. "We'll eat in about ten minutes."

Mac followed Hunter to the upper level of the house and walked into a clean, tidy bedroom. Two trophies given for participation in a youth soccer league sat on his dresser next to a Frisbee and a large conch shell. An old teddy bear rested his frayed head at an angle against his pillow.

"Is your room always this neat?" Mac asked. "I'm impressed."

"Of course not. Mom told me to pick up everything before you came, but that would have been impossible. I dumped most of it in the closet." Hunter slid back the door to reveal a jumbled conglomeration of personal belongings.

"Where are your baseball cards?" Mac asked.

"Under the bed." Hunter lay on the floor and pulled out a pair of boxes. "I have some old cards from the 1980s to show you."

"1980s? That's not old."

"It's before I was born."

Mac didn't try to argue.

They sat on Hunter's bed and looked at the cards until Anna called them to supper.

"Since Mr. McClain is here," she said, "we'll eat in the dining room."

Anna sat at one end of the dining room table with Hunter to her left, Jean on the right, and Mac at the other end. In the center of the table sat a baked chicken filled with cornbread stuffing, green beans garnished with almonds, carrots in a butter and brown sugar sauce, corn on the cob, and yeast rolls.

"Do you want tea?" she asked.

"Yes."

"I'll pour your drink if you'll carve the chicken,"

Anna handed Mac a carving knife and fork.

"White meat, please," Hunter said.

The meal was delicious. Mac especially enjoyed the moist stuffing and the carrots.

"Hunter, do you eat this well all the time?" he asked.

"Uh, sometimes. Mom doesn't fix carrots unless we have company."

Mac speared a carrot with his fork. "The company appreciates the carrots."

Mac asked Jean questions about her life and learned that she never married, spent most of her life as a fifth-grade schoolteacher, and had retired the year before receiving the call from Anna to come to Chattanooga. "It's been a blessing for me to live with Anna and Hunter," she concluded.

Mac cleaned his plate. Hunter left a few carrots. "I'll eat my pie later," the boy said and ran upstairs.

"I left room for pie," Mac said.

"Coming up," Anna responded.

In a minute Jean presented Mac with a generous slice of warm apple pie topped with vanilla ice cream, then set a cup of black coffee at his elbow. She and Anna fixed smaller portions for themselves.

When they finished, Jean said, "I'll clean up."

While Jean worked in the kitchen, Anna turned in her chair and picked up a sheet of paper from a small table behind her chair. "Can we talk business for a minute?" she asked.

"Okay."

"I have the name of another drug that could have caused Pete's amnesia. It's called gamma-hydroxybutryate, or GHB."

"Never heard of it."

"Listen to this." She read from a sheet paper, " 'Used years ago by serious bodybuilders to stimulate muscle growth, GHB had serious side effects and was pulled off the market in 1990. In higher doses it can cause dizziness, confusion, and memory loss. Usually seen in a liquid form, GHB is colorless and odorless, and although much less publicized than Rohypnol or flunitrazepam can have the same or worse effect.' "

She handed the sheet to Mac, who studied it for a minute. "Looks like another blood test is in order," he said.

"I thought so. Enough business. Bring your coffee into the living room."

Glancing toward Hunter's room to check his escape route, Mac followed Anna through a pair of wooden French doors. The living room contained a short ivory-and-blue couch, a pair of dark blue side chairs, an antique coffee table, and a shiny grand piano.

"That's quite a piano," Mac said.

"It's too much for this room."

"Do you play?"

"Jean and I both play. Hunter's just a beginner."

"I'd love to hear something."

"You don't want to play Scrabble instead?"

"Positive."

Anna slipped onto the bench. "Old or new music?"

"Classical." Mac sat down in one of the chairs.

The psychologist launched into a Chopin sonata that transformed the cozy living room into a miniature concert hall. Her nimble fingers sped up and down the keyboard, and her small hands demonstrated surprising strength and vigor when the music demanded forceful emphasis. Mac closed his eyes and listened.

The last note faded and Mac said, "Superb. How did you learn to play like that?"

"Practice and genes. It's the way I relax and relieve stress."

"I like to split wood to relax and relieve stress. I've had a lot of practice, but it doesn't match Chopin."

Anna took a sip of coffee from her cup resting on top of the piano. "Now, it's your turn."

"Turn for what? I can barely play 'Chopsticks.'"

"Your life story."

"No, it's too long and boring."

"It's barely eight o'clock, and I don't bore easily."

Mac realized that his plan to bolt for Hunter's room wouldn't work. He didn't start with his first memory, but he took her through his early years in Dennison Springs, college, and law school. He hesitated, then told about meeting and marrying Laura.

"Laura is a beautiful name," Anna said.

The room was relaxed and peaceful. With a full stomach and a compassionate listener, Mac's protective shield cracked open. His reservations about unwrapping his life didn't seem so vital. He talked about his sons. "Zach was like your Hunter, easygoing and positive. Ben was smart and tenacious."

"Like his dad."

"I guess so. He looked more like me, too. Ben graduated near the top of his high school class and went to Georgia on a full scholarship. Zach was in his senior year of high school and on his way to Georgia Tech."

"How long ago was this?"

"Nine years this coming December." Mac's eyes got a faraway look, and like a plane on autopilot the story went forward under its own initiative. "Ben was home on Christmas break. There was a cold snap, and the weatherman predicted a light dusting of snow in the mountains near Dennison Springs. We had a four-wheel-drive Jeep at the time and decided to head into the mountains until we reached snow. We left home about ten o'clock in the morning and by eleven-thirty we were surrounded by soft falling flakes. There is a small lake on top of the mountain, and we found a place to park, bundled up in our coats, and walked around the lake as the snow began to accumulate on the trees. Ben and Zach played like little boys, throwing snowballs at each other and catching snowflakes on their tongues. Laura and I walked together under the trees. It was beautiful, like a fairyland."

Mac was with his family again. "After we completed a loop around the lake, we had a snack at a table under a picnic shelter. The temperature kept dropping and even with the Jeep I was concerned about the safety of the roads. We got in and started down the mountain.

"We hadn't gone far when I realized that I'd forgotten to engage the vehicle's four-wheel drive. When I leaned over to flip the switch, the right front tire slipped off the roadway. I jerked the steering wheel and almost straightened it out but hit a slick spot. We went off the road, down an embankment, and into the trees."

Mac's voice became flat. "A huge limb shattered the windshield and ripped through the interior. Laura and Ben died instantly. Zach suffered a severe head injury. I broke my right leg and had some minor facial injuries from exploding glass but remained conscious. The scene inside the Jeep was indescribable," he stopped as his voice cracked.

A single tear rolled down Anna's cheek.

Mac closed his eyes for a moment before continuing, "I knew Laura and Ben were dead, and I could hear Zach's groans in the seat behind me. In a few minutes, paramedics were on the scene, but we had to wait for the fire department to bring the Jaws of Life to cut Zach and me out of the vehicle. By that point, I was hysterical, and they gave me a shot to knock me out. Zach died in the ambulance. They brought him back once, but his heart stopped a second time and they couldn't revive him. I woke up in the hospital, hoping it was all a terrible nightmare but having to face the fact that it wasn't. I left the hospital in a wheelchair to attend the funeral and went back in the next day for surgery on my leg. The whole time is fuzzy in my mind now, and I'm sure I was in some kind of shock. The drugs they gave me for pain probably contributed to my haze.

"I thought about—" he paused. The tear Anna had earlier wiped away was joined by others. She wiped her cheeks with the back of her hand.

"Do you want me to stop?" he asked.

"No, go ahead," she said. "I thought I could listen with enough professional detachment to avoid emotion, but I can't. I'm human."

"There's not much more to tell. I still have a recurring nightmare in which I'm trapped inside the Jeep, unable to catch my breath and screaming for help."

"How long were you in the hospital?"

"A couple of weeks. After I was walking again, I tried to live in our home, but it didn't work, so I sold it and built a house north of town. I've gone on, but recently, I've found myself thinking more and more about quitting."

Mac meant ending his life, but Anna thought he was referring to his law practice. "What is the typical retirement age for a lawyer?" she asked.

Mac shrugged. "Several methods are used to calculate the best time to hang it up. Too much money, too much booze, or too many divorce cases are common yardsticks. A few weeks ago I dressed in the dark and put on two different types of black shoes. I didn't discover my mistake until I was arguing a motion in front of the judge. Maybe that was a sign to hang it up."

"Or a sign to turn on the light when you go into your closet."

They sat in silence for several moments.

"I'm sorry," Anna said simply.

Mac looked at her still-moist eyes. "Somehow," he said, "I knew I was going to tell you all this. Why?"

Anna got up from the piano bench and pulled a tissue from a box on the coffee table. "Not because I'm a psychologist," she said.

"That didn't enter my mind."

Anna touched her eyes with the tissue. "I can think of a couple of reasons. First, you heard my story. I'm no stranger to pain."

Mac nodded.

"Second, I care."

NINETEEN

Have we eaten on the insane root that takes the reason prisoner?
MACBETH, ACT 1, SCENE 3

WHEN HE ARRIVED HOME, Mac let Flo and Sue out for a late-night romp through the woods. Then he went inside the house to check the messages on his answering machine. A bothersome client had called wanting to know the status of his case. The machine beeped, and the next message started.

"Mr. McClain, this is Lieutenant Cochran at the correctional center. Your client, Peter Thomason, was taken to the hospital tonight for a suspected drug overdose. Please contact the jail as soon as possible."

Mac fidgeted while the machine played three more messages, but there was nothing else about Pete, and he quickly dialed the number for the jail.

"Booking department, Sergeant Fred Davidson."

"Fred, Mac McClain. I had a message on my answering machine from Lieutenant Cochran. What happened with Thomason?"

Fred lowered his voice. "It looks like he scored some speed and decided to get high."

"It wasn't a suicide attempt?"

"Not from what I heard. He just went on an amphetamine joyride for a few hours and started acting crazy. Second shift took him to the hospital to make sure he was okay. He's in one of the drunk tanks now."

"Did he pass out?"

"I don't think so. I peeked in a few minutes ago and he was sitting on a bench."

Mac called David and told him the news. "This doesn't make any sense," David said. "After what he told us about not using any drugs. How—"

Mac interrupted him. "Remember what you told me after Pete failed the stipulated polygraph?"

"That he might be guilty?"

"Yeah."

"To me, this is worse than the polygraph. But it still doesn't change our job description."

"Should we go to the jail tonight?"

"I've tried to talk to stoned clients in the past, and it doesn't work. You have to repeat everything the next day."

"Did he pass out?"

"No, the booking officer said he was sitting on a bench in the drunk tank when I called."

David hesitated. He'd thought his midnight prayer session with Pete less than twenty-four hours before had been on target. Now this. "I still think we should see him," he said.

Mac sighed, "You're probably right. Can you meet me at the jail in thirty minutes?"

"Yes."

Mac and David arrived at the same time and got out of their cars.

"What are you going to do?" David asked.

"Try not to yell at him," Mac said grimly. "Hopefully, he'll tell us what's going on."

Mac watched Pete walk down the hall. Eyes glued to the floor, the big redhead looked more beaten down than the first time Mac saw him.

"Sit down." Mac said. "How are you feeling?"

"Tired."

"Did you see the State's psychiatrist this afternoon?"

"Yeah."

"How was it?"

"He seemed okay."

"How long did he spend with you for the evaluation?"

"I don't remember."

"Don't start that 'I don't remember' stuff with me tonight," Mac said, his voice rising a few decibels.

Pete shifted in his seat. "I don't have a watch. He wasn't here too long. He left a long time before supper."

"When did you get high?"

"I don't know."

"What do you mean?" Mac's face started turning red.

"I didn't get high."

It was Mac's turn to slam his fist on the table. The sound echoed in the tiny room.

"You were hauled off to the hospital with your bloodstream full of amphetamines!"

"I don't know what happened."

"I don't want any 'I don't know' answers either! What are you trying to prove?"

Pete looked up for a second and then dropped his head without answering.

"Were you trying to kill yourself? Was it an intentional overdose?"

Pete didn't move.

Mac leaned forward. A judge might not let him yell at a witness, but there was no judge in this tiny room. "Answer me! Yes or no?"

"No."

"Then why did you do it?"

"I didn't do anything. I felt rotten. It was not a good time."

"That's interesting." Mac's voice dripped with sarcasm. "You got stoned but didn't have a good time? I'm glad you're beginning to recognize that amphetamines are not good for you."

"It wasn't like with Angela."

"What do you mean?"

"I don't remember anything about the night Angela died. I remember everything that happened tonight. I just don't remember taking any drugs."

Mac's face flushed and he looked at David. "You try."

"You said you felt bad?" David began.

"Yeah."

"How?"

"My heart was beating fast and everything was jumping around. I started talking in a loud voice and felt very shaky on the inside. One of the deputies tried to talk to me, but I couldn't make him understand. I thought I was making sense, but they took me to the hospital."

"What happened at the hospital?"

"They strapped me down on a gurney and drew some blood out of my arm. I don't know how long I stayed there, but they brought me back to the jail and put me in the drunk tank. I fell asleep for a while then woke up before you got here."

"You didn't take any pills?"

"I don't remember taking any." Pete looked sideways at Mac who made no move to come across the table and grab him.

"And you don't know why you had speed in your system?"

"That's right."

"Pete," David said slowly. "Mr. McClain and I are working as hard as we can to save your life, but we need your help. The best way you can help us is to tell us the truth, the whole truth, and nothing but the truth."

"That's what I've done."

David held Pete's gaze across the table for a few seconds. "Okay. I don't have anything else to ask you."

"That's all," Mac said. "I'll ask the guards to take you back to your regular cell."

Watching their client shuffle down the hall, Mac said to David, "The more I'm around our client, the more confused and messed up I think he is."

—

Ray Morrison sat in his truck and yawned. He'd been waiting outside the Club Now, a high-class singles' bar in north Atlanta, for almost four hours. The previous day, he'd stopped by the *Echota Express* and located a back issue of the newspaper that contained a photo of Spencer Hightower standing in front of the County Mental Health Center after he and Alex had donated the money to build a drug treatment facility. The quality of the black-and-white picture was poor, but Ray hoped it was sufficient to ensure a positive identification. Nothing was worse than spending hours following the wrong person.

He had arrived outside the gated neighborhood where Spencer lived at about eight o'clock in the morning. A high brick wall decorated with fancy ironwork ran parallel to the roadway. Two guards in a small building kept unwanted intruders away from the residents. Ray parked around the corner from the entrance and took an orange measuring wheel from the bed of his truck. Putting on a white hard-hat, he held the measuring wheel in one hand, a clipboard in the other and started down the sidewalk. When he came within view of the guardhouse, he stopped, pretended to write something important on the sheet of paper, and continued in the direction of the entrance. One of the men came to the door of the guardhouse.

"I need to do some work in the neighborhood," Ray called out.

The guard waved him through. Ray turned a corner and walked past several large stucco-and-stone houses that overpowered the small parcels of land on which they were built. The homes were jammed so close together that it reminded Ray of a mobile home park on the outskirts of Dennison Springs, although, of course, on a much grander scale. In a few minutes, he found Castlewood Lane, the short street where Spencer Hightower lived.

Spencer's house was at the end of the street. The garage door was open and Ray saw two cars: a dark green Jaguar and a red Corvette convertible. Ray slipped a camera out of his pocket and quickly snapped several pictures. Unless he was out for an early morning drive, Spencer Hightower did not own a midnight purple Lincoln. The morning paper was still on the front steps. Ray walked slowly past the house and retraced his steps to the entrance. He waved to the guards, put his diversion devices back in his truck, parked at a deli across from the entrance to the neighborhood, and waited. And waited. And waited.

At 6:00 P.M, the green Jaguar nosed through the gate and turned left. Spencer was driving. Ray quickly fell in behind him and followed him to a bar, where Ray continued his vigil. At 10:00 P.M., Ray went inside to look around and saw Spencer having a drink in a corner with two girls. It was 1:00 A.M. before Spencer strolled out of the bar alone and headed home. Ray drove to a Motel 6 and went to sleep.

At 8:30 the next morning, he resumed surveillance. Five minutes later, the Jaguar zipped through the gate and sped through the lightly traveled Saturday morning streets. Ray followed in hot pursuit and almost lost his prey at a traffic light. Spencer pulled into a bagel shop, and Ray watched him through a pair of small, powerful binoculars. Spencer ate a bagel with cream cheese and drank a cappuccino. "No grits," Ray wrote on his summary sheet. Next, he followed the young man to an office tower near a local hospital. Spencer went inside, and Ray followed him into the building. There was a bank of three elevators and Spencer entered one and disappeared before Ray could slip in behind him to see which floor he selected. Ray took a high-resolution picture of the building directory with a compact camera and waited in his truck. Two hours later, Spencer emerged and drove to Phipps Plaza, an upscale shopping mall. Ray tailed him on foot inside. Spencer went into Saks Fifth Avenue, bought a shirt, and left.

It was past lunchtime, and Ray's stomach was growling so loudly that he could hear it over the sound of the truck's motor. Spencer didn't stop for lunch. He turned onto West Paces Ferry Road and drove a mile or so before pulling into his brother's long driveway. Ray parked along the street. An hour later, Spencer drove back to the same office tower where he stayed a few minutes before driving home. Ray waited until 9:00 P.M. before breaking off the surveillance.

The private detective stopped by KFC, bought an eight-piece meal for himself, and returned to his motel room. After he finished eating, he licked his fingers and called Mac at home.

"If Spencer Hightower's weekends are typical for the rich and famous, there is more going on in Dennison Springs than Atlanta."

"Any sign of the Lincoln?"

"Negative, he has a green Jag and a red Corvette ragtop."

"How does he spend his time?"

"I can't tell you much. He went to a bar for several hours last night, made two trips to an office tower today, and went by his brother's house."

"What did he do at the office tower?"

"I don't know. It's near Piedmont Hospital. Most of the tenants are doctors with a few other businesses thrown in. There wasn't a listing for anything with the Hightower name in it on the building directory."

"Okay. Hang around Sunday and unless something interesting happens, come home in the afternoon. The Lincoln was my primary question. We've had some bad news on our end." Mac told him about the latest incident with Pete.

Ray listened, then said, "That guy can get in more trouble in jail than most people can out on the street."

"He's strange and very frustrating to talk to. I don't know what to make of him."

"Oh, you had another question about Spencer," Ray said.

"What?"

"He doesn't eats grits for breakfast. He's a bagel and cream cheese guy."

"That figures. Did you eat one?"

"Mac, there are limits to what I will do, even for you."

The next day Ray once again drove to Spencer's neighborhood and waited until noon without seeing the younger Hightower venture forth.

Several hours later, he was sitting in Mac's office.

"Not much here," he handed Mac his notes. "Sorry it was a bust. I wish the Lincoln had been in his driveway."

"Me, too. But it's out there somewhere. We just need to find it."

TWENTY

The people living in darkness have seen a great light;
on those living in the land of the shadow of
death a light has dawned.
MATTHEW 4:16 (NIV)

LATE MONDAY MORNING, Bert Langley faxed Mac a copy of Dr. Louis Newburn's psychiatric evaluation of Peter Thomason. It was worse than Mac expected.

After reciting a couple of pages of background information, Dr. Newburn stated his summary and conclusions:

> Mr. Thomason presented as an alert, twenty-two-year-old male who understands his present situation and can provide competent assistance to legal counsel acting on his behalf. The subject is depressed, but he denied any suicidal ideations, plans, or intent. Rapport for purposes of this evaluation was easily established, and this report reflects an objective assessment of his current level of functioning and mental status.
>
> Based upon the diagnostic assessment and utilization of cross-verifying interview techniques, it is my opinion that Mr. Thomason is suffering from episodes of violent sociopathic behavior based upon significant underlying antisocial tendencies. These antisocial tendencies are directed against authority figures and in Mr. Thomason's mind justify violent action against such figures and those within their sphere.
>
> This individual's conduct is not outside the realm of conscious control so as to render him incapable of differentiating between right and wrong as defined by recognized standards of criminal conduct, and he chooses to

follow antisocial impulses as his means of response to authority. His attempt to deny recollection of the events forming the basis for the charges against him is a diagnostic indicator of the deception which buttresses his sociopathic behavior. For example, on a surface level, he adamantly maintains that he has never used illegal drugs or committed violent acts against other persons; however, a review of his past conduct would, in my opinion, reveal episodic binges of drug use coupled with violent, antisocial behavior. The success rate of treatment for individuals with Mr. Thomason's level of sociopathic tendencies is very low, and it is virtually certain that he will engage in drug abuse and violent acts in the future. Documented case studies of individuals with similar profiles would include Theodore "Ted" Bundy and David Berkowitz.

For his own safety and that of other prisoners, it is my recommendation that Mr. Thomason be isolated from other inmates as long as he is incarcerated. Guards and prison officials should exercise extreme caution in personal contact with him. Should he be convicted of any criminal offense, the sentencing authorities should be aware of his potential for violent acts against authority figures within the governmental structure.

I hope this information is sufficient. If I can be of further assistance, please contact me.

Respectfully submitted,
Louis Newburn, M.D.
Diplomate, American Board
of Neurology and Psychiatry

Mac felt as though he had been punched in the stomach. Within hours of the psychiatrist's prediction of future drug abuse, Pete Thomason had been stoned out of his mind on amphetamines. If the drug incident had been coupled with an assault against the deputies or medical personnel, the psychiatrist could have added "clairvoyant" to his professional qualifications.

One of the guards in the bull pen of the Echota County Jail called out, "Church meeting in fifteen minutes!"

Jailhouse church services in Dennison Springs weren't held on Sunday mornings. The meetings were scheduled to accommodate the jail administration and the volunteers who came in from the community. After all, the prisoners weren't going anywhere. Behind bars, the days of the week lost significance, so Monday morning at 10:30 had been church time at the Echota County Jail for many years.

One of Pete's cellmates, a man named Leroy, tapped him on the shoulder.

"Why don't you come? It beats sitting in here."

Pete had never gone to the church services, but the events of the weekend had left him open to anything.

"Okay."

Grabbing a Bible from a stack of books in the corner of the cell, Leroy said, "Here's a Bible. Can you read?"

"Yes, I can read."

"They might ask you to read a verse."

Twenty of the inmates followed a guard downstairs to the indoor basketball court that served as the general assembly area for the prisoners. The men sat in three rows on the concrete floor. Metal chairs weren't allowed since they could be used as weapons.

Charles Gallegly, a short, slightly overweight man with thick dark hair, a wrinkled face, and a compassionate smile, coordinated the activities of the volunteers. Twenty years before, Mr. Gallegly had convinced jail officials to allow Christians from the community inside the jail to encourage the prisoners. He'd been coming ever since.

Today, six volunteers joined him, and after Mr. Gallegly said a brief prayer one of them strummed a guitar and led the men in a couple of halfhearted songs. When the sound of the last note faded, a Baptist minister in his thirties named Mitchell Kane walked to the front of the group and opened his Bible.

"If you want to follow along, I'm going to read from John 4 about a woman who met Jesus at the well of Samaria." His voice rising and falling, Reverend Kane read with deep emotion. To an outsider his style might have seemed overdramatized at first, but within a few seconds, the flow of the story drew the prisoners into the events of a hot noontime two thousand years before.

Kane read, "'And Jesus told the woman to go call her husband and come back to the well.' 'I have no husband,' she replied. 'You're right,' Jesus said. 'You've had five husbands, and the man you're living with now is not your husband.' 'Uh-oh,' she thought, 'They've had surveillance on me and I'm busted.'" A few men chuckled.

"But she was honest; she didn't try to deny what Jesus said. 'Sir, I see you are a prophet.' You see, Jesus knew her past without her saying a word to him about it.

Kane looked over his congregation. The men were sitting much as the crowds who first heard Jesus. "Men, it's the same today. Jesus knows everything you've done. The D.A. doesn't know everything you've done. The sheriff's department doesn't know everything you've done. Your mama doesn't know everything you've done. Most of you have tried to forget a lot of what you've done. But you can be sure of one thing—Jesus knows everything about you. Every hidden, secret thought. Every act of violence. Every lie. Every lustful thought. Every selfish, evil thing."

Kane paused for a few seconds. "Some of you know my past. When I was a kid I spent time in juvenile detention. In my early twenties I spent a couple of nights in this place. I was as rotten on the inside as a man could be. I lived for myself in rebellion against a God who loved me. I thumbed my nose at Jesus. And you know what I deserved?"

"Jail," one man spoke out.

"Hell," said another.

"Right on both counts. All of us are sinners. No one is righteous in the sight of a holy God. But you're not a sinner because you're in this jail. There are a lot of people in big houses driving expensive cars who may be further from the kingdom of God than you are. At least you know you need God.

"You see, it's not a matter of money. It's not a matter of where you grew up. It's not a matter of how smart you are. It's a matter of something twisted and wrong in each and every one of us. We sin because we're sinners. It's our nature, as natural as the sun coming up in the east. And we need a Savior from sin who will forgive us and change us on the inside so we can live a different life."

The room was quiet. Men in jail have no self-righteous illusions.

"Jesus didn't die for your excuses. He died for your sins. Do you want to be forgiven; do you want to change? I've asked the Holy Spirit to make all of you convicts today—not in the way you think, but to convict you of your sin so that you might be saved and born again. What did Jesus say to the woman at the well? He knew her life inside and out. But he didn't tell her to get away from him and not come near his holy presence. Did he shake his head and say, 'There is no hope for you; get your act together and come back later'?"

"No," a voice said from the back of the room. Pete looked at the speaker. It was Leroy.

"That's right." Kane's voice took on a softer tone. "Jesus offered the woman the waters of eternal life right there by the side of the road. He said, 'If you knew who I am, you would ask me for waters which would well up in you to eternal life.' How many of you need a drink of living water from the Holy Spirit? How many of you are willing to be honest before God? How many of you would like to have your sins washed away? How many of you are ready to yield control of your life to the Lord Jesus Christ? How many of you know that the voice of God is calling you this moment to come to Jesus and be transformed by the power of his death on the cross and his resurrection from the grave?"

Kane waited as his final questions settled in the hearts and minds of his hearers. "We're going to pray. But I don't want you to bow your head and close your eyes. I want everybody's eyes open so you can look around the room and see who's got the guts to respond to God's invitation. If there is anyone who wants to repent of his sins and give control of his life to Jesus Christ, stand up in full view of every other man here and ask Jesus Christ to be your Savior and Lord."

Two men immediately stood and a third followed more slowly.

"God bless you," Kane said. "Let's pray together . . ."

When the preacher said, "Amen," three of the volunteers went to those who were standing and led them to the side of the room. Several others came up with questions or to ask someone to pray for them. Leaning against the wall, Pete stayed toward the back of the group. Simple as it was, the preacher's message had stirred his emotions. The thought of Jesus taking personal interest in him was something new. Mr. Gallegly made a beeline straight toward him.

"I'm Charles Gallegly. I don't think I've seen you here before."

"Pete Thomason."

He extended his hand. "Pleased to meet you, Pete."

Charles Gallegly's dark brown eyes were pools of love, and when Pete looked into the older man's face, he couldn't restrain his own emotion. Several tears forced their way into his eyes and rolled down his cheeks.

Mr. Gallegly didn't speak but reached out and put his arm around Pete's broad shoulders. In a few seconds, Pete slid down to the floor and put his head between his knees to hide his face from the other prisoners. Mr. Gallegly sat next to him: one man desperately trying to release pent-up frustration and hurt, another silently asking God to work in the secret place of the heart where no one but Jesus can go.

Pete lifted his head and wiped his nose on the sleeve of his jumpsuit. "I'm in a big mess."

Mr. Gallegly didn't respond. Wisdom and experience kept him quiet.

Pete continued, "I've heard this message before, but I've never really believed it. What do you think I should do?"

Without probing for facts or details, Mr. Gallegly said, "Ask Jesus to reveal himself to you. The Bible says that Jesus will never leave you nor forsake you. Even if everyone gives up on you; even if you give up on yourself. Jesus is still there. This is true in the cellblock or wherever you go."

"I've had some black nights when no one was there."

"The Bible describes Jesus as the light of the world."

Pete shook his head. "I don't know. It's so vague."

"It's understood in here." Mr. Gallegly tapped Pete on the chest. "Not up here." He pointed to his own forehead.

Pete nodded.

"Do you have a Bible?"

"Yes. There are several in my cell."

"Read the Book of Romans. I believe it will speak to your heart."

"Okay."

"Could I pray for you?"

Pete nodded and Mr. Gallegly bowed his head.

In a few minutes, a loud buzzer sounded and ended the volunteers' time with the prisoners.

—

Leroy walked with Pete down the hall and up the stairs to the cellblock. "I asked Jesus to save me three weeks ago when Preacher Kane was here," Leroy said.

"Was it the first time?" Pete asked.

Leroy looked puzzled. "Can you get saved more than once?"

"I don't know. I meant was it the first time you asked Jesus to save you?"

"I've prayed before when I was in trouble, but it was the first time I knew God was calling me person to person. It was like the preacher said—I heard the voice of God and right then and there knew it was my time to jump in."

"How has it been since then?"

"It's been weird."

"Weird?"

"I mean, I know it sounds crazy. I'm looking at three to five years as a habitual violator for DUI, but I know I can make it. I'm going to use the time in jail to get stronger in the Lord."

Two hours later, David met Mac, and they prepared to go inside the jail.

"How are you going to handle this?" David asked.

"Carefully," the older lawyer responded.

Mac asked a guard to stay close to the interview room door. He didn't totally discount Dr. Newburn's opinion that Pete might react violently to an authority figure, including his own lawyer telling him something he didn't want to hear.

Pete read the report but didn't blow up or bang his fist on the table. He handed the sheets back to Mac and said simply, "That's garbage."

"Tell me your side of the interview."

"Just a bunch of questions."

"How did he treat you?"

"Okay."

"It wasn't like the polygraph exam with the GBI?" David asked.

"No, he was a bald-headed, wimpy little guy. He didn't get on my case at all. I'm surprised at the report."

"Did you take any tests like the ones Dr. Wilkes administered?" Mac asked.

"No. We just talked. No big deal. He even got me a Coke."

"Did you tell him you thought about hurting people or had problems with authority figures?"

"He asked about my family. I told him how rough it was when my father left us and that my mother and I got along okay. She did her best, but she couldn't be both a dad and a mom."

"That's it?"

"Pretty much. I think he made up all that other stuff."

"I sent a copy of the report to Dr. Wilkes for her comments."

"She spent a lot more time with me than he did. I wouldn't mind talking to her again."

"That can't happen. It was a one-time evaluation." Mac straightened the sheets of the report by tapping them against the table. "Also, when the judge gets this report, he may tell the sheriff's office to move you out of the general cellblock into isolation."

"Why?"

Mac paused. "In order to protect the other prisoners."

TWENTY-ONE

On that day they will fast.
MARK 2:20 (NIV)

CELESTE JAMISON SPENT the last two hours before dawn in the sunroom. Concern for Mac McClain had been with her for several days like a gnawing hunger pang in her stomach that refused to go away. She'd eaten more, but the discomfort wasn't satisfied by food.

"What should I do?" she prayed, leaning forward in her chair. "Please tell me."

"Fast and pray."

Celeste stayed bent over. The ache came again, severe enough that she groaned. But the remedy for hunger was to eat, not fast. This couldn't be right.

"Fast and pray." The words came more slowly and deliberately. She waited again.

Then, as the first rays of the sun streamed through the wall of windows on the east side of the room, she understood. The ways of the kingdom of God are contrary to the ways of this world. Fast instead of eating. Do the opposite of her natural, fleshly inclination.

"How long?" she asked.

"Until you have no hunger."

Mindy buzzed Mac. "Dr. Wilkes on line one. She sounds like a nice person."

Mac swiveled in his chair. "Don't let her fool you, Mindy. I've heard

Dr. Wilkes has a terrible temper if someone disagrees with her, so be careful not to make her mad."

"Right," Mindy said curtly.

Mac picked up the phone.

"Did you read the report?" he asked.

"Yes. None of my testing indicates anything close to a psychotic or sociopathic personality disorder. Dr. Newburn is expressing an opinion that he can't back up with any objective data."

"What if I told you that Pete was high on amphetamines Friday night and had to go to the hospital?"

The line was silent for a few seconds. "I'm surprised, but it doesn't change the results of my testing."

"Does it support Newburn's report?"

"Yes, but Pete's performance on the psychological tests is not consistent with Dr. Newborn's overall conclusions."

"How can you be so sure?"

"To use ordinary language, Pete is not as 'crazy' as Dr. Newburn claims. Depressed, yes; angry, at times; psychotic, no. Mass murderers like Ted Bundy and David Berkowitz were unquestionably in another world of their own demented creation when they committed their crimes. And even for them change is possible. Bundy gave a convincing testimony of Christian conversion before he was executed, and Berkowitz has made a video about his relationship with Christ."

"Let's not talk about execution."

"Sorry. I just mentioned it to show that I disagree with the psychiatrist's conclusions."

Mac was relieved. "I hope you're right, but the more I'm around Pete the less in touch with the real world he seems to be."

"When will the case be tried?"

"A couple of weeks. The judge asked me the other day if I was ready, and I told him we were still interviewing witnesses."

"Anything good?"

"So far I have a few wisps of smoke, but it's going to take more to give us a reasonable shot at an acquittal."

"Does Pete know about the latest report?"

"Yes."

"How did he react?"

"He said it was garbage."

"A nontechnical but accurate assessment."

Spunky, Mac thought as he hung up the phone.

Sergeant Davidson rapped on the bars of Pete's cell.

"Thomason. Grab your stuff. You're moving."

Pete rolled out of his bunk. "Where to?"

"Isolation."

"Why?"

"Just get your stuff. I'll explain it to you on the way."

Pete put his meager possessions into a pillowcase and followed the officer down the stairs to the newer wing of the jail.

"Some shrink thinks you're a danger to the other men," Davidson said when they were alone.

"That's not true."

"They didn't ask my opinion. I'm just following orders."

They passed by the interview area and through a double set of steel doors. The isolation wing held three, single-man cells. As soon as the second set of doors clanged behind them, Pete heard screams.

"What in the world is going on in here?" he asked.

"That's Crazy Cal Musgrave. He's waiting for a padded cell to open up at the psychiatric unit in Milledgeville. Get used to it. You two are the only inmates here."

"Fresh meat! Have you brought me fresh meat?" the deranged man yelled. "Come here, you fat pig! I want a piece of you!"

"Shut up, Cal," Davidson said.

They passed by the cell, and its inhabitant spit through the bars, hitting Pete on the arm.

"A redhead! What you in for, boy? Murder? Armed robbery? Shoplifting?" He laughed in a high-pitched voice.

Davidson opened the door to Pete's cell. "We can let you out for an hour of exercise, two times a day. Otherwise, you're here"—he nodded toward the adjacent cell—"with him."

Judge Danielson summoned Mac and Bert Langley to his chambers.

"Gentlemen, I have a traverse jury pool scheduled to report for service in two weeks, and I want to put Thomason on the trial calendar."

"Unless Joe Whetstone has a conflict, the State is ready to proceed," Bert said.

"Mr. McClain?"

Mac nodded. "We have some out-of-town subpoenas that need to be served and a few more witnesses to track down."

"So you'll be ready to go?"

"Yes, sir."

"How is Moreland working out?"

"Fine."

"Good. I've approved payment on all the fees and expenses submitted thus far."

"Thank you, Your Honor."

Back in his office, Mac immediately phoned David and asked him to come over. When he arrived the two of them gathered in the library with Vicki. Mac, pacing back and forth, fired off orders to his paralegal.

"Copy the list of potential jurors at the courthouse so you and Judy can look it over and identify any familiar names. Make a note about each one and discuss it with me."

"Do you want Mindy to have a copy?" Vicki asked.

"Yes, she may know someone on the printout. What about the Lincoln owners?"

Vicki handed Mac four sheets of paper. "Here is the list of the people in Atlanta and Chattanooga who bought midnight purple Lincolns."

"How many are there?"

"Sixty-six."

"Any names look familiar?"

"Not as in Hightower."

"We don't have time to locate sixty-six people and interrogate them about their activities on August second, but make a copy for Ray Morrison, and I'll go over it with him."

"Okay."

"Have you contacted Joan Brinkley at Hollins about testifying at the trial?" Mac asked.

"Yes, she asked me to call her parents and explain everything to them. I told Joan we would fly her down the day before she testifies and to make sure she brings her computer."

"Give me the number. I'll call her parents," Mac said. "It should come from me."

Vicki continued, "I also have the name and phone number of a former GBI polygraph examiner who is willing to talk with you about the differences between the two tests. His background info and phone number are on my desk." She left to retrieve the number.

Just then the phone in the library buzzed.

"Ray Morrison is here to see you," Mindy said over the speakerphone.

"Send him in."

The detective peeked around the door. "This looks like a high-powered lawyer meeting. Is it safe for me to come in?"

"Probably not, unless you want to work. The judge says we're going to trial in two weeks."

Ray laid a manila envelope on the table. "I brought you some pictures."

Mac slid the photos out on the table.

"Here's Spencer's house. You can see the two cars. I ran the license plates, and he owns both of them. Doesn't owe a dime to any finance company."

"What's this?" David asked.

"That's the directory for the office tower where Spencer spent a bunch of time."

David picked up the picture, which had been enlarged so that the names could be read. After a few seconds, he said, "Look at this."

Mac put on his glasses and peered over David's shoulder.

"Right here," David pointed. "Can you read it?"

Mac moved the picture but couldn't bring it into focus. "No, it's too fuzzy."

"It's not too fuzzy to me," David said. "It says, 'Newburn Psychiatric Clinic, Suite 1210.'"

"What is Newburn Psychiatric Clinic?" Ray asked.

"The office for Dr. Louis Newburn, the psychiatrist who examined Pete and said he was America's next mass murderer," Mac said.

"That's who Spencer was seeing," David said. "Probably paying him off for his evaluation of Pete."

Ray shook his head. "There are a lot of offices in the building."

"But only one with a connection to this case," Mac said. "Spencer was relaxing on the doctor's couch while you waited outside."

"Listening to the doctor dictate a report designed to fry Thomason for the family of his rich patient," David concluded.

Pointing to David, Mac said, "We need the names and numbers of visits for Dr. Newburn's patients during the past three years. That should tell us how often Spencer or some other member of the Hightower family has been to see him." Mac grabbed the phone and buzzed Vicki. "Bring a copy of the list of Lincoln owners into the library. We have another name to check."

Vicki brought Mac the list, and Ray and David looked over his shoulder while he quickly scanned the names. "It's not here."

"Spencer borrows the doctor's car to commit a crime?" David asked.

"Yeah, it was an idea."

"You're beginning to think like a real investigator, Mac," Ray said, smiling. "It didn't pan out, but you're still in the running for that job as my sidekick and bodyguard."

"Speaking of real investigators," Mac said. "Can you locate the sixty-six people on this list and find out where they were on August second?"

"By next March?"

"In ten days."

"No."

"I didn't think so. The Lincoln owner we need may not even be on the list, and I have a better use of your time. A road trip."

"Where?"

"To interview a man named Harry O'Ryan."

"Who is he?" Ray asked.

"An acquaintance of Pete's from Parris Island days."

"A fellow Marine? Where is he now?"

"All I know is that he isn't in the Marine Corps."

"Great," Ray sighed. "Is he on the list of Lincoln owners?"

TWENTY-TWO

And there wasted his substance with riotous living.
LUKE 15:13 (KJV)

MAC GAVE RAY all the information in the file about the incident involving the three Marines and the two young women from South Carolina and told him, "Go fetch." But finding Harry O'Ryan was considerably more challenging than tracking down Rodney McFarland on his lonely hilltop near Morganton.

Working the phone, Ray found an address where O'Ryan landed a job as assistant chief of security for a small chain of banks in Corbin, Kentucky. O'Ryan lost his job for reasons Ray couldn't discover and left Corbin for parts unknown.

Hoping to pick up the trail where it ended, Ray left Dennison Springs before the sun came up the next morning and drove through east Tennessee and southern Kentucky to Corbin, home of the original Colonel Sander's Kentucky Fried Chicken Restaurant. He stopped by the main office of the Corbin Community Bank and Trust and asked to speak to the chief of bank security.

"Mr. Shepherd is at one of our branch offices this morning," the receptionist said. "Could his assistant, Nicole Meadows, help you?"

"Possibly. Is she available?"

Ray waited a few minutes until an attractive, well-dressed blonde in her late twenties came to the waiting area and introduced herself. "Nicole Meadows. How may I help you?"

"I'm Ray Morrison, a private detective. Could I talk to you for just a minute? I have some questions about a man named Harry O'Ryan, a former employee."

The woman lost her pleasant expression and looked to the ceiling for help. "Not again. Come back to my office."

She led Ray through a labyrinth of hallways and offices. Punching in a security code on a grid panel, she opened a heavy brown door and Ray followed her into the suite of offices used by the security department of the bank.

"Have a seat. Would you like some coffee?"

"Thanks. Black with one sugar, please."

Ms. Meadows handed him the cup. "Why are *you* asking for Harry O'Ryan?" she asked.

Ray took a hot sip. "I'm not the only one?"

"No, just the most recent."

"I'm at the beginning of my search. How can you help me?"

"I'll tell you what I told the others. Harry O'Ryan floated out of town two years ago in a boat of bad checks on a river of cheap vodka."

"Not a good recommendation for a future employer. How well did you know him?"

"Too well. He's a charming guy on first appearances, but you know what they say about first impressions."

"That they're lasting?"

"No, that they're deceptive. But I feel sorry for Harry. If he's still alive, he's probably lying in a gutter."

"Why would other people be looking for him?"

"Probably more bad checks. The bank covered his bogus paper here in Corbin, but he didn't change his ways after he left town. We've been in contact with skip tracers and collection agents from California to New York."

"Do you know his first stop after he left Corbin?"

"He went to the Fort Pendleton, California, area."

"The Marine base?"

"Yes. Harry was an ex-Marine having trouble re-entering normal society. He liked to hang out with active duty and former Marines."

"Did he ever mention a man named Walter Monroe?"

"He had a friend named Buster Monroe, probably the same guy. Buster came to see him before leaving to go overseas somewhere."

"Okinawa?"

"I don't know."

"Did you meet Buster?"

"I think Harry brought him by the office for a minute, but it could have been one of his other friends."

"How about another Marine named Peter Thomason?"

"No, I never met him," she said. "But I heard Harry talk about him."

"What did he say about him?"

Nicole looked quizzically at Ray. "Did you tell me why you're looking for Harry?"

"No, but I will. I'm working for a lawyer representing Pete Thomason. Pete is charged with first-degree murder in Georgia."

Eyes open wide, she asked, "What does Harry have to do with it?"

"That's a long story. It's something that happened between Harry, Pete Thomason, and Buster Monroe when they were in boot camp together."

"Start your version of the story. I'll compare it with the account I heard."

When he finished, Nicole shook her head. "What a jerk."

"No doubt about that."

"It's not true."

"What's not true?"

"It makes more sense now."

Ray waited.

"I never heard the whole story, but Harry admitted that he and another Marine, who must have been Buster Monroe, double-crossed a fellow recruit named Peter Thomason and got him kicked out of the military."

"What did he say about it?"

"For obvious reasons he didn't tell me all the details you mentioned. Harry and I dated a few times, and one night when he was in the process of getting drunk, he started confessing some of his sins to me. There were many, but one he felt bad about was lying to the camp commander so that an innocent man named Pete took the rap for something another Marine had done."

"No other specifics."

"No. Have you talked to Buster Monroe? Is he in Okinawa?"

"No and yes. He's on the State's list of witnesses, so we have to assume he's going to tell the original story and help convict Thomason. That's why we need to talk to Harry."

"Did your client kill someone?"

"That's not my call; I'm just doing my job."

Nicole wrote "Harry" on a notepad on her desk and drew an X across it. "This is a lot more serious than a few bad checks. How long are you going to be in town?"

"How long do I need to be?"

"I could do a search on our network and see if I can establish an up-to-date bad check trail on Harry."

"How long would that take?"

"Two or three hours. All the information I need is in our personnel files."

"Thanks. I'll get a bite to eat and come back. Where is the original KFC?"

Ray decided that an extra-crispy four-piece meal was the same at the original KFC in Corbin as at the local outlet in Dennison Springs. He sat in his truck listening to a country music station until a full three hours had passed. Then he meandered into the lobby of the bank and found a comfortable chair to sit in. He didn't want to rush his blonde helper.

In a few minutes, Nicole appeared with a folder in her hand.

"Come into the conference room," she said.

Closing the door, she put the folder on the shiny table.

"This has everything I could find. Harry wrote some bad checks two months ago to a bar in Columbus, Ohio. Here's the name and address. That's the last place he turned up in the system. I also made a color copy of his employment photo. Whether he still looks as clean-cut is doubtful, but it may help."

"Very helpful." Ray held up the picture. Square head, close-cut brown hair, firm jaw, impassive, dead stare. "He looks every inch a Marine except for his eyes."

"Alcohol had knocked the life out of him. When liquor wasn't around, he was someone worth knowing."

"Do you need me to return any of this information?"

"No." She paused. "If you find him and he's sober . . ."

"Yes?"

"Tell him I asked how he is doing."

Ray stayed on I-75 through Lexington, crossed the Ohio River at Cincinnati, and turned north on I-71. It was a hundred miles from Cincinnati to Columbus, and Ray enjoyed the well-kept Ohio farms that divided the rich, dark flatland into giant checkerboard squares. He passed sign after sign urging travelers to "Eat More Pork—The Other White Meat." The sun was low in the sky when the Columbus skyline rose up out of the plain ahead.

He took the High Street exit. Located in the midst of rundown factories and decaying retail stores, the South End Bar looked like a place where the going-home-from-work crowd could stop off for a cold one before spending the rest of the night vegetating in front of the TV. Ray shut off the engine, got out of the truck, and stretched. Photograph of Harry

O'Ryan in his hand, he went inside. The jukebox was cranking out Garth Brooks, and a light gray cigarette haze hung suspended a foot below the ceiling. He went up to the bar.

A man sitting with some friends at a small round table called out, "Butch, how about a couple of drafts down here?"

The bartender dried two large mugs with a dingy towel and filled them with beer. After he served his customer, he came over to Ray.

"What do you want?"

Ray put a five-dollar bill on the counter. "To ask you a five-dollar question."

"Go ahead," the man put the five in his shirt pocket.

He handed the picture to the bartender. "Have you seen this man?"

The man sneered, "Yeah, did that deadbeat write you a bad check, too?"

"No, more serious."

"Are you a cop?"

"Not anymore."

"Whatever. He doesn't come around anymore. I finally got my money last week with a little help from some friends with baseball bats, but he is no longer allowed to come in here. You know, he's a person non gratuity."

"Okay," Ray made a mental note to include the bartender's last comment verbatim in his report to Mac. "Where else did he hang out?"

"Hey, I don't go to other bars. I own ten percent of this place."

"What else do you know?"

"The meter is up on your five dollars."

Ray made himself smile and put another five on the counter.

The man pocketed the five and wiped up a wet spot on the bar with the gray towel. "He was staying with some drinking buddies in an apartment at the corner of Front and Baxter Streets. The landlady is named Delores Potowsky; she lives next-door in a brown brick house. Tell her you got her name from Bernard at the South End Bar."

"Bernard?"

"Everyone here calls me Butch, but Mrs. Potowsky knew me when I was a kid."

The apartment was a couple of miles closer to the center of the city, and it was dark when Ray pulled into Mrs. Potowsky's driveway. He rang the doorbell and heard the deep-throated growl of a large dog on the other side of the white wooden door. The door opened three inches and a thin, wrinkled face peered over a thick metal chain.

"Quiet, Popeye," she said to the dog, who was trying to force his massive jaws through the door opening so that he could gnaw on Ray's leg. "What do you want?"

"Mrs. Potowsky?"

"Yeah."

"Bernard at the South End Bar said you might be able to help me locate Harry O'Ryan."

"Harry who?"

Ray slid the picture through the opening. "O'Ryan. Here's a picture."

"Oh yeah. People come and go so much I don't remember names. He's staying in Apartment B-1. You may be too late, though."

"Why?"

"It's Wednesday night, isn't it?"

"Yes."

"Fifty-cent beer night at the Old Irish Pub down the street. If he's not in his apartment, he'll be at the pub."

"Thanks. I'll check the apartment first."

Popeye made one last frustrated lunge as the door closed.

The rooming house had four apartments on the ground floor and four on the second floor. Apartment B-1 was at the top of the stairs on the right. Ray knocked, and a voice yelled out, "I'll be ready in a minute. Come on in."

Opening the door, Ray hesitantly stepped across the threshold. "Harry O'Ryan?"

A stocky, bleary-eyed man came out of a bathroom rubbing his wet head with a towel. "Hey, who do you think you are coming in here?"

Ray held his hands in front of him and stepped back. "I knocked on the door and you said, 'Come in.' "

"Well, back out of here." The man threw the towel toward a chair. It missed and landed on the floor.

Ray obliged and stepped back into the hallway. "Are you Harry O'Ryan?"

"Yeah, why?"

"I'm Ray Morrison. I drove up from Georgia today to see you. Do you have a few minutes to talk to me?"

"I'm in a hurry. I have an appointment."

"I know. It's fifty-cent beer night at the Old Irish Pub."

Harry's scowl disappeared and he grinned, giving Ray a glimpse of faded charm that once graced the young man's face and had attracted Nicole Meadows's attention. "Okay. Come in."

Ray came into the drab room and shut the door.

"I don't know anybody in Georgia."

"What about Pete Thomason?"

Harry picked up the towel and draped it across a rickety wooden chair. "How do you know Pete?"

"You could say I'm working for him. I wanted to talk to you about something that happened at the end of boot camp involving you, Pete, and Buster Monroe."

"Oh, that. Hey, the statute of limitations ran out on those charges a long time ago." Harry pulled a navy blue sweater over his T-shirt. "I'm sorry about that deal, but I can't help him now. It's over and done with, and I have more immediate problems."

"It's still very immediate for Pete. He needs your help."

"Like you said. It's fifty-cent beer night, and I have to be on my way."

Ray didn't budge. "You are free to walk down the street and drink beer in a few minutes, but I need to tell you where Pete is tonight."

"You've got five seconds."

Ray started, and Harry listened to the end. The young man shook his head. "Pete has always been a hard-luck guy, but this is unbelievable. Unless he's changed, he's not a killer."

"That's good to hear."

Harry sat in the ricketty chair. "The whole thing with the girls was Buster's idea. He slipped them the drugs and dropped me off at another bar. I had to get a cab back to the base. Like an idiot, I agreed to back him up when everything hit the fan. Pete didn't know anything. And Buster will lie. He's still in the Corps and will say anything to keep his record clean."

"Which is why Pete needs you."

Harry waved his hand at the apartment. "Look at me and where I live. Do I look like a believable witness?"

"I believe you. There are even people who care about you."

Harry snorted. "Name one."

"Nicole Meadows."

"Did she help you find me?"

"Yes, and she told me to ask how you were doing."

"Lousy."

"Are you working?" Ray asked.

"Are you kidding?"

Ray knew he had to catch this fish but wasn't sure which bait to use. He made a quick decision to spend some of Mac's money. "If you'll go back to Georgia with me, the lawyer I'm working for will put you up at the nicest place in town for a couple of weeks until the trial is over. All you have to do is tell the truth when your time comes on the witness stand."

"You came all the way up here to find me?"

"Yes."

"I don't know."

"You're a Marine," Ray said. "Let me ask you something."

"Okay."

"Did you look out for the other men in your unit in the Marine Corps?"

"Uh, of course."

"If some local tough guys jumped one of your buddies in a nightclub, would you stay on the sidelines or help him out?"

"Yeah, but that was a bunch of gung-ho stuff."

"And this is real-time. It's not about a drunken brawl that no one remembers in a couple of weeks. Pete could be sent to the electric chair unless the people who can help step up."

Harry leaned over and closed his eyes. "This thing has eaten at me for a long time."

"It's time to make it right."

Harry opened his eyes. "Okay. I'll do it."

"Good. When can you leave?"

"If I start with the beer, maybe never. Let's go now."

"Do you need to pack?"

"Nothing except my clothes. Do you have room for two suitcases?"

On the way out, they met a man coming up to the second floor. He stopped when he saw Harry and Ray. "Hey, man, sorry I'm late."

"I'm not going." Harry said.

"But it's fifty-cent beer night."

"I know it, Sal, but something else has come up. Something more important than fifty-cent beer."

TWENTY-THREE

Let me love river and woodland.
VIRGIL

MAC AND DAVID spent Thursday morning at Mac's office. Fingers pecking on the keys of the computer, David did research while Mac worked on an outline of questions for the State's witnesses. Midmorning, a very sleepy Ray Morrison stumbled into the room.

"Don't interrupt me," he said. "If I don't talk, I'll fall asleep on my feet. Harry O'Ryan is in Room 315 at the Jackson Inn. I told the desk clerk to charge the room to you, Mac."

Mac started to speak, but Ray held up his hand. "I'm warning you. You don't want me snoring in here while you try to work. I found O'Ryan in a cheap boardinghouse in Columbus, Ohio. He is going to testify that Pete was not involved in the incident with the two girls in South Carolina. The whole thing was instigated and carried out by Walter 'Buster' Monroe. O'Ryan helped Monroe frame Pete. He's sorry and wants to make it right."

Mac snapped his fingers. "Great work."

"Don't celebrate until we're able to keep O'Ryan in town and sober through the trial. He's only a few gallons away from living on the streets or dying in a gutter somewhere. And don't call me until tomorrow. Good night." Ray turned around and left.

David stood up. "I have a few things to do at my office before I leave to visit my folks this weekend."

Mac worked for another hour in his office. Putting down his legal pad, he propped his feet up on the edge of his desk and glanced at the picture of Jacks River Falls on the wall of his office. The preparation for the trial was moving forward. With David handling all the legal research and cranking out a series of well-reasoned memos, Mac was free to think and plan his trial strategy.

He looked again at the picture of the falls. The leaves would be a bit past peak, but it would be a gorgeous time of year to take a walk in the woods. He picked up the phone.

"Dr. Wilkes, please. This is Mac McClain."

He waited. A now-familiar voice came on the line. "Is everything all right?"

"As well as can be expected. The trial is scheduled to start in two weeks. How does that fit with your calendar?"

"Let me see. I have appointments, of course, but nothing that can't be moved around. Just let me know the specific day I need to be there as soon as possible."

"Okay."

"Thanks for calling."

"That's not all," Mac said quickly. "Do you remember the photograph of the waterfall in my office?"

"Sure."

"Would you and Hunter like to see it on Saturday?"

The phone was silent for a second "I'm sorry, but I can't. I'm speaking at a seminar."

Disappointed, Mac said, "Maybe another time."

"Would you like to take Hunter?"

Mac considered the idea for a moment. "It's the perfect trail for a boy his age. Not too strenuous and something to look forward to at the end. I can come pick him up early Saturday morning."

"No, no. I'll drive him to Dennison Springs, but could you bring him home?"

"That will be fine. Can you have him here at eight o'clock? It's a full day's outing."

"Yes. Once Hunter finds out about this he will be wide awake by six-thirty."

The mountains of north Georgia had been logged by timber companies around the turn of the century, and the massive old-growth timber that amazed the first settlers in the region was lost forever. However, with nature's relentless persistence and the protection of the Georgia Department of Natural Resources, the forest was making a comeback, and there were groves of one-hundred-year-old trees atop the steep ridges and along the river valleys created by the Conasauga and Jacks Rivers. If left alone for another hundred years, the glory of the primeval, southern Appalachian forest might be restored to the region known as the Cohutta Wilderness. But Mac and Hunter couldn't wait that long. Forty-five minutes after leaving Dennison Springs they bounced along on a gravel road that led toward the entrance to the wilderness area.

"How much farther is it?" Hunter asked through rattling teeth as they drove over a recently washed-out section of road that created a scrubboard effect of rapid bumps.

"You can't drive sixty miles per hour on this road. Average speed is about fifteen, and we have ten miles to go before we reach the trailhead."

"About forty-five minutes?" Hunter asked in a few seconds.

"Yeah," Mac said with an approving look. "We should be there in another forty-five minutes."

Their first view of the river was from an old iron bridge. Mac slowed to a stop in the middle of the span, and they listened to the sound of water rushing over and around the rock-filled stream.

"In the spring and summer, people will come from all over to fish along here," Mac said.

"It doesn't look very deep."

"That's because the water is so clear. Several times I've stepped off a rock thinking the water was a few inches deep and found out it was two feet deep."

"Will we wade across the river on the hike?"

"No, only cross a few little tributaries that are very shallow. If you're careful you won't even get your feet wet."

Fifteen trails crisscrossed the wilderness. One of the most popular followed the river basin for fourteen miles and required hikers and backpackers to wet their thighs forty times at fords along the rocky waterway. If a summer thunderstorm dumped a quick inch or two of rain, the river could become impassable in a matter of minutes, stranding hikers for hours until the water receded.

Mac had chosen a much easier access route for Hunter. Pulling into the parking lot for the Beech Bottom Trail, he set the emergency brake on the truck.

"Last stop for civilization. It's a four-mile hike from here to the falls."

Hunter grabbed his backpack from behind the seat in the truck.

"One rule of the trail is never carry anything you don't need," Mac said.

Putting down the gate on the old pickup, he put his pack on it and motioned for Hunter to do the same.

"Whose pack do you want to check out first? Mine or yours?" he asked.

"Let's do one thing from yours and one from mine," Hunter said.

"Okay. Water bottle." Mac pulled out a thirty-two-ounce water bottle.

"Water bottle." Hunter had a smaller one.

"Trail map."

"Compass."

"Two apples," Mac said.

"Three apples," Hunter responded. "I think I can eat three."

"If you carry them, you can eat them. Four granola bars."

"Peanut butter and jelly sandwich."

Mac held up the plastic bag containing the sandwich, which was neatly cut into four squares. "Good-looking sandwich. Could I trade you a granola bar for one of these squares?"

"I'll have to think about it," Hunter said.

"No pressure. Extra pair of socks in case I slip into the stream."

"My mom made me bring an extra pair of socks, too."

"Your mom is a smart woman. University of Georgia hat."

"University of Tennessee hat."

Mac cringed at the sight of the offensive orange cap. "Do you have another hat?"

"No, sir. I like Tennessee. I watched the game on TV a few weeks ago when they beat Georgia."

"We won't talk about that here on neutral territory. I'll do my best to tolerate the hat. Half-used roll of toilet paper."

"My mom said you would bring some toilet paper."

"What else?"

"I have my knife."

Mac inspected the red-handled pocketknife. The edge was shiny. "Did you sharpen it yesterday?"

"Yes, sir."

"Good. It has a lock blade."

The little boy pulled out a backpacker's poncho stuffed into a bag the size of a man's hand. "Plastic poncho."

"I forgot my poncho. I hope it doesn't rain."

"I also brought a little boat to float in the river."

"We'd better leave that behind. It would get away from us and end up along the bank downstream. I've also brought some twine and a few feathers."

"Why?"

"In case we need to trade with the Indians."

"No, tell me."

"You'll see later. Anything else?"

"I have eight homemade chocolate-chip cookies." Hunter showed the bag to Mac, whose mouth watered.

"Okay."

"Four for me and four for you."

"Are you sure?"

"Yeah. Aunt Jean made extra."

"Do you want me to carry the cookies in my pack?" Mac asked.

"That's okay. They're not heavy."

"All I have left is a water purifier," Mac said. "We will drink the water in our bottles and then get some from the river."

"We can't drink the water in the river?" Hunter asked. "I thought you said it was clean."

"It's clear but not safe to drink. I'll show you how the purifier works."

"That's all."

"Good job. Let's go."

Beech Bottom Trail wound southeast along an old roadbed. Multicolored leaves still covered many of the limbs, and Mac pointed out the different types of trees and the resulting variations in color. Birch, yellow poplar, several varieties of oak, basswood, maple, and hickory trees lined the trail and paraded up the hillside to the left and stair-stepped down the slope to the right. After walking gently downhill for half an hour, they climbed sharply up and followed the path as it hopped from hilltop to hilltop. Mac loved ridge trails, especially in winter when the trees were bare and the view in two directions unobstructed by leaves.

"Break time," Mac said.

Sitting on a log, they drank some water and each ate an apple.

"I'm thirsty. It's a good thing you brought your water thing," Hunter said.

"The purifier? Without it we'd have to use iodine tablets to kill the bacteria and germs."

Once they resumed their hike, the trail began a long gradual descent to the river. Hunter stayed beside Mac and matched his pace.

Mac limped slightly.

"What's wrong with your leg?" Hunter asked.

"It aches every so often but not enough to keep me home." Mac stopped. "Listen."

They stood still. As the rustle of the leaves died down, Mac asked, "Do you hear it?"

Hunter looked through the trees. "I hear something. What is it?"

"The waterfall. We won't be there for another forty-five minutes, but you can hear it from here."

It took another thirty minutes to reach Beech Bottom, the trail's namesake and the site of an old homestead that had been abandoned for many years. The wooden buildings had long ago served as supper for woodland termites, and the forest had reclaimed most of the evidence of man's intrusion.

"In the spring, daffodils planted by a rugged pioneer woman more than one hundred years ago bloom here," Mac said.

Not far from the homestead, they crossed two tiny streams by stepping from rock to rock.

"It's not far now," Mac said.

In fifteen minutes they stood on the banks of the river. The Jacks River was really a large mountain stream, no more than thirty to forty feet wide and four to five feet deep. There were a few pools over a man's head, but in most spots the stream could be crossed by someone not intimidated by the prospect of risking a spill on the slick rocks.

Mac and Hunter followed a trail along the river for half a mile to their destination—the Jacks River Falls. They left the trail and climbed up on a large rock.

"That's it," Mac said.

"I can feel the spray on my face from here," Hunter responded.

The scene wouldn't rival Livingston's first glimpse of Victoria Falls on the Zambezi, but for an Appalachian mountain river, the explosive twenty-five-foot freefall of water between two massive boulders was worth the three-hour trek. Other hikers were spread out on the surrounding rocks, enjoying the sun and the scenery. Mac let Hunter select a resting place on a large boulder above the falls. They took off their backpacks and sat down so they could watch the river as it rocketed down the steeply ridged gorge. No place on earth was more beautiful to Mac than a mountain stream in the woods.

"Do you have enough water?" he asked Hunter.

"Yes. I'll need more after we eat."

They unpacked all the food. Mac was about to bite into a granola bar when Hunter asked, "Are you going to pray?"

"Sure. Take off your hat."

Mac started to close his eyes but changed his mind. Hunter's brown head was bowed. Mac looked up into the clear sky and said, "God, thank you for this place you created. Thank you for this food. Thank you for Hunter. Keep him safe. Amen."

Hunter started eating his sandwich, but Mac sat still, suddenly remembering another crisp fall day many years before when he sat on a nearby rock with two brown-haired boys and watched them eat peanut butter and jelly sandwiches. Forgotten memories bubbled to the surface. They too had walked Beech Bottom trail together, stopped on the hillside to listen for the distant roar of the waterfall, and talked for a minute at the old homestead. Mac and Ben made it across the two little streams, but Zach had slipped and soaked a pair of old tennis shoes. When they reached the falls, Zach took off his shoes and socks, laid them on a warm rock to dry, and wiggled his white toes in the sun.

Mac watched his boys that day and wondered what they would become, what paths they would follow, what mountains they would climb, where the river of life would take them. He even wondered if someday he would bring grandsons and granddaughters down the familiar trail and point out the places he had first shown their fathers.

His loss was more than he could bear.

Mac turned away from Hunter and looked upstream. Eighteen years earlier he had not foreseen the Niagara-like precipice that would sweep his family to sudden destruction. What would he have done differently if he had known that death lay in ambush only a few years in the future? Could he have done anything? Was it all his fault? Tears stung his eyes. Grief was not unfamiliar to him, but it had a thousand different faces. Today, it pierced his soul through memories triggered by the brown head of a little boy on the rocks above Jacks River Falls. Was there no healing for inner wounds by the balm of time? Who could blame him if he chose to stop the pain?

"I'll trade you a square of my sandwich for a granola bar." The boy's voice called him back.

Pretending to squint into the sun, Mac turned around and handed Hunter a granola bar and received the sticky sandwich. "Thanks," he said hoarsely.

They ate in silence. When they finished, Mac refilled their water bottles with cold water pumped quickly through his purifier. Leaving the rock, they walked a few hundred yards downstream. Mac stopped beside the trail.

"Let me use your knife for a minute," he said.

He cut a three-foot section of a slender sapling, sat down beside the path, and sliced notches in each end of the flexible piece of wood.

"What are you making?" Hunter asked.

"You'll see."

Unzipping his backpack, he took out the piece of twine and looped a hitch around one end of the stick.

"A bow and arrow," Hunter said.

"That's right. While I finish the bow, you look for some straight sticks for arrows."

Hunter returned with various sticks, some straighter than others, and Mac selected the three best ones. He let Hunter sharpen one end of each stick and showed him how to cut slits for the feathers. Nearby was a deserted campsite that offered an open space for target practice. They took turns trying to hit a large poplar tree and a bear-size rock.

"This is neat," Hunter said after hitting the "bear" in the hindquarters.

"The feathers are the key. They don't seem important, but they keep the arrows on a straight flight."

"My mom could make a lesson out of that."

"What would she say?" Mac asked.

"I don't know. You'd have to ask her."

"Speaking of your mom, it's time to start back so I can take you home."

They retraced their steps to the waterfall and climbed steadily out of the river valley. Hunter didn't stay as close to Mac on the return journey. This was familiar territory to him now, and he would run ahead, shoot an arrow or two, and wait for Mac to catch up. He lost one arrow but found two more sticks, and when they stopped for a drink, Mac helped him outfit two new arrows.

It was late afternoon when they arrived back at the truck and jerked and bumped down the road to civilization. Once they reached a paved road, Mac stopped at a country store and bought Hunter a snack and drink. The owner also worked as a taxidermist, so the store was filled with animals trapped or killed in the nearby forests. Hunter asked question after question.

The sun had set by the time they reached Chattanooga, and a tired Hunter, his hand wrapped around his best arrow, was asleep with his head on the seat next to Mac. Pulling into the driveway, Mac gently shook him.

"Wake up, you're home."

Hunter stretched. Mac carried the boy's backpack and followed him into the garage and then into the kitchen.

"I'm home," Hunter called.

Anna greeted Hunter with a hug and Mac with a smile.

"Come in."

Hunter showed her his bow and began describing the trip. When he finished, he said, "Thanks, Mr. McClain." He ran upstairs to show his bow and arrows to Jean.

"Would you like a cup of coffee?" Anna asked.

"No, thanks. I need to go home."

"Are you sure?"

"Another time. I enjoyed Hunter."

"Thanks for giving him a day to remember."

Mac's face grew serious. "I hope he has this memory for a long, long time."

TWENTY-FOUR

Great is thy faithfulness.
LAMENTATIONS 3:23 (KJV)

MAC HAD PROGRAMMED his VCR to record the Georgia football game while he was on the hike with Hunter. After he fed and watered Flo and Sue, he watched the first two quarters of the contest before his eyelids grew heavy. He fast-forwarded to the last two minutes of the fourth quarter. His beloved Bulldogs won on a last-second field goal, and he rolled into bed, determined to go to Sunday school in the morning.

Mac's Sunday school class turned out en masse wearing their triumphant red jackets. It was a joyful time. Mac decided not to skip the eleven o'clock church service, and as he sat in the pew before the start of the service, he thought about David Moreland's claim that God communicated with him.

Of course, Mac had his doubts about David's theories, but he decided to give the Almighty an opportunity to speak to him during the next hour. *God,* he said internally, *I'm listening.*

The minister of Poplar Avenue Presbyterian Church was Reverend Archibald Faircloth, a jovial, bearded man from Wilmington, North Carolina. Everyone who knew the minister called him Archie. Reverend Faircloth didn't fit his looks or his personality, and no one had called him Archibald since his mother summoned him into the house for a spanking when he was eight.

The church bulletin on the pew beside Mac announced that today's sermon, "Tasting God," would be based on Psalm 34:1–8. Mac listened to the minister read the Scripture passage with special emphasis on verse 8—"Taste and see that the Lord is good." To Mac, the concept of tasting God was as ephemeral as a bag of cotton candy at the county fair.

After several minutes of background information, Archie asked the question of the morning. "How do you taste and see that the Lord is good?" He then gave a number of possible answers, including the opinions of two famous theologians whose names were completely unfamiliar to Mac. Continuing, he said, "I've thought about this question myself, and although my purpose this morning is not to criticize the ideas of other people, their explanations of this verse left me, shall I say, still hungry.

"Let me ask a personal question. It's not designed to shock you but to give you a perspective. Did your mother try to poison you at the dinner table when you were growing up? If so, raise your hand." He waited but had no takers. "No, you trusted your mother's cooking because you knew that no one loved and cared for you more than she did. She fed you good food, and, for the most part, what she fed you tasted good and established preferences that remain with you today.

"It's the same with the Lord. Some of you view God with as much desire as you did Brussels sprouts when you were a child. 'There's no way I'm putting that slimy green thing in my mouth. It'll kill me.'" A few laughs came from the pews. "Now, I won't debate the flavor of Brussels sprouts with you this morning, but I am asking you not to believe any lies about how the presence of God will taste to your soul. You can trust your Creator to give you something good more than the most loving earthly mother. Open your spiritual mouth and say, 'Come in, Lord Jesus.' Taste, and you will see that he is very, very good.

"And when you taste the Lord, what happens? You receive food for your spirit. Food that fills a hunger within you that only the goodness of God can satisfy. Those who skip a few meals during Lent know that the first few bites of food after not eating are an exhilarating experience. Imagine the thrill to your soul of a taste of divine goodness after months or years without a morsel from heaven."

Archie stepped away from the pulpit and held out his hands to the congregation. “How hungry is your soul this morning? Are you hungry enough to come to the table the Lord has prepared for you? God is not in the force-feeding business. He extends an invitation to dine. Do you hear his invitation this morning? How will you RSVP? Let us pray.”

His head bowed, Mac felt an unfamiliar nervous tightness inside his chest. In his prayer, Archie asked the congregation to open wide their hearts to the goodness of God, and when he said, “Amen,” Mac found himself offering a softly spoken, “Amen” of his own.

On his way out of the sanctuary, he stood behind Celeste and Bob Jamison.

Mac tapped Bob on the shoulder. “How’ve you been, Bob?”

The Jamisons turned around. “Fine,” Bob said. “And you?”

“Up and down. That was a good sermon, wasn’t it?”

“In what way?” Celeste asked.

“Oh, I’ve never thought about tasting God, but Archie did a good job of explaining it to me. It sounded almost as good as the creamed corn at Josie’s Restaurant.”

Bob laughed and excused himself to join a small group of men that included his younger brother, Don.

“Is your circle still praying for the people involved in the murder case?” Mac asked Celeste.

“Yes.”

“Uh, thanks.”

Mac stepped toward the door and shook the minister’s hand. “Good sermon, Archie.”

Celeste watched Mac disappear into the throng outside the door. Catching Bob’s eye, she pointed toward the prayer room and held up five fingers for five minutes. Bob nodded.

Celeste had smiled when she read the title of Archie’s sermon. She was in the middle of the sixth day of her fast, and she knew what it meant to feel hunger, both physically and spiritually. Several times over the years she'd gone without food for a day. Twice, she'd fasted for three days. But this was new territory for her. When she told Bob the Lord had called her to an open-ended time of fasting, he listened then went to the exercise room in the basement, where he prayed. Thirty minutes later, he came upstairs and said, "I'll support you." Since then, he'd eaten out or fixed his own meals, thus freeing her from the need to prepare food for him while doing without herself.

The ache in her stomach was not continuous; her body had gotten the message that no food was on the way. Her hunger pangs, like a spiritual barometer, only returned when she asked each morning if she were to continue the fast for another day. Saturday afternoon, she'd felt weak and dizzy and asked Bob to pray for her. After he prayed, the dizziness left, and by Sunday morning she felt a little bit stronger.

Unlocking the bookcase in the prayer room, she opened the index for "M" and found "McClain." There were multiple references for Mac, Laura, Ben, and Zach.

She placed several journals on the table and began reading. Celeste and Laura spent six years together in the group, and as she read, she could almost hear Laura's soft voice carefully choosing her words as she talked to the Lord. Recorded on the yellowing pages was the group's prayer for Ben before he attended a church camp when he was fourteen and the answer after he returned and told his mother that Jesus had come into his heart. Later, a similar prayer for Zach was answered when he started meeting with a group of Christian athletes at the local high school. Opening another volume, she found the oldest entry that specifically mentioned Mac. It was Laura's prayer voiced almost twenty years before. "Father, reveal your goodness to Mac. Let him come to know your love. May he taste and see that the Lord is good."

Tears quickly clouded Celeste's vision and she closed the book. *God is good. God is faithful. He will answer the prayers of a loving wife. Even after she leaves earth for heaven.*

TWENTY-FIVE

A few good men.

U.S. MARINE CORPS RECRUITING SLOGAN

HARRY O'RYAN SWALLOWED a perfectly seasoned bite of mashed potatoes and gravy fixed by Peggy Morrison. Ray had picked Harry up from the motel and brought him over for Sunday dinner.

"I got a little stir-crazy in my room yesterday," Harry said. "If I'd had some wheels and cash I might have hit the liquor store."

"I was worried about you," Ray said. "Old demon rum is a stubborn rascal to evict once he gets inside the house."

Harry cut a piece of roast beef. "I was thinking about getting some help while I'm here. I don't have anything better to do."

Ray looked at Peggy and raised his eyebrows.

"I know the man who runs the local Alcohol and Drug Abuse Center," Peggy said.

"Would you like us to contact him for you?" Ray asked.

"I don't have any money to pay for it."

"It's funded by the State, a typical twenty-one day program for problem drinkers," Ray responded. "Peggy could take you in the morning, and I'll pick you up in the afternoon."

"I'd be happy to," Peggy said.

Harry nodded. "I'll think about it. Coming here to try and make things right with Pete has taken a weight off my shoulders, and I wouldn't mind losing a few more tons of the baggage I've been carrying around on my back."

Later, Harry waited in the den while Ray and Peggy cleared the table. A big brown recliner with its cushions permanently compressed to match Ray's posterior sat in a corner of the friendly room. On a bookcase shelf were some pictures of Ray and Peggy's grandchildren. Harry stepped over to take a closer look. Next to a photograph of a chubby, dark-haired boy in a football uniform was a picture of a slimmer, younger Ray Morrison standing ramrod straight in his Marine Corps dress blues. Beside it in a small frame was a silver star and two purple hearts. During the long ride from Ohio, the private detective never told Harry he was a fellow Marine, much less a Vietnam war hero.

Pete Thomason put a single potato chip in his mouth and chewed it slowly. Sunday lunch in jail was just another milestone of monotony. Pete couldn't order what he wanted from a menu at a nice restaurant or gather with family for a leisurely meal. He ate a processed American cheese sandwich, eight potato chips, applesauce, and chocolate cake without icing. His meal was not enlivened by interesting conversation or the spontaneous entertainment of children or grandchildren. Instead, every so often Crazy Cal pushed his face against the bars of his cell and screamed at the top of his lungs. The sound echoed off the concrete walls of the short hallway. The guards couldn't threaten Cal with further punishment if he refused to be quiet; he was already in isolation.

It took Pete an hour to eat his lunch. He took small bites, chewed slowly, and didn't leave a bit of food on his plate. Falling back on the prisoner-of-war training he received in the military, he adopted a strict routine soon after he arrived in the isolation unit. He brushed and flossed his teeth after every meal, made his bed better than boot camp specifications, and didn't allow a speck of dust to rest in his ten-by-ten-foot cubicle. Twice a day, a guard took him to the basketball court. Pete turned the court into a private parade ground and practiced different types of slow, fast, and double-time marching. He would get into a rhythm and repeat some of the chants used during his training. To a casual observer, it looked more and more like Pete belonged in a cell next to Cal Musgrave.

And Pete started reading his Bible. Following Mr. Gallegly's recommendation, he studied the Book of Romans in the morning. In the afternoon he read one of the Gospels and in the evening focused on Psalms and Proverbs. Eventually, Cal's ranting faded into the background, and Pete paid as much attention to the noise as he would to the air conditioner cycling on and off at his apartment. Pete even started to pray, writing down prayers on pieces of paper with a stubby pencil and reading them back to God while kneeling on the cold, hard floor.

At 10:25, a deputy came to take Pete from his cell.

Cal screamed, "They're taking you to the chair, boy! It's your day to die!"

"Shut up, Cal," the deputy said. "It's Monday morning. He's going to church."

"Boy, don't believe him! They're going to shave your head, strap you in, and turn on the juice!" Cal's voice faded as they closed the door to the isolation block.

"How do you stand it?" the deputy asked as they walked down the hall to the basketball court.

Pete shrugged. "Mostly, I tune it out, but sometimes he reminds me of a drill instructor I had at Parris Island."

The guard unlocked the door to the assembly area and let Pete in. Mr. Gallegly came over and shook Pete's hand.

"The sheriff said you could keep coming to these meetings, and he agreed to let me spend some time with you by myself."

"Thanks," Pete said. "Every opportunity to get out of my cell for a few minutes is worth more than you know."

The preacher of the day was a tall, young African-American man named Francis Young who had served six years as a missionary in Togo, a small, French-speaking country in west Africa. In Togo, Francis saw a brand of Christianity similar to the events recorded in the Book of Acts, and it changed his life. He was a popular speaker with the men at the jail, many of whom had never heard an African American preach.

Opening his Bible, he turned to the Book of Hebrews. "In Hebrews 7:25 it says that Jesus 'is able also to save them to the uttermost that come unto God by him, seeing that he ever liveth to make intercession for them.' *Uttermost* is an old-fashioned word that means 'completely,' and the verse is telling you that Jesus is able to completely and totally save you."

Francis closed the Bible and looked directly at the men before him. "But the enemy of your soul has a boast this morning. He is boasting about some of you in this room. What is he boasting? What is he claiming? He's not boasting that Jesus can't save you. He knows that Jesus saves. He's not claiming that the blood of Jesus can't cleanse you from sin. He knows it can. What is his boastful lie?"

"You can't live it," a voice said.

"It won't work for you," another added.

"That's right. The devil is saying to the Son of God, 'You can save them, but you can't change them. You can keep them out of hell; you can take them to heaven, but you can't make them fit to live as Christians on earth.'"

His voice rising, the preacher asked, "Does the testimony of your life prove the devil's case? Could he call you to the witness stand to prove that Jesus can't change a person from the inside out? That's not what God wants for your life. It says in Hebrews that Jesus is able also to save to the uttermost those who come to God by him. The power of Jesus Christ in your life can deliver you from every evil thought, word, and action. Jesus is able to save 'to the uttermost.' That means all the way, without limit, no matter what you've done or how much you need to be changed. There is nothing too deep, dark, or devilish to be beyond the ability of Jesus to reach in and forgive, cleanse, and change. Now, that's good news!"

One of the volunteers, a man from Francis's church, called out, "Preach it!"

Francis didn't need much encouragement, "Jesus has the power to save! Jesus has the power to change! It says in the Book of Philippians that 'he which hath begun a good work in you will perform it until the day of Jesus Christ.' It is the promise of Jesus Christ that he will continue working in you to change you according to his pattern and purpose for your life. How serious is Jesus about helping you? What does the rest of Hebrews 7:25 say? 'Seeing that he ever liveth to make intercession for them.' Jesus is not up in heaven kicked back in an easy chair eating a powdered donut.

"He is working hard," Francis said, then added with emphasis, *"praying for you.* How many of you haven't had a visitor or received a letter since you were locked up?"

Half the men raised their hands. "Jesus knows your address, and he is talking to some of you this morning. Will you listen to him?"

Francis put his hand on his chest. "All of you. Put your hand over your heart and realize Jesus is praying today for the man who lives inside your body. Does God the Father hear and answer the prayers of his Son? Of course, he does. Would anyone listening to me like to agree with the prayers the Son of God is praying for him? Does anybody in this room hear the voice of God calling them to believe that Jesus is able to save to the uttermost—no matter what you've done, no matter how much you need to change? If you know the message this morning is for you, stand up and claim it."

Two men stood up immediately. "God bless you. Speak out and ask Jesus to save and change you."

"Jesus, save me; change me," one said, his words cracking with emotion.

"Jesus, save me and change me," Pete Thomason said in a calm, confident voice.

When the volunteers began to mix and talk with the men, Charles Gallegly came over to Pete and was rewarded with the first smile he'd seen on the prisoner's face.

"It happened," Pete said. "I heard the voice of the Lord calling me." He pointed to his chest. "Just like you told me."

"That's the way it works."

"But something had already been happening to me all week. It was like a coffeepot percolating. I'd read my Bible, stop and think about it, and go on. Different sections began to have meaning to me."

"Any part in particular?"

"I've been studying Romans every afternoon since they transferred me to the isolation cell. I mean, it's as if it were written for me."

"The words leaping off the page?"

"Yeah. And I'm changing. Even the isolation cell has been a positive thing. I'm focused, disciplined, and organized—all the qualities that helped me in school and in my job before I ended up here and gave up."

"God has spoken to a lot of people in jail."

Pete hesitated. "There's something else I'd like to talk to you about . . . privately, without anyone around."

Mr. Gallegly checked his watch. "Time is almost up, but I'll ask if I can stay after everyone leaves. We could go to one of the interview rooms."

"That would be better. This may take awhile. I need to tell you some things that no one knows."

TWENTY-SIX

For we know that in all things God works for the good of those who love him, who have been called according to his purpose.
ROMANS 8:28 (NIV)

VICKI HAD PUT together multiple copies of the 126 names on the potential juror list from the courthouse. She, Mac, and Judy went over the names one by one in the library. After talking to Mindy in the reception area for a few minutes, David joined them. As lifelong residents of Echota County, Mac and Judy collectively knew more than one-third of the prospective jurors.

"Number 6, Maynard Johnson is a no," Mac said. "I sued him for failing to finish the work he started on a client's house. He was real sour about the deal."

"Number 18 lives two doors down the street from me," Judy said.

"What's she like?" Mac asked.

"Independent and opinionated. Once Mrs. Kidwell makes up her mind she would be tough for either side to move."

"Number 24 is Doug Kendrick's eldest boy," Mac said.

"What's your connection with him?" David asked.

"Doug is a local plumbing contractor and longtime client. He's a good man, but I don't know his son very well."

"Number 39 worked for years as a housekeeper for Cecil Hightower," Judy said.

"What will you do about employees of Hightower-controlled companies?" Vicki asked.

"Good question," Mac responded. "I will probably keep current employees off the jury unless I have a stronger connection with them as their attorney or from representing a member of their family. Former employees could be good for us, especially if they believe they were mistreated in some way by the Hightowers."

"Here's one of those," Judy said. "Number 34, Lyman Bakerfield. I know he lost his job at Dalconex when the Hightowers took over the company."

"Make a note on him, Vicki," Mac said.

"Number 97 died three weeks ago at the nursing home," Judy said.

By the time they finished, they had twenty-one former clients or personal acquaintances checked as favorable and nineteen individuals with close connections to the Hightowers or other significant factors listed as unfavorable.

"It only takes a couple of strong jurors to turn the rest of them," Mac said.

Gazing out the window of his corner office on the fourteenth floor of the Peachtree South Office Tower, special prosecutor Joe Whetstone lit a cigar. After their last meeting, Alexander Hightower had sent over a box of Davidoff "double-R" Dominican cigars. At twenty-two dollars apiece, the cigars were a rich man's substitute for a ten-cent stick of candy. Joe and his staff had just finished going over the Echota County jury list. Mac's methods of jury research were musket ball and muzzle-loading rifle; Joe's techniques were computer-guided Tomahawk missiles.

On his desk were 126 neatly stacked sheets of paper, each sheet containing a wealth of known and lesser-known information about each juror. Joe was already aware of ten people Mac had represented in the jury pool. They would be eliminated. But he also had a detailed summary of other types of data regarding every juror's personal and public life—what organizations they belonged to or supported, where they worked, the extent of previous jury service and the result of that deliberation, their relationship with anyone associated with the case, whether they or a family member had been victims of a crime, how much they owed, and other details that revealed a bias for or against the prosecution. Joe knew which former Hightower employees to avoid. He was not worried about Lyman Bakerfield; in fact, he hoped Lyman made it on the jury. It was true Lyman lost his job when Hightower & Co. bought Dalconex; however, he had received a severance package that had tripled in value because of the increase in value of shares he owned in other Hightower-related companies. Lyman had written a note of appreciation to Alexander Hightower two years after he lost his job and thanked him for the way in which the termination of his employment was handled.

The Hightower's former housekeeper was a dangerous negative. After working for Cecil Hightower for twenty years, she committed a petty theft at the Dennison Springs estate, and Cecil immediately fired her. Because of her long years of service no criminal charges were filed, but the woman told her family that she had been framed. Ten years later, she believed her own lies and harbored a considerable grudge against the Hightower family.

Doug Kendrick's son would never sit on the jury. Joe knew Doug and Mac were friends and former schoolmates who had maintained a friendship for more than forty years. Judy's neighbor was one of his stars. Her sister's nephew had been shot in Birmingham five years before, and the killer escaped justice on a legal technicality. It wouldn't take much to convince Mrs. Kidwell that another murderer did not need to avoid responsibility for his crimes.

Joe knew about the juror who had recently died, but he was also aware that numbers 57, 90, and 102 had sick family members, which would make it difficult for them to serve. Numbers 21 and 123 had criminal records even their spouses might not know about. Number 33 had been charged with murder in Idaho and acquitted after a jury deliberated for three days. Numbers 64 and 94 were former Marines who would respond favorably to Walter Monroe's testimony. Number 78,

Mrs. Lola Hawkins, was the daughter of a career prosecutor with the Cook County, Illinois, district attorney's office and had probably heard enough of her father's war stories to know better than to buy into a defense lawyer's attempts to smoke screen the jury with half-baked theories designed to create reasonable doubt.

Like Napoleon on a hilltop, Joe was carefully marshaling his forces from a distance to coordinate his attack with measured confidence. The forensic evidence was solid. The law enforcement testimony and procedures meticulous and professional. The circumstances surrounding the discovery of the body convincing. The psychiatric report a tour de force. The stipulated polygraph a devastating blow to the defense. He would move forward deliberately, cut the throat of the defense's case with surgical precision, and watch it bleed to death on the courtroom floor.

—

First thing Tuesday morning, Mac phoned Bruce Wilcox, the former Georgia Bureau of Investigation agent who had agreed to examine the charts of the two lie-detector tests taken by Pete.

"Mr. Wilcox. Mac McClain here. Did you review the charts we sent by FedEx last week?"

"Yes. I can see how the examiners reached dissimilar conclusions."

"How do you explain the different results?"

"One of two possibilities. The subject is schizophrenic or one of the pretest interviews was significantly tainted."

"If we omit schizophrenia, can you tell which one was based on a faulty interview?"

"Maybe. There is a big difference between the subject's normal physiological response to the control, or nonthreatening questions, on the two tests. He was much calmer during the first than the second. Abnormal stress during control questions on the second test could make the responses to the relevant questions on that test unreliable. Frankly, based only on the charts, I found the results of both inconclusive."

"Do you know either of the examiners?"

"I've seen Larry Waters at some training seminars, but I'm unfamiliar with Sergeant Laird."

Mac wrote some notes on a pad. "If shown the two charts in court, could you explain the differences in a way the jury could understand?"

"If you ask the right questions."

"You understand my dilemma?" Mac asked.

"The admissibility of the second polygraph is stipulated and the first is not," Wilcox responded. "You need a backdoor way to let the jury know the results of the first test because at least it supports an argument that the subject didn't use any drugs."

"Exactly," Mac said.

"I've seen this situation twice in twenty-five years. It's not common, but if you can convince the judge to let me testify, I'm willing to render an opinion."

"The trial begins next week. What's your schedule?"

"I can juggle my responsibilities with forty-eight hours' notice."

"I'll send you a subpoena and place you on call."

After hanging up the phone, Mac went to the jail to brief Pete on the events of the past few days. When his young client came down the hall, he looked more like a recruit coming in from the parade ground than a bedraggled prisoner.

"You're looking sharp this morning," Mac said.

"Thanks."

Once they were seated, Mac briefly told him about Bruce Wilcox and gave a detailed account of Harry O'Ryan's latest version of the boot-camp incident. "Harry is staying at a local motel until the trial."

Pete nodded. "My life would have been different if he'd told the truth five years ago. But maybe it's better I left the Corps and went to college. Did you know they moved me to isolation last week?"

"I figured they might. Do you want me to ask the judge to move you back upstairs with the other prisoners?"

Pete hesitated. "I'm not sure. There is an insane man in the cell next to me. He yells and screams several hours a day."

"What's his name?"

"Cal Musgrave."

"Oh yeah. He's been causing trouble around town for years."

"But I'm able to tune him out most of the time. When I went to the isolation cell, I decided to live as if I was in a prisoner-of-war camp and let the old Marine Corps training kick in. You know, develop a daily routine, discipline my time, keep mentally focused. Part of that has been reading the Bible every day, and I'm doing better now than before."

"Okay."

"I've even gone to the past two church services and talked with Mr. Gallegly."

"Charles Gallegly has been coming to the jail for years."

"He's a kind man," Pete said. "Anyway, I was a mess last week. All we'd had was bad news on top of bad news, but Mr. Gallegly helped me have a little hope."

"That's good."

Pete scratched his ear. "Do you ever read the Bible?"

A month earlier Mac would have given a glib, "Yes." But after being around David Moreland, he knew there were different ways to read the Scriptures than flipping through a few pages once or twice a year. "I go to church occasionally, but to be honest, I'm learning myself."

"There's a verse I've been wondering about—it's Romans 8:28. I memorized it."

"What does it say?"

Pete looked straight into Mac's eyes. "'And we know that in all things God works for the good of those who love him, who have been called according to his purpose.'"

"God works all things for the good?" Mac asked.

"'For those who love him and have been called according to his purpose.'"

Mac mentally ran a condensed replay of the last ten years of his life—his wife, his sons, his pain. Finally, he said, "I can't see it."

"It makes sense in the deal with the Marines," Pete responded. "I'm glad I went on to college. But this"—he gestured to the walls surrounding them. "I want to believe, but I can't."

"I can't help on that one," Mac said. "There's too much suffering in the world for me to make any sense out of it. But let me tell you one thing I have learned recently while sitting in a church service. Was your mother a good cook?"

"Yeah. She made the best squash casserole."

Thirty minutes later, Mac walked out of the jail, shaking his head in amazement. He'd done a lot in his career, but he'd never talked to a client about religion, much less the idea that he could taste God.

Mac McClain was the topic of preliminary conversation for the Tuesday morning meeting of the Mable Ray Circle. Celeste told about her brief encounter with Mac as they walked out of the sanctuary and read the old prayer journal about Laura's prayer, spoken so many years before and now answered so specifically in the present. Several women wiped away tears.

"Amazing," Kelli said. "I wasn't even in first grade when Mrs. McClain prayed for her husband."

"This is what it's all about," Naomi said, wiping her eye with a tissue. "Praying a matter through to its fulfillment."

The women grew quiet and waited.

In a few minutes, Kathy Howell began, "Father, thank you for your love and faithfulness to your children. Help us in this time of prayer to enter into the power of agreement with one another and with you for Mac McClain."

Then, one by one they joined in. Some quietly prayed a verse or two of Scripture. Others proclaimed with confidence the manifestation of God's will over Mac's life. Celeste saw a simple vision of Mac on a ladder and prayed that he would have the courage to climb higher. For an hour they continued in alternating periods of silence and spoken words, knowing from experience that the unity of the Spirit would weave a tapestry of prayer through their collective sensitivity to the Lord that more completely revealed the will of God than the perspective of a single individual. The number of words spoken in prayer was not their measure of success. They realized that a simple cry for help at the right time and place attracted the attention of the only One whose assistance was worth seeking.

"Mac also asked us to pray for the Angela Hightower murder case," Celeste said. "Let's ask the Lord for something on behalf of the Hightower family."

Another period of silence followed. Then Naomi prayed in her slightly tremulous voice, "Father, we ask you to bring the members of the Hightower family together for healing during this time of tragedy and sorrow. Open their eyes. Where there has been rejection, bring acceptance. Where there has been isolation, bring relationship. Where there have been," she paused, "hidden deeds of darkness, bring the revelation of your light . . ."

TWENTY-SEVEN

Man looks at the outward appearance,
but the L*ORD* *looks at the heart.*
1 SAMUEL 16:7 (NIV)

VICKI HAD BEEN WORKING for several days on the "list of sixty-six," as they called the midnight purple Lincoln owners. She eliminated one-third of the purchasers as retired couples who posed no threat to anyone except perhaps a stockbroker who gave them bad advice on commodity futures. However, information about two-thirds of the individuals was too sketchy to form an opinion about their potential for criminal activity. She and David met with Mac in the library.

"What do you want me to do?" she asked.

"Do the best you can," Mac said. "We don't have the time or resources to investigate forty people in less than a week, but we can go as far down the list as possible. Maybe something will turn up that connects a person on the list to the Lincoln that struck Mr. McFarland's truck."

Vicki turned to go.

"One other thing," Mac said. "Do you have the number of the Peachtree Lab? I have a final piece of work for them to do."

"I'll try to get them on the phone."

After Vicki left, Mac turned to David. "I've been working on my direct and cross-examination of every potential witness. I want you to do the same thing. Prepare an outline of information you think is important, and I'll supplement it from my point of view and frame the exact language of critical questions."

"Yes, sir. Will I question any witnesses?"

"Do you want to?"

David thought about the responsibility. "I'm not sure."

"We'll work up the whole case before delegating any responsibility."

"Okay."

Vicki buzzed the phone in the library. "Dr. Gary Ogden from the lab in Atlanta is on line three."

"Dr. Ogden, do you have enough of Thomason's blood to run another test?"

"What type of test?"

"For the presence of gamma-hydroxybutryate, GHB. I need to know as soon as possible."

"Yes, I can do it. I'm familiar with the drug and its effects," the chemist responded.

"How soon?" Mac asked.

"I'll go into the lab myself and call you before five o'clock."

Several hours later, Mindy buzzed Mac. "Dr. Odgen on line two."

Mac's heart sped up an extra couple of beats. He desperately needed a physical explanation for Pete's claim of memory loss. His client's "I don't remembers" and "I don't knows" were as convincing as the excuses offered by war criminals at Nuremberg.

"What did you find?" he asked.

"GHB was present at a significant level—over five hundred milligrams."

"What effect would that have on a two-hundred-pound male?"

"In combination with the other drugs in his system, he could have gone to the moon and not remembered it."

Thank you, Anna Wilkes, Ph.D., Mac thought as he dialed David's number to give him the news.

Mac and David met at the jail to tell Pete the news. He listened as Mac explained how they would present the evidence then asked the obvious question, "But why was GHB in my bloodstream in the first place?"

Mac stopped. "All I'd thought about since the call from the lab was proving your mental condition on the night of Angela's death. I don't have any idea how the drug got in your system."

"That's what I thought," Pete said. "I don't remember and you don't know."

—

Back at the office, Mac left a message for Anna Wilkes.

She called close to 5:00 P.M. Mindy buzzed Mac's office. "Dr. Wilkes on line two. We had a nice chat."

"You what?" Mac asked, but Mindy had already disconnected.

He punched the phone button. "Hey. I've talked with the lab in Atlanta. Pete's tested positive for GHB."

"I'm surprised."

"Surprised?" Mac asked. "You suggested the test."

"I didn't know I would be right. It was a guess."

"Guess or not. You hit the jackpot. It answers some questions but raises others."

"It's like starting at the end and working your way backward."

"Exactly."

"How is the overall trial preparation going?" Anna asked.

"I'm in good shape." Mac paused. "My last chance to breathe freely will be Saturday night, and I'd like to spend it at a nice restaurant in Chattanooga. Any suggestions?"

"Are you looking for gourmet chicken livers?"

Mac laughed. "No, I was thinking more about steak or prime rib."

"Then it's Kincaid's on the river. They have good steaks and great grilled salmon."

"Would you like to join me?" Mac asked.

"Are you sure that's wise?"

"What do you mean?"

"So close to the trial. Fraternizing with your expert witness."

Mac realized he was being teased. "Maybe you're right."

"Maybe I'm not," Anna shot back. "You've made my mouth water thinking about the salmon. What time?"

"Seven?"

"That's good."

Anna hung up the phone. Ever since her conversation with Celeste Jamison outside the courthouse, she'd kept Mac at the forefront of her thoughts and prayers. But in praying for his needs, she'd found herself caring more and more about him in a different light. As a man.

By late Friday afternoon, Mac and David were ready for a break. They'd sent out subpoenas, arranged airplane flights, prepared motions, written hundreds of questions, pored over the jury list, and made sure they had enough extra sheets of blank paper in their trial notebooks for any surprises along the way. Mac had spent Thursday evening with Harry O'Ryan, and he hoped the now-sober ex-Marine's testimony would soften the anticipated blow from Buster Monroe.

Mac brought the mugs and drinks into the library. For a snack he'd found a jar of fresh peanuts in the break room.

"I missed our little ritual last week," David said. "I told my dad about it."

"Did he think I was corrupting you?"

"No, he'd like to meet you."

"I'd like that, too." Mac poured his beer and handed David a spring water. "It's a nice rite of passage into the weekend. Although this weekend will be a bit more stressful than normal."

"Are you working all day tomorrow?" David asked.

"Yes. But I have dinner plans."

"Me, too." David took a drink of water. "Is there a decent Chinese restaurant in town?"

"The Canton District on Hamilton Street is good. Do you have a date?"

David nodded toward the reception area. "Mindy."

"You're kidding." Mac set down his mug. "I mean, is she your type?"

"What is my type?" David smiled.

"Well, I guess, uh—"

"Someone dressed in a long brown skirt with thick glasses and an IQ over 150?"

Mac held up his hand. "Okay, so I'm wrong. But Mindy?"

"You hired her. Surely you know more about her intelligence and personality than I do."

Mac thought a minute. "Actually, I don't know much at all. She's a hard worker, and as long as she answered the phone and did the filing, I didn't try to find out anything else."

"That's your loss."

They sat quietly for a few minutes, drinking and munching peanuts.

Mac's curiosity about Mindy rose to the surface. "What is she like?" he asked.

"She really understands people," David said. "Including you."

"What does she say about me?"

"That you're a hard worker."

"That's all?"

"No, the rest is privileged."

"Oh."

David smiled. "She thinks you're a neat guy—for someone your age."

"I don't like the way this questioning is going," Mac said. "Tell me more about *her,* not her ideas about me."

"Okay. She is willing to help someone else even if it inconveniences her. I call it a servant's heart."

Mac looked at David. When he was twenty-five years old, identifying whether a woman had servantlike qualities never appeared on his radar screen. Yet Laura had been much the same. He'd always considered himself extremely lucky that she gave him a second look.

"She's cute, too." David added. "And funny. I like being around her."

"Take her to the Canton," Mac said. "They have a great selection of south China dishes. Ask for Lu and tell him you know me. He'll recommend something good."

Mac drained the last drops from his mug. "By the way, how many white shirts do you own?" he asked.

"Three."

"Do you wash and iron them yourself?"

"That's kind of a personal question, isn't it?"

Mac smiled. "David, you do as good a job ironing shirts as any young male on a tight budget I've ever seen. However, for purposes of the upcoming trial, I want you to have your shirts laundered and starched." Mac pulled out his wallet and handed David four new one-hundred-dollar bills.

David's eyes opened wide when he saw the amount of money in his hand. "Are you sure? I don't need this much to get extra starch in my collars."

"Buy three more shirts and three more ties. I like the tie you wear every day, but I have the pattern completely memorized and would like a change in landscape. Pick out whatever you want, except no cartoon characters or pictures of food. There is a one-hour cleaner open Saturday afternoons on Jackson Street."

"I've seen it."

"And buy Mindy some flowers. She deserves a big bouquet after working for me."

Mac pulled his car into Anna's driveway. Hunter was playing basketball. His face lit up when he saw Mac.

"Hey," he said. "I've made some new arrows."

"I want to see them later. First, let's play a game of horse."

"Don't you want to go inside?"

"Not yet. Your mother probably isn't ready."

"Yeah. It always takes her a long time to get ready when we go somewhere."

"You first." Mac loosened his tie.

Mac was rusty, and if he hadn't been able to shoot a backward over-the-head shot, perfected years before in previous games of horse, Hunter would have made short work of him. They were tied at h-o-r-s when Anna, dressed in a fancy black dress and white pearls, opened the front door.

"It was his idea," Hunter yelled quickly. "I told him to go inside."

"I believe you," Anna answered. "Finish him off, Hunter. Try one from the drain spout."

Hunter stood on the concrete splash block and swished the net. The pressure on Mac mounted. He was almost too large to stand on the block, but he took aim and banked in a lucky shot. Hunter missed his next attempt and Mac stood in the middle of the driveway and turned away from the goal.

"Watch this, Mom. He's only missed once."

Looking over his shoulder at the goal and then staring down the driveway, Mac threw the ball over his head and through the net. Marking the spot with his toe, he waited for Hunter to stand in his footsteps. The boy imitated Mac's every move, but when he let go of the ball, it bounced off the front of the rim.

"You win," Hunter said. "I'm going to work on that backward shot before we play again."

"Come in the house before you give him any more ideas," Anna said. "If Hunter learns how to hit that crazy shot, it means I'll have to work on it, too."

"Or you can outlaw it," Mac said. "That's what my boys did until they learned how to shoot it better than I could. Then they made it legal, and I never won again."

Mac followed Anna into the living room. She looked very elegant, not like any psychologist Mac had ever seen. "We can go as soon as Jean gets back from an errand," she said.

Before Mac could sit down, Hunter returned with his new arrows. Mac took the multicolored straight sticks and inspected them. "Good work. Have you shot them yet?"

"Not much. I was waiting for you. It will be light outside for a few more minutes."

Mac looked to Anna. "Do Hunter and I have time to shoot a few arrows in the backyard?"

"Dinner can wait a few more minutes. Just be sure to keep your eyes open and don't try to shoot behind your back. I'll come referee."

Anna's small backyard sloped up gradually away from the house. On a large cardboard box Hunter had drawn the outline of something that vaguely resembled a wild boar with long tusks. The side of the feral beast was decorated with a bull's-eye and numbered rings from ten to one hundred.

"Nice target," Mac said. "The bull's-eye would be a hard shot. How far away do we stand?"

"At the edge of the patio. You go first."

Pulling a long-forgotten phrase from his memory bank of childhood etiquette, Mac said, "No, it's your house."

"But you're my guest," Hunter answered correctly.

Mac picked an arrow, took careful aim, and let it fly. It missed the target area but struck the animal in the eye.

"I didn't get any points, but I think I killed it. Are you sure you want to watch this?" he asked Anna. "It could get gory."

"I'm fine as long as it's cardboard."

Hunter took the bow and lodged an arrow just outside the ten-point ring.

Mac made a ten-point shot and handed the bow back to Hunter, who also shot his next arrow into the same area.

"One more each," the boy said.

Mac thought about deliberately missing the target. When his sons were very young, he often played below his capability to encourage them, but Hunter was eleven, and Mac decided to play it straight. He took his time and hit the twenty ring.

"Thirty points," Hunter said. "I need to hit a thirty or better."

Mac held his breath and hoped for a thirty as he watched Hunter, one eye squeezed shut, draw down on the target. The arrow hit the line between the twenty and thirty rings. Hunter ran up to the target. "What do you think?" he asked.

Mac pulled out the arrow and inspected the hole. "It's more toward the thirty than the twenty. We always played if it's on the line it goes up, not down."

"Yes," Hunter pumped his fist. "That was my best arrow."

"Jean's here," Anna said.

"I want a rematch on a sunny day," Mac said. "I think the dim light bothered my shot."

To reach downtown Chattanooga, Mac drove west on Brainerd Road to a tunnel cut through a long hill named Missionary Ridge. The restaurant was situated on a bluff overlooking the Tennessee River, and a sharp wind swept off the water and buffeted them as they walked across the parking lot toward the front door.

Kincaid's was a small, intimate, very expensive place. Mac had made reservations, and the maître d' seated them at a table with an unobstructed view of the beautiful panorama. The lights of a long, narrow barge reflected off the water below.

"This is perfect," Anna said, settling into her chair.

"Good."

A young waiter brought water and menus. Anna ordered the salmon, and Mac chose a steak.

After they ordered, Mac told Anna about David Moreland. "He's been an asset in preparing for the trial—very intelligent, but he has some unusual ideas about religion."

"What kind of ideas?"

"He talks to God."

"That's not odd; it's a simple definition of prayer."

"But he believes that God talks back. Do you he think he might be delusional?"

Anna laughed. "Maybe, or he could be a normal Christian."

The waiter brought their meal. The salmon was fresh and the steak a shade under medium.

"Good steak," Mac said after his first bite. "How's the salmon?"

"As good as I remembered."

They ate in silence for a few moments, enjoying the food and the view.

"Do you cook?" Anna asked after a few bites.

"Nothing fancy. I eat out during the day and snack at night; it helps keep my weight under control."

"I bet I can guess your age and weight," she said.

"Go ahead," Mac braced himself.

"Two hundred and fifty-six," she said confidently.

"Do I look that fat?" Mac put down the bite he was about to eat.

"No, two hundred pounds and fifty-six years."

"That's close on the weight and exact on the years."

"I had some help."

"Who?"

"Your receptionist."

They watched a cabin cruiser tie up for the night at the docks. Lights ablaze, other boats moved slowly across the water,

"Have you ever wanted to do that?" Anna asked.

"Ride in a motorboat down the Tennessee River?"

"Yes."

"Maybe if it was as wild as the Mississippi in Mark Twain's day, but there is too much development along the river to suit me. How about you?"

"I'm not a river or lake person. I love the beach, and I'd like to see tropical fish in their natural habitat and do some snorkeling."

"Where would you go?"

"The Caribbean, Australia, the Red Sea."

They talked. Mostly about Hunter. Mac gave Anna his perspective on their hike to Jacks River Falls, leaving out the memories of his own past.

"Hunter remembered everything you told him," Anna said. "He wants me to see the daffodils at the abandoned homestead when they bloom next spring."

"It's a nice spot."

They finished their meal with a pair of cappuccinos and split a piece of cheesecake.

It was cooler when they stepped outside. Mac turned on the car's heater.

"Let's drive over the ridge," Anna said.

"Okay."

There was a way through and a way over Missionary Ridge. Bypassing the road to the tunnel, they quickly climbed until the lights of the city were spread out in the valley below.

"Turn here," Anna said as they approached a side street.

Mac made the turn.

"Go past two streets on the left and take the third left."

"Don't get us lost."

"You're in my territory now."

Mac took the turn.

"Go to the end of the street. There is a gray stone house built near the edge of the bluff. Turn there."

Mac turned into the driveway and stopped the car.

"Now what?"

"Some friends of mine live here, but they're out of town. I wanted you to see the city from this vantage point. Do you have a coat I could borrow?"

"My red Bulldog jacket is still in the backseat."

"That will do. It's too dark for a Tennessee fan to see me and fire his squirrel rifle at me."

Anna put on the red coat, and they walked along a slate path to a white gazebo that seemed to hang in space over the cliff. It was a spectacular nighttime panorama. They could see the river in the distance; its winding course traced by the lights of buildings along the bank. To the northwest, Chattanooga's modest skyscrapers were clustered in a huddle of silver and gray spires, and across the whole landscape, a twinkling carpet of streetlights illuminated the slopes of Lookout Mountain.

The wind was blowing harder across the top of the ridge, and as they stood in the gazebo, Anna wrapped her arms tightly around herself and stood in front of Mac to block some of the wind. Mac stood watching the lights below them.

"Thank you for telling me about your family the other night," she said.

Mac looked straight ahead; the tiny sparkles slightly blurred before his vision.

"There is a perspective on things from up here," she continued, her back still to him.

"What is it?" he asked.

"That God is over everything. He can see the end from the beginning."

"If he knows the future, why doesn't he do something about evil?"

"He did. He sent Jesus."

"That's not an answer. Bad things still happen."

"And he offers healing to those who come to him."

Mac thought again about Archie's sermon, but its impact had faded. "I want to believe that God is good, but I can't see that he's helped me. I've been waiting on time to heal my wounds."

Anna turned and looked up into Mac's face. "Time doesn't heal wounds; it only watches them take different shapes and forms until they look so different that where they came from is often obscured. The real capacity to heal inner wounds comes from heaven, not earth. Only the power of Jesus can go to the deep places and bring healing."

Mac listened without responding.

They were quiet on the drive back to Anna's house. Mac was troubled. He had opened long-closed doors to another person and faced again what lurked behind them. Not that Anna Wilkes meant to hurt him, but like a doctor probing a sore place, she kept putting her finger in a wound as wide and deep as the Missionary Ridge tunnel. It didn't take a degree in psychology to figure out that a part of him died on a cold December afternoon nine years before. And then she told him Jesus was his only source of help—how vague. Counseling might give perspective. A pill he could understand. A bullet would end everything. But Jesus. How did that work? His frustration built.

Turning into Anna's driveway and stopping the car, he said, "I don't want every time we talk to be a religious counseling session."

Surprised, Anna said, "Of course. I wasn't—"

Mac cut her off. "Thanks for your concern, but don't try to fix me."

"Sorry. Thanks for dinner."

She was out the door and up the steps before he could say another word.

Mac stared at the closed door for a few seconds. Mad at himself, he jerked the car into reverse and backed quickly down the driveway.

Inside the house, Anna leaned against the door and closed her eyes. She went into the darkened living room and sat on the piano bench. She lightly touched a couple of random keys. Wrapped in her bathrobe, Jean appeared in the doorway.

"What happened?" she asked.

"Great time at dinner, but then I pushed too hard about the Lord as the source of his healing. He rejected it."

"Don't jump to conclusions. Give him time."

Anna shook her head. "No. I think time is his enemy, not his ally. He's probably opened up with me as much as he has with anyone, but there's something deeper gnawing away at him, and I don't know what it is."

"How is *your* heart?"

"Confused about the whole situation and my role in it. He's a decent man who has problems, but that doesn't mean I'm supposed to help fix them. That's what he just told me in the driveway. Maybe he's right."

Anna softly struck another sequence of notes on the piano. "He hides his depression, but I know it's there. It's familiar to me; I can almost touch it, but I'm missing an obvious key."

Suddenly, Anna put her hand over her mouth. "Oh no!"

"What is it?" Jean asked sharply.

"The other night, he asked me if I wished it had been quicker . . ."

"What?"

"Jack's death. It makes sense now." She looked up at her aunt. "Mac is thinking of suicide, too."

TWENTY-EIGHT

In all criminal prosecutions, the accused shall enjoy the right to a speedy and public trial, by an impartial jury.
UNITED STATES CONSTITUTION, AMENDMENT VI

MAC DIDN'T HAVE TIME to ruminate about his time with Anna. A young man's life was in his hands, and he hoped Dr. Anna Wilkes was professional enough not to allow any personal conflict between them to interfere with her testimony on behalf of Pete. He skipped church on Sunday and spent several hours at the office making final preparation for the opening stages of the trial.

The following morning, the citizens of Echota County required to report for jury duty began arriving at the courthouse shortly after 8:00. Jurors' cars and trucks lined the streets in front and to the sides of the city square, and by 8:50 A.M., the normally quiet courtroom took on the air of a giant family reunion. In a small Southern town like Dennison Springs, a week of court involving a murder case generated a lot of local interest. No matter the jurors' backgrounds—retired, unemployed, textile worker, businessman, homemaker—the things that normally shaped their individuality had to take a backseat to their designation as members of the jury pool. For some, jury duty offered an excuse to be off work; for others, it was a major disruption of personal and business plans. It was a time when American society made clear the jobs with the highest intrinsic importance for the future of the nation—schoolteachers and mothers of young children were routinely excused from jury service. CEOs of corporations were not.

—

The lawyers stood in the open area in front of the judge's bench. Pete Thomason, dressed in a suit and freed of manacles and leg chains, sat alone with a deputy by his side on a bench against the wall.

Joe Whetstone introduced his two assistants to Mac. Mac did the same with David.

Sheriff Bomar stood and announced in a loud voice, "All rise."

An immediate hush stilled the noisy room and everyone stood as the Honorable William L. Danielson swept into the room in his black robe, took his place, and said, "Be seated."

"Ladies and gentlemen," he began, "I want to thank you for your willingness to serve as jurors for the fall term of Echota County Superior Court. We will be trying criminal cases during the next two weeks. We have a capital murder case on the docket that will take most or all of this week, and our first order of business will be to select a jury in that case. Madam Clerk, please administer the oath to the jurors."

In a high-pitched voice that carried to the back of the large room, the clerk, a tall, middle-aged woman with black hair, called out, "Raise your right hand. Do you solemnly swear or affirm that you shall give true answers to all questions as may be asked by the court or its authority, including all questions asked by the parties or their attorneys, concerning your qualifications as jurors in the cases now pending before this court? So help you God."

A chorus of "I do's" from more than one hundred throats gave assent to the oath.

"Mr. Langley, please proceed," the judge said to the district attorney.

"Judge, we have several cases to resolve by plea agreements. We'd like to handle those before striking the jury in the Thomason case."

"Proceed."

Bert called the name of the first defendant, a young man who didn't look a day older than eighteen. Everyone watched closely as he walked forward. His mother started crying, and a friend put an arm around her. When the judge sentenced him to ten years in prison for drug-related charges, the mother had to be helped from the courtroom. The second defendant received probation. Four more defendants followed in short order.

"That's all the preliminary matters, Your Honor," Bert said. "At this time I call *State versus Thomason,* case number 76932."

All the other lawyers cleared out of the courtroom. Mac and David set their briefcases on the defense table. In seconds, stacks of papers and legal pads took their assigned place. Because she knew so many people in the community, Judy joined them to help Mac with jury selection.

On the opposite side of the room, the prosecution table underwent a similar metamorphosis. Bert Langley and his staff removed their files and Joe Whetstone and company assumed center stage.

When the commotion stilled, Judge Danielson addressed the jurors again, "Ladies and gentlemen, in case number 76932, Peter Thomason is charged with the murder of Angela Hightower. The State has indicated its intention to seek the death penalty."

Any festive atmosphere in the courtroom immediately vanished, and the room became completely quiet.

Pete's mouth, already dry, became more parched, and he poured a glass of water from a pitcher on the table in front of him.

"When the clerk calls your name, please come into the jury box so the court and lawyers can ask you questions to determine your qualifications to serve as jurors. These questions are not asked in an effort to embarrass you but to provide information so that a fair and impartial jury can be selected to try this case."

The clerk stood to call the name of the first juror when the back of the courtroom door opened. Alexander and Sarah Hightower walked together down the aisle. Alexander Hightower, dressed in a dark suit, looked straight ahead, nodding slightly to the judge and Joe Whetstone before taking a seat on the wooden bench behind the prosecution table. He did not look in the direction of the defense. Sarah stole a glance at Pete before looking away.

Then the court clerk called the names of twelve persons who came forward into the jury box, and the judge began asking the preliminary questions required of all prospective jurors.

"Are any of you related by blood or marriage to Peter Thomason, the defendant in this case, or Angela Hightower, the victim?"

No response.

"Have any of you, for any reason, formed or expressed any opinion in regard to the guilt or innocence of the accused?"

A heavyset man on the back row raised his hand.

"Your name, please?" the judge asked.

"Roscoe Wilson, judge. When I got my jury notice I told two of my friends I thought the man who killed the Hightower girl ought to be strung up, the sooner the better."

Mac quickly stood. "I ask that Mr. Wilson be excused for cause, Your Honor."

"Just a minute, Mr. McClain. Mr. Wilson, is your opinion so fixed that it could not be changed by the evidence?"

"I reckon not. I mean, if the defense lawyer proves his client didn't do it, I would vote to turn him loose."

The judge tapped the arm of his chair with his fingers. "Mr. Wilson, the law presumes a defendant is innocent until proven guilty. The burden of proving guilt beyond a reasonable doubt is on the State. The accused does not have to prove his innocence. Could you follow those instructions in this case?"

Obviously, Roscoe had not watched enough law-and-order shows on TV.

Shaking his head, he said, "That doesn't make sense to me, Judge. It seems like both sides ought to put up what they have and let us pick whichever one is right."

The judge leaned forward. "I understand your position, Mr. Wilson, but I am going to excuse you from jury service. Please stop by the clerk's office to receive your pay voucher on your way out of the courthouse."

Roscoe Wilson muttered to himself as he walked up the aisle.

"Has anyone else on this panel formed or expressed an opinion about the guilt or innocence of the accused?

Apparently everyone else had learned the lesson the judge tried to teach Mr. Wilson and kept his or her mouth shut.

"Have you any prejudice or bias resting on your mind either for or against the accused?"

No response.

"Is your mind perfectly impartial between the State and the accused?"

No response.

"Are any of you conscientiously opposed to capital punishment?"

A small, white-haired lady in the front row raised her hand so slightly it took the judge a moment to notice her.

"Yes, ma'am. Your name please?"

"Mildred Dexter."

"Why did you raise your hand?"

"I'm not sure I could vote to kill someone."

"Do you have any religious reason for opposing the death penalty?"

"No, sir. I'm a Methodist."

A few laughs greeted her response.

"Let me ask you another way. Are your reservations about capital punishment such that you could never vote to impose the death penalty regardless of the evidence and the instructions of the court?"

"You mean, you would tell us how to vote?"

"No, ma'am. At the conclusion of the case, I will instruct the jury on the law to apply to the evidence. It will be up to the jury to decide if the death penalty is appropriate."

"Well, I'd rather not decide that if I don't have to."

"But you could do so if supported by sufficient evidence?"

"Yes, sir."

"Anyone else?"

No one raised a hand, and the judge looked at Joe Whetstone. "Mr. Whetstone, you may ask."

While the judge was asking the standard questions, Joe's staff had taped a summary of each juror's profile to a notebook-size chart of the jury box. Joe quickly put it to good use.

After introducing himself and his assistants, Joe turned to Mildred Dexter.

"Mrs. Dexter. Would it be a hardship for you to be away from your husband for a week?"

Startled, she said, "Yes, it would. I've been sitting here worrying about it. He's got Alzheimer's, and I guess I could get my niece to come over and stay with him, but she has two small children—"

Joe interrupted, "Your Honor, the State asks that Mrs. Dexter be excused."

"Granted. You may leave, ma'am."

Having established himself as the champion of little old white-haired ladies with sick husbands, Joe moved to another area.

"Do any of you know the defendant, Peter Thomason?"

A young woman in the back row raised her hand. Quickly noting her name on his sheet, Joe said, "Yes, Ms. Kerney."

"I work as a waitress at a restaurant. I've seen him there."

"Thank you. Would your contact with the defendant affect your ability to fairly weigh the evidence and find him guilty of murder at the conclusion of the case?"

"No."

"The defendant has not been in the area very long. Does anybody else know him?"

No response. Mac scribbled a reminder on his pad.

Joe proceeded with his questions. He didn't ask Jason Patterson, the young man on the front row, about his criminal record of petty thefts and shoplifting in New York, but he did connect for a few seconds with Mrs. Lola Hawkins, the daughter of the Chicago prosecutor, by asking her some questions about her work experience. Four of the twelve jurors knew Mac either professionally or socially. One, Spears Avery, was not on Joe's list of people to be avoided, but Joe politely uncovered the fact that Mac represented Mr. Avery almost twenty years before in a condemnation action.

"I'm sure Mr. McClain did a good job."

"He was okay," Avery responded grudgingly. "But I had to get together most of the paperwork and pay for the survey."

Mac couldn't remember the man at first, but Judy leaned over and whispered, "He was a pill. You made me talk to him. He received a good settlement from the power company but resented paying you a dime of it."

"That's all for this panel, Your Honor. Thank you, ladies and gentlemen. Now, Mr. McClain is going to ask you some questions."

"Proceed, Mr. McClain," the judge said.

Mac stood and moved slowly to a spot directly in front of the jury box. By the time he stopped, he'd established eye contact with every juror and recognized a few familiar faces. He introduced himself and those seated at the defense table, saving Pete for last. "Ladies and gentlemen, this is Pete Thomason," he motioned toward his client who, as previously instructed, nodded toward the jurors.

Throughout the course of the trial, Mac would never call Pete "the accused" or "the defendant." He wanted the jury to realize that Pete was a human being.

"Do any of you know Mr. Joe Whetstone?" he began. "He is not from this area."

No one knew Joe or his assistants.

Mac continued asking questions and in a few minutes he was in an easy, conversational relationship with the jurors. David leaned over to Pete. "He's smooth, isn't he?"

"Yeah," Pete muttered. He listened to Mac's questions, but his attention was on the faces of the people. He knew some of those faces would decide his fate.

Five panels of twelve came into the jury box. Ten jurors were excused for legal excuses ranging from uncorrectable bias against the defendant to one man who said he would never believe a police officer under any circumstances.

Mac could tell that the Hightowers' former housekeeper was antagonistic toward Joe. Dennis Kendrick gave Mac a big grin, which was duly noted by one of Joe's assistants. Lyman Bakerfield was harder to decipher. He didn't change expression or give any hint of his attitude toward the Hightowers during questioning, and both Mac and Judy had a big question mark beside his name. Judy's neighbor whose nephew's murderer was freed on a technicality was excused for cause, and Joe sadly watched her walk out of the courtroom. She would have been a great juror for the prosecution.

The judge didn't stop for lunch and, except for a couple of bathroom breaks, moved the proceedings along as rapidly as possible. It was 2:00 P.M. when Mac asked his final questions to the fifth panel. There were fifty qualified jurors left to pick from.

"Mr. Whetstone and Mr. McClain, we are going to choose twelve jurors and two alternates. Because the State has announced its intention to seek the death penalty, the defendant will receive twenty strikes and the prosecution ten strikes for the initial twelve jurors and two strikes to one for the alternates. Any questions?"

"Could we have a recess to prepare?" Joe asked.

"Yes." The judge raised his voice. "The court will be in recess for thirty minutes. Please do not leave the building. Reassemble in the courtroom at two-forty-five."

Like opposing football teams, each group went into immediate huddles around the notes and information that now lay scattered across their tables. It was a time of short but intense debate. Accept, cut, don't know. Some decisions were easy: a business associate of Alexander Hightower, a loyal client of Mac's who thought Mr. McClain was the greatest lawyer on two legs. Others were more difficult. Lyman Bakerfield topped Mac's list; Joe expressed concern about an intelligent-looking young man who worked for a local CPA.

The primary participants in the defense debate were Mac, Judy, and Vicki, who joined them with notes she'd taken during voir dire. They moved through the list in a series of short but intense debates. Mac always cast the deciding vote. They were left with three unknowns.

"Do you have any opinion about these?" Mac asked Judy.

"No."

He turned to David. "Any intuitive reactions?"

The young lawyer responded without hesitation. "Yes to Vera Black, no to Quinn Mashburn, yes to Lance Patrick."

"That's confident. Why do you say yes to Lance Patrick?"

"His name has a decisive ring to it. I think he'll be a strong juror."

"Very scientific," Mac said.

Plans and guesswork complete, everybody took a five-minute break. The jurors wandered back into the courtroom, and the judge brought the group to order precisely at 2:45 P.M.

"Ladies and gentlemen, we are now ready to select a jury in the case of *State versus Thomason.* As your names are called, please stand. If you are accepted by both the State and the defense, come forward into the jury box. Madam Clerk, please proceed."

The court clerk had furnished a revised list of jurors to both sets of lawyers so they could see the order of selection and plan their strategy accordingly. "Beatrice Lancaster."

"The State excuses Mrs. Lancaster," Joe said.

"Gary Kanolin."

"The State accepts Mr. Kanolin."

"Mr. Thomason excuses Mr. Kanolin," Mac said.

On it went. Like jack-in-the-boxes, people popped up and sat down. A few became red in the face when they were rejected; others showed signs of obvious relief. Those accepted by both prosecution and defense took a seat in the jury box. There were eight jurors when the State used the last of its ten strikes. Mac accepted the next two jurors then quickly struck six in a row. He had used a total of eighteen strikes when Lyman Bakerfield's name was called. Of the next three jurors on the list, two were unfavorable. If Mac had known Joe Whetstone was holding his breath, it would have made his decision easier. But he didn't.

"Mr. Thomason accepts Mr. Bakerfield."

Joe wrote a big "Yes!" on his legal pad.

Mac excused the next two jurors and exhausted his strikes. The final juror, a retired schoolteacher, took her seat in the box.

"Gentlemen, we will now select two alternates."

Joe rejected the first juror. Mac struck one, accepted Lance Patrick as first alternate, and allowed the next juror on as second alternate without using his final strike.

When the jury was seated, the judge turned to the lawyers. "Is this your jury?"

"Yes, Your Honor," they answered in unison.

"Ladies and gentleman of the jury, please stand and raise your right hands while I administer your oath for this particular case."

Everyone in the courtroom stood as the oath was issued.

"You shall well and truly try the issue formed upon this bill of indictment between the State of Georgia and Peter Thomason, who is charged with the crime of murder, and a true verdict give according to the evidence. So help you God."

A smaller chorus of "I do's" responded.

"At this time, the bailiffs will take you to the motel, where you will be given opportunity to contact your families and make necessary arrangements to obtain your personal belongings. Any assistance you need will be provided by the bailiffs, and if you experience any difficulties that they cannot handle, please let me know. You are not to discuss the case among yourselves or with anyone else from this moment forward.

You will not seek information about the case from any media source. Your deliberations and decision in this case must come solely from the testimony and evidence presented to you in this courtroom upon proper instructions from the court. Do any of you have any questions?"

The weight of responsibility already settling in, no one spoke.

"Very well. The court will be in recess until nine o'clock in the morning."

TWENTY-NINE

The men of war which went to the battle.
NUMBERS 31:21 (KJV)

AS THEY WALKED through the front door of the office, Mindy cried out, "Help!"

"What is it?" Judy asked.

"You think it was tough being in court trying a murder case. You should have been here handling everything else by myself."

"What happened?" Judy asked.

"Phone calls, people coming by. I had to give legal advice. It was terrible."

"What kind of legal advice?" Mac said sharply.

"Oh, I told a man whose textile machine was repossessed that he didn't owe the deficiency if the bank failed to send him the proper notification under the security agreement and the Uniform Commercial Code."

"How did you know that?" Mac asked.

"I read it off the letter you sent to Mr. Portsmouth. That's right, isn't it?"

"Yes."

"I try to pay attention and learn." Mindy pushed her hair behind her ears.

"Until you pass the bar exam, just take the calls," Mac said. "It will keep the State Bar of Georgia and my malpractice insurance company happy."

"What do you think?" Mac asked David when they were seated in the library.

"I think you should send Mindy to law school."

Mac chuckled. "How was the Chinese restaurant Friday night?"

"There's more to Mindy than you realize. She can use chopsticks with either hand and recently read an article in a travel magazine about Cantonese cooking."

"It's easier to order in Chinese than to select jurors," Mac said.

"Definitely. And my stomach reacted better to the food than it did to court this morning. I was tied up in knots all morning."

"Watching is harder than doing. I've had lawyers from out of town ask me to assist in local trials at my highest hourly rate, but I can't be a spectator. Be patient, I'll get you involved."

"What do you want me to do?"

"Review the cross-examination of Sergeant Laird about the stipulated polygraph exam."

"Okay."

"Also, get ready to muffle Dr. Newburn's squeal when he gets the subpoena for the names of his patients for the past three years. The process server in Atlanta delivered it to his office while we were in court this morning."

"Ditto."

"One other thing."

"Yes, sir?"

"Nice tie."

"Thanks." David ran his hand over it. "You can borrow it sometime."

The bonding process between the different participants in the trial began in earnest the next morning at 9:00. In stark contrast to the throng of jurors the previous day, the courtroom was empty except for Pete, the lawyers, the jury, a pair of sleepy old bailiffs, Alexander and Sarah Hightower, and two newspaper reporters, one from the *Atlanta Journal Constitution* and Barbara Williams of the *Echota Express.* Now that the trial was underway and the jury sequestered, the media blackout was over.

The judge described the unique, two-part procedure in a death penalty case. "Ladies and gentlemen, there are two potential parts to this trial. First, you will decide whether the State proves the guilt of the accused beyond a reasonable doubt. If the State does not meet its burden and you acquit the defendant, there would, of course, be no need to determine any punishment. However, if you find the defendant guilty, each side will have opportunity to present additional evidence related to the punishment to be imposed, and you will deliberate a second time to decide if Peter Thomason should be sentenced to life in prison or put to death.

"The lawyers are going to make opening statements. Neither the opening statements nor the indictment by the grand jury is evidence in this case. Evidence is what you hear from the witness stand and the documents and exhibits which I allow you to consider. Mr. Whetstone will go first, followed by Mr. McClain."

The lawyers' first chance to outline the evidence would set the tone for all that followed in the trial. First impressions are lasting, and the brief speeches by each side would be the first beams in a bridge of trust between the attorneys and the individuals in the jury box.

Joe began by reading the formal language of the grand jury indictment charging Peter Thomason with the murder of Angela Hightower "with malice aforethought contrary to the laws of the State of Georgia." He held the indictment toward Pete before putting it down on the prosecution table. Pete didn't change expression, but his jaw tightened and he ground his teeth together.

Joe continued, "This trial is necessary because a beautiful, nineteen-year-old woman named Angela Hightower is dead. I wish we weren't here today. Mr. and Mrs. Alexander Hightower, Angela's parents, desperately wish they weren't here today. I'm sure that you, together with Judge Danielson and Mr. McClain, feel the same way. Even the defendant, for different reasons, wishes he was not in this courtroom."

"Objection, Your Honor." Mac normally didn't object during opening statements, but Joe had flagrantly crossed the line into argument at the starting gate.

"Don't argue your case, Mr. Whetstone," said the judge. "There'll be time for that later."

"Of course, Your Honor."

Joe proceeded to bring Angela back from the grave to tell her story. "In a murder case, the victim can become depersonalized after repeated references by law enforcement officers, medical personnel, and defense counsel to 'the deceased,' 'the body,' or 'the decedent.' With your help, I am determined not to let that happen to Angela. Until her brutal death, she was a beautiful young woman with a lovely name. Let me speak for Angela and tell you the events that led up to her murder through her eyes."

After describing Angela's background and her first contacts with Pete Thomason, Joe moved to the night of the murder.

"The defendant won Angela's trust and the trust of her parents. On August second, he came by the Hightower home, spoke briefly with Mr. and Mrs. Hightower, and took their daughter to Atlanta in Angela's yellow Porsche. I don't know what Angela and the defendant talked about on the way to Atlanta. I don't know what they ate at a quiet little Italian restaurant on the north side of Atlanta. But I do know that Angela never came home. Sometime after leaving the restaurant, she called from her car phone and left a message on her parents' answering machine that she would be late getting home. Her last words were, 'I love you.'"

Mrs. Hightower stifled a sob. Everyone in the courtroom turned and watched as she covered her face with a lace handkerchief and walked quickly out of the room. Joe waited until the door closed behind her.

"At some point, the defendant gave Angela something to drink. It could have been a soft drink. It could have been a cup of coffee. Whatever it was, it was not an ordinary beverage. Inside the glass were a few drops of an odorless, tasteless drug called Rohypnol or, as it's known in drug circles, 'roofies.' How do we know that? A chemist at the state crime lab will testify that he found this drug in Angela's blood. Could Angela have voluntarily taken this drug? Not likely. Rohypnol is used by sexual predators to render their victims unable to resist unwanted advances. And the defendant is no stranger to roofies. The State will present evidence that he has relied on Rohypnol to take advantage of young women in the past."

Joe let his words hang in the air. Pete was finding it harder to sit still than he thought and squirmed in his seat. Mac leaned over to him and whispered, "Remember what I told you. Don't believe what Whetstone says. He has to prove it, and we'll get our chance."

Joe continued, "The evidence will also show that the defendant took drugs on August second—amphetamines and barbiturates—that fueled the evil within him and that the marks of violence on Angela's body are irrefutable witnesses that the defendant cannot silence. For some reason, perhaps because she resisted the defendant's advances, Angela was strangled. The autopsy report reads 'death by asphyxiation.' "

Joe brought his hands together tightly. "'Asphyxiation.' A big word to describe someone putting his hands around her neck and choking the life out of her.

"Around midnight, sheriff's department deputies responded to a call on Norton Mountain Road and discovered Angela's car over the side of a cliff at an overlook point. Climbing down the rocks, they reached the car and found Angela inside, dead. The defendant was taken into custody along the highway near the place where the Porsche went over the edge of the mountain.

"Is that all the evidence? No. A psychiatrist will give you an understanding of the defendant's mental capacity to commit this horrible crime. A polygraph expert will give you the results of a lie-detector test the defendant failed. Police investigators will help you piece together what happened on August second. And when all the evidence has been presented, I will stand here and ask to do your duty—to find the defendant guilty of murder."

Joe let his words linger in the air for several moments before turning on his heels and returning to the prosecution table. A couple of jurors appeared ready to send Pete straight from the courtroom to the electric chair at Reidsville State Prison for an afternoon appointment. Joe had pushed the edge of the envelope and in doing so ran the risk of promising too much to the jury. Later, if he didn't deliver, he would face a counterattack from Mac that "the State didn't do what it promised."

Mac didn't rush. He slowly scooted back his chair and stood up. He was not going to launch a vigorous counterattack. His case was going to have to develop gradually and indirectly. Mac couldn't accuse Spencer Hightower of the murder in his opening statement or tell the jury that the State's polygraph test was flawed by a coercive pretest interrogation. He wanted to tell about the presence of GHB in Pete's blood, but the impact of his statement would have been insignificant to a jury still absorbing the horror of Rohypnol in Angela's body. He didn't know whether Harry O'Ryan would be effective in countering the testimony of Walter Monroe, and he wasn't sure how Anna Wilkes would compare to Dr. Louis Newburn. Mac had to follow a different tack, showing just enough to begin the process of undercutting Joe's forceful presentation of seemingly incontrovertible facts.

"Ladies and gentlemen, I can't think of anything more serious than deciding the fate of another human being. When we walked into the courtroom this morning, the clock started ticking on an experience none of us will ever forget. My job is to help you through this process. Not to tell you what to think. Not to bully you. But to treat you with the respect that service on this jury deserves. Will you let me do that?"

Mac released his words like a gentle shower.

As he talked, he made eye contact with every juror.

"First, please remember what Judge Danielson said before Mr. Whetstone spoke to you. Nothing the lawyers say to you is evidence in this case. Oh, we both want you to pay attention to us and give careful consideration to our points of view, but whether the prosecution proves beyond a reasonable doubt that Pete Thomason committed this horrible crime will not depend on a lawyer's eloquence. It will be the result of what you hear from the witness stand and any other information the judge decides is worth your consideration.

"Second, I agree with everything Mr. Whetstone told you about Angela Hightower. She was cut off from life before she had a chance to live it, and *someone* should be brought to justice and punished for this crime. However, we believe the evidence will show that the most likely person or persons responsible for the death of Angela Hightower are not in the courtroom today. Not yet."

Thus, in a calm way Mac dropped his bombshell. He wanted the jurors always looking toward the back door to see who came in next.

"Third, please keep an open mind and listen to all the evidence. The prosecution presents its side of the case first. In the Book of Proverbs it says, 'The first to present his case seems right, till another comes forward and questions him.' That is wisdom from the ages, and I would ask you to apply it to your responsibilities today. Thank you very much."

Mac's opening statement loosened the spring of inner tension in Pete that had wound to the breaking point during Joe's remarks. He sat back in his chair and breathed easier.

"The court will be in recess for fifteen minutes," the judge said.

Celeste had been awake since early in the morning. It was day fourteen of her fast, and she had begun to lose enough weight that friends were complimenting her on a successful diet. She smiled and thanked them. She no longer felt a strong physical hunger, but an occasional ache that was more spiritual than physical let her know that her assignment wasn't complete.

She began the Tuesday morning meeting of the Mable Ray Circle by reading one of the most important scriptures for the group—Isaiah 62:6–7:

> I have posted watchmen on your walls, O Jerusalem; they will never be silent day or night. You who call on the name of the Lord, give yourselves

no rest, and give him no rest till he establishes Jerusalem and makes her the praise of the earth.

Dennison Springs was their Jerusalem, and the watchmen on its walls were a small group of faithful women. They became quiet and waited. A heavy stillness settled in the room, a time when heaven held its breath in anticipation.

Then the divine wind came. There were no visible tongues of fire resting on their heads, but the manifestation of the Holy Spirit was immediate and intense. Like ripe stalks of wheat before a coming storm, the women bowed down and began to pray aloud with passion and zeal. Spirit-inspired phrases and Scripture passages rolled out of their hearts and through their lips in a gushing river of intercession. "Expose the deeds of darkness, loose the chains of injustice, break the bands of the oppressor, proclaim freedom to the captives, cast down the accuser, establish truth and integrity, save the perishing, shine forth the light, reveal your glory." There were ebbs and flows, tears and sighs, but for more than an hour one after another would come to the head of the column and push forward the advance until yielding to the next in line.

When Naomi said, "In the strong name of Jesus Christ, amen," they sat back in their chairs and looked at one another in amazement.

"That was different," Kelli said.

"*That* was a prayer meeting," Naomi responded.

"I couldn't keep up writing notes," Kathy said.

"Don't worry," Celeste said. "You can do it later. The important record is written in heaven."

THIRTY

Cannon to the right of them, cannon to the left of them.
THE CHARGE OF THE LIGHT BRIGADE

PROCEED WITH THE State's case, Mr. Whetstone," the judge said.

"Officer Bryce Gordon," Joe said.

Joe called Officer Gordon, then Detective Kenneth Mason to the witness stand. Joe stood behind a podium beside the jury box and asked his questions. The men who found Pete alongside the road near the overlook methodically delivered their testimony without a hitch.

When Joe finished questioning Detective Mason, Mac began, "Detective Mason, how severely impaired was Mr. Thomason at the time of your first contact?"

"Physically or mentally?"

"Both. Start with physical problems."

"He had been able to walk a couple hundred yards from the overlook to the place where we saw him alongside the road. So I would say his physical capacity was only mildly impaired."

"Did you see him walk a couple hundred yards?"

Mac began pacing back and forth as he asked questions.

"No, but we measured the distance from the point where we apprehended him to the overlook. It was more than two hundred yards."

"But how far did you *see* him walk?"

"We stopped the car next to him. He was at the edge of the woods."

"How far was it to the edge of the woods?"

"About twenty-five feet."

"So the only distance you saw Pete walk would have been from the woods to your car, correct?"

"Yes."

"And he fell down before he could make it to the patrol car?"

"Yes."

Mac stopped.

"So you're not telling this jury that you saw Pete Thomason walk from the overlook to the place where you and Officer Borden first saw him?"

"No."

"Is it possible Pete never went to the overlook?"

Joe stood. "Objection, Your Honor. That's speculation."

"Your Honor," Mac responded. "I think Detective Mason has already speculated about Mr. Thomason's activities beyond his ability to observe."

"He has the witness on cross-examination, Mr. Whetstone. Objection denied."

"Please answer the question."

"I don't know where he was before I saw him."

"Someone could have put him out of a vehicle at the edge of the road near the spot you found him, couldn't they?"

"I don't know."

"Did Pete try to run away when Officer Gordon stopped the patrol car?"

"No."

"When you got out of the car, did Mr. Thomason walk away from you or come toward you?"

"He came out of the woods."

"When you told him to come over to the car, did he cooperate?"

"Not really."

"Did he try to run away?"

"No, he took a couple of steps and fell down. I almost had to carry him to the car."

"Did you or Officer Gordon talk with him before putting him in the backseat of the patrol car?"

"No."

"Why not?"

"He passed out as soon as we put him in the backseat."

"How long did he stay unconscious?"

"All the way to the hospital."

"So, from a physical standpoint, he didn't demonstrate much capability while under your observation and custody, did he?"

"No."

"What about mental capability?"

Detective Mason obviously did not want to repeat another long line of questioning before admitting the obvious.

"He was impaired."

"How impaired?"

"Disoriented, confused, pupils dilated. He looked stoned, to put it in street language."

"He was so impaired you didn't think it necessary to advise him of his legal rights, did you?"

"I didn't read him his rights."

"That's all I have."

Joe called Officers Morris Jefferson and Tim Logan to paint a word picture of the gruesome scene at the overlook. Mac didn't ask Jefferson any questions. Tim Logan testified about his discovery of the damaged guardrail and described how he climbed down the cliff to the place where the Porsche had come to rest. He identified a picture of the yellow car, its top caved in, and three large pictures of Angela as he first found her.

The photos had the desired effect on the jury. Joe laid them on the jury rail and the jurors in the second row leaned forward to see them. Several men looked grimly at Pete. A couple of women began to cry.

—

Mac went softly when it was his turn to question Tim Logan. "Were there many cars on Norton Mountain Road that night?"

"No. It's not heavily traveled."

"Do you recall seeing any cars on your way down the mountain to the overlook?"

"I'm sure there were several, but only one I remember."

"Why do you remember it?"

"It was traveling too fast and came over into my lane. I had to swerve to avoid it."

"Can you describe the car?"

"It was a large dark sedan."

Joe asked a few questions on redirect examination.

"Did you see any connection that night between the dark sedan and what you found at the overlook?"

"No."

"Today, do you have any evidence linking this car and Angela Hightower's murder?"

"No, sir."

—

After lunch came the parade of forensic experts. Joe spent quite a bit of time with each witness; Mac only asked a few questions.

The pathologist professionally and graphically described Angela's injuries and the cause of death. In his opinion, she had been dead for at least two hours before the car went over the edge of the cliff. It was the hardest time yet for Pete. More pictures of Angela's body lined the rail in front of the jury. The stark reality of the photographs and the doctor's description of death shocked Pete as much as it did anyone in the courtroom. Even though he was charged with the murder, he'd felt disconnected from the night of the murder because he couldn't remember it.

Now, when he glanced up, he occasionally met the eyes of a juror who looked at him with obvious disgust.

Next came the fiber expert, a woman named Dr. Karen Mead, who testified that there was fiber from Pete's clothes in the car. On cross-examination, Mac asked,"Dr. Mead, were there fibers present in the vehicle that did not match any clothes samples from either Angela Hightower or Pete Thomason?"

"Of course. Unless a vehicle has been very carefully vacuumed, there would be stray fibers from any number of sources."

"Did you identify and retain the 'stray fibers,' as you call them, from the yellow Porsche?"

"Yes. They are lumped together in a container labeled 'extraneous residue.' "

"How many different types of extraneous residue did you find in the vehicle?"

"I can't tell you exactly because we didn't count. Our instructions were to search for specific fibers, but I can tell you there was as much extraneous residue as there were fibers linked to the victim and the defendant."

"So if you added other specific fibers to your search list, they might be in the extraneous residue container."

"Correct."

Harold Kolb, the fingerprint evaluator, was a former FBI analyst with a shaved head and bushy gray mustache. Kolb obviously loved his work. To him, the lines on a fingerprint were as intriguing as the brush strokes on a Winslow Homer seascape. Joe had trouble restraining the witness's enthusiasm.

When it was Mac's turn, he tried to focus Kolb's testimony on a couple of points.

"Mr. Kolb, did you dust the entire vehicle?"

"Yes. I used a number-fourteen, synthetic extra fine-brush and a special powder developed last year by a German laboratory."

"But there were no fingerprints on the steering wheel. Is that correct?"

"Right."

"Could you tell if the steering wheel had been wiped clean?"

"Only by deduction. The steering wheel is normally a fertile site for fingerprints, but in this case there was nothing on it."

"And there were other prints beside those of Pete Thomason and Angela Hightower in the vehicle."

"A plethora."

"A what?" Mac asked, looking up from his notes.

"I'm sorry. A lot. A lot of variety. There was an unusual swirled left index finger unlike anything I have ever seen and a right thumb with a pronounced scar that must have really hurt at some time in the past and a—"

"Mr. Kolb, if I may stop you. Did you submit any of these other prints to the FBI national fingerprint database?"

"No."

"But a search might reveal if someone else who had been in the car had a criminal record, wouldn't it?"

"Possibly."

Mac nodded, checking off a question on his pad. "That's all."

It was close to five o'clock when Mr. Kolb left the witness stand.

"The court will be in recess until tomorrow morning at nine o'clock," the judge said. "Let me remind the jury not to discuss this case among yourselves until all the evidence is presented and you receive your instructions from the court. You can talk about the weather, your children and grandchildren, or what you plan to do with the twenty-five dollars a day the county is paying you to serve as jurors, but do not talk about the case."

After the jury followed the bailiffs out of the courtroom, the judge addressed the lawyers. "Gentlemen, we have a matter to discuss before tomorrow morning. The clerk's office received a motion to quash a subpoena served by Mr. McClain on a psychiatrist, Dr. Louis Newburn. The motion was filed by Dr. Newburn's attorney in Atlanta. My secretary was unable to reach the lawyer, and I wanted to know your positions on this matter."

Joe spoke, "I intend to call Dr. Newburn on behalf of the State during both the initial and sentencing phases of the trial. I don't know why he would want to avoid appearing in the case."

"Mr. Moreland can explain our position, Your Honor," Mac said.

David had been anticipating this moment all afternoon, trying to rehearse and visualize it in his mind. He stood and nervously cleared his throat.

"Go ahead," the judge said.

"Your Honor, I served a subpoena duces tecum requiring Dr. Newburn to appear and bring a list of all the patients he has treated in his psychiatric practice for the past three years."

"That's confidential and irrelevant," Joe quickly responded. "The State joins in the motion to quash the subpoena filed by Dr. Newburn's attorney."

The judge's eyes narrowed. "I would tend to agree, Mr. Moreland, unless you can convince me otherwise."

"The defense believes the doctor has a conflict of interest which could bias his testimony in favor of the State and against Mr. Thomason."

"Explain."

"Our investigation indicates that Dr. Newburn may be the personal psychiatrist for members of the Hightower family. On at least two occasions within the past two weeks, Spencer Hightower, the younger brother of Alexander Hightower, was observed going into the building where Dr. Newburn's office is located in Atlanta."

"Dr. Newburn's office is part of a medical complex containing more than a hundred doctors." Joe said. "Did anyone see Mr. Hightower's brother go into the doctor's office?"

"No, our investigator couldn't verify the precise office Spencer Hightower visited."

The judge held up his hand. He didn't want a free-for-all in front of the bench. "What does the complete patient list for three years have to do with one or two possible patients? You're using a cannon to do the job of a rifle, counsel."

"Dr. Newburn is subject to the rule of sequestration," David said, referring to the prohibition of communication between the witnesses once the trial began. "He does not, and should not, know the purpose behind our request for records. A complete list is necessary for two reasons. First, it will increase the likelihood that we receive an accurate list of patients if the doctor is unaware of the names of the people we are seeking to identify."

"That's an insult!" Joe sputtered. "He has absolutely no basis for insinuating that Dr. Newburn, a board-certified psychiatrist, would falsify his records to conceal the identity of a patient."

"If I may finish?" David said. Mac smiled at the sign of the young lawyer's poise. "We are willing to inspect the list of patients under Your Honor's supervision with instructions not to reveal the names unless you determine it is relevant to the case. Second, there is the possibility that other individuals with a connection to the State's case may be Dr. Newburn's patients."

"Your Honor, this is harassment and a fishing expedition that should not be sanctioned by the court."

"I understand," the judge said. "Anything else, Mr. Moreland?"

"No, Your Honor."

"Mr. Whetstone?"

"No, sir."

"Mr. Whetstone, I am inclined to agree with your position in this matter and at most allow the defendant to obtain information about any doctor-patient relationship between the psychiatrist and members of the Hightower family. However, the State is asking for the death penalty, and I am going to make sure the defense has the opportunity to conduct a thorough cross-examination of every witness called by the prosecution. Since Dr. Newburn may play a significant role in supporting the State's case, I am going to deny the motion to quash. Mr. Whetstone, please notify Dr. Newburn and his personal attorney of my ruling, keeping in mind the rule of sequestration."

"Of course, Your Honor."

"That's all."

"Good job, David," Mac said as they walked back to the office. "How did it feel to face Goliath?"

"Not too bad. Once the rock left my sling, I enjoyed watching it fly."

THIRTY-ONE

O true apothecary! Thy drugs are quick.
ROMEO AND JULIET, ACT 5, SCENE 3

ONCE THE JURY settled in the next morning, Joe called George Doolittle III to the witness stand and asked the forensic chemist to take the jury for a stroll through the drugstore coursing through Pete's veins on the night of the murder. Then he moved to his real purpose for calling the witness.

"Did you also perform tests on a blood sample taken from Angela Hightower?"

"Yes."

"What were the results?"

"Negative for the drugs we found in the defendant's blood. No amphetamines, barbiturates, cannabinoids, or opiates. There was a trace of alcohol."

"Which means?"

"She had a glass of wine or beer within three hours of her death."

Joe paused before asking his next question. "Did you conduct additional tests?"

"Yes."

"Why?"

"Because of the circumstances surrounding the victim's death, we tested her system for the presence of flunitrazepam, a drug originally marketed by Hoffman-La Roche Pharmaceuticals under the trade name Rohypnol."

"Please tell the jury about Rohypnol."

"The drug was developed to sedate patients before surgery and to treat severe cases of insomnia. It is similar to Valium but about ten times stronger. It is legal in about eighty countries and illegal in more than sixty, including the United States and Canada."

"Why was it banned in the United States?"

"In the mid-1990s, Rohypnol's potential for abuse was publicized when it was linked to several sexual assaults, primarily on college campuses. It dissolves easily in a hot or cold drink and is colorless, odorless, and tasteless. Within twenty to thirty minutes, the victim suffers from impaired judgment, drowsiness, dizziness, disorientation, and memory loss. It takes several hours for the drug to leave the system, and the victim frequently has no memory of the events which take place while under the influence. It has several street names: roofie, mind eraser, forget pill, party poppers."

Finished with the pharmacology lesson, Joe put down his legal pad and walked to a spot near the jury box. The chemist turned so that he was looking directly at the jury before Joe asked his next question.

"What were the results of your testing for Rohypnol with the blood sample from Angela Hightower?"

"Positive for Rohypnol at a clinically significant level, which means for a period of time before her death she would have suffered from the side effects I described."

"Disorientation?"

"Yes."

"Impaired judgment?"

"Yes."

"Dizziness?"

"Yes."

Joe held his hand out toward Pete. "Inability to protect herself?"

Doolittle followed Joe's direction and looked directly at Pete before answering. "Yes. She was helpless."

Joe dropped his hand. "Your witness, Mr. McClain."

Mac stepped forward to question the man whose marriage to Gene Nelson's sister triggered Mac's involvement in the case of *State v. Thomason.*

"Mr. Doolittle, did you test Peter Thomason's blood for Rohypnol?"

"No. It is not part of any recognized protocol for blood taken from a male."

"But it would have the same effect on a male as it does on a female: dizziness, disorientation, memory loss."

"Yes, if present in high enough concentration."

"Are there any other drugs that produce a similar effect as Rohypnol?"

Doolittle stroked his chin. "Yes. A very high dose of Valium could be comparable, and there are drugs used by anesthesiologists that render a person completely unconscious for prolonged periods of time during surgery."

"Did you test Mr. Thomason's blood for any of these additional drugs?"

"Yes. A Valium screen was performed, and it was negative."

"Are there any other drugs which mimic Rohypnol?"

The chemist shook his head. "None that I can recall."

"Have you ever heard of gamma-hydroxybutrate?"

"Yes, I forgot about that one. It's not very common," the chemist said. "It's known by the initials GHB."

"Do you know how it operates?"

"It has the same effect as Rohypnol."

"Did you test Peter Thomason's blood for the presence of GHB?"

"No."

Mac expected Joe to call Dr. Newburn as his next witness, but instead the prosecutor asked the bailiff to send Sergeant Tom Laird into the courtroom. Mac leaned over to David. "Get ready."

The polygraph examiner came prepared with some impressive statistics about the accuracy of lie-detector testing. He described in detail the testing process and explained the triple-check system of charting respiration and movement, changes in responses in the skin, and relative blood pressure and pulse rate. Finally, he testified about the purpose of control and relevant questions.

"Sergeant Laird, please tell the jury the questions asked the accused, his responses, and your findings."

"There were four relevant questions. I went over these several times with the defendant before administering the test to make sure he understood and was comfortable with the wording."

Pete leaned over to Mac. "That's a lie. I wasn't comfortable. It was an interrogation."

Mac nodded. "We know. David is going to bring that out on cross-examination."

Joe asked, "Did he object or change anything?"

"No."

"Go ahead."

Sergeant Laird looked down at a sheet of paper he'd brought to the witness stand. "I'll read the questions exactly as they were worded at the time of the examination:

"Did you give Angela Hightower Rohypnol on August second? Did you physically harm Angela Hightower on August second? Did you strangle Angela Hightower on August second? Did you kill Angela Hightower on August second?"

Joe nodded. "And what were his answers to these questions?"

"He answered, 'No' to each."

"Sergeant Laird, please tell the jury your opinion about the truthfulness of his responses."

The witness answered slowly. "The defendant was deceptive on every question."

"Can you evaluate the level of the defendant's deception?"

"Yes. Deception is shown by deviation in two out of the three scales. In this case there was deception indicated on all three scales on every question."

"Exactly how many times were the relevant questions asked during the testing?"

Laird answered in a tone that left no doubt that he considered Pete a bona fide liar. "Three times with identical results. Deception, deception, deception."

"Based on your experience and the results of other polygraphs, how would you compare the charts produced in this test with other tests?"

Mac could have stopped the witness from answering but didn't object because he wanted to talk as much as possible about "other tests," especially the one performed by Larry Davenport.

"In the test administered to the defendant there was a high level of deception."

David whispered to Mac, "Deception by whom?"

"Thank you, Sergeant Laird." Joe concluded.

It was David's cue to come onstage. Confident of his preparation but nervous about his delivery, he stood with a legal pad in his hand and walked toward the witness stand.

"Is it true that the pretest interview is an important part of the test?"

"Not really. All it does is make clear the questions that will be asked."

"But can't the way the pretest interview is conducted affect the results of the test?"

"No. The validity of the test is based on data outside the ability of the subject to control."

David was learning his first lesson in questioning an expert witness—not only could their conclusions vary, but they didn't always agree about the basics.

"So, you don't believe an antagonistic atmosphere during the pretest interview would affect the test?"

"It's not what I believe," Sergeant Laird said. "It's what I know. Weren't you listening when I explained the operation of the equipment used in conducting the test?"

"I'm asking the questions," David said, his face flushing.

"Of course. I just thought I already covered this for the jury."

"Could two examiners look at the same charts and reach different conclusions?"

"Not likely."

David stepped back to the defense table and retrieved the charts from the test administered by Larry Davenport and had them marked as defense exhibits.

Joe joined him at the court reporter's seat, quickly read the results of the other polygraph test, then turned to the judge. "Your Honor, may we approach the bench?"

The judge nodded.

In a low but intense voice, Joe said, "Mr. Moreland is trying to introduce the results of a nonstipulated polygraph. I realize he may not have much experience in trying cases—"

"That's not true," David interrupted. "I mean, the part about trying to introduce the results of the test. I want to show that one examiner can look at another examiner's charts and render an opinion about the test. I'll not mention that this is a test performed on Pete Thomason."

"Judge, this is too close to the edge."

Judge Danielson glared at David. "Counsel, I'll let you ask generic questions, but do not in any way intimate that these charts are for a test administered to the defendant. If you cross the line, I'll hold you in contempt of court. It that clear?"

His knees a little wobbly, David answered, "Yes, sir."

"Very well. Proceed."

David took the exhibits from the court reporter and handed them to Sergeant Laird. "Can you review these charts and tell whether the individual taking the test was truthful or deceptive?"

The examiner looked over the readings for a minute. "No. Unlike the results from the test administered to the defendant, these test results appear inconclusive, and I would question the competency of the examiner. There is insufficient distinction between the control questions and the relevant questions."

David leaned over to Mac and whispered. "What do I do now?"

"Cut him loose. He's not going to give you anything."

"That's all from this witness, Your Honor."

David sat down. His first cross-examination of a witness in a jury trial had as much zip as an unsalted cracker. At least he hadn't joined Pete in a cell.

Joe stood. "May I approach the bench, Your Honor?"

"Yes."

Mac joined him for a conversation that the jury could not hear.

"The witnesses who are going to testify about the defendant's prior similar conduct are staying about fifteen minutes from the courthouse. Could we break for lunch now and hear from them first thing this afternoon?"

The judge checked his watch and addressed the jury,

"Ladies and gentlemen, the court will be in recess until one o'clock."

Mac, David, and Vicki organized the papers that had become scattered during the morning's proceedings.

"What about Dr. Newburn?" David asked.

Before Mac could answer, Joe called out, "Mac. Can I talk to you a minute?"

Mac walked over to Joe, who was leaning against the prosecution table. "What is it?" he asked.

The prosecutor straightened a stack of papers. "I know Bert Langley talked to you about a guilty plea in return for a life sentence without parole."

"Yes. My client wasn't interested."

"I talked to Bert this morning and can offer life with the possibility of parole. With good behavior, Thomason might be out of prison by his midthirties."

"Why the change?" Mac asked.

"Why not? I think I have a good chance at a conviction, but we both know nobody can predict what a jury will do."

"I'll talk to Pete before one o'clock."

After Mac left, Joe snapped shut his briefcase. His interview with Spencer Hightower the previous evening had been very disturbing. Ever since Mac's dramatic claim in his opening statement that the real killer was not in the courtroom, Joe had been working through the list of people who might be the object of Mac's allegation, and Spencer Hightower had moved to the head of the class. The younger Hightower brother acted furtive and evasive when interviewed, and Joe was suspicious about Spencer's relationship with Angela. Personally, he thought Spencer was a harmless idiot. But if Mac had something that linked Spencer to Angela's murder, Joe knew his case might disappear as quickly as an April frost on a north Georgia pasture.

As soon as they were outside the courtroom, Mac told David and Vicki what Joe had said.

"Well?" Vicki asked. "It's not a bad offer."

"But he didn't do it," David said.

"He says he doesn't remember anything," Mac corrected him. "We have some suspicions about Spencer Hightower, but we can't let our theories become so real in our imaginations that we put on blinders to the strengths of the State's case. I'm not saying I think Pete should accept a deal, but we have to let Pete decide after we give him an unbiased perspective. His life, not ours, is on the line."

After grabbing a snack at the office, Mac and David went back to the courthouse to talk to Pete in the holding cell where he spent his breaks. Standing in front of the bars, Mac explained the special prosecutor's offer and finished by saying, "We have an obligation to communicate the offer to you. What do you want to do?"

Pete shook his head. "I'd have to say that I killed Angela, wouldn't I?"

"Yes," Mac said. "The judge would ask you, point blank."

Pete looked down at the scuffed tile floor of the cell for several seconds before answering. "A few weeks ago I was so depressed that I might have accepted a deal just to get the whole thing over with. That's what I did when I was kicked out of the Marine Corps. I avoided the hassle of a fight and accepted the dishonorable discharge. This is a million times worse, but I didn't kill Angela. I'm not going to lie and plead guilty even though it would save my life and stop the torture of the trial."

"So, your answer is 'No,'" Mac said.

Pete looked steadily into Mac's eyes. "My answer is 'No.'"

When Joe returned to the courtroom, Mac told him Pete's decision.

"The offer is withdrawn," Joe said curtly. "And there won't be another."

"It doesn't matter," Mac responded. "The boy is not going to plead guilty."

Joe began the afternoon's testimony by calling Sally Neland, formerly Sally Tompkins, of Beaufort, South Carolina. Dressed conservatively in a brown plaid skirt and dark sweater, Mrs. Neland obviously did not want to be on the witness stand. At least Dennison Springs was six hundred miles away from her new husband and home in Fairfax, Virginia. She would answer questions and get out of town as soon as possible.

"Ms. Neland, where were you living during the month of July five years ago?"

"With my parents in South Carolina."

"How old were you at the time?"

"Twenty. I was a student at the College of Charleston and home for summer vacation."

"Have you ever met Peter Thomason, the defendant in this case?"

Sally looked at Pete with a disgust that signaled more to the jury than any words could have communicated. Pete stared back without flinching, determined not to look as though he had something to hide.

"Yes," she said.

Mac stood. "Your Honor, may we approach the bench?"

"Come forward."

Joe joined Mac in front of the judge. Mac leaned forward. "I want to make an objection before this witness gives any testimony."

The judge turned to Joe. "What is the nature of the testimony?"

"Prior similar conduct, Your Honor. I mentioned it briefly in court the other day." Joe quickly outlined the incident in the bar.

"It's highly prejudicial," Mac responded, keeping his voice low. "There was no criminal conviction."

"Is that true?" the judge asked Joe.

"Yes, but the defendant's use of Rohypnol in both instances ties them together."

"If this comes in, I'll have to move for a mistrial," Mac said a little louder.

The judge hesitated for several seconds before deciding. "Mr. Whetstone, I am going to allow the testimony based on your representation that you can tie it to the defendant. If you don't, I will give serious consideration to a motion for mistrial."

"Yes, sir."

Mac returned to the defense table. "It looked like the judge considered keeping it out," David said.

Mac shrugged. "So what. There's no such thing as partial victory."

Grim-faced, Sally proceeded to tell about meeting the three Marines.

"Did the defendant buy you a drink?"

"Yes. He went to the bar and brought me a strawberry daiquiri."

"Was he out of your sight for a period of time?"

"Yes. We were talking, and I didn't pay attention to what he did."

"Do you recall if the defendant also got a drink for your friend Patricia Rawlings?"

"I believe he did. She and the defendant were both drinking margaritas."

The young woman's anger changed to tears when she told about the effects of Rohypnol on her. She ended by describing her middle-of-the-night visit to the hospital.

Mac walked softly when he asked his questions.

"Were the names of the other two Marines Walter Monroe and Harry O'Ryan?"

"I think that's right."

"Have you talked to either of them since all this happened?"

Sally shook her head vigorously. "No. I didn't ever want to see anyone from that night again."

"I understand. Just a few more questions. Who were you with when you left the bar?"

The young woman furrowed her brow. "That is fuzzy, but I think it was the two men you mentioned."

"Not Pete Thomason?"

"No, I think he followed in another car."

"If it's unclear to you, how can you recall that he followed in another car?"

"I think, uh, it's been a long time."

"Whose car were the four of you in?"

"Patricia's car. She had a blue Camaro."

"How did you get home?"

"When Patricia and I came around, we were alone in her car near the beach."

"Pete Thomason wasn't there?"

"No one was there but us."

"That's all I have, Your Honor."

Sergeant Walter Monroe was all spit and polish. His dark hair was not more than a quarter-inch long at any place on his head, and the big Marine sat so straight in the witness chair that everyone in the courtroom subconsciously adjusted their posture. Pete watched him walk to the witness stand, but Monroe kept his eyes straight ahead, never looking in Pete's direction. Every other word was "Yes, sir," or "No, sir," as he told his version of the events leading up to Pete's discharge.

"Did you know the defendant was going to spike the girls' drinks with Rohypnol?" Whetstone asked.

"No, sir. He had mentioned it, but I considered it a joke. I never suspected he would carry it out and don't know where he got the drugs. I thought the girls were just drunk."

"Now tell the jury what happened after you left the bar."

"Thomason drove the girls in one of their cars toward the beach area. O'Ryan and I decided to go back to the base. Thomason came in later that night, bragging about what he had done."

"What happened the next day?"

"We reported the incident to the camp commandant, and Thomason was dishonorably discharged."

Monroe was a good liar, but most fabricated stories had a few loose strings in the details. Mac's job was to pull a few strings out and show them to the jury until they could be tied together with other testimony.

"Sergeant Monroe, do you have a nickname?" Mac asked.

"Yes, sir."

"What is it?"

"Buster, sir."

"Does the Marine Corps have a code of conduct which requires you to report misconduct by fellow marines?"

"Yes, sir."

"Were you aware of this requirement when Pete Thomason returned to the barracks and told you about the incident with the girls?"

"Yes, sir."

"Did you immediately contact your superiors to report what you learned?"

"Yes, sir. The next day."

"But not that night?"

"No, sir."

"Did you tell your story before or after the girls' parents contacted the base commander?"

"After, sir."

"Were you summoned to the base commander's office?"

"Yes, sir."

"Who else was present?"

"Thomason, O'Ryan, Colonel Baxter, and Lieutenant General Lietner."

Mac walked back toward the jury box as he asked his next question. "Sounds like you were in serious trouble."

"Thomason was in trouble, sir."

"Did you talk about the situation with Harry O'Ryan before you met with the commander?"

"Yes, sir."

"What was said?"

"We discussed what we ought to do."

"What did O'Ryan suggest?"

"He didn't want to come forward at first."

"I see." Mac moved closer to the witness stand. "Did you report this violation of the rules of conduct to Colonel Baxter or Lieutenant General Lietner?"

"Uh, no, sir."

"Because O'Ryan was your best friend?"

"Yes, sir. But compared to Thomason, he didn't do much wrong."

"I see. What kind of car did Pete Thomason own?"

"An old Nissan."

"Who drove you and O'Ryan to the bar?"

"Thomason drove."

"What kind of car were the girls in?"

"A Camaro."

"So Thomason let you drive his car back to the base?"

"Yes, uh, wait a minute . . ." Monroe paused. "I can't remember."

"Did you drive the Camaro back to the base?"

"No. He would have gone with the girls."

Mac raised his voice and looked toward the jury, "So the semiconscious girls drove Thomason back to the base, dropped him off, and went back to the beach until the effects of the drug wore off. Is that what happened?"

"I don't know how Thomason got back to the base."

"How far is it from the beach to the base?"

"Ten to twelve miles."

Mac took off his reading glasses and laid them on the defense table. "Sergeant Monroe, would it surprise you to learn that an hour ago in this courtroom Sally Tomkins-Neland testified that you and Harry O'Ryan drove her and Patricia Rawlings from the bar to the beach?"

Monroe gave Mac a puzzled expression, and for a second a crack appeared in his steely veneer before he quickly closed it.

"Uh, that's not what I remember."

"Is it possible Harry O'Ryan may recall additional details you have forgotten?"

"Yes, sir."

"That's all," Mac said and returned to the defense table.

Joe announced in his best courtroom voice, "As its final witness, the State calls Mrs. Sarah Hightower."

David leaned over to Mac and whispered, "What about Dr. Newburn?"

"He's not going to use him until later," Mac responded.

"Which means we won't need Dr. Wilkes?"

"Maybe not."

Sarah Hightower was impeccably dressed in a dark navy dress with a heavy gold necklace and a very large diamond ring. She remained poised as Joe asked her about Angela and the events leading up to August second. She identified a beautifully posed photograph of Angela taken soon after her eighteenth birthday. Sarah seemed almost reluctant to give it back to Joe so that he could present it to the jury as an exhibit.

"Tell us about that night," Joe continued.

"Alex and I had gone out to dinner and returned home about nine-thirty. When I checked our answering machine, we had a message from Angela."

Joe faced the judge. "Your Honor, I would like to play the tape so Mrs. Hightower can identify it."

"Proceed."

Joe placed the cassette player on the railing in front of the jury box and pressed the play button.

The tape scratched to life and the "beep" of the answering machine came through the speaker.

"Mom. Pete and I were stuck in traffic because of a wreck on the expressway. We'll be home a bit later than I thought. I love you. Bye."

Hearing her daughter's voice, Sarah touched her eye with a tissue she had been clutching in her hand.

"Was that the call recorded on the evening of August second?"

"Yes. It was about seven-thirty in the evening."

"And was that Angela's voice?"

"Yes. That's the last time—" Sarah's trailed off.

Mac straightened his tie and stood a respectful distance from the witness stand. In a calm voice that nevertheless carried across the courtroom he began his cross-examination.

"Mrs. Hightower, who are the other members of your husband's family?"

"His parents are deceased. He has a younger brother and some cousins."

"What is the brother's name?"

"Spencer Hightower."

"How old is Spencer?"

"I think he's twenty-six or twenty-seven."

"Mrs. Hightower, are you aware of any personal conflicts between Spencer and Angela?"

"No," she said sharply.

Mac let the answer rest in the air while he walked to the defense table and picked up a copy of the letter about Spencer from Angela to her parents. He held the sheet in his hand while he asked his next question.

"Who was Angela's roommate in college last year?"

"A girl from North Carolina named Joan Brinkley."

Mac handed the letter to Joe, who quickly looked at it and kept it.

"Your Honor," Joe said, rising to his feet. "We need to discuss a matter outside the presence of the jury."

"Approach the bench."

It was Joe's turn to raise an intense objection. "Your Honor, the defense is attempting to use a libelous letter that could be a complete fabrication."

"Let me see it." The judge read it and handed it back to Mac. "How do you intend to prove the authenticity of this letter, Mr. McClain?"

"Angela used Joan Brinkley's laptop computer to write the letter. Ms. Brinkley has firsthand knowledge about the letter and is arriving in Chattanooga from Virginia this afternoon. She will be available tomorrow to testify about the legitimacy of the document and the circumstances surrounding it."

The judge leaned forward. "Gentlemen, I do not want a mistrial in this case because of the introduction of inflammatory material that would so prejudice the jury that an impartial consideration of the case becomes impossible. Mr. McClain, I am going to instruct you not to ask the witness about the letter at this time. If it is admitted into evidence during the presentation of your case you may recall Mrs. Hightower and cross-examine her about its contents."

Mac stepped back from the bench. "Your Honor, in light of the court's ruling, I reserve my right to ask more questions of the witness at a later time." Mac walked past the jury with the sheet of paper in his hand and put it, faceup, on the corner of the defense table.

"Very well," the judge said.

"That concludes the State's case, Your Honor," Joe said with a lot less confidence than he had hoped to convey two minutes earlier.

Thus, with more of a pop than a bang, the prosecution ended its case, and the jury was left wondering what was on the sheet of paper in Mac's hand and why they couldn't find out.

THIRTY-TWO

Find out where your enemy is. Get at him as soon as you can. Strike at him as hard as you can and as often as you can.
ULYSSES S. GRANT

THURSDAY MORNING WAS the coldest day of the fall season, and everyone hurried up the sidewalk to the courthouse. The previous evening, Mac and David had made their final decisions and preparations. They had debated again whether Pete should be called to the witness stand and decided they had only one option. On his way home from the office, Mac had met with Joan Brinkley at the Jackson Inn and stopped in to chat a few minutes with a still sober Harry O'Ryan. The troops Mac was assembling for battle were ready.

Mac wanted to give the jury an alternative theory for the murder of Angela Hightower. It was only a theory, but it would be the basis upon which everything the defense presented would rest. The cornerstone for this foundation would be the testimony of his first witness, a nervous, scatterbrained girl.

The jury filed into the jury box. Judge Danielson nodded to Mac. "Proceed on behalf of the defendant."

"The defense calls Miss Joan Brinkley."

A bailiff opened the witness-room door and summoned Angela's former roommate. Joan looked small and young as she walked into the large courtroom. She nervously twisted her hands together and lifted her left hand instead of her right when asked to repeat the oath. After giving her name and a little bit of background, Mac asked her about Angela.

"How did you know Angela Hightower?"

"We were roommates. Really, like, best friends. At least I thought so. Angela had lots of friends, so I don't know if she thought of me as her best friend."

"Did you and Angela ever study together?"

"Sometimes. We both took zoology second semester and shared notes, after class and all." Joan's eyes suddenly teared up.

"Are you okay?" Mac asked.

A big tear rolled down Joan's cheek. "It just hit me again, you know, that she's gone forever."

It hit Pete, too. He looked down at the table, wishing for the ten thousandth time that he could wake up and find that the past few months had never happened. But this was not a nightmare; it was cold, ruthless reality.

"Joan," Mac said gently. "Did Angela ever borrow your laptop computer?"

Joan nodded as another tear escaped and fell from her face.

Mac handed her the letter from Angela to Spencer Hightower. "Do you recognize this letter?"

"Yes, sir."

"Who wrote it?"

"Angela."

"How do you know that?"

"She used my computer. I was with her in the library when she typed it."

Mac stepped back toward the jury box. "Please read the letter to the jury."

In her high, childlike voice, Joan cleared her throat and read, "'Spencer. Do not call or write again. I do not want to see you or talk to you. If I hear one more word from you, I will tell my parents. I mean it. Get some help. Angela.'"

The normally quiet courtroom was even more silent.

"Who is Spencer?"

"Her uncle in Atlanta."

"Do you know what happened to the letter after Angela typed it on your computer?"

"She printed it out and addressed an envelope."

"Whose name and address were on the envelope?"

"Spencer Hightower."

"What happened to the envelope?"

"She asked me to mail it, and I took it to the campus post office the next day."

"Was there another letter written at the same time?"

"Yes, you know, the one to her parents."

Mac handed her a second piece of paper.

"Please read it for the jury."

"The whole thing?"

"Yes."

"Okay. 'Dear Mom and Dad. I don't know how to tell you this except to just come out and say it. Spencer has been bothering me. Last fall at the steeplechase in Dunwoody, he followed me around all day, stood too close to me, and said some things he shouldn't have said. Then he started writing me letters, telling me how much he cared for me and saying he wanted to come see me here at school. I called and told him to stop, and he left me alone until I was home for Christmas. Then he started back, only worse. One night, he made a pass at me in the downstairs hallway and I slapped him—hard. He got mad, and I hoped that was the end of it. Now I have started getting more letters, and he has left three phone messages for me in the past week! This has got to stop. Can't his psychiatrist do something for him? Do his doctors know what he's doing? I'm mad, frustrated, and scared. I don't want him showing up on campus and embarrassing me in front of my friends. Dad, please take care of this.' "

Joan choked up again and stopped reading. Mac waited. The two newspaper reporters in the room were furiously taking notes.

"There's not much more," she said after a few moments. "The last line of the letter says, 'I'm sorry, but it's not my fault, and I want it to stop. Love, Angela.'"

Mac took the letter from her and held it up in front of the jury as he asked his next question. "What happened to the letter you just read?"

"I don't know."

"Did Angela send it?"

"I never saw it printed out, and she didn't ask me to mail it."

"So as far as you know it was never mailed?"

"That's right. I don't know why. Maybe she didn't want her parents to blow up at her uncle."

Joe had no grounds to object to admission of the letters into evidence but quickly tried to salvage something from the witness.

"Did Spencer Hightower ever come to the campus?" he asked.

"I don't think so."

Joe paused and took a chance. "Did you have any contact with Angela after you left school for summer break?"

"Yeah, we talked on the phone a couple of times."

"What did you talk about?"

"You know, different stuff. She was working at a camp for kids, and I was spending a lot of time at the beach."

"Did she mention Spencer Hightower?"

"Uh, I had forgotten about that," she looked at Mac sheepishly.

Joe pressed her. "What did she tell you?"

"She said she saw Spencer, and it was no big deal."

"What did that mean to you?"

"Let me see. Like, I guess that there wasn't a big problem anymore, but then she was killed, and I didn't know what to think."

"Miss Brinkley, you don't know much about the evidence linking Peter Thomason to Angela's murder, do you?"

"No."

"Are you accusing Spencer Hightower of killing Angela?"

"No. I don't know who did it."

"I understand. Thank you."

Rodney McFarland arrived in the courtroom wearing brown polyester pants, a white shirt, and black tie. His wispy white hair was plastered to his head, and he was wearing a strong cologne that smelled like liniment. The aroma wafted across the courtroom as he walked to the witness stand. Mac asked the old man to describe his drive down the mountain.

"It was a dark night. There wasn't much of a moon showing, so I had on my bright lights. My truck has the old-style headlamps, the kind that look like big eyes when they're coming at you down the road. It was a warm night, and I'd rolled down my window so I could stay cool and spit out the window instead of into a cup I keep in the front seat."

Mac decided it was time to regain control of the witness.

"How fast were you going?"

Mr. McFarland looked up at the judge. "Judge. I won't lie to you. I had been over the speed limit. I wanted to get here before my granddaughter had her young-un, but I'm a good driver. I haven't had a speeding ticket since . . ." Mr. McFarland scratched his chin. "I think it was 1958. I had a blue Plymouth with more engine than it needed—"

"Please tell us what caused you to run off the road," Mac said.

"Oh yeah. That road has a lot of curves. I had moved my hands up on the steering wheel to make sure I stayed in my lane." Mr. McFarland began turning an invisible steering wheel as he talked to the jury. "I was having to turn this way and that way, when all of sudden this yellow car came barreling around the curve. I jerked it to the right, then back to the left, but I couldn't keep it on the road and scooted off into the ditch.

Man, was I mad." He looked up at the judge again. "Judge, I said some things I wouldn't want to repeat in front of the ladies here in the courtroom." He stopped.

Mac waited for him to mention the dark sedan. Mr. McFarland sat staring blankly. Finally, Mac asked, "Is that all?"

"You want me to repeat what I said?"

"No. Is that all you saw?"

"Oh, you want me to tell about the other car?"

"Yes. That might be helpful."

"There was another car burning up the road behind the yellow one. It nicked the tail end of my truck. Ray scraped off some of the paint and sent it to a scientist somewhere. He told me—"

"Don't tell what he told you," Mac stopped him before Joe could object. "What color was the car?"

Mr. McFarland smiled. "Well, I told Ray it was a dark purple, but he said it was burgundy. Now he admits that I was—"

Joe stood. "Any testimony about what someone named Ray may have told the witness is hearsay."

The judge turned toward Mr. McFarland. "Tell what you saw or said. Not what anyone else said."

Mr. McFarland looked puzzled. "I'll try, but it won't make much sense telling just one side of a conversation."

Several jurors laughed out loud. Mac enjoyed the sound. A laughing jury was less likely to convict a man of murder. "So it was dark purple, correct?" he asked.

"I thought I was right."

"How close were the two cars to each other?"

"Real close. I'd guess they were together."

"Objection," Joe said. "Speculation."

"Sustained," the judge said. "The jury will disregard the witness's last comment."

"I'm not one hundred percent sure," Mr. McFarland said, quickly defending himself. "But if they had been much closer, the purple car could have hooked on to the yellow car's bumper for a tow."

"That's clear enough," Mac said. "No further questions."

"No questions," Joe said. He knew when to keep his mouth shut and leave a witness alone.

Mac had time for one more witness before the lunch break. He asked the bailiff to see if Gary Ogden from Peachtree Labs had arrived. In a minute the chemist, a short, stocky man with a large handlebar mustache came into the courtroom. Mac's questions covered two topics: analysis of the paint sample from Mr. McFarland's truck and the drug tests of Pete's blood. He quickly moved through the identification of the midnight purple Lincoln that Mr. McFarland had so effectively introduced to the jury. Primarily, he wanted Dr. Ogden to reveal the presence of GHB, the memory-loss drug, in Pete's blood.

"Did you conduct additional tests on the blood sample taken from Mr. Thomason?"

"Yes, on two occasions. First, I tested his blood for the presence of Rohypnol."

"What were the results?"

"Negative."

"And the purpose and results of the second test?"

Mac stepped next to the jury box so that the chemist's answer would project to the farthest seat.

"At your request, I tested his blood for the presence of gamma-hydroxybutyrate, or GHB. This drug was present in the blood sample at a significant level."

"What do you mean by significant?"

"It would have produced changes in Mr. Thomason's mind and body for a period of several hours."

Pete looked at the jurors, wanting to exert his will so that they would pay attention to the chemist's conclusions. He couldn't tell what they thought. One man on the front row was slouched down in his seat and a woman on the back row was looking through her pocketbook. In a few seconds the woman pulled out a nail file and gave one of her fingers a few quick strokes.

"What is the effect of GHB?" Mac asked.

"It is the same type of drug as Rohypnol. It makes a person confused, disoriented, and passive."

"What is its effect on memory?"

"It causes short-term amnesia."

"Dr. Ogden, if you assume the level of GHB you found in Pete Thomason's blood sample to be accurate, how long would he have been confused, disoriented, and passive?"

"Two to three hours immediately before the sample was drawn."

"What about amnesia?"

"The same. There would be the potential for total memory loss."

"During this period, how difficult would it have been for Mr. Thomason to drive a car on a winding mountain road?"

"Very difficult, even for a short period of time."

"Your witness," Mac said to Joe.

Joe walked forward, trying to exude more confidence than he felt.

"Dr. Ogden, were you hired and paid by the defense to perform tests on the paint sample from Mr. McFarland's truck and the defendant's blood?"

"Mr. McClain's office contacted me and I submitted my bill to him, but my file indicates Echota County is responsible for paying for my services."

"And you do not work for the state crime lab?"

"No. I have an independent company."

"So you do a lot of tests that have nothing to do with criminal proceedings?"

"The majority of my work is for private companies and individuals."

"Have you ever testified in a murder trial before?"

"Twice."

"Who hired you in those cases?"

"Counsel for the defendant."

"So the State has never hired you to testify?"

"Oh yes. I have testified at least twenty or thirty times for the prosecution in complex criminal drug cases. I worked with the U.S. Attorney's office on several cases when you were with them in Atlanta."

Having asked one question too many, Joe slunk back to the prosecution table.

After the lunch break, Mac called polygraph expert Bruce Wilcox. As a former GBI agent and trainer of polygraph examiners, Wilcox shot down some of Sergeant Laird's testimony about polygraph theory and, after reviewing Laird's charts, mildly criticized the test that indicated Pete was deceptive.

"Mr. Wilcox, please compare the chart from the polygraph test administered by Sergeant Laird with a set from another examination and tell the jury if they support different conclusions."

Joe quickly responded, "Objection, Your Honor."

"Come forward," the judge said. The lawyers came close to the bench. "Mr. McClain, I warned Mr. Moreland about trying to introduce a nonstipulated polygraph into evidence and threatened him with contempt if he crossed the line. You know better."

Mac kept his cool. "Of course, Your Honor. I have no intention of trying to introduce testimony that connects the other chart with the defendant."

"That's bogus," Joe snorted. "This whole line of questioning is a backdoor way to violate the rules of evidence. Any talk about 'another examination' is meant to send a message to the jury that there is another polygraph of the defendant."

The judge nodded. "Mr. Whetstone, I agree. Objection sustained. Mr. McClain, move on to something else."

Mac backed away from the bench. "That's all from this witness," he said.

Wilcox stepped down from the witness stand.

"The defense calls Harry O'Ryan," Mac said.

Harry, dressed in a new suit purchased by Peggy Morrison, looked more like his file photo from the bank in Corbin, Kentucky, than the bar-hopping bum tracked down by Ray. If confession was good for the soul, Harry's soul got a double dose of goodness as he recanted his previous lies and completely exonerated Pete from any responsibility for the incident involving Sally Tompkins and Patricia Rawlings.

"Did Pete Thomason put any drugs into the girls' drinks?" Mac asked.

"No. Buster did it. I saw him pour something into their drinks from a bottle he took from his pocket while the girls were in the rest room."

"Did you know what he was doing?"

"Yeah," Harry admitted. "He told me, but I didn't think he was serious."

"What happened next?"

"The four of us left together in a Camaro owned by one of the girls."

"Where was Pete?"

"He stayed at the bar."

"Where did you go?"

"The girls passed out in the backseat, and I got scared. I told Buster to drop me off at another bar, and I'd catch a cab back to the base. That's what I did. The next morning Buster woke me up and said someone was going to get in a lot of trouble about the deal with the girls. We decided to blame Pete and told the base commander it was all Pete's fault."

"Why are you telling the truth five years later?"

"When I found out Pete was charged with murder and that Buster was going to testify against him, I decided to come forward and clear the record."

"Your witness," Mac said.

Joe placed a stack of papers on the edge of the prosecution table.

"Mr. O'Ryan, how many different stories have you told about what happened with Sally Tompkins and Patricia Rawlings?"

"Two."

"And in both versions you didn't do anything wrong, did you?"

"It wasn't my deal," Harry shifted in the witness chair. "Buster slipped the stuff in their drinks."

"And you didn't go along for the ride?"

"Not very far. I went to another bar."

"Speaking of bars. You've spent a lot of time in bars, haven't you?"

"Uh, yeah."

"And you're an alcoholic, aren't you?"

Harry glanced toward Mac, who had seen similar looks many times from witnesses who saw a train coming around the bend in their direction. But there was nothing he could do. Joe Whetstone was on solid ground.

"Do I need to repeat the question?" Joe asked.

"No, uh, yes. I mean, what do you mean?'

"If an alcoholic is someone who drinks almost every day, would you qualify?"

"I don't drink every day."

"When did you stop?"

"About a week and half ago."

"Up until then you were drinking every day?"

"I drank regularly. Maybe not every day."

Joe moved forward. "Every day you had money to buy it, isn't that the way it was, Mr. O'Ryan?"

"Sometimes, but now I'm in a recovery program."

"Recovery program?" Joe acted surprised. "Recovery from what?"

"My drinking problem."

"Have you told the other people in the program that you have a problem with alcohol?"

"Yes. We have group sessions."

"Did you tell them you were an alcoholic?"

"Uh, yes."

"So, now you've told two different stories about whether you're an alcoholic? Which one do you want the jury to believe?"

Harry looked at Mac again with a silent plea for help. Mac stood up. "Objection, Your Honor. He's being argumentative with the witness."

"Overruled," the judge responded. "He has him on cross."

"He's trying to crucify him, all right," David whispered when Mac sat down.

"Answer the question," the judge said to Harry.

"What was it?" the witness asked.

"I'll be happy to ask it again," Joe said. "Mr. O'Ryan, you've told two different stories about whether you're an alcoholic. Which one do you want the jury to believe?"

"I'm trying to get straightened out," Harry said.

"Or dried out?"

"Yeah."

"Has Mr. McClain paid you to come here?" Joe asked.

"He is paying for my room and food."

"And all you wanted to do was help Pete Thomason and return to wherever you came from. Correct?"

"I'm here to tell the truth about the deal with Buster Monroe."

"Really?" Joe asked, raising his eyebrows. "But you've had problems telling the truth in the past, haven't you?"

"I don't know what you mean."

Joe picked up a sheet of paper from a stack on the corner of the prosecution table.

"Are you the same Harry O'Ryan convicted of issuing a false writing, a bad check, to Southside Convenience Store in Corbin, Kentucky?"

"Yes."

"Are you the same Harry O'Ryan convicted of issuing a false writing, a bad check, to Westside Pawn Shop in Boiling Springs, Kentucky?"

"Yes."

Joe flipped through the stack of papers. "Do you know how many false writings are represented by these papers?"

"Are they all on me?" Harry asked.

"Do you want to look them over?"

Harry sighed. "Not really."

"Would you be surprised to learn that you have written 137 bad checks during the past two and half years?" Joe lifted the stack and let it fall back on the table with a thud.

"I didn't know it was that many."

"That's almost one lie a week, Mr. O'Ryan."

"I've had problems." Harry coughed.

"Are you aware how many outstanding warrants have been issued for your arrest since you left the Marine Corps?"

"No."

"I may be off a little, but it appears you've been subject to arrest thirteen times in six states. That's quite an accomplishment."

"Like I said, I've made some mistakes, but I want to make things right."

"Do you want to add a perjury charge to the list of crimes you call mistakes?"

Mac jumped up. "Objection, Your Honor."

"Overruled."

"Answer the question, please."

"No."

"Where are you going from here?"

"I don't know."

"You don't have a job?"

"No."

Joe stopped. He was having a lot of fun, but a few of the jurors were beginning to look restless. They'd obviously heard enough.

"That's all," he said.

Relieved, Harry left the witness stand.

Pete sighed, not sure if his former comrade had done more harm than good.

"Your Honor, the defense recalls Mrs. Sarah Hightower."

Mac had to do everything in his power to convince the jury of Pete's innocence—even if it detonated an explosion in what remained of the already fractured Hightower family.

Not as poised as the previous day, Sarah Hightower shifted nervously in the witness chair. She obviously had no idea what was coming.

"Mrs. Hightower, your previous testimony stopped after I asked you about your husband's brother, Spencer. Let's pick up where we left off. What contact did Angela have with Spencer?"

"Occasional."

"How often would that be?"

"A few times a year. Usually over the holidays or at large gatherings for employees of my husband's companies."

"Nothing regular?"

"No. She was in school, and we didn't socialize with Spencer. He had his own life."

Mac took a deep breath. "Were you aware that Spencer made improper advances toward Angela?"

"Of course not. That's ridiculous." Sarah looked at Joe, as if expecting him to object, but all Joe could do was grip the arms of his chair until his knuckles turned white. Several members of the jury moved closer to the edge of their seats.

"Mrs. Hightower, it is not my intent to upset you, but I have to show you a letter typed by Angela on Joan Brinkley's computer in April and ask if you received it." Mac handed her the sheet of paper and stepped back.

Her hands trembling, Sarah read the letter. "No! Oh, no!" Her face contorted with anguish, then she bolted out of the witness chair and left the courtroom. Alex followed her up the aisle.

For several seconds no one moved.

"The court will be in recess for thirty minutes," Judge Danielson said.

THIRTY-THREE

Still questioned me the story of my life.
OTHELLO, ACT 1, SCENE 3

THE BARB WAS GONE from the hook Joe Whetstone was trying to sink into Pete. When everyone reassembled in the courtroom, Sarah Hightower, her face still contorted in anguish, sat in the witness chair. Mac addressed the judge. "Your Honor, the defense has no more questions for Mrs. Hightower."

Joe quickly responded. "No questions. Mrs. Hightower, you may come down."

Without looking at Pete or Mac, Sarah walked out of the courtroom a second time.

Mac leaned over to Pete. "Are you ready?"

Pete nodded. "Yes."

Mac turned to the judge. "At this time we call Peter Thomason."

It was a risk, but the potential benefits made the decision an easy one. The jury needed to hear Pete's voice, watch him move, share his thoughts, and realize that he was not a cold-blooded name on a murder indictment but a human being who didn't look or talk like a person capable of taking the life of Angela Hightower. The minds of the jurors might wander during the course of a trial, but when a defendant took the stand, they knew it was their solemn duty to listen carefully to everything that was said.

Pete was ready. Mac and David had conducted three role plays of his testimony with him and taught him when to look at the jury, how to wait before answering Joe Whetstone's questions, and covered every conceivable topic that might be brought up in court.

Mac didn't begin with the moment of Pete's birth, but he opened the door to the life of Pete Thomason soon thereafter. After a few minutes the questioning became more like a conversation between friends with the jury having the opportunity to listen in.

"My dad left home when I was in the first grade and never came back," Pete said. "After that it was just my mother and me."

"Tell us about her."

"My mother worked in the payroll department of an auto parts factory. We lived in a one-bedroom apartment, and I slept on the couch in the living room until I was in the seventh grade"

"Where did you go to school?"

"Public schools on the south side of Atlanta. After graduating from high school, I joined the Marine Corps."

"You've heard the two versions of the incident that led to you leaving the military," Mac said. "What do you want to tell the jury about it?"

Pete looked directly at the jurors in the box. "The only mistake I made was not fighting to clear my name and my record. I panicked under pressure. I didn't do anything wrong, and I shouldn't have agreed to a discharge."

"You didn't give Sally Tompkins or Patricia Rawlings any Rohypnol?"

"No. I'd never heard of it until I was in the commandant's office the next day."

"What did you do after leaving the Marine Corps?"

"I went home and worked in a grocery store for a couple of months. My mother had always wanted me to go to college, but I didn't think I could handle it. She finally convinced me to apply to Auburn. I was accepted into a work-study program and graduated four years later with a degree in computer science. My mother died suddenly of a brain hemorrhage two months before I graduated."

As Pete talked, Mac watched the jury out of the corner of his eye. Several faces seemed less hard and unyielding than when the young man took the witness oath.

"Why did you move to Dennison Springs?"

"I didn't want to go back to Atlanta. Auburn is in a small town, and I liked the small-town atmosphere. I interviewed with Aeromart here in Dennison Springs, and they offered me a job. It was a great opportunity."

"How did you meet Angela?"

Pete took a deep breath. "It was at a picnic for new professional-level employees of Hightower companies. Angela was there. We started talking and ate our meal at the same table. All I knew was that her name was Angela. After she walked away, one of my coworkers came up and asked me if I knew I'd been talking with Angela Hightower."

"When did you see her again?"

"The same day. She came over before she left and gave me her phone number. I called her a few days later, and we went to dinner a couple of times before, uh, she died."

"Was there any romance between you and Angela?"

"No, we were friends. Nothing else had developed."

Mac asked softly, "Tell the jury about August second, the last day."

Pete looked at the jurors before answering. "Angela suggested that we go to dinner at an Italian place she knew in Atlanta. I went to her house to pick her up, and she offered to let me drive her Porsche. I thought it would be fun to drive a fancy sports car, so we took her car and arrived at the restaurant in Atlanta around seven-thirty."

"What happened next?"

Pete's face clouded. "We ordered our food, but after that I don't remember anything until I woke up in the hospital the next day with a deputy sheriff in my room, and found out"—Pete bit his lower lip—"that she was dead."

Mac waited, wanting the jury to remember the look on Pete's face. It was not the face of a murderer.

"What can you tell the jury about the drugs in your system?" Mac asked after several more seconds passed.

"I never took any drugs, and I never gave Angela any drugs."

"And the murder?"

Pete glanced at Alex Hightower, who was sitting stone-faced behind the prosecution table. "I never harmed or hurt Angela in any way, and I really hope the police find who killed her."

Joe began by asking obvious questions to develop a rhythm of response, then moved into the strongest evidence that supported the State's case.

"You don't deny that you were with Angela on the evening of August second?"

"No, sir."

"And you don't dispute the testimony of the officers who apprehended you near the overlook where Angela and her car were found?"

"No, sir. I don't remember."

"Of course, you remember with great detail events from your childhood, but when it comes to the reason for this trial you can't remember anything that would help this jury decide if you're telling the truth, can you?"

"I wish I could. But I can't."

"And do you know the results of the lie-detector test you agreed to take?"

"Yes, sir."

Joe raised his voice. "A test that showed deception every time you answered a question about Angela Hightower?"

"I think Mr. Wilcox explained that the test was not performed as it should have been."

"You're only saying that because you weren't able to lie and get away with it, aren't you?"

"No. I would take another test if the examiner was fair."

"But the test showed you were lying when you said you didn't take any drugs, didn't it?"

"Yes."

"And that you were lying when you said you didn't give Angela any Rohypnol?" Joe spoke more rapidly.

"Yes, but I didn't do it."

"And that you were lying when you said you didn't harm Angela?"

"Yes."

"And that you were lying when you said you didn't kill Angela Hightower?"

"I didn't harm or kill Angela," Pete's voice got louder and his eyes flashed. Mac squirmed in his seat, wanting to give Pete a break from the onslaught, but there was nothing he could do.

"Your attempts to lie didn't fool the polygraph machine, did they, Mr. Thomason?"

"I told the truth then, and I'm telling the truth now."

"Just like your friend Harry O'Ryan always tells the truth?"

"I didn't do anything to the two girls in South Carolina."

"Or is it that you don't remember?"

"I remember what I didn't do," Pete shot back.

"Do you have what they call selective memory recall?"

"No."

"Is that why you forgot to mention to the jury your most recent incident of illegal drug usage while you have been a prisoner in the Echota County Jail?"

Mac was on his feet in a flash. "I object and move for a mistrial, Your Honor. The State has improperly placed Mr. Thomason's character at issue."

"Overruled and denied. He has him on cross-examination," Judge Danielson said evenly.

"I didn't take any illegal drugs," Pete persisted.

"Would Lieutenant Cochran, the officer in charge at the jail, Officer Bailey, the deputy who took you to the hospital, and Dr. Randolph, the doctor who tested your blood at the hospital, verify your story?"

"Uh, no." Pete dropped his head.

"So, Mr. Thomason, everybody in the world is out to get you by either lying about you or forcing drugs down your throat against your will. Is that what you expect this jury to believe?"

Pete's face turned noticeably red. "No."

"Based on your prior conduct, you may not remember anything tomorrow, but that's what you've told us today, isn't it?"

"No."

While Joe was hammering Pete, Mac debated whether to try to rehabilitate his client or let him come down from the witness stand. He decided to attempt a few questions they'd worked out beforehand.

"Pete, is there something more you would like to tell the jury about your inability to remember the events of August second?"

Pete took a deep breath to calm himself down. "For weeks and weeks, I didn't know why I suffered from amnesia. It was driving me crazy, trying to wrack my brain and understand what had happened the night of Angela's death. Then, they identified the drug that was in me—GHB. And I knew that there was a chemical reason why I couldn't remember. It's still frustrating, but there is nothing I can do about it."

"Anything else about your testimony on direct or cross-examination that you want to clear up?" Mac asked.

Pete nodded toward the prosecution table then faced the jury. "I know Mr. Whetstone's job is to convince you that I'm guilty. He's a good lawyer, but I did nothing to harm Angela. Nothing."

Mac checked his notes one last time, then announced, "The defense rests, Your Honor."

"No further questions," Joe said. "We'll refute the defendant's contentions with our rebuttal witnesses."

"How long will you take in rebuttal, Mr. Whetstone?"

"No more than two or three hours, Judge."

"All right. We will adjourn until the morning. Gentlemen, please be prepared to discuss the court's instructions to the jury and present closing arguments tomorrow immediately upon completion of the evidence."

The next morning, Joe called Lieutenant Cochran, Officer Bailey, and Dr. Randolph to testify about Pete's overdose at the Echota County Jail.

"Lieutenant Cochran, was there any indication that someone forced the defendant to take the amphetamines which were found in his system?"

"Of course not," the officer answered, looking as if he thought the idea was the most absurd thing he'd ever heard.

"How did he obtain the drugs?"

"We don't know. Unfortunately, even the jail is not immune from traffic in illegal drugs if an inmate wants it badly enough."

Mac walked to a spot about ten feet from the witness stand.

"How long has Mr. Thomason been in jail?" he began.

"About four months."

"Have there been any other disciplinary problems involving him?"

"No."

"Was he violent or aggressive the night he was taken to the hospital?"

"No."

"In fact, he wouldn't have attracted any attention if he hadn't become confused and disoriented?"

"I don't know if that's true or not. I was in my office downstairs when one of the deputies upstairs called me on an internal phone line."

"And told you Pete was confused?" Mac asked.

"Yes. He was talking nonsense, and they were concerned something was wrong with him."

"Is it possible that someone could have put some amphetamines in his food or drink?"

"Anything is possible, but I've never had that happen at the jail during the twelve years I've been there."

"At least that you know about?" Mac stopped and faced the witness.

"Well, yes."

"Was Mr. Thomason charged with possession of illegal drugs as a result of this incident?"

"No."

"Has he been searched on a regular basis since this happened?"

"Yes."

"Have any drugs been found?"

"No, but Thomason has been moved into isolation."

The questioning of Officer Bailey was even more brief. Dr. Randolph took less than ten minutes.

Although risky, Joe had decided to bring Spencer Hightower out of the shadows and put him on the witness stand for the jury to see. The prosecutor couldn't let Mac create a phantom killer for the jury to blame; the defense lawyer would have to confront Spencer in flesh and blood.

In a voice that sounded more confident than he felt, Joe announced, "The State calls Spencer Hightower."

Once again, the jurors knew it was their sworn duty to pay close attention to every detail, and they sat a little straighter in their seats when Spencer walked into the courtroom. Although shorter than Pete and without the defendant's rugged build, Spencer's reddish-brown hair and facial features made the two men look more like brothers than two people from totally diverse backgrounds. Spencer wore rimless glasses that gave him a studious look.

"State your name please," Joe said.

"Spencer Hightower," he said, his voice slightly cracking with nervousness.

"How old are you, Spencer?"

"Twenty-six."

"And what is your relationship to Alexander Hightower?"

"He's my older brother."

"And Angela?"

"She is, or I guess was, my niece," he said. "I need a drink."

One of the bailiffs brought Spencer a cup of water, and everyone in the courtroom could see Spencer's hand shake as he raised it to his lips.

Joe asked a fairly lengthy series of questions that emphasized Spencer's achievements while skimming over his problems. Then, he walked slowly up to the court reporter and retrieved the letter Angela had written to Spencer on Joan Brinkley's computer.

"Let me show you a letter written by Angela in April," he said quietly. "Please explain the reason for the letter."

Spencer avoided looking toward his brother, Alex. "It's a misunderstanding."

"Go ahead," Joe prompted.

"I was kidding around with Angela, but I can understand how she took it the wrong way."

"What happened between you?"

"Nothing really, except I wrote some letters."

"Did she slap you at a Christmas party?"

"It was more of a push." Spencer shrugged.

"Did you keep writing after you received the April letter?"

"Only once more. I told her I was sorry for bothering her and promised to leave her alone."

"Is that what you did?"

"Yes."

"Did you see her over the summer before her death?"

"A couple of times. There wasn't any problem between us."

Joe stepped back toward the jury box. "Now, where were you at the time Angela was murdered?"

"I was in the Caribbean for ten days."

Joe motioned toward the jury with a sweep of his hand. "Please tell this jury whether you had anything to do with Angela's death?"

"No," he said, and looking toward Mac added, "and anyone who claims I did should have their head examined. The whole idea is ridiculous nonsense cooked up by the low-rent lawyers—"

Mac jumped to his feet. "Objection, Your Honor. Nonresponsive and improper."

The judge looked down at Spencer. "Answer the questions and avoid characterizations of the defendant or his counsel."

"How did you learn about the murder?" Joe asked.

"I received a shore-to-ship phone call from my sister-in-law and immediately came home."

Perry Mason would have obtained a courtroom confession between commercial breaks. Mac set his sights on something more reasonable—to make clear Spencer's motivation and opportunity to commit the crime.

"Mr. Hightower, were you upset when Angela refused your advances and wrote you the letter Mr. Whetstone showed you a few minutes ago?"

"There were no 'advances,' as you call them. It was no big deal. Just a misunderstanding."

"There's no misunderstanding what Angela wrote, is there?"

"You don't know the whole story. She was just a little upset."

"Is that how you characterize the letter—'a little upset'?"

"Yeah. You don't know our family. That's how we communicate."

"Isn't it true that both you and Angela were more than 'a little upset' about what had taken place between you?"

"No. It was no big deal."

"Is that what you expect this jury to believe? That it was 'no big deal' and the two of you were 'a little upset'?"

"That's the way it was." Spencer nodded toward the jury. "They can believe what they want to."

"How are you employed, Mr. Hightower?" Mac asked.

"I'm on the board of directors for some of the companies owned by my family."

"So you don't get up and go to an office every day, do you?"

"No."

"Are you a wealthy man?"

"I think that's my business," Spencer said testily.

Mac looked at the judge, who spoke before Mac could say anything. "Answer the question, Mr. Hightower."

"Well, compared to Bill Gates, I'm not wealthy."

"How about compared to most people in Echota County?"

"Most people in Echota County live in trailers."

Mac's face flushed. "Are you trying to be funny?"

"Listen, Mr. McDonald, or whatever your name is, I shouldn't be here answering your stupid questions."

Judge Danielson cut in, "You are here because Mr. Whetstone called you as a witness, and you will answer Mr. McClain's questions unless I instruct you not to. Do you understand?"

"Yeah."

Mac pointed his finger directly at a spot between Spencer's eyes. "Did you hire someone to kill Angela?"

Spencer rolled his eyes in disdain. "No. That's a stupid question. But the answer is 'No.'"

Mac kept his hand outstretched. "Did you arrange the murder to make it look like Peter Thomason was responsible?"

"No. I've never heard of Peter Thomason before this happened."

"Is that your answer?"

"You heard me."

"And I guess to you this case is 'no big deal,' is it?"

"It's a big deal to your client, and the sooner he goes to the electric chair the better I'll like it."

Mac lowered his arm and walked back to the defense table. "No further questions."

"That's all our rebuttal, Your Honor," Joe said.

"Mr. Hightower, you may leave the courtroom."

A slightly crooked smile on his face, Spencer stepped down from the witness stand.

—

"Ladies and gentlemen," Judge Danielson said, "The court will be in recess until one o'clock this afternoon. Gentlemen, please be in my chambers at twelve-fifteen to discuss the instructions for the jury. We will begin closing arguments when the jury returns."

THIRTY-FOUR

He will maintain his argument.
HENRY V, ACT 3, SCENE 2

THE LAWYERS DIDN'T leave the courthouse to eat lunch. An army might march on a full stomach, but when the fiercest moments of conflict arise, they don't take time to dine on meat loaf, two vegetables, and cornbread.

Mac decided there were two legal principles not already covered in Defendant's Requests to Charge. He huddled with David and explained what he needed. "Go to the office. You should be able to find what I need in the blue form book in the library."

"Okay."

David walked quickly to the office. Mindy was at her post near the front door. "Is Judy here?" he asked.

"No, she took Joan Brinkley to the airport," Mindy replied. "Vicki is gone, too. Can I help?" she asked.

David looked at her upturned face. "I have a couple of requests to charge that need to be typed right away."

"I can do it. I'll use Judy's computer."

"Are you sure?"

"I can do a lot more than answer the phone," she said pertly.

They went back to Judy's desk.

"Do you know how to access her files?" David asked as the screen blinked on.

"Of course. It should just take a second."

"Okay, I'll get the book that you'll need to type the charges."

"I'm ready," Mindy said when David returned in a couple of minutes. "How much are you going to charge and what hourly rate do you want me to use? Mac usually charges $125 an hour for time in the office and $225 an hour for time in court."

David burst out laughing. "I am not talking about time and billing. I wouldn't rush over here in the middle of a murder case to send someone a bill for two hundred dollars. Requests to charge are the instructions on the law the judge gives to the jury before they begin deliberation."

"Oh," Mindy said, chewing her fingernail. "Why didn't you say the judge's instructions to the jury? You lawyers do more to confuse the English language than anybody. I mean, you charge batteries, you charge something at the store. A request to charge sounds like a nice way to bill a client. How was I supposed to know the difference?"

"Okay," David said, still chuckling. "It's just the thought of handing the judge a sheet of paper so he could explain to the jury how much we should be paid."

"I'm glad you think it's so funny," Mindy said in a hurt voice.

"I'm sorry. You're right—I wasn't clear. Here's what you need to type."

Mindy completed the rest of the task without a hitch, and after profusely thanking her, David scurried back to the courthouse. Mac and Joe were about to go into Judge Danielson's chambers when David handed Mac the papers.

At 12:58 P.M., Mac and Joe walked back into the courtroom from the judge's chambers.

"How did it go?" David asked.

"We got almost everything we wanted. The judge is going to tell the jury what we wanted them to hear."

"Are you ready?"

Mac straightened his tie. "Yes, along with the usual nervousness. Do you wish it were you, not me?"

"Not yet, but I'll be praying for the right words to come out of your mouth."

"Pray for the jury. My words won't do any good if they don't go into their ears and persuade their minds."

When the jury was seated, Judge Danielson addressed them. "Ladies and gentlemen, the lawyers will now present closing arguments and after receiving instructions from the court, you will decide the guilt or innocence of the defendant. You are not being asked at this time to determine punishment. As I told you at the beginning of the case, if you acquit the defendant, the trial will end at that point. If you find the defendant guilty of murdering Angela Hightower, each side will have opportunity to present additional evidence and you will deliberate a second time to decide if the defendant should be sentenced to life in prison or put to death." The judge nodded to Mac. "You may present your argument, Mr. McClain."

It was no use fighting the butterflies. The only remedy was to begin talking and keep going until they gave up and flew away. Mac thanked the jury for their service and attention during the trial, then began his argument more like a schoolteacher helping his students prepare for a test than an advocate seeking to bend their wills to his.

"In a few minutes, Peter Thomason's future will be in your hands," he said. "I don't have to tell you the importance of your responsibility. You will leave and return to your homes and families after this trial is over. Mr. Whetstone and I will return to our offices and represent other clients. Judge Danielson will preside over other cases. But this is Peter Thomason's only day in court, and on his behalf I am entrusting his future into your hands."

Mac motioned toward the judge. "Before you begin your deliberations, the judge will instruct you that Pete is presumed innocent. This means that being charged with a crime does not in any way prove that he is guilty. For hundreds of years, our legal system has held the position that it is best not to jump to conclusions but to begin with the belief that someone like Pete is innocent of any wrongdoing. That's what I would ask you to do. When you think about Pete, think of him as you would want to be viewed yourself, an innocent man or woman who is protected from accusation and punishment by a shield that can only be removed by proof of guilt beyond a reasonable doubt. If that shield is not overcome by the evidence, your decision is an easy one, and you should acquit Pete Thomason of this charge."

The afternoon sun streaming through the courtroom windows created a rectangle of light on the floor at one end of the jury box. Mac stood at the edge of light and continued, "Judge Danielson will also tell you that the State must prove each and every element of the crime beyond a reasonable doubt. *Reasonable doubt* are two words we rarely use in everyday conversation, and it is not the standard we apply in many common situations. Those of you who have children know that if you are at least fifty percent sure a child did something wrong you will decide an appropriate punishment. Such a test works fine in raising children, but it is not the way you will be instructed to decide this case. A reasonable doubt is exactly what it says—a doubt for which you have a reason. It is the doubt of a fair-minded, impartial juror, honestly seeking the truth. It is a doubt based upon common sense and reason. Some portion of your mind may think Peter Thomason is guilty, but if, after considering all the evidence you remain wavering and unsettled due to weakness, insufficiency, or conflict in the testimony or evidence, it is your duty to give Pete the benefit of the doubt and find him not guilty of these charges."

Beginning with the midnight purple Lincoln that sideswiped Rodney McFarland's truck and crossed over into the path of Tim Logan's patrol car, Mac outlined twelve grounds for reasonable doubt about Peter Thomason's guilt. He paced back and forth, sometimes talking directly to the jury, at other times looking straight ahead then turning sharply to emphasize an important point. Facing the jury, he came several steps closer to the jury box, rested his hands on the rail, and said, "Peter Thomason was not mentally capable of forming the intent to harm Angela or physically able to carry out this crime because he was a victim himself, a victim subject to the devastating effects of GHB, a first cousin to the drug found in Angela. The amount of GHB in Pete's bloodstream made him confused, disoriented, unfit to drive, and unable to remember what happened. Did the State make any effort to disprove the testimony of Dr. Ogden, the chemist who performed the test? No. Why not? Because they know it is the truth.

"Ladies and gentlemen, how likely is it that the same person or persons who drugged and killed Angela Hightower, also drugged Peter Thomason? Why was Pete drugged? I can suggest at least three very good reasons. You may think of others. First, Pete was not able to remember and identify the killer or killers. I say killers because it took at least two people to drive the Porsche and the Lincoln to the overlook. Second, the effect of the drugs made it easy to set up the circumstances surrounding the discovery of Angela's body and frame Pete as the murderer. Third, it is possible the killers intended to end Pete's life as well. Why they didn't, I don't know. Perhaps, the police officers arrived on the scene before they could finish their plans. But, please, whatever the reason, do not allow the wicked deception of the real killers into the jury room to influence your decision. It is horrible enough that Angela is dead. Don't let those who hatched this evil scheme take another life."

Mac didn't use any notes. He had lived with the case and organized his thoughts for weeks. He knew precisely what he wanted to say and how he wanted to say it. He discussed the polygraph test and discounted Walter Monroe's allegations about the Marine Corps incident, then moved to Spencer Hightower.

"In my opening statement, I told you that the person most likely responsible for the murder of Angela Hightower was not in this courtroom. Now you know why I made that statement. I am not here to prosecute Spencer

Hightower. My job is to defend Peter Thomason. But it is easier to ask you to acquit Pete than it would be to defend Mr. Hightower. It's not necessary that you choose between the two men in deciding who murdered Angela. In fact, to do so would violate the judge's instructions. But the circumstances surrounding Spencer Hightower's harassment of Angela and his financial capability to hire someone to kill her is enough by itself to support the presence of a reasonable doubt as to the guilt of Peter Thomason."

Mac held up the letters hidden for months in Joan Brinkley's computer. "Read Angela's letters in the jury room. Hear her cry to be left alone. Ask yourself if she considered Spencer Hightower's stalking behavior 'no big deal.' You have had the opportunity to view both Pete Thomason and Spencer Hightower from the witness stand. Which one did you find more believable? Which one had the greater motivation and capability to commit this crime? Has the prosecution removed all reasonable doubt from your minds about the guilt of Peter Thomason?"

He walked over and stood near where Pete sat at the defense table. "Because we presented evidence in this case, Mr. Whetstone will have the opportunity to make the last argument you hear before retiring to the jury room. Listen to him carefully. That's right. Listen to him carefully. Then ask yourself if he has answered to your satisfaction each and every one of the twelve grounds of reasonable doubt I've mentioned. He can't do it because the truth is that Peter Thomason did not kill Angela Hightower, and on his behalf I ask you to find him not guilty."

Mac sat down.

Pete leaned over and said, "Thanks." He was relieved. Mac had riddled the State's case with so many holes that no reasonable person could convict him of Angela's murder. Now, all he had to do was endure Joe Whetstone's final diatribe and wait for the news that would set him free. He offered a silent prayer of thanksgiving.

Joe Whetstone wasn't praying. His source of strength was an abundance of the inner confidence, ego, and concentration it took to be a successful trial lawyer. He could listen to everything an opposing lawyer said and simultaneously block out the persuasive power of an adversary's position so that it didn't weaken his capacity to present his argument with zeal and fire. He alone in the courtroom was unmoved by Mac's argument, and when he stood to speak he had no doubt that he could convince the jury to convict Peter Thomason of murder.

"You may proceed, Mr. Whetstone," the judge said.

Joe stood. Every hair was in place, and Joe's expensive suit and tie were billboards proclaiming his success. He positioned himself directly in front of the jury and began.

"Ladies and gentlemen, Mr. McClain is an excellent lawyer and delivered a fine closing argument. I applaud his eloquence and the passion with which he spoke." He nodded in Mac's direction. "I don't expect you to forget what Mr. McClain has told you, but on behalf of the State and Angela's parents, I ask you to consider what I have to say as well.

"We are not here so that Mr. McClain and I can try to impress you with our oratory or legal skills. We are not here at the request of Alexander and Sarah Hightower. We are here because the life of Angela Hightower was brutally ended before it had time to blossom. Hear her voice. Because only you can make sure her voice is heard and her life given the respect and dignity denied her on the night of August second."

Joe picked up the indictment. "This is the legal document charging Peter Thomason with murder. The defense technique used by the defendant and his lawyers against these charges is called a red herring defense. A red herring is a fish that protects its eggs from predators by boldly darting in front of its enemy to divert attention from the place where the eggs are hidden. In this trial, the defendant views you as an enemy because you have the power to take away his freedom. He is desperate and has resorted to skillful measures to distract you from your rightful goal. The red herring is a very smart fish. It knows just how close it can come to an enemy without letting the predator catch it for supper. The key tactic it uses is distraction." Joe put the indictment behind his back and held his other hand away from his body and moved it back and forth. "The red herring gets the eye of the other fish away from what's important."

Joe brought the indictment out from behind his back and placed it in the center of the jury rail. "Every one of the defenses raised by Mr. McClain is a red herring calculated to divert you and keep you from focusing on the common-sense, reliable evidence that proves beyond reasonable doubt that Peter Thomason murdered Angela Hightower. It's only on a one-hour TV show and in cheap novels that the real killer is lurking in the shadows, waiting to be exposed in the final five minutes or last ten pages. Reality is different from fiction, and the case laid out by the State is logical and supported by every reasonable interpretation of the evidence presented to you."

Joe replayed a lengthy summary of the evidence and countered most of Mac's points along the way. The only thing he didn't discuss was the presence of GHB in Pete's blood. That was a briar patch he didn't enter.

"On behalf of Angela, I have complete confidence in your ability to sift and weigh the evidence within the guidelines Judge Danielson will provide in a few minutes and render the only just verdict possible in this case—a verdict of guilty."

Judge Danielson had memorized sections of the instructions given to juries in criminal cases but to be sure he didn't swap an "and" for an "or," he read everything directly from the sheets of paper submitted by the lawyers and the sections of the law he had chosen himself. He used the same phrases mentioned by Mac about presumption of innocence, circumstantial evidence, and reasonable doubt. Mac hoped the jury would conclude that because he accurately foretold the words of the judge, the rest of his argument would be the guide for their deliberations.

The judge concluded, "Let your decision be unanimous and signed and dated by the person selected as foreperson. You may now retire to the jury room and begin your deliberations."

Everyone stood as the jury filed out.

THIRTY-FIVE

The jury, passing on the prisoner's life,
may in the sworn twelve have a thief
or two guiltier than him they try.
MEASURE FOR MEASURE, ACT 2, SCENE 1

DURING THE FIVE DAYS they'd spent together, the jury in *State v. Thomason* had divided into two camps, one led by Lyman Bakerfield, the former Hightower employee, and the other influenced by John Terry, the owner of a janitorial cleaning service.

After listening to Judge Danielson's instruction, the jurors were escorted back to the jury room they'd occupied during breaks in the trial. They took their customary seats around the table. One of John Terry's followers immediately spoke up.

"I nominate John Terry to serve as foreman of this jury. We talked about it over lunch yesterday, and he is willing to serve."

Another of Terry's followers, a woman named Florence Stone, piped in, "I second the nomination and call for a vote."

Lyman kicked Paul Sumter under the table, the signal they had agreed upon for Paul to nominate Lyman to head the jury.

"Ouch!" Paul said.

"What?" John Terry asked.

"I mean, I nominate Lyman Bakerfield as foreman of the jury."

"I second the nomination," said another.

The room was silent as they waited to see if any other frogs rose to the surface of the little pond.

"Well, I guess we need to vote," Lyman said.

"I don't see how this is going to work, " said Florence Stone. "The judge said our decision had to be unanimous."

"Don't be ridiculous," Lyman quickly responded. "That only applies to the verdict."

"Hold on there, Lyman," John Terry said. "Show Mrs. Stone a little respect. I was listening closely to the judge, and he told us our decision had to be unanimous."

"We could be here a long time," someone groaned.

"Why don't we flip a coin?" another suggested

"I don't think that would be legal," Lyman said.

"Maybe we should ask the judge to settle this?" someone else suggested.

"I think that would be okay," said John.

"Fine with me, too," said Lyman. "We need to write out a question and send it to him."

So, after several more minutes of discussion and a few minor disagreements, Florence Stone wrote on a sheet of paper, "We are having trouble selecting a foreman. Does the vote have to be unanimous? One person wants to flip a coin if we can't agree."

Lyman handed the sheet of paper to the bailiff sitting outside the jury room door.

Judge Danielson was in his office sorting through the pile of paperwork that had accumulated on his desk during the course of the trial when the bailiff knocked on his door. "The jury has a question, Your Honor."

"Already? Gather the lawyers in the courtroom."

David was sitting at the defense table. Mac and Joe Whetstone were coming up the stairs when the bailiff found them.

Once everyone was present, the judge said, "Gentlemen, the jury has not been able to elect a foreperson. Apparently, there are several jurors who believe the vote must be unanimous and one who wants to flip a coin. Unless there is an objection, I will not have the jury brought out to the courtroom but simply write a response that the foreperson is elected by majority vote and that no aspect of the case should be decided by a coin flip."

"That's fine, Your Honor," Mac said.

"I agree," said Joe.

"That's crazy," David whispered to Mac.

"Welcome to the insane asylum of trial by jury," Mac replied.

Ten minutes after the bailiff delivered the judge's response, the jury, by a vote of eight to four, elected Lyman Bakerfield foreman. As soon as the votes were counted, Florence nominated John Terry to serve as vice-foreman. Paul Sumter was poised to object when Lyman kicked him under the table again and shook his head.

"I think that's an excellent idea," Lyman said.

The vote was unanimous.

With the jury deliberating, activity in the courtroom came to a screeching halt. The trial of the case was as intense as driving a racecar at 150 miles per hour through the streets of Monaco. Waiting for the jury was like sitting at a Dennison Springs red light that never seemed to turn green. David walked to the spectator section of the courtroom and sat down next to Mindy, who had come in the back door during Mac's closing argument.

"The judge really liked the charges you typed," David said. "I think he enjoyed reading them to the jury."

"Right," she said, sticking out her tongue. "Watch out because I owe you one."

"I'll be careful."

"How do you think it's going to turn out?" she asked.

"Not guilty," David said confidently. "I don't think Whetstone answered the questions raised by Mac about the State's case. It would only take one of Mac's points to create a reasonable doubt."

Pointing toward Mac and Joe, who were quietly talking in front of the jury box, Mindy asked, "They look like best friends. How can they act as if nothing has happened?"

David smiled. "Oh, lawyers are like professional wrestlers. They pretend to get mad and fight, but then they socialize after a trial is over."

"Lawyers are strange."

"They live in an artificial world," David admitted.

Mindy stood up. "I'd better get back to the office. Vicki is answering the phone calls for me."

Mac motioned to David, who walked over to the railing that separated the two areas of the courtroom. "Call Dr. Wilkes and tell her the status of the case."

"Yes, sir."

David caught up with Mindy at the bottom of the stairs. "I'll walk with you," he said.

They stepped outside into a brilliant afternoon.

"It's a beautiful day, isn't it?" she asked as they passed through the ring of crepe myrtles. "Not the sort of day for a murder trial."

"What do you mean?" David asked.

"Oh, it should be overcast with a misty rain and clouds on the mountains. That's the right weather for a murder case."

David looked sideways. He couldn't tell if this was payback time or not.

"I'll try to get Dr. Wilkes on the line for you," Mindy offered when they reached the office.

"Okay. I'll be in the library."

After several minutes, David stuck his head into the reception room. Mindy was on the phone and silently mouthed, "Just a minute."

David went back to the library.

The phone buzzed. "She's on line two," Mindy said. "We had a couple of things to talk about first."

David introduced himself to Anna.

"Mac told me about you," she said. "What's happening in the trial? I've been thinking about it all day."

"It's with the jury."

"Dr. Newburn didn't testify?"

"No. We subpoenaed his patient list and could have shown his bias because of the doctor/patient relationship with members of the Hightower family. Also, he can't testify about Pete's alleged psychopathic tendencies unless the jury returns a guilty verdict."

"But the trial went well?"

"Mac did a great job. He was very smooth but had passion when it counted. It beat *Judge Judy* by a mile."

Anna laughed. "Maybe I can talk to him about it later."

"Sure. Where can we reach you this weekend?"

"At home. Mac has the number. I've reviewed the proposed questions he sent me."

"Actually, I prepared the questions. How did they look?"

"Fine."

—

In the jury room, Lyman Bakerfield took off his glasses and rubbed his eyes. "Let's take a vote before we talk any more and see where we are. John, please tear up twelve pieces of paper and give one to everyone. Write 'guilty' or 'not guilty' and pass them around to me."

In a minute Lyman had two equal stacks in front of him. "That's six to six. I guess we have some more things to discuss."

An hour later it was eight to four. An hour after that it was nine to three. By then, it was after six o'clock, and the judge sent a message by a bailiff asking if they wanted to continue into the night or come back in the morning.

"Let's give it another hour," Florence said.

After another hour and a very heated discussion, they took another vote. It was ten to two.

"Let's sleep on it," one of the holdouts said. "We can come back in the morning, and if everything is as clear to all of you then as you think it is now, I'll reconsider."

"I'm ready to get it over with," Paul Sumter said.

"No, in fairness to everyone we ought to sleep on it," Lyman said. "We'll come back in the morning."

"Yeah, I can use one last night of free room and board," the other holdout said.

THIRTY-SIX

It is better that ten guilty persons escape than one innocent suffer.
SIR WILLIAM BLACKSTONE

DAVID LAY IN BED and catalogued his thoughts from the day. The trial had been different than he anticipated. He hadn't been as content watching Mac do most of the work as he thought he would. Every young lawyer expects to serve a time of apprenticeship, but time and time again he wanted to be the one who stood to his feet to question a witness or explain the applicable law to the judge. He'd even fantasized about arguing the case to the jury and felt a touch of disappointment when he realized that his hard work on the sentencing phase would not be needed. But that was fine. An acquittal was, of course, their goal for Pete. David's time to be a full-fledged trial lawyer would come. Someday.

He fell asleep but woke up in the night and couldn't go back to sleep. He turned on the light, and read some of the verses from Psalm 35 that he'd been using as prayers during the trial. "Contend, O Lord, with those who contend with me . . . May those who seek my life be disgraced and put to shame . . . Vindicate me in your righteousness, O Lord my God . . . May those who delight in my vindication shout for joy and gladness."

Slipping out of bed, he walked from room to room in his apartment, praying and imagining the scene in the courtroom when the jury announced its verdict of not guilty. "My tongue will speak of your righteousness and of your praises all day long."

Yes, in the morning, God would vindicate one falsely accused. And David, like his biblical namesake, would rejoice with all his might.

An hour after they resumed deliberations in the morning, and four hours and thirty-six minutes after they elected Lyman Bakerfield foreman, the jury sent word to the judge that they had reached a verdict. After reporting to the judge, the bailiff stuck his head in the courtroom and announced, "Jury's ready."

Everyone scrambled to their seat.

The deputy assigned to Pete quickly brought him from the holding cell. Mac's heart began to pound. He looked across the courtroom and saw the muscles in Joe Whetstone's jaw twitch.

Pete sat down between his lawyers. "Is this a quick decision?" he asked Mac.

"Somewhat. I've waited up to two days for a verdict."

Pete's hands were sweaty. He stole a glance at Mr. and Mrs. Hightower, who were sitting behind the prosecution table. Joe Whetstone, grim-faced, leaned over and said something to them seconds before the first juror came back into the courtroom.

Everyone stood as the jurors filed into the jury box. Pete looked closely at the now-familiar faces, seeking a hint of their decision. None of them looked directly at either the prosecution table or the defense.

Judge Danielson cleared his throat. "Ladies and gentlemen, have you reached a verdict?"

Lyman Bakerfield stood. "Yes, Your Honor."

"What is your verdict?"

Bakerfield looked directly at Pete and said in a clear voice, "We find the defendant, Peter Thomason, guilty of first-degree murder."

Sarah Hightower began to sob. In total shock, Pete stared sightlessly down at the defense table.

Mac gripped Pete's arm for a second before he rose. "I ask that the jury be polled, Your Honor."

The judge asked each juror whether he or she consented to the verdict to make sure there had been no undue pressure in the privacy of the jury room. One by one the jurors stood and responded, "Yes," when asked if they supported the decision.

"Mr. Foreman, have you signed and dated the verdict on your copy of the indictment?" the judge asked.

"Yes, sir."

"All right. Hand it to the clerk of court."

The clerk took the sheet from Lyman.

The judge continued, "Ladies and gentlemen, we will begin the sentencing phase of the trial in one hour. Court will be in recess until that time."

Mac felt as if he had been punched in the stomach, but he showed no emotion. There was still a job to do—a young man's life was at stake.

All the color had drained from David's face. Mac turned to him and said calmly, "Call Anna Wilkes and tell her to come immediately to the courthouse." He patted Pete on the shoulder. "Do you want us to use Charles Gallegly? He said he would testify if you needed him, too."

Pete nodded.

Mac turned back to David. "Also, contact Mr. Gallegly. He's been on standby. Vicki has his number."

David walked quickly to the office. He was quiet on the outside, but inside he was shouting at the top of his lungs, *Why, God? Why? You promised!*

"Guilty," he announced soberly to the women at the office. "Mindy, please get Dr. Wilkes on the line. Mac needs her to come ASAP. Vicki, do the same for Charles Gallegly."

"It will take an hour and a half for me to get ready and drive down there," Anna said.

"That will be fine," David replied. "The State won't finish before lunch."

"What happened?" she asked.

"I don't know. We can't talk to the jurors because the case isn't over. I thought I had a promise from the Lord about an acquittal," David said, discouraged. "I don't know what to think."

"How is Mac?"

"He's focused on what we need to do next."

"I'll come straight to the courthouse."

"Thanks. One of the bailiffs will show you where to wait."

David returned to the courthouse with thirty minutes to spare.

"Are you ready?" Mac asked as soon as he sat down at the defense table.

David's mouth suddenly went dry. "You want me to handle the witnesses we discussed?"

"That was our plan. You're ready, and I'll be here. The jury needs to see a new face; some of them apparently don't like mine."

"Okay," David said.

"Let's check on Pete before the judge reconvenes," Mac said.

Standing outside the bars, neither of them asked how Pete felt. Their client sat with his head in his hands. He didn't look up until Mac started talking.

"As we discussed the other day at the jail, David will take primary responsibility for the sentencing phase," Mac began. "He's done most of the preparatory work, and there is a possibility that some of the jurors have developed a negative reaction to me during the trial. I don't want any bad feelings toward me to carry over into what lies ahead. I think it's best for a fresh face and voice to speak on your behalf."

"Okay," Pete said, turning his head sideways so that he could look into David's eyes. "I know you will do a good job."

David tried to swallow, but there was nothing but cotton in his mouth. "Are you sure?" he asked.

"Yes. I know you'll do your best."

In the courtroom, the imaginary bell for round two sounded, and Joe Whetstone rose to his feet. "The State calls Dr. Louis Newburn."

Taking a step toward the bench, David asked, "Your Honor, may we approach the bench?"

"Yes," the judge replied.

Joe joined him in front of the judge. Mac came alongside David.

"We want to know whether Dr. Newburn has brought the patient records we subpoenaed," David asked.

Joe walked back to the prosecution table and returned with a slim stack of papers that he handed to the judge. "Here they are. I renew my objection on the grounds that this is privileged information with no relevance to this case."

"Your objection is noted." The judge handed the sheets to David. "Proceed, Mr. Whetstone."

The short, balding psychiatrist had a generous doughboy belly and entered the courtroom wearing a white medical coat with his name embroidered on the pocket. His eyebrows, permanently arched from years of peering over his glasses while listening to stories about the bizarre behavior of his patients, created an appearance of perpetual puzzlement and surprise.

Joe began by asking questions about Dr. Newburn's educational and professional qualifications. During the introductory questions, Mac quickly scanned the patient list, looking for familiar names beginning with "H."

"Dr. Newburn, did you perform a psychiatric evaluation of Peter Thomason, the man this jury has found guilty of murdering Angela Hightower?" Joe asked.

"Yes, I did."

"Where and when was this evaluation performed?"

"Three weeks ago at the Echota County Jail."

"Please tell the jury about your findings and conclusions."

The psychiatrist knew how to communicate. He explained the reasons for his opinion that Pete had sociopathic behavior patterns based on significant antisocial tendencies. He dissected Pete's troubled upbringing and identified factors that he claimed triggered violent, antiauthority behavior.

"Dr. Newburn, when the defendant testified before this jury, he did not exhibit any of the tendencies you have identified. Could you explain why?"

"Yes, I can," the psychiatrist said. "The defendant has a level of conscious control that enables him to present himself in what a layperson would call a normal manner. He knows what he is doing; it is not outside the realm of his will to control. I've described his particular form of psychosis as ingenuous."

"What does *ingenuous* mean?"

"In the defendant's case, it means initially friendly, yet deceptive and homicidal. Mr. Thomason is able to act in a nonthreatening or even engaging manner, thus winning the trust of those around him. Then, once a false sense of trust is established, the door is open for him to act out his violent behavior in a way he hopes will avoid detection by the authorities."

"How does this relate to Angela Hightower's death?"

"It explains the entire sequence of events." Dr. Newburn held up his fingers and counted off the ways Pete set the stage for Angela's murder. "He established a friendly relationship with Angela in June, won her trust and that of her parents during the next few weeks, lured Angela into a situation where she was isolated from help, murdered her, and then attempted to make the murder look like a tragic automobile accident." He closed his fist.

Joe moved closer to the jury. "Do you have an opinion about the danger Peter Thomason poses to society in the future?"

"Yes, I do."

"What is your opinion?"

"His predisposition to violence is deeply ingrained. I am not aware of any treatment program with a statistically significant success rate for individuals with his diagnosis. He should be isolated from the general prison population and if released from custody would pose a real threat to kill and kill again. Angela was his first identified victim. There may have been prior victims, and if he is in contact with the general population the likelihood of additional homicides would be significant."

David stood. "I object to that as speculative, Your Honor."

"Overruled. He can express his opinion, and you can cross-examine him."

"What other murderers have had similar psychological profiles?" Joe continued.

Still standing, David objected again. "Your Honor, Dr. Newburn is not qualified to testify about people he hasn't evaluated."

Joe responded. "Dr. Newburn has studied evaluations performed by other psychiatrists on serial killers and can render a comparative opinion about the defendant."

"Objection overruled."

"Go ahead, Doctor," Joe said.

"I have closely evaluated nonpublic case studies of serial killers like Theodore 'Ted' Bundy and David Berkowitz, the 'Son of Sam' killer. Their profiles are markedly similar to Peter Thomason's."

"Thank you, Doctor."

"Judge," David said, "May I have a few minutes to discuss the patient list with Mr. McClain before I begin questioning the witness?"

"Yes. I'll give the jury a short break."

Mac and David huddled at the defense table.

"There's not a Hightower on any of these sheets," Mac said.

"Are you sure?"

"I checked it twice during his testimony. None of the other witnesses for the State is here, either."

"What do I do?" David asked anxiously.

"Go with what you prepared."

When the jury returned, David, feeling much less confident in the courtroom than he had in the security of his bedroom the night before, began the second attempt at cross-examination in his young legal career. He stood behind a small podium near the jury box. A legal pad covered with neatly written questions lay in front of him.

"Dr. Newburn, did you perform any psychological tests when you evaluated Mr. Thomason?"

"I utilized a comparative clinical interview."

"Could you list the psychological tests you performed?" David asked again.

"I utilized a comparative clinical interview."

"Is that a psychological test?"

"It is an indicator of psychological status."

"Is it a uniform test that can be given to people and the results compared with other tests?"

"No, it is not a multiple choice or fill-in-the-blank test," the doctor said with a hint of condescension in his voice. "It depends on the experience and expertise of the psychiatrist performing the interview."

"An interview means you talk to someone, correct?"

"Yes, talk with a diagnostic goal in mind."

"So, during your time with Pete Thomason, the two of you were sitting in a room talking."

"Yes."

"For how long?"

"Three hours."

"Did you do anything else beside talk?"

"No."

"Did he cooperate in answering your questions?"

"Yes."

"Did he threaten you or exhibit any of the violent antisocial behavior you claim he has while you were having your three-hour talk?"

"No, but that is consistent with my diagnosis."

"An ingenuous psychopath?"

"That's just a descriptive term."

"I see." David decided to venture out from behind the safety of the podium. Leaving his notes behind, he took a few steps toward the witness. "Am I correct in saying that an ingenuous psychopath is someone who is a psychopath but doesn't act like one when you meet him?"

"Unless you meet him on the wrong day," the doctor pointed out.

David changed directions. "What is the DSM IV, Dr. Newburn?"

"The Diagnostic and Statistical Manual, Fourth Edition."

"Who uses the DSM IV and why do they use it?"

"Mental health professionals use it. It lists the different types of mental disorders and conditions with information about them."

"Is ingenuous psychopath listed in the DSM IV?"

"No, but I think it is a concise, accurate way to categorize the defendant's mental condition."

"So your diagnosis of Pete's condition is something you made up?"

"No." A little color appeared in the psychiatrist's thick neck and spread up into his cheeks. "It is analogous to other antisocial, psychotic conditions, but it has its own unique characteristics."

"Would one of those characteristics be your convenient ability to diagnose the condition even when an individual demonstrates no obvious signs of psychotic illness?"

"No, that's the purpose of the clinical interview."

David held up his hands. "I feel like we're on a merry-go-round, Dr. Newburn."

"Objection," Joe said.

"Ask questions, Mr. Moreland," the judge said.

David crossed his arms in front of him. "Would you agree that the clinical interview is the primary basis for your opinion?"

"I was the only psychiatrist in the room at the time."

"Is that a 'yes'?

"Yes."

"Did you record the interview?"

"No, that is not standard procedure."

David looked at the jury while he asked his next question. "So there is no way for another psychiatrist to listen to the tape of the interview and decide if your yet-unrecognized diagnosis of 'ingenuous psychopath' was correct?"

"There is no tape recording. But another psychiatrist could reach the same conclusion using different terminology."

David faced the witness again. "Would other psychiatrists consider the availability of other mental health records helpful in diagnosing an individual such as Pete Thomason?"

"Possibly."

"Did you have any additional records?"

"No, none were provided to me."

David went over to the defense table and picked up a folder. "Did you have the psychological test results from Dr. Anna Wilkes, the psychologist who tested Pete a week or so before your evaluation?"

"Oh, yes. I had those records, but they were not helpful."

"Is the reason they weren't helpful because they did not support the opinion you had already decided to give about Pete Thomason's mental status?"

"Of course not. I reviewed the report."

"Did you perform any of the same tests?"

"No. I'm not a psychologist."

"I understand. You talk. Psychologists test, correct?"

"We have different types of training. I am a medical doctor; a psychologist is not. I have the ability to treat patients by prescribing medication; a psychologist cannot write a prescription for even the mildest type of psychotropic drugs."

"Speaking of drugs, are you familiar with gamma-hydroxybutyrate, or GHB?"

"Somewhat."

David took several steps toward the witness. Keeping his voice low to avoid an objection from Joe Whetstone, he asked. "Dr. Newburn, were you aware GHB was found in Mr. Thomason's system at the time of his arrest?"

"No."

"What are the effects of GHB?"

"I'm not sure. It's not a drug prescribed by psychiatrists."

"Would it surprise you to learn that GHB causes confusion, temporary memory loss, and disorientation?"

"I'm not that familiar with it."

"Dr. Newburn, is Spencer Hightower one of your patients?" David quickly switched gears in his questioning.

"No."

"Where is your office located?"

"400 West Lenox Towers, Suite 358, Atlanta."

"Can you explain why Spencer Hightower would visit your office on a regular basis?"

Perspiration appeared on the psychiatrist's forehead, and he wiped his face with a handkerchief. "You would have to ask him."

"I'm asking you."

Dr. Newburn looked at Joe, who didn't move.

"Uh, he's a client."

"I thought you had patients?" David glanced at Mac who raised an eyebrow.

"He's not really a client or a patient." The doctor shifted in his chair and looked up at the judge.

"What is he?" David took a step closer.

"I told you. He's a client. Ah, I'm his financial advisor."

David stopped in his tracks. "Dr. Newburn, are you a stockbroker, too?"

"No."

"Are you a certified financial planner?"

"No."

David came as close to the witness as he thought the judge would allow.

"Exactly what are you to Spencer Hightower, Dr. Newburn?"

"Well, you see," the doctor hesitated, "I'm cotrustee of a trust set up by his father."

Mac put down his pen.

David retreated to a spot near the jury box. "So you control his money?"

"Not really. Just some of it. I do it to help Spencer."

"You're on a first-name basis?"

"Yes."

"Are you paid for your help?"

"Yes, there is a fee authorized by the trust."

"How much were you paid last year?"

The doctor's cheeks grew redder, and he wiped his face again with the handkerchief. "I don't remember exactly."

"Can you give an estimate?"

"It was less than $100,000," he said, then quickly added, "but that had nothing to do with my evaluation of the defendant."

David was silent for several seconds. "Dr. Newburn, are you being *ingenuous* with this jury? Friendly, yet deceptive?"

If it hadn't been a murder trial, Mac would have burst out laughing.

"Objection, argumentative," Joe said.

"Overruled. The witness will answer the question."

"No," the doctor said.

"So you're saying there is no possibility whatsoever that your role as cotrustee of Spencer Hightower's trust influenced your evaluation and opinion of Pete Thomason?"

"Yes."

"Because you based your opinion solely on your clinical interview and nothing else?"

"That's correct."

David stared at the witness for several seconds before turning and walking back to the defense table. "No further questions," he said.

THIRTY-SEVEN

Who shall decide when doctors disagree?
ALEXANDER POPE

MAC LEANED OVER to David when he returned to the table. "The doctor will need a session with his own therapist after that cross-examination."

David was about to ask Mac a question, when Joe said, "The State calls Alexander Hightower."

His face set like granite and dressed in a dark blue suit, Angela Hightower's father walked into the courtroom with the same air of authority that had dominated countless board meetings. But today, there was a crack in the Hightower coat of arms and a sense of brokenness in Alexander.

David's dissection of Dr. Newburn may have encouraged his lawyers, but it didn't move Pete. Still reeling from the verdict, he didn't know how many more attacks he could stand before he had to jump and scream. He watched Alexander Hightower raise his hand to take the oath.

Before the start of the trial, Pete had only seen his former employer from a distance at the picnic where he met Angela and for a five-second handshake once when he came by to pick her up. Now, the most powerful man in Echota County had one desire—to hear a jury sentence Pete to death.

Alexander answered Joe Whetstone's questions in a quiet, somber voice without looking in Pete's direction.

"Angela was everything to us," Alexander said. "I still wake up in the morning thinking she is asleep in her bed or that I will see her later in the day. Unless you've lost someone in your family, there's no way to describe what you feel."

Mac nodded imperceptibly. He knew.

"To say we'll miss her sounds so inadequate," Alexander finished.

"What do you want to say to the jury at this point?" Joe asked quietly.

Alexander looked directly at the jurors. "I want to thank them for the verdict of guilty. My wife and I could not have been able to endure the thought that our daughter's killer could be walking the streets while Angela—" he stopped and looked away.

Joe waited for Alexander's emotion and words to find a secure resting place in the hearts and minds of the jurors, then asked, "What about punishment?"

Alexander spoke slowly. "I trust the jury will do the right thing, not only because of Angela but for the good of us all. I don't want anyone else to go through what my family has suffered, and unless the defendant is put to death, there will always be a fear in the back of my mind that he might get out of jail and kill again."

"That's all I have from this witness."

David had a series of questions prepared but, with an instinct many lawyers don't have or never acquire, he decided to keep his mouth shut.

"No questions of Mr. Hightower," he said.

"The State rests," Joe said.

"Ladies and gentlemen," the judge said, "we will break for lunch. Counsel, if you could remain behind for a couple of minutes."

After the jury and Mr. Hightower were gone, the judge addressed Mac.

"Mr. McClain, do you intend to handle the balance of the defense during this phase of the trial?"

"I am available to assist, but Mr. Moreland is going to present our proof and argue to the jury."

The judge picked up his gavel and tapped it lightly against his palm. "I do not want any conduct that would support a claim of ineffective assistance of counsel."

It was a known tactic of a few defense lawyers to purposely commit legal errors in a death penalty trial in order to increase the likelihood of a reversal down the road in the appellate courts. Mac resented the judge's implication.

"I understand your point, Your Honor," he said, controlling his emotions. "Let me assure you that every decision has been made with a goal of providing the best defense for Mr. Thomason. Mr. Moreland's cross-examination of the prosecution psychiatrist should speak for itself."

"I want to know if the defendant has been consulted about this matter," the judge persisted.

"Of course, Your Honor," Mac said

"Mr. Thomason," the judge addressed Pete. "Do you want Mr. Moreland to assume primary responsibility for this phase of your case?"

"Yes, sir. We discussed it earlier."

"Very well. Mr. Moreland, how long will your side of the case take?"

"Two to three hours," David said.

"All right. Gentlemen, be prepared to discuss requests to charge at the close of the defense's case and argue to the jury by late this afternoon."

Before Pete was taken back to the holding cell, he turned to David. "There is no way the psychiatrist spent three hours with me. It was more like an hour and a half."

Anna Wilkes was due to arrive in a few minutes and David wanted to go back to the office to get some papers he'd forgotten to put in his briefcase. Walking up the sidewalk, he asked Mac, "Would the jail have a record of the amount of time Dr. Newburn spent with Pete?"

"Possibly. Do you want to check?"

"Is there someone you can call?"

Mac thought a moment. "Yes, there is."

When they returned to the courthouse, Dr. Anna Wilkes, dressed in a tan suit, was standing in the room where the witnesses waited until called to testify.

"Am I late?" she asked.

"No. We're on lunch break," Mac said.

Concern etched on her face, she said, "I'm sorry about the verdict."

"It's a hard one to figure," Mac shook his head. "Juries are so unpredictable; you never know what they are going to latch on to from the testimony."

"How's Pete?"

"Devastated."

"Did Dr. Newburn testify yet?"

"Just finished. He started out as a big piece of marble, but David chiseled away at him until he was a little pebble."

Twenty minutes later the bailiffs led the jury back into the jury box, and the lawyers reassembled at their tables. Fred Davidson, the correctional sergeant whom Mac had called, stuck his head in the back of the courtroom. Mac quickly walked over to him.

"Here it is," Fred opened the jailhouse log and showed it to Mac.

Mac quickly read it. "This will help," he said. "David Moreland will be the one to call you to the witness stand and ask you a few questions about it."

David called Fred as his first witness and, after having him explain his position at the jail, asked him about the day of Dr. Newburn's visit.

"Were you on duty?"

"Yes, sir."

"Were you in charge of keeping the log of people coming in and out of the jail to meet with prisoners?"

"Yes."

"Do you have the official record with you today?"

"Yes." Fred put the open book on the edge of the witness stand.

"Please tell the jury about the entry for Dr. Newburn's visit with Peter Thomason."

"Okay. Dr. Newburn arrived at 4:11 P.M. and left at 5:40 P.M."

"How much of that time would he have been with Pete Thomason?"

"It takes at least three or four minutes to bring a prisoner down to the interview rooms, so he was with Thomason for about an hour and a half."

"Not three hours?"

"No."

David put his hands behind his back. "By the way, do you also have the record of the visit by the psychologist who evaluated Mr. Thomason?"

"That was sometime before the psychiatrist?"

"Yes."

Fred flipped a few pages back in the log. "Here it is. Dr. Anna Wilkes arrived at 1:08 P.M. and left at 5:52 P.M."

"Would that mean she spent more than four and a half hours with Pete?"

"Yes."

Joe didn't have enough questions to build up a head of steam.

"Sergeant Davidson, do you know what happened during Dr. Newburn's interview of the defendant?'

"No, sir. I was at my desk outside the interview room."

"And your desk can be a busy place, can't it?"

"Sometimes it's very hectic."

"So could the accuracy of your records be affected by the number of other distractions that occupy your attention?"

Fred narrowed his eyes. "One of my main jobs is to monitor the visitors coming in and out of the jail. If I don't keep accurate records, I could lose my job."

Joe took a step back. "And you don't know how much time the psychologist spent actually testing the defendant, do you?"

"No. I just know when she arrived and left."

David stood and called out, "The defense calls Dr. Anna Wilkes."

The bailiff went to the witness room, and in a few seconds Anna appeared, walked directly to the witness stand, and raised her hand. At the conclusion of the oath, she said, "I do," in a clear voice.

David asked the necessary questions about her educational and professional qualifications, then moved to her evaluation of Pete.

"What was the nature of your psychological evaluation of Pete Thomason?" he asked.

"Clinical interview and testing."

"Do you have a copy of your report with you today?"

"Yes, sir."

"What tests did you perform?"

Anna propped her glasses on the end of her nose and referred to the summary portion of her evaluation. "WAIS IQ testing, Rorschach, Beck's Depression Inventory, and General Achievement Testing."

"Please explain the purpose of each test for the jury."

Anna gave a brief description of the origin, purpose, and methodology of each test.

"What were your findings?

"I can summarize by telling you that Mr. Thomason is not psychotic, had an emotionally deprived upbringing, and is above average in intelligence. At the time of the evaluation, he was seriously depressed."

"Would other psychologists agree with the results of your testing?"

"Objection," Joe said. "She can't testify about the opinion of another psychologist."

"Sustained. Rephrase your question."

David glanced down for a second to organize his thoughts. "Could you explain the standard of review for the tests you administered?"

"Any psychologist trained in reading the answers would reach the same or virtually the same results."

"Is a psychiatrist trained to review the tests you administered?"

"They are familiar with the tests and rely on them to help patients, but it would depend on the training received by the individual."

"What other observations did you make?"

"The absence of any memory of the night of the murder. There had to be a reason for it."

"And did you reach a conclusion?"

Anna leaned forward in her seat. "Yes. Mr. Thomason was either faking memory loss or it was the result of a foreign substance in his system, some drug or combination of drugs."

"Are you familiar with gamma-hydroxybutyrate, GHB?"

"Yes. I was the one who suggested that a chemical analysis be performed to determine if GHB was in Mr. Thomason's system. A positive finding would give a clear reason for his temporary amnesia."

"Do you have an opinion whether Pete Thomason has violent, anti-authority, psychopathic behavior patterns?"

"Yes."

"What is your opinion?"

Anna put her report in her lap and looked directly at the jury. "I didn't see any of those characteristics. He is depressed, but not psychotic or psychopathic."

"Based on your testing, would he be a danger to society in the future?"

Anna shook her head. "He can make choices that could harm others, but there is no psychological dynamic operating that makes that type of choice or behavior more likely."

"That's all. Thank you." David returned to his seat.

Joe stood and began by asking, "Ms. Wilkes, who hired you in this case?"

David objected. "It's *Dr.* Wilkes, Your Honor."

"Sustained. The witness has been qualified as an expert with appropriate qualifications."

Anna, her hands folded in her lap, continued in the same level voice she used during David's questioning. "I was contacted by Mr. McClain's office and paid by Echota County for my work. A copy of my report was sent to you, Judge Danielson, and Mr. McClain."

"And you have talked several times with Mr. McClain and Mr. Moreland about this case after preparing your report, haven't you?"

"Yes."

"How many times have you talked with me or my staff?"

"You never contacted me, so we never talked."

Joe stepped closer to the witness stand. "Would it be fair to say that your contact with Mr. McClain has exceeded the typical level for a psychologist working on a case for a lawyer?"

Anna's face flushed. "We've seen each other in social settings on several occasions."

"Could you tell us about that?"

Anna described the lunch at Rock Springs, the meal at her house, and dinner at Kincaid's. Mac ground his teeth.

"Was Mr. Moreland present at any of these meetings?"

"No."

"Did you and Mr. McClain discuss your testimony?"

"No, we talked about personal matters."

"What does that mean?"

"We talked about our lives and backgrounds."

Joe waited a few seconds before asking his next question. "Would you characterize yourself as romantically involved with Mr. McClain?"

David wanted to object, but Joe had the right to uncover a reason for partiality in favor of the defense. Dr. Newburn had his potential for bias. So did Anna Wilkes. Meanwhile, Mac kept grinding his teeth. If the questioning didn't end soon, he would need dentures.

Anna smiled. "Mr. McClain is a fine man. My social contact with

Mr. McClain did not develop until after I performed the testing on Peter Thomason and prepared the report I sent to the parties in this case. My testimony today is based on that report and that report alone."

"But couldn't your relationship with Mr. McClain influence your evaluation of his client in subtle ways?"

"My opinion is based on testing and generally accepted standards of psychological analysis."

"So your assessment is based solely on cold-blooded facts?"

"Not totally," Anna said. "There is a degree of opinion in every evaluation, but I think mine in this case is as objective as possible."

"Really?" Joe raised his eyebrows. "Dr. Wilkes, are you being ingenuous with this jury?"

"Ingenuous? No."

"Just checking," Joe said. "No further questions."

David called Charles Gallegly. When Pete saw him walk into the courtroom, he suddenly teared up. The kind, little man had shown him nothing but God's love and acceptance in the midst of circumstances that were harsh and cruel.

David asked Mr. Gallegly to describe his twenty-year ministry at the jail. He then introduced Pete into the story as a continuation in the line of lives that had been changed by the power of the gospel.

"How often have you been meeting with Pete?"

"Every evening this week. Before that I saw him on at least a weekly basis."

"How would you describe him to the jury?"

"I believe his conversion is real and his desire to grow as a Christian is genuine."

"Why do you say that?"

Mr. Gallegly leaned forward in the witness chair. "The Bible says you know a tree by its fruit. It's the same with a Christian whether they've been born again two weeks ago or thirty years ago. Pete is studying, praying, telling me about changes in his conduct and attitude. I've been around a lot of 'jailhouse conversions' and admit that many of them don't stick, but I believe this young man is a new person in Jesus Christ."

"What else can you tell the jury about Pete?" David asked.

Mr. Gallegly looked to Pete, who nodded.

"He told me about some incidents in his childhood. Difficult times with a man who lived with his mother and physically abused Pete when he was between the ages of eight and ten. He asked me to pray with him about what he'd gone through. That's what I did, and we closed the book on that part of his past."

"Do you believe Pete is a danger to society?"

Mr. Gallegly looked at the jury, which saw the same face that had welcomed scores of prisoners into the kingdom of God. "I'll answer this way. All my children are grown, and I would let Pete come to my house and stay with me as long as he needed a roof over his head. I would go to sleep at night without any fear and wake up the next day glad that I could be around him."

Pete rubbed his eye. Mr. Gallegly's words of trust, even in the face of the jury's verdict, were like water to his thirsty soul.

Joe was respectful in his probing, making Mr. Gallegly admit that two weeks is a short time to predict someone's future behavior and re-enforcing the often transitory nature of jailhouse religion.

"Mr. Gallegly, would you agree that physical abuse of the type you mentioned can cause a child to resent authority?"

"Yes."

"And the defendant considered this an important part of his upbringing. Important enough to mention it to you."

"He did, so we could pray about it."

"But before you prayed with him, the problem was unresolved, wasn't it?"

"I guess so," Mr. Gallegly said.

"And the defendant could still have harbored anger and resentment against authority figures based on what he suffered as a child, couldn't he?"

"Yes, that's possible."

"So, you're not telling this jury about Peter Thomason's mental state prior to your contact with him at the jail. Only your opinion about him after you met him."

"I didn't know him before."

"That's my point. Thank you." Joe took his seat.

"That's all on behalf of the defense, Your Honor," David said.

It was almost three o'clock.

"We'll take a thirty-minute break to go over the charges and proceed to closing arguments."

THIRTY-EIGHT

The winepress of eloquence.
ST. JEROME

MAC FOUND ANNA outside the courtroom.

"I apologize about the other night," he said, standing close to her so he wouldn't be overheard. "And I'm sorry about the questioning by Joe Whetstone, too. You handled it well."

"That's okay on both points," she smiled wryly. "I've testified many times, but I've never been cross-examined about my personal feelings toward one of the lawyers in the case."

Relieved that she wasn't upset with him, he said, "You also said some kind things about me that aren't justified."

"I'm entitled to my opinion. How did he know to ask about our social contacts?"

"Either a lucky guess or he's had me followed to see who I was talking to."

"Would they do that?"

"If money isn't an issue, they can do almost anything. Are you going to stay for the closing argument?"

"Yes. Are you going to do it?"

"No. It's in David's hands," Mac said.

"And God's," Anna added.

Mac pointed to the ceiling. "I'm not sure I trust him. David thought he had a promise from the Almighty that Pete wouldn't be convicted."

Anna put her hand on Mac's arm. "Don't lose hope. God can make a way where there seems to be no way."

The lawyers went into Judge Danielson's chambers to go over the jury instructions. Anna sat by herself on a bench toward the back and waited. Celeste Jamison cracked open the door of the courtroom and joined her.

"I heard about the verdict on the radio and thought I should come," Celeste said. "How long have you been here?"

"Today. I testified during the sentencing phase. All that's left are closing arguments."

"Have you talked to Mac?"

"Just for a minute."

"How is he doing?"

"Discouraged. David Moreland, the young lawyer who is helping him try the case, is going to give the closing argument."

They sat silently for a few moments.

"How have you been handling the burden of the Lord for Mac?" Celeste asked in a quiet voice.

Anna sighed. "I don't think I've cooperated very well." She told Celeste about the night at Kincaid's and finished by saying, "After I came inside the house, I had the strange feeling that there was a similarity between Mac and my husband, Jack, who committed suicide ten years ago. I'm probably off-base, but I felt Mac was a suicide risk. I haven't been able to get it out of my mind since."

"You may be right," Celeste said. "Several weeks ago, I believe the Lord told me that Mac was *'hanging by a thread.'* That sounds like life and death to me."

"Yes, it does," Anna responded soberly.

"And it explains why the Father has assigned both of us to help in our different ways."

"What is your way?" Anna asked.

Celeste didn't hide the truth. "To fast and pray. And you?"

Anna thought for a few seconds. "To show him the way home."

After meeting with the lawyers, the judge returned to the courtroom and said, "Ladies and gentlemen, the lawyers will now present their closing arguments. Mr. Whetstone, proceed for the State."

Joe thanked the jury again for the guilty verdict. "In sentencing the defendant, you may consider all the evidence presented during the first part of the case and rely on the factors that convinced you beyond a reasonable doubt of his guilt. Please show this community that you have the courage to do the rest of your duty.

"Your duty is an opportunity," Joe explained. "Because you have the power to prevent Peter Thomason from killing again. You heard the request of Alexander Hightower. He is not asking for vengeance at the loss of a daughter but pleading for the safety and security of other nineteen-year-old girls, innocent children today but potential victims of the defendant if he is allowed to live and walk the streets of Dennison Springs or some other unsuspecting town in the future. Only you can provide the protection that society needs."

As Joe talked about the aggravating circumstance of kidnapping and how it was demonstrated by the circumstances, David felt a weight come over his mind and found it difficult to jot notes. He shook his head, but the heaviness remained and he felt that his brain was running at one-tenth its normal speed. The confusion continued until he realized Joe was coming to the conclusion of his argument.

"Do not compromise with evil," the special prosecutor said. "There was no compromise with death for Angela Hightower, and none should be granted to the man who killed her. Do the right thing. Do the courageous thing. Do the just thing. Do what you need to do for your family, friends, and neighbors."

Standing directly in front of the jury box, Joe made eye contact one last time with every juror. "On behalf of all that is good and decent,

I ask you to sentence the defendant to death for committing this horrible crime."

Still trying to gather his final thoughts, David looked out one of the tall windows that lined the wall of the courthouse. It was a clear day and the mountains in the distance were etched against a pale blue background. Suddenly, out of the memory bank of a long-ago Sunday school lesson came strength from a verse in Psalm 121. "I will lift up mine eyes unto the hills, from whence cometh my help. My help cometh from the Lord, which made heaven and earth." His mind cleared, David stood to face the jury.

"Ladies and gentlemen," he began, "In many places in our world, human life is cheap. Men, women, children, and babies die, and no one seems to care, no one seems to notice. But in this country, you are not part of a mindless killing machine run by a wicked dictator. You are part of a process of American justice that affirms life as incredibly valuable, a gift from God that should not be taken away except in the most extraordinary circumstances of wanton cruelty. Today, at this moment, you hold someone's life in your hands. By your decision, Pete Thomason will live or die."

David walked over to the defense table. "We have presented the testimony of several witnesses to help you make your decision. Please consider what you heard from the witnesses who testified during the first stage of the trial and those who have come before you this afternoon." David summarized the testimony of the witnesses called by the defense, linking them together and hoping that some of the doubts that might remain about Pete's guilt would influence the jury's deliberations about his sentence. "And in addition to the testimony of Officer Davidson, Dr. Wilkes, and Mr. Gallegly, I ask you to consider something else when you retire to the jury room. I ask you to think about a single word—a word that will guide you in deciding Pete's fate.

"What is that word? It's not *mercy,* because whatever happens, Pete Thomason will be punished for the rest of his life. It's not *forgiveness,* because only those who have been wronged can extend forgiveness to those who've hurt them. It's not *revenge,* because our society has rejected the anarchy of the lynch mob."

Pete leaned forward. He didn't know what David was going to say. But somehow, he knew that the word would have significance for him, regardless of whether the jury heard it or not.

"The word I want you to think about is an ordinary word. It's not a word that standing by itself inspires emotion or pulls at your heart strings, but it's a word that is important in choosing what you do with the power entrusted into your hands. That word is *life.*

"There is no question that most or all of Pete Thomason's remaining days on earth will be spent in a penitentiary. Does a life in prison have a potential for good? Has anybody ever made a difference in society from behind prison bars? Can life have meaning no matter where it's lived?"

The nervousness David had felt at the beginning of his argument was gone. He was speaking from his heart. "In deciding your answer to my questions, please consider a few individuals who have shaped history for good from a prison cell. For two hundred years the most influential book beside the Bible among English-speaking people was written by a poor Englishman imprisoned for his religious beliefs. That book was *Pilgrim's Progress.* Millions of people have been inspired by John Bunyan's simple yet profound account of the Christian's journey through life toward the Celestial City of God. Yet that book was written in a smelly stone cell inhabited by more rats than people.

"Sixty years ago," David continued, "Dietrich Bonhoeffer wrote from a Nazi prison about the nature of Christian discipleship and the responsibility of God-honoring people to oppose tyranny. Bonhoeffer's powerful words were forged in the crucible of a prison cell."

David's voice increased in intensity. "And who can deny the influence of the apostle Paul? A self-confessed murderer, the chief of sinners, yet there has never been a man whose letters from prison have inspired more people and produced greater change for good in a world that desperately needs it. The chains that bound him proved to be the links to his most enduring influence."

David stopped, put his hands on the railing in front of the jury box and, like Joe Whetstone, made sure he had the full attention of every juror. "I can't promise you that Pete Thomason will be another John Bunyan, Dietrich Bonhoeffer, or apostle Paul. But I can promise you this, if his life is ended in an electric chair, we'll never know. *Life!* May that word echo in your hearts and minds until it becomes your answer to the issue before you."

In the hushed silence of the courtroom, David returned to his seat.

Judge Danielson cleared his throat. "Ladies and gentlemen of the jury, I will now instruct you on the law that will guide your deliberations."

Mac leaned over to David, "Good job. I couldn't have said those things and believed them the same way you do. I hope they heard you."

While the judge talked, Pete examined the now-familiar faces of the members of the jury—the faces that had unanimously decided he killed Angela. Several jurors yawned as the judge's voice droned on.

Pete didn't want to die, but the possibility of life in prison without parole was a black hole of never-ending despair. David had said life had value wherever it was lived, but the thought of spending the rest of his life incarcerated with the Cal Musgraves of the world was a terrifying prospect. Early that morning, Cal's ranting had followed him down the hallway as he left for the courthouse.

"Today's your day to fry, boy. I saw it in the night. It's a jury of death. There wasn't nothing but skeletons in the jury box. You've got a hangin' jury, and they are going to hang you high."

"Let your decision be unanimous," the judge concluded. "Notify the bailiff when you finish your deliberations."

The jury filed out for the second time.

THIRTY-NINE

God's finger touched him.
TENNYSON

THE DOOR CLOSED, and Lyman Bakerfield assumed immediate command of the jury.

"The judge said we have three choices," he said. "I'll write them on the blackboard, and we can discuss them one at a time." He found a stubby piece of chalk and listed their three options:

Death
Life without Parole
Life with Parole

Lyman pointed to one of the possibilities. "Let's start with this one."

Everyone had an opinion, but after an hour of discussion it became clear that one of the choices could be eliminated. They voted, and Lyman erased it from the blackboard.

At that point the debate became more intense. Another hour passed.

"Let's take a vote, and see where we stand," Lyman said. He put a number beside each of the remaining options on the blackboard. "Vote by the number."

John Terry tore up twelve pieces of paper and passed them around the table. Several members held the slips in their hands for several moments before making a final choice. John Terry wrote down one number, thought a moment, then changed his mind. When the slips came back to Lyman, he opened each one, called out the result, and stacked it on the table.

The vote was nine to three.

"Do you think we need to sleep on it?" one juror asked.

His proposal was greeted by a chorus of "No's!" from the others.

"Hey, I'm in the majority," he said quickly. "It was just a suggestion."

There was no movement for almost an hour, until one of the three holdouts remembered a line from one of the closing arguments and changed the minds of the other two.

"Let's have another vote to make sure," Lyman said. "All agreed raise your hand."

Twelve hands went up. "Anyone want to change their vote?" Lyman asked. "This is a huge responsibility."

Silence.

"Okay. Let's do it. John, please tell the bailiff we've made a decision."

As the jury filed in, Pete's heart was beating so loudly he wondered if Mac and David could hear it. He'd had hope before, but after the jury's verdict finding him guilty, it was hard to summon hope again. The next few moments would determine if Cal Musgrave had been right when he called down prophecies of death. Pete glanced at David, but David was battling his own demons of fear. A death sentence for Pete would haunt him for the rest of his life, bringing constant accusations of things he could have said or done differently to save his client's life. For the next few seconds, the two young men's futures were linked at a depth unknown except to those who share the most perilous circumstances.

"Have you reached a decision?" the judge asked.

Lyman Bakerfield stood. "Yes, sir."

"What is it?"

Once again, Lyman looked at the defense table. "We recommend a life sentence with possibility of parole."

Pete, David, and Mac let out a collective sigh.

It was Joe's turn to request that each juror stand and assent to the verdict. It was unanimous.

There was relief on one side of the courtroom. Anger on the other. No celebration by either.

"The defendant will come forward," Judge Danielson ordered.

Pete slowly walked forward and stood before the judge. Mac and David joined him.

"Peter Thomason, according to the verdict of the jury, I hereby sentence you to life in the Georgia State Penitentiary subject to review by the Georgia State Board of Pardons and Paroles."

The gavel fell, and Pete was quickly escorted toward the back door of the courtroom. His face red, Alexander Hightower made a move to say something to him, but one of the bailiffs stepped between them.

Mac and David watched Pete disappear from view into the Georgia prison system. Putting his papers in his briefcase, Mac asked, "Do you want to talk to any of the jurors?"

"Not now," David said. "I'm very, very tired. I probably won't be able to sleep, but I know I need to try. How about you?"

"I've talked to enough juries to last a lifetime, but it obviously didn't do me any good when it came time to pick this one."

They were clearing off the defense table when one of the alternate jurors came over to them.

"Excuse me," he said.

"Yes," Mac said.

"I would never have found your client guilty if I had been able to vote. The case against him didn't add up in my mind."

"Then I'm sorry you were an alternate," Mac said.

"Me, too. Both of you did a good job."

It was dark and chilly on the sidewalk outside as Mac and David walked slowly back to the office.

"I believe an innocent man is going to prison," Mac said bitterly. "But then, anyone who expects life to turn out right hasn't lived very long."

"Remember what I told you?" David shook his head. "I thought Pete was going to be acquitted."

"Looks like you got your wires crossed between here and heaven. It's a big universe, and with everything he has to do, God must have forgotten about Pete Thomason and Dennison Springs."

When the deputy took Pete back to his cell for the night, Crazy Cal was wide awake and raring to go.

"Did they give you the chair, boy? I know it would fit you perfect."

"Shut up, Cal," the deputy said. "He got life. He'll be out long before they unlock you from the padded cell where you're going."

"I ain't talking to you, buttercup," Cal sneered. "A life sentence is good, redhead. You ought to be shouting and jumping for joy."

Pete went quietly into his cell, but Cal refused to settle down. Pete had learned to recognize the different voices that came from the troubled man. There was the mocking voice that greeted him upon his return from court. An angry voice that cursed anyone and everything. An insane voice that talked nonsense. And the most difficult to ignore, a weeping voice that cried, wailed, and moaned pathetically for up to an hour at a time.

When it was time for lights out in the isolation block, Pete couldn't sleep. There was a small security light in the hall that cast a beam onto his bunk, and if he positioned his Bible at an angle, he could read a third of a page at a time. Turning to the Book of Exodus, he read about the miraculous deliverance of an entire nation from bondage in the land of Egypt. With tears running down he cheeks, he silently cried out to God, *Why would you do that for them and not for me? Why am I in bondage when I ought to be free?*

Mac turned off the lights and stayed at the office after David left. The adrenaline from the trial had drained out of his veins, and the black bear of depression came out of hibernation to cast its dark shadow over Mac's soul. David's speech about the potential of Pete Thomason's life in prison may have persuaded the jury, but it didn't persuade Mac. A message of hope for the future didn't have any relevance to Mac McClain. There were deeper, darker prisons than those built by men, other types of death sentences in which juries had no say.

A glimmer from a streetlight cast a beam onto the bottom drawer of Mac's desk. He pulled it open, reached in, and felt the cool weight of the pistol in his hand. Slowly, methodically, he put six bullets in the clip and snapped it into place. Holding the fully loaded gun, Mac's life-and-death debate reached a new level. He'd thought loading the gun would give him a feeling of regret and sadness, but he was surprised when it had the opposite effect. He felt excited, almost exhilarated. Now he understood how someone could end his life. It was a good thing. It wouldn't be hard to stop the pain. It would be very, very simple.

Taking a deep breath, he raised the gun up to his right temple, the open end of the barrel resting lightly against his skin. One quick inward flex of his index finger and all his pain and nightmares would end.

His excitement increased. He squeezed slightly on the trigger, but it didn't move a millimeter. He pressed harder, sure that the next sound in the room would be one that his mind wouldn't have time to process. Nothing happened. He lowered the gun and stared at it in the darkness. Turning on the lamp on his desk, he discovered the problem. He hadn't flipped off the safety.

In the lighted area of his desk beneath the lamp was a slip of paper with Anna Wilkes's car phone number on it. He should have spoken to her before he left the courthouse. Putting the gun on the table, he decided to play roulette. If the psychologist answered the phone, he would put the pistol back in the drawer. If not, the safety would not stop him a second time. He dialed the number. One, two, three, four rings.

He slowly took the phone away from his ear and lowered it toward the cradle when a voice came across the open space, "Hello."

Mac froze.

"Hello? Is anyone there?"

He raised the receiver. "It's Mac."

"Are you okay? Where are you?" Anna asked anxiously.

"At the office," he said dully.

"I'm on the road back to Chattanooga, but I'd like to talk with you. I can come back to your office."

"I'm tired. I should probably go home."

"I'd like to see you. When could we get together?"

Mac paused, debating whether he wanted to step back from the precipice of death.

"Mac? Did you hear me?"

"Yeah. I guess I'll be sleeping late tomorrow."

"How about in the afternoon?"

Mac reluctantly put the still-loaded gun back in the drawer. "What time?"

"About three o'clock at my house. You need a break, and I'd like to take you on an outing."

"Are you sure?"

"Yes," she said. "If you want to come."

"Okay."

Anna gripped the steering wheel so tightly her hands hurt. The other cars on the highway were blurs. Not since her struggles with Jack had she felt such a heaviness of heart for another person. "Please, God," she prayed. "Help him."

Mac kept his promise and pulled into Anna's driveway at three o'clock the following day. Anna came out before he could ring the doorbell. She was dressed in jeans and a sweater.

"Good afternoon," she said with a hint of uncertainty at his mood. "Jean has taken Hunter to a friend's birthday party."

"Okay," Mac said flatly. "Where to?"

"A surprise. I'll drive," she responded.

Circling to the south, they drove for several miles along a highway that followed the broad expanse of the Tennessee River.

They rode in silence. Mac was numb. The morning light had not dispelled the darkness that lay like a blanket over his soul. Anna took the Lookout Mountain exit.

"We're not going to Rock City, are we?" Mac asked. "I'm not in the mood to visit a tourist attraction."

"I wouldn't do that to you," Anna replied. "I know you're hurting."

Lookout Mountain was the name given to the end of a long ridge that stretched eastward for many miles from its beginning in Alabama to its end above the Tennessee River at Chattanooga. Driving higher, they passed homes built to catch glimpses of the spectacular views that gave the mountain its name. Many of the older houses were made from rocks chipped away from the sides of the ridge and reshaped into human dwelling places.

The most prominent feature on top of the mountain was Covenant College, a small Presbyterian school. The college's trustees had converted a bankrupt resort hotel and casino into a place of higher learning. The main casino, built in the early 1900s, housed the cafeteria, and the blackjack tables had given way to the faculty dining room. The bar where illegal liquor flowed during Prohibition now served iced tea and 2-percent milk. Some of the best spots for viewing the surrounding area were from the college campus, and unlike Rock City, there was no charge to see seven states. It was sunny and warm in the late afternoon sun. A light breeze stirred the few remaining dead leaves on the trees.

Anna parked the car, and they walked along a path that ran behind a dormitory to an overlook point on the east side of the ridge. They sat down on a concrete bench. From their vantage point, they could see the massive shadow of the mountain inch forward across the city and valley that stretched out before them. Neither spoke as they let their eyes roam back and forth across the panorama.

Anna turned toward Mac. "Can we talk?" she asked.

"Yeah," Mac sighed. "I won't bite off your head. There's not much fight left in me right now."

"Do you like the view?" she asked.

Mac nodded. "There's no place like a mountaintop."

"This is another place of perspective," Anna said. "Like Missionary Ridge. When I come here, I see the things of life as very small and God as very great."

"I see the small part," Mac grunted. "People are very small—too small for God to notice or care about."

"Are you saying that because of the trial?"

"Yes," he said, staring straight ahead. "And other things . . ."

Anna sat quietly for several moments. "It's your family, isn't it?"

Mac nodded without looking at her.

There were many things Anna Wilkes could have said, but out of the stillness of her spirit came the answer for Mac McClain.

"Mac, you've been wounded beyond the ability of the mind to comprehend. I don't have an explanation for what has happened in your life, but I believe God wants to heal you."

Mac stared at the ground. "It's not possible."

Two tears streaked down Anna's cheeks and made tiny dark spots on her jeans, but when she spoke, her voice remained calm. "Let God touch you," she said slowly.

And Mac's world stopped.

Let God touch you. The right words in the right time have the power to change the course of a human life. *Let God touch you.* Something inside Mac reached out its hand to grasp heaven's healing for his broken heart. He stood and took a couple of steps forward. It wasn't an explanation he needed; it was a touch. But how? He began his usual process of internal debate. How did it work? What would replace the pain that had become such a familiar companion? Familiar pain can be better than an unknown alternative. Letting go of brokenness held its own fear. But the divine message cast down every opposing argument. *Let God touch you.* Although he couldn't analyze it, Mac knew this was his chance to come out of the darkness of depression and into a sunrise of hope. Four simple words halted the suicidal lunacy that had been hurtling Mac toward self-annihilation.

Looking along the tree line, he saw a hawk perched on top of a twisted old hickory tree. The bird spread its wings as if to take flight but only fluttered them for a few seconds before folding them back in place. Mac watched and waited for the bird to leave the barren limb and launch out over the valley below. The bird didn't move. Mac knew the bird was meant to soar above the earth. But it refused to let go of a dead branch and glide on the wind over the valley. *You can do it*, Mac thought.

You can do it, came the internal response. Mac pondered the reply for a moment and made up his mind. He had nothing to lose but the pain that had threatened to destroy his life. Taking a deep breath, he silently prayed, *Lord, touch me.*

And God answered—washing away in a river of healing the ancient heartache of Mac McClain's soul. In a moment of unhindered insight, Mac realized that lifeless, dead sorrow didn't honor his wife and sons or nurture his memories of those he'd cherished. God touched him.

When Mac opened his eyes, the bird had risen, sweeping in a broad arc through the air, sustained by unseen currents beneath its wings. And a weightlessness entered Mac's soul. He knew that he, too, could release his grip on the pain of earth. Healing flowed. Hope followed. Peace settled into his spirit. Stress and tension flowed out of his body. Turning, he faced Anna, her outline framed by the setting sun behind her.

"You're right." he said, putting his hand on his chest. "He did it. God touched me."

FORTY

A covenant with death and an agreement with hell.
WILLIAM LLOYD GARRISON

MIKE AND BART CONAN sat across from each other at the glass-topped table in the furnished apartment. The brothers had eaten a late lunch: two frozen microwave Salisbury steak dinners with mashed potatoes, green beans, and a soggy dinner roll. Piles of lottery tickets covered one end of the table. In four months they had spent $20,000 playing every game available at the convenience store near the entrance to the apartment complex. Currently, they were only down $8,000. The two men bought so many tickets some of the regular customers complained to the manager about waiting in line, but nobody had the nerve to say anything directly to the brothers. This week the eight-state jackpot known as the Big Game would reach $40,000,000, and they were going to buy $2,000 worth of tickets. On the counter in the kitchen were the keys to a midnight purple Lincoln.

"He was convicted but didn't get the chair," Mike said, looking closely at the article in the Atlanta paper.

"Life without parole?" Bart asked.

"Naw. With parole."

"Ricky Banner only served twelve years on his life sentence."

"But that was armed robbery, not murder. Nobody in my cellblock with a life sentence for murder served less than twenty years."

"Well, whatever time he does, I think we need to drink to his health."

Bart went to the kitchen and poured two eight-ounce tumblers of whiskey.

"Here's to hard time at Hardwick Correctional Institute," Mike said, referring to the facility where prisoners Pete's age were kept until they turned thirty.

A grim-faced Alexander Hightower backed out of Spencer's driveway for the last time. Devastated and distraught by Angela's letters produced during the trial, Sarah Hightower had come home and not left the house since the verdict. Alexander had a colder, but no less intense fury.

"Okay," Spencer said, stepping back from Alex, who had barged through the front door as soon as it opened. "I'll never come over to your house again. I won't phone either."

Alex pointed his finger at Spencer's chest. "I don't want you on the boards of any of the family businesses. I never want to walk in a room and see you again. I'll pay your director fees, but don't come to the meetings. You can live off your trust income. Do you understand?"

"Yeah."

"As of today, forget you have a brother."

Spencer held up his hands. "Okay, but don't make me sound like I was the murderer."

"I don't know what you are, Spencer," Alex said with disgust. "I just want you out of my life—forever."

Shaken, Spencer called Dr. Newburn as soon as Alex left and told him what had happened.

"Alexander may cool down after time passes," the psychiatrist said, trying to calm the waters. "I'll wait for a good time to talk to him and Sarah, too."

"The sooner the better. In the meantime, I want you to increase my monthly distribution."

"Why?" the doctor asked. "You receive a generous allowance already."

"Because I want more money. I'm not in high school. And who knows, Alex may change his mind and cut off my other sources of income."

"Why do you want more money? Is there anything you need?"

"It's not what I need; it's what I want. I've had some extra expenses recently."

The doctor hesitated. "I'll have to think about it and get back to you."

"What is there to think about?" Spencer said angrily. "I'm old enough to make my own decisions. There's no way my rate of withdrawal has touched the main portion of the trust."

"Of course not." Dr. Newburn reassured him. "I need to get an update from the investment people, but you're set for life. The stock market has been going through the ceiling."

"Then, follow my orders," Spencer demanded.

"I have a responsibility to protect you," the doctor said, making one last effort to reason with the beneficiary of the trust.

"You can fulfill your responsibility by doing what I tell you to do with my money."

"I hear you," the psychiatrist said soothingly. "I'll check and get back with you."

Spencer paused. "And you'd better calm Alexander down before he changes his will."

"Did he mention that?"

"No, but I don't want him changing the spillover provisions of his trust into my trust."

"That trust would never come into play unless Alexander and Sarah were killed in a common disaster. Something like a car wreck or plane crash."

"I know, but people need to plan ahead."

"Okay," the doctor said. "I'll talk with the investment firm and call you back later in the week."

Late Sunday night, Mike answered the cell phone they kept in the apartment. Only one person had the number.

"What?" he asked, motioning for Bart to come closer and put his ear near the phone.

"Are you ready for number two?" the voice asked.

"So soon?"

"Things are happening that could cause problems."

"We need to talk before we do anything else," Mike insisted.

"What do you mean? We had a deal—$100,000 each plus the car."

"Well, the car makes me nervous. I read in the paper that they lifted a paint sample from the pickup that almost ran us off the road."

"That was stupid, driving like moonshiners up the mountain. Just sell the car and buy something else."

"If I sell it, I'll take a big loss and can't get anything as nice."

"Okay. I'll toss in another $10,000, but no more. I can get someone else to do this for less than you two."

"Some crack head maybe," Mike said.

The speaker ignored the comment. "Leave the car unlocked tonight. There will be $55,000 in a briefcase waiting for you in the backseat in the morning. The balance when the job is done. And I want it done quick."

"You're the man."

The phone clicked off.

"Are we really going to sell the car?" Bart asked.

"Not yet. I need it for one more job."

Monday morning, Mac came in late to the office. The weight was gone from his chest, and the new hope he'd received on Lookout Mountain had not fled as he feared. God's touch remained.

He opened the top drawer of his desk, took out the bottle of pills, and held it in his hand for several seconds. Their power was broken. He dropped the bottle into the trash can. In a few seconds they were joined by the bullets from his father's pistol. Case closed. Mac shut the drawer, checked the time on the old grandfather clock, and began the rest of his life.

The phone buzzed. "Judge Danielson phoned earlier and wants to see you this morning," Mindy said.

"Thanks. I know what he wants. Call David and ask him to come over here immediately. I want to talk to him before I see the judge."

Mac walked down the hall to the library. In a couple of minutes, there was a knock on the door and David came in.

"Have a seat," Mac said. "The judge wants to see me this morning. My guess is that he is going to relieve us from further representation for Pete. Now that the trial is over and questioning Mr. Doolittle is no longer an issue, Gene Nelson can handle the appeal. What do you think?"

David shook his head. "The case isn't over."

Mac nodded. "I agree. But the county will not pay us to do an appeal when Gene is already on the payroll."

"So it would be pro bono?" David asked.

"Only in part," Mac answered. "I want to make you an offer you can't refuse. I'm going to hire you to assist with the appeal and pay you $5,000 to write the brief for the appellate court. The county will give us the transcript of the trial free since Gene would have needed one anyway."

David's mouth dropped open. "I don't know what to say."

"Try, 'yes.' Can you use an extra five grand?"

"I don't have to think about that." David smiled broadly.

"Okay, it's a deal?"

"Yes, sir."

"Let's go talk to the judge together."

When they were seated in the familiar office, Judge Danielson said, "I didn't want to waste any time approving payment for your work and releasing you from the Thomason case. You both did a good job."

Leaning back in his chair and, looking at David, he added, "You're going to be a fine lawyer, Mr. Moreland."

"Thank you, sir."

Mac spoke, "Judge, David and I talked this morning. We'd like to keep the Thomason case and handle the appeal pro bono."

Surprised, the judge sat up. "Are you sure?"

"Yes."

"You don't want to think about it for a few days and decide after the trial gets out of your system?"

Mac shook his head. "We believe we need to keep going."

"All right," the judge said. "File your motions, and I'll have the transcript prepared at county expense. Mac, you've made Gene Nelson's day. Again."

Mac dictated a motion for new trial and spent the rest of the morning opening mail neglected the previous week.

He called Ray Morrison.

"Yeah," the detective said, "I read about the verdict in the paper. Tough loss, but you can't ever tell with a jury. Did you talk to any of them afterward?"

"Only an alternate who said he wouldn't have convicted."

"That figures."

"I'm going to handle the appeal," Mac said. "Would you have any interest in further investigation? You'd be working for me, not the county."

"Could I get my new investigator to help if it doesn't cost you extra?"

"New investigator? I didn't know you were thinking about hiring someone."

"It came up kind of sudden," Ray drawled. "The guy needs a temporary job, and I was tired of waiting on you to make up your mind."

"Who is it?"

"He's new to town, but he'd be a good one to work on the Thomason case. It's Harry O'Ryan."

Mac laughed. "You're another Mother Teresa, taking in homeless kids off the street."

"Her group has their hands full in India, so I thought I would pick up the slack in Dennison Springs. Harry is finishing up the alcohol treatment program and will be able to start as soon as I need him."

"Okay. Let me give you your first assignment. You remember the Italian Restaurant where Pete and Angela ate the evening of the murder?"

"Yeah, I talked to the manager a couple of times on the phone. He said it was a busy place and no one remembered anything."

"I want you to visit in person."

"Sounds good. I like spaghetti."

"Get a double order, but keep Harry away from the vino."

—

Monday evening Charles Gallegly visited Pete.

"How long will it be before you're eligible for parole?" he asked.

Pete sighed. "Mac said the minimum is about eighteen years, but it could be longer. Right now, a year seems like forever. I read in the Bible this morning that each day has enough trouble of its own. That's the way I feel."

"Take it one day at a time."

"I know that." Pete tapped the table with his fingers. "I've also been thinking a lot about the closing argument David made in my case. You know, about doing something good while I'm in jail."

"Any ideas?"

"Cal Musgrave. Have you ever tried to talk to him?"

"I remember one of the first times he was locked up," the older man said. "It's been at least fifteen years ago. He was angry back then and wouldn't have anything to do with me. From what I hear he's in worse shape now than he was then."

"Do you think he could be helped?"

Mr. Gallegly nodded. "As long as someone is breathing, there is hope."

"I'm crammed next to him twenty-two hours a day," Pete said thoughtfully. "Maybe the reason I'm in the isolation block is to help Cal."

"You're not starting out easy." Mr. Gallegly smiled. "Cal reminds me of a hopeless case in the Bible. Everybody had given up on this man until he met Jesus."

Mr. Gallegly read the story in Luke 8 of the demon-possessed man who lived among the tombs.

When he finished, Pete said, "That's Cal all right."

"Do you want to pray about it?" the older man suggested.

"Sure."

So, with the simple faith of a young believer unspoiled by doubt or failure, Pete Thomason asked the Lord Jesus to do the same thing for Crazy Cal Musgrave that he did for another tortured soul two thousand years before.

When Pete returned to his cell, Cal was quiet. Pete sat down on the floor beside the opening in the door.

"Cal. Are you awake?"

"I'm awake now. Why don't you shut up?"

"Hey, did you know Jesus could set you free from all the junk that's driving you nuts?"

Cal spewed a long string of profanity, then said, "Does that answer you?"

"No. I'm not talking to that voice, I'm talking to Cal," Pete said.

"Redhead, you're crazier than I am. Go to sleep."

"That's the real you, isn't it, Cal?"

"Who do you think is in here with me?"

"Cal, I read in the Bible about a man who was more tormented than you are. Jesus can set you free."

"Okay. Why don't you tell your friend Jesus to come by in a couple of hours and get me out of this stinking cell. That would be a big help."

"It's a different kind of freedom," Pete persevered. "Something that happens on the inside so you can have it wherever you go."

Cal delivered another string of profanity and started crying out in the weeping voice.

Pete tried to say a few more things, but it was no use. Cal's body was in his cell, but the rest of him was in a place where Pete couldn't and didn't want to go.

Pete picked up his Bible and found several other passages that described the ministry of Jesus to people like Cal. Trying to reach Cal would be a goal. A goal would give him a reason for living—a reason to be behind bars, a purpose for each day.

FORTY-ONE

Italia! O Italia!
LORD BYRON

CHARLES GALLEGLY and his volunteers had a special meeting with prisoners on Tuesday. Pete spoke for a couple of minutes to the group. After he finished, several inmates came up to him and asked questions. Charles Gallegly stood to the side and enjoyed watching the young disciple take his first steps. As the older man was leaving the jail, one of the deputies stopped him.

"Mr. Gallegly, the sheriff wants to see you before you leave."

He followed the deputy to Leonard Bomar's office.

"Have a seat, Charles," the sheriff said. "Did you have a good meeting with the men?"

"Yes. Pete Thomason spoke for a few minutes."

"Glad to hear it, and Thomason is the one I wanted to talk to you about. Normally, I would handle this myself, but the officers on duty tell me you're visiting Thomason on a regular basis, and I wanted your input before I took any action."

"How can I help?"

"I'm thinking about moving him back in with the general jail population. His lawyer has filed a motion for a new trial so he's going to be here for a while during the appeal, and I don't think he poses a threat to the other prisoners. There is only one problem."

"What?"

"He says he doesn't want to go, claims he has a plan to help Cal Musgrave. Do you know anything about this?"

"Yes. We talked about it."

"Crazy Cal? Why?"

"Pete's praying that Cal will be set free from whatever is tormenting him."

Sheriff Bomar's face went totally blank for a moment. "Did you put him up to this, Charles?"

"It wasn't my idea, but I didn't discourage him. Pete's motivation is good, and who else cares about Cal?"

"Cal is a hopeless case," the sheriff said matter-of-factly. "We're expecting authorization any day from Atlanta to send him to Milledgeville for psychiatric detention."

"Then, there is no harm in Pete praying for Cal until he leaves.

The sheriff rubbed his chin. One thing about law enforcement—something new popped up every time he thought he'd seen and heard it all. "Oh, why not," he said. "It can't hurt anything."

Dr. Newburn called Spencer. "I have a surprise for you."

"What is it?"

"A trip to London this weekend. Doctor's orders. I think you could use a break from all that's been going on."

"And stay at the Savoy?"

"Of course. I remember the junket you enjoyed so much last year. This one should be even better. A limo will take you to the airport at ten on Tuesday. I checked with the investment people, and I have an extra fifty grand to give you as spending money for the trip."

"Sounds better and better," Spencer said. "I need to get out of town and forget about all that's happened."

"And don't give up on Alexander and Sarah," Dr. Newburn added. "Leave that to me."

Thursday morning Ray and the newest graduate of the Echota County Alcohol and Drug Abuse Program were on their way to Atlanta. Peggy had fixed breakfast for them, and they each had a fresh cup of coffee nestled in the drink holders in Ray's truck.

"Now that we're comrades in arms, I can give you a full report of my work on Pete's case," Ray said. He spent the next fifty miles telling Harry all he knew about the Thomason investigation.

Alberto's Restaurant didn't open until 11:00 A.M., and Ray gave Harry a quick tour of the places of interest to those involved in the case. They drove past the driveway that led to Alexander and Sarah's mansion.

"The house is back there somewhere," Ray said. "Old Mr. Hightower bought it and left it to Alexander after he died."

Harry leaned forward and peered down the twisting, tree-lined drive. "What about the younger brother who testified at the trial? Where does he live?"

"Spencer. That's our next stop."

They parked at the surveillance point across the street from the entrance to the neighborhood as a white limo drove through the gate.

"Spencer has a nice place but nothing like his brother," Ray said. "I've seen it up close, but we won't try to get past the guards today."

"And you think Spencer is the one who arranged the murder?" Harry asked as Ray turned around in the parking lot and pulled back onto the roadway.

"Probably."

"But other than anger at Angela for telling him to bug off and jealousy of his older brother, you don't have a motive?"

"From what Mac told me about Spencer, either of those reasons would be enough. He's got money to burn and could pay professional hit men. Based on the way Pete was set up, that's what happened."

Harry ate the last biscuit he'd been saving since they left Dennison

Springs. "Too bad you couldn't track down the car that ran the old man off the road," he said.

"Yeah, Mac and I felt it would have blown the State's case out of the water. We can still try to locate it, but testimony about the car was mentioned in one of the newspaper articles about the trial. If the real killer reads the article, the midnight purple Lincoln will be repainted or locked up in a garage somewhere by now."

"What next?" Harry asked.

Ray checked his watch. "On to Alberto's. We can beat the lunchtime crowd."

A plain-looking, one-story red-brick building surrounded by an asphalt parking lot, Alberto's was an ugly duckling on the outside. A fluid neon sign, "Alberto's Italian Restaurant," burned in red at an angle above the darkly stained wooden front door. Inside, Ray felt as if he had stepped out of the United States into a café in Naples or Venice. White tablecloths, a bottle of imported wine on each table, original paintings of Italian scenes on the walls, waiters who spoke English as a second language—it was not the place for Chicago pizza or West Coast vegetable lasagna.

Ray asked the first busboy who walked by to take him to the manager and received a blank stare. On his second try, he was rewarded with a nod, and in a few minutes, a small, olive-skinned man with a thin mustache appeared from the back of the restaurant.

"Mr. Giovanelli?" Ray asked, using the name Vicki had given him.

"Yes. How may I help you?"

Ray introduced himself, then said, "I talked to you a couple of times on the phone, and I'm sorry to bother you again. But I was wondering—"

"Ray, come here," Harry interrupted. "You need to see this."

Harry was still in the foyer. On one wall were several framed newspaper articles praising the restaurant and a black-and-white picture of Mr. and

Mrs. Giglio, the smiling owners of Alberto's. On the opposite wall was a bulletin board covered with pictures of patrons eating at the restaurant. At the bottom left-hand corner of this pictorial collage was a Polaroid snapshot of a young couple sitting at a cozy table. It was Pete and Angela.

"This is the couple," Ray said, pointing to the picture. "Who would have taken this photo?"

Mr. Giovanelli squinted at the picture. "That's Luigi's table. I'll get him."

Luigi was helping in the kitchen during lunch and understood only enough English to wait on tables where everything on the menu was in Italian.

"Ask him about the couple?" Ray asked.

Mr. Giovanelli translated, listened to the reply, then said, "Yes, he took the picture with a camera we keep at the restaurant. They were such a nice-looking couple, he thought about the bulletin board and wanted to include their photograph."

"What else does he remember about them?"

Mr. Giovanelli asked the question, and Ray waited while Luigi told what sounded like a long, involved story.

"The girl had been to Milan, Luigi's hometown, and knew a few words in Italian."

"Is that all he said?"

Mr. Giovanelli smiled. "You have to understand. When Luigi talks about Milan, he is talking about a place he loves. He told me about every place the girl had visited and added his own comments and memories."

Ray saw two half-full wineglasses and a tall bottle on the table in front of Pete and Angela. Pointing at the glasses, he asked, "Can you tell from the picture what they had to drink?"

Mr. Giovanelli asked the question and another long answer followed, complete with gestures and hand motions.

"Luigi says a couple of men in the restaurant called Luigi over and bought a very expensive bottle of wine that comes from Luigi's home province. The grapes are unique to a small section of northern Italy and—"

"So two men bought a bottle of wine," Ray interrupted. "What else does he remember?"

"Sir, I'm only translating for you."

Ray apologized, "I'm sorry. Take your time. If I need a lesson on rare wines of northern Italy to find out what Luigi knows, I'm your student."

The restaurant manager continued, "The men had a glass of wine themselves then asked Luigi to take a complimentary glass to the young man and woman. Luigi took over two glasses of wine and snapped the picture you see on the board."

"Who poured the glasses of wine?"

In a moment, the manager said, "He doesn't know. There have been a lot of bottles of wine opened here since then."

Ray and Harry exchanged a look.

"Does he remember what the men looked like?"

Once again a long dialogue took place in Italian. Even Mr. Giovanelli seemed surprised by Luigi's comments and asked several questions himself. Ray went past the point of frustration into a state of enforced calm.

Finally, Mr. Giovanelli turned toward him. "The police never talked to Luigi—he wasn't working when they came to the restaurant asking questions. And I didn't know the girl in the picture was the one who was murdered when you called before."

"What did he say about the two men?" Ray said through slightly clenched teeth.

"Oh, the two men were in their late twenties or early thirties, both with blond hair cut very close to their heads. What do you call it? A buzz?"

"Yes."

"The men went over to the table where the couple was sitting. Apparently the young people had too much to drink because the men helped them out of the restaurant. Luigi was concerned and looked out the window in the kitchen. They drove off in two cars. One was yellow and the other one was—" he asked Luigi a question.

"Did I hear the Italian word for purple?" Ray asked.

"That's right," Mr. Giovanelli said with a puzzled look. "He said it was a big, dark purple car. The couple sat in the backseat. One of the men drove the yellow car, and the other drove the purple car. Luigi guessed they all knew each other and were helping the couple get home safely."

"Who paid for the couple's meal?"

A brief exchange followed, and Mr. Giovanelli said, "He's not sure."

"Does he know that the girl was killed that night?" Ray asked.

"Should I ask him that?"

Ray studied Luigi's face for a second. He couldn't see the point of making the waiter regret that he should have done something else to avert a horrible murder.

"No. It may be necessary later, but not now. May I have the picture?"

"Of course. We take them down from time to time and replace them with new ones. This one would have been thrown away in a few days anyway."

Back in the truck, Ray said, "They put Rohypnol in one glass and GHB in the other. Then they watched. When the drugs began to take effect, they took Angela and Pete out to the parking lot and dumped them in the back of the Lincoln."

"Let's call Mac," Harry said, delighted that he had participated in a major breakthrough in the case. "This real private detective stuff is better than what I've seen on TV."

Ray, thinking about all the dead-end leads he'd followed over the past thirty years, rolled his eyes and didn't respond.

After Ray gave his report to Mac, he asked, "Is there anything else you want us to do in Atlanta?"

"Not now. You've hit a home run already. Come home and we'll decide what to do next."

Later that evening, Mac and David met at the jail to talk with Pete. Their client listened intently to the summary of Ray's conversation with the waiter at the restaurant.

"No, I can't remember anybody," he said. "Were the two men hired by Spencer Hightower?"

"It's looking more and more that way," Mac said. "They knew what they were doing and waited until the drugs took effect before approaching you and Angela."

"Are you going to tell the police?"

"Not yet. They think they have the killer in this jail, and it will take more than theories to open the door to your cell."

FORTY-TWO

How are the mighty fallen!
2 SAMUEL 1:25 (KJV)

ALEXANDER HIGHTOWER was a creature of habit. Three mornings a week he exercised at the Buckhead Fitness Club, but every Saturday he woke up at 5:00 A.M. for a five-mile run along the tree-lined streets where Atlanta's richest inhabitants lived. By 5:10, his high-tech running shoes were hitting the sidewalk down a hill and around the corner from the entrance to his house.

Mike and Bart knew the route Alex followed and selected their spot with care. Near the three-mile point there was a break in the sidewalk as the street went up a steep hill and passed in front of a vacant lot that sloped abruptly away from the roadway. Mike parked the Lincoln around the corner. Bart waited behind a large tree in the center of the curve with his weapon of choice for the day, a thirty-two-inch metal baseball bat, tightly gripped in his black-gloved right hand. He peered around the tree, straining to see any movement coming up the hill. Through the morning mist, he saw Alex's head bowed down as he began the ascent up the hill, and in a few seconds he heard Alex's labored breathing as he neared the spot where he waited.

The first blow smashed Alex's right ankle and cut him down like a blade of grass underneath a lawn mower. The second, which followed so quickly that there was no time for a scream of pain to escape his lips, landed on the left side of his skull about two inches above his ear. Alex fell forward onto the pavement, and blood spurted from his head onto the roadway. Bart grunted and swung the bat twice more, striking Alex in the lower back.

Hearing the thud of the blows through the open window of the car, Mike put out his cigarette and drove around the corner. Bart jumped out of the way of the car, and his brother aimed the left front tire of the heavy vehicle at Alex's head. In the predawn light, Mike misjudged the position of the wheel, and instead of hitting the unconscious man's head, ran over his outstretched left arm. The bones in Alex's wrist snapped like dry twigs.

Mike stuck his head out the window and hissed at Bart, "I missed him! I've got to back up and make another run at him."

Bart opened the passenger door and got into the car. "Forget it! He's dead! Let's get outa here."

"No!" Mike jerked the car in reverse and backed up several feet. He looked in the rearview mirror and saw headlights coming up the hill. "Someone's coming!" Mike stopped the car. "Don't move. The car will block the body from view," he said.

A delivery truck for the Atlanta paper rumbled over the top of the hill and around the Lincoln.

Bart dropped the bat in the floorboard. "Let's go! We don't have time to do anything else!"

Mike pulled into the driveway of a large, three-story brick house located across the road from the vacant lot, quickly backed out into the street, and drove around the corner.

Bart looked over his shoulder, "Do you think the paper guy saw anything?"

Mike looked in the rearview mirror. "No. It's dark and the body was on the ground. Was he still alive?"

"He's road kill. But man, we've got to get rid of this car."

"Yeah. First thing this morning."

Hidden in the ivy that gracefully wrapped itself around the mailbox beside the driveway where Mike turned around, a surveillance camera that started running as soon as Mike pulled into the driveway recorded the car's movements for fifteen seconds with silent, impersonal passivity. The owners of the house, Mr. and Mrs. Bertram Kingsley, had decided on the spur of the moment to fly to New York and attend a couple of Broadway shows. They would not be back until Monday evening.

A bleary-eyed, tense Sarah Hightower had been sitting in the surgical waiting room of Piedmont Hospital for four hours, not sure if she could endure the loss of another loved one. She stood up when two doctors, dressed in surgical scrubs, came through the door and called her name.

"Mrs. Hightower?" a small gray-haired man asked.

Sarah nodded and her voice shaking said, "Yes. Is he—?"

"He's alive. I'm Dr. Thurman, a surgeon."

"How bad is it?" Sarah asked anxiously.

"Your husband had a severe concussion with a subdural hematoma or bruise that is approximately four inches square. He is unconscious and heavily sedated. If the blow to his head had been forward another inch he would have died instantly. The amount of swelling he experiences over the next few hours will be critical."

"So he's in a coma?" Sarah put her hand on the back of the chair to steady herself.

"Yes, but I'm more optimistic than when we first saw him. It was touch-and-go for a while. This is Dr. Rankin, an orthopedist."

A younger doctor, the orthopedist, said, "Your husband also suffered comminuted fractures to his right ankle and left wrist. *Comminuted* means there were multiple, broken bone fragments. We put the pieces of bone back in place and secured them with screws and pins. It's impossible to predict exactly, but he should have reasonable function and mobility for everyday purposes."

"But a new problem has developed," Dr. Thurman added.

"What?" Sarah asked, not sure how much more she could bear.

"Both of his kidneys were severely damaged, and we cannot save them. They're gone."

"That won't kill him, will it?"

"No. He could survive by using a dialysis machine for the rest of his life, but dialysis causes its own host of problems."

"Could he receive a transplant?"

"Probably yes. We wanted to ask you about that. Are his parents alive?"

"No."

"Siblings?"

Sarah paused. "He has a younger brother."

The Sunday morning sunlight exploded into Mac's bedroom. Propping up a pillow to shield himself from the intrusion, he rolled over and went back to sleep. When he got up a couple of hours later, his plan for the day was three cups of coffee and the newspaper. As he walked up the driveway with the paper, he thought about Pete, a young man wrongfully deprived of even a short stroll down a country road.

Mac dropped the paper on the kitchen table, walked into the living room, and stared out the large window beside the fireplace. Restless, his lazy agenda didn't match his mood. He didn't want to stay home; he wanted to go out. It was Sunday, and the only place to go on Sunday in Dennison Springs was church. Mac checked the clock. It was too late for Sunday school, and the class would be in the doldrums after Georgia's disappointing loss to Florida the previous day. But he could still make it to the eleven o'clock worship service at church. He went into the bathroom to shave and shower.

The church was more crowded than usual, and Mac had to sit in the second row, so close to the front that he could see a spot where Archie cut himself shaving earlier that morning. The minister read a passage from Isaiah 53 that sounded as obscure to Mac's ear as "taste and see that the Lord is good" had several weeks before.

"Look at verse six," the minister said. "'We all, like sheep, have gone astray, each of us has turned to his own way.' 'We all' is the Bible's way of saying 'you all,' and that means everybody. Most Presbyterians are well-fed, well-clothed, financially secure, and don't think they've wandered from the fold. They feel safe and secure, but worldly security is not the same as spiritual safety. You can be debt-free with enough zero-coupon bonds to keep you comfortable if you live to be a hundred." Mac winced at the mention of zero-coupon bonds—he had a drawer full. "But there is no abiding safety for a sheep apart from a close relationship with the Good Shepherd."

Archie swept his hand across the congregation. "We were created to live in close, obedient relationship with a loving God. We go astray when we insist on self-focused control of our lives. We are so used to seeking and maintaining selfish control at home, work, and in relationships with others that it sounds radical to suggest there is another way to live.

"How serious is this problem?" he asked, raising his voice. "Read the rest of the verse, 'and the Lord has laid on him the iniquity of us all.' That's serious. Going our own way is not a casual choice of lifestyle that escapes God's notice. It is a fundamental part of the burden of sin placed upon Jesus Christ as the sacrifice for our sins. Iniquity speaks of the deepest level of sin within us, and for most of us, that means exercising control over our lives to the exclusion of God's authority and influence."

Mac was feeling very, very uncomfortable. He looked at his watch and wondered how much longer Archie would keep probing. Mac had never been unfaithful to his wife, misappropriated a client's funds, or stolen anything since he was twelve. But there was no doubt that he had exercised control over his life. It had never dawned on him that this was wrong. The day before, he had asked God to touch him with healing power; but was there something more?

As if hearing Mac's silent inquiry, Archie said, "Some of you are wondering how to respond. You're hesitant or afraid to take a step toward God. Don't be. Submit your will to God, yield control of your life to the Lord Jesus Christ, and begin the adventure of living as a member of the kingdom of God."

Mac was wiggling in his seat like a schoolboy waiting for recess on a beautiful spring afternoon. When Archie ended the sermon and said, "Let's pray," Mac quickly closed his eyes and bowed his head to shut out the unsettling sensations of the moment. But instead of relieving his inner turmoil, closing his eyes sealed him in with his own thoughts. At the center of his thinking, he saw the truth that he had never, ever yielded control of his life to Jesus Christ. He believed intellectually, but yielding his will was something totally different.

Archie prayed, "Lord, if there is anyone this morning who wants to relinquish control of their life and submit to the loving authority of Jesus, enable them to cross that line. In their own words, in their own way, hear their prayer." He paused.

For Mac, it was a moment of decision. He waited. Archie waited. God waited. Mac made his choice.

Okay, he prayed.

Mac's one-word prayer may have been one of the shortest prayers of surrender ever recorded in heaven, but a prayer doesn't have to be long-winded or theologically precise to satisfy God. It only has to be an honest response of the human heart to the influence of the Holy Spirit. On those counts, Mac scored 100 percent.

After the service, Celeste Jamison came up to him in the foyer.

"Good morning, Mac. Are you recovered from the trial?"

"Partway," he shrugged. "I saw you at the courthouse but didn't want to talk to anyone after the verdict."

"I understand."

"What did you think of Archie's sermon?" Mac asked, shaking his head. "I mean, it was the story of my life."

Celeste opened her eyes wider and nodded. "It's everyone's story."

"I admit I was uncomfortable when he talked about giving up control of my life to God, but in the end I saw it was the only real option any of us have . . ."

Celeste waited.

Mac looked at Celeste, and she saw something new in his eyes yet familiar to her heart. "During the prayer at the end, I did what he suggested. Imagine," he said a bit sheepishly. "A fifty-six-year-old man like me reacting like this to a sermon."

Tears instantly welled behind Celeste's eyelids. "No. It makes perfect sense," she said.

Still focused on what he'd heard and his reaction to it, Mac didn't notice and moved away through the crowd toward the door.

"See you later," she said hoarsely as he disappeared.

Celeste went into the prayer room, sat down, and dried her eyes with a tissue. She unlocked the bookcase containing the prayer journals, and after opening several books, found the volume where, many years before, Laura's prayer for Mac's salvation had been recorded. In the margin, Celeste wrote the day's date, followed by the word, *"Answered!"*

Her husband stuck his head in the door of the prayer room. "Are you all right?"

"Yes," she said. "Let's go out to lunch. I'd like some soup."

FORTY-THREE

The finger of God.
LUKE 11:20 (KJV)

EARLY MONDAY MORNING, David, sitting in the now-familiar surroundings of Mac's library, was organizing the exhibits from the trial. Three neat stacks of papers containing lists of names lay on the table: the Lincoln owners, the members of the jury pool, and Dr. Newburn's patients. Getting up, he went into the reception area.

"Mindy, could you help me for a few minutes?" he asked.

"Is this another plan to make fun of me?" she asked, looking down her nose.

"No, it has nothing to do with any kind of charges."

Mindy followed him into the library. He handed her the list of Lincoln owners and picked up the sheets of paper containing the names of the people summoned for jury duty.

"Please read the names on your list so I can see if there are any matches with the members of the jury pool."

Mindy slowly read the sixty-six names while David kept the names of the jurors in front of him.

"That's it," she said in a few minutes.

There were no matches.

"Okay. Let's compare your list of midnight purple Lincoln owners with Dr. Newburn's patients."

Because neither the patient list nor the Lincoln owners' list was in alphabetical order, it was a tedious process. Mindy made another copy of the car owner list, and they each went through the six pages of psychiatric patients, frequently flipping papers back and forth.

There was a Brenda Morgan who bought a Lincoln and a Brandon Morgan treated by Dr. Newburn, but neither found an identical match until Mindy turned over her last sheet of paper.

"This looks familiar," she said. "Michael Stenson Conan. I think he's on the Lincoln list, too."

David quickly ran down the sheet of Lincoln owners. "Here it is. Mike Conan."

Mindy circled the name with a pen. "It's close enough for me."

"Yeah. I'll tell Mac when he gets here."

Mac arrived a few minutes later. He'd heard the news about the attack on Alex Hightower on the radio while driving to work and gathered everyone in the library to tell them what had happened.

"He's in the hospital in Atlanta with multiple broken bones, a concussion, and internal injuries."

"That's not all," David spoke up. "Mindy and I discovered something else this morning." He pulled out the sheets and showed them the match between Newburn's patient list and the Lincoln owners. "Should we report this information to the police?"

Mac shook his head. "Not yet. It all makes sense to us, but without the background information in our file, I'm not sure how serious the investigators in Atlanta will consider the connection."

"Do you think Spencer met Michael Conan through Dr. Newburn's office?" Vicki asked.

"Probably," Mac nodded. "And then recruited him to kill his niece, brother, and—" Mac set down his coffee cup. "Sarah Hightower. We've got to warn Sarah Hightower."

Mac called Joe Whetstone and plowed through a receptionist and two secretaries before Joe came on the line. He told him everything that had surfaced since the trial.

"Sarah Hightower needs to be warned," Mac said.

"I haven't had much contact with the Hightowers since the trial," the prosecutor said. "I'll try to reach her at home in Buckhead or at the hospital and advise her to take steps for her own security."

"What about forwarding our information to the Atlanta police?"

"I'll handle that, too. I know several detectives. Thanks for calling."

"Will he follow through?" David asked.

"He'll call Sarah. And if he thinks he can get some favorable publicity by helping exonerate Pete, he may help us with the police in Atlanta."

"I can see the headline," David said. "Former U.S. Attorney Successfully Prosecutes Man For Murder Then Uncovers Evidence of His Innocence."

"Too long. And we can't count on Joe Whetstone to do our job."

Burton Grable, president of a blue-jean manufacturing company owned by Alex Hightower, was waiting for Spencer when he arrived in Atlanta from London on Monday afternoon.

"What are you doing here?" Spencer asked when he saw the balding businessman waiting at the gate with an anxious look on his face.

"Let's get a drink. There's something I need to tell you. It's about Alex."

They walked into a bar located on the concourse and sat down.

Spencer listened to Burton's summary of events without changing expressions. "Is he going to make it?"

"He'll live. He's still unconscious, but the worst has passed, and the doctors don't think there will be any permanent brain damage. The broken wrist and ankle will improve with time. But the kidney damage is irreversible."

"Can they do a transplant from someone who signed an organ donor card?"

Burton took a drink. When Sarah had asked him to meet with Spencer, he couldn't refuse, and he didn't want to fail now.

"That's possible, but the success of a transplant is much greater if the donor is a close relative."

Spencer jerked back his head. "Don't look at me! Last week Alex told me to forget I even had a brother. Now he wants to harvest one of my kidneys! They can put him on one of those machines until a corpse with a suitable kidney comes through the system."

"Don't make a quick decision," Burton pleaded. "Sarah would like to talk with you, too."

Spencer stood. "Forget it."

"Please think it over, Spencer. What would Alex do if you were lying in the hospital?"

Spencer's face grew hard. "I know exactly what he'd do."

When Mac showed Ray and Harry the common name on the two lists, Ray let out a low whistle. "This is getting hot, Mac. The cops need to get involved."

"I know. That's why I called Joe Whetstone. He promised to pass along the information to the Atlanta police. But that doesn't mean anybody is going to do anything to help Pete."

"Except yours truly," Ray said.

"Right. Are you willing to go back to Atlanta and try to track down the car and find out everything you can about Michael Stenson Conan?"

"Yeah."

"Okay, but be careful. Very careful."

"I've been shot at more times than I can remember, and I don't need a new one to add to those I've forgotten."

"More times than you can remember?" Harry asked.

"Not recently," Ray reassured him. "What about Spencer?"

"You know where he lives. Check him out again. Do you need some money?" Mac asked.

"Harry, do we have grocery money?" Ray turned to his apprentice.

"You always seem to have enough to feed us both."

"All right," Mac said. "But keep track so I can pay you every penny."

"Be careful with your promises, Mac. We can spend a lot for fried chicken when we get really hungry."

A few hours later Ray and Harry passed the entrance to the Hightower mansion and turned onto the street where Alex was attacked. They drove up the hill and saw a small area that had been cordoned off with yellow police tape.

"That's it," Ray said.

A police car was exiting the Kingsley residence and Mr. Kingsley, a small, birdlike man, stood on the sidewalk in front of his house. Ray pulled into the driveway and got out of the car. Mr. Kingsley walked over to them.

"Are you detectives?" he asked.

"Not with the police," Ray introduced himself and Harry. "We're working on the Angela Hightower case, and there may be a link between the assault on Mr. Hightower and the men who killed his daughter."

"My wife and I were discussing that this morning."

"Were you home when Mr. Hightower was attacked?" Ray asked.

"No, we were in New York, but when we checked the surveillance tape we called the police."

"Surveillance tape?"

"Yes. I gave it to the officer who just left. He said the detectives needed to see it. Here, I'll show you the camera."

They followed him over to the mailbox. Mr. Kingsley brushed the ivy back with his hand. Ray knelt to get a better view of the camera angle.

"I understand it was still dark when Mr. Hightower came by here," he said.

"Yes, but the camera compensates for dim light."

"What could you see on the tape?"

"The camera was not positioned to pick up activity across the street so it doesn't show anything about the attack. It started running when the car turned into the driveway."

"What kind of car?"

"Like mine." Mr. Kingsley pointed to a shiny black Lincoln parked in front of the broad steps leading up to his house.

"Oh boy," Harry said. "This is hot, Ray."

"Was the picture in color?" Ray continued.

"No, but it was a dark-colored car."

"Did the camera pick up the driver?"

"Not from that angle."

"Any license plate number?"

The little man shook his head. "Not that either. All I know is that it was a dark Lincoln."

Ray patted the top of the camera for a job well done. "That's very helpful."

Oblivious to the swirl of events, Pete continued praying for Cal Musgrave. It had been six days since he started, and there had not been any tangible signs of progress in Cal. However, several things had happened in Pete's heart as he focused his attention on his fellow prisoner. First, he discovered that he cared about Cal. Not fake, not sentimental, not manufactured. When Pete looked inside himself, he saw a genuine concern for the troubled soul next-door. Cal's rantings now saddened him more than irritated him. Second, without any outward encouragement due to visible changes, Pete had developed a hope for Cal's future. Pete didn't label his hope, but others might call it a miracle-producing faith. Third, Pete was angry with a righteous indignation against the forces of darkness and evil that tormented Cal and tossed him about like a spineless rag doll. He knew those forces were from the pit of hell.

Cal had been quiet all morning. About nine o'clock, Pete was lying on his bunk with his eyes closed and heard someone call his name.

"Pete."

Thinking it was the imaginary voice that prisoners occasionally hear, he didn't answer. It came louder.

"Pete!"

"What?" he said. "Where are you?"

"It's me. Cal." The sound of the voice was so different from the various noises that had come from the adjacent cell, Pete double-checked to make sure he was awake.

"Hey. How are you?" he asked.

"I'm better."

"That's good."

"I had a strange dream last night," Cal said in a level voice that didn't hold the threat of ranting and raving. "Do you want to hear about it?"

Pete got out of bed and sat down on the floor so he could be nearer to the opening to Cal's cell.

"Yeah. I'm here."

"I dreamed that a man came into my cell and put his hands on my head."

"What did he look like?"

"Just an average-looking guy."

"Did he do or say anything?"

"Yes, it was so real. He said, 'Jesus is Lord. Be free.' "

Pete's jaw dropped open. "Anything else?"

"Yes. 'Go and tell.' Then he left. Went right through the bars. Do you think I'm crazy?"

Pete leaned his head against the wall of the cell and looked through the ceiling of the jail directly into heaven. "No," he said. "You're not crazy. Not anymore."

"Yeah. I feel like I've been somewhere else for twenty years and I just woke up."

Pete smiled. "Rip Van Winkle."

"Who?"

"Never mind. This is great."

"Yeah."

"Can we pray together?" Pete asked.

"Okay."

As they prayed back and forth, Cal's voice grew stronger and stronger. Pete read Bible verses to him, and they talked until lunchtime. When the food trays came at noon, the deputy quickly slid Cal's through the slot at the bottom of his door and moved out of the way. Sometimes Cal would throw his food out into the hall.

"Thanks, deputy," Cal said.

"What?" the startled guard replied.

"Thanks for lunch."

"Uh, you're welcome."

The guard slid Pete his food and whispered, "What's up with Crazy Cal?"

Pete pointed toward heaven. "Ask Jesus."

On the glass-topped table was an Atlanta newspaper opened to an article about the assault on Alex Hightower. According to the report, the police believed a blunt object was used in the attack. Robbery did not appear to be the motive. Michael Stenson Conan, a.k.a. Mike, answered the cell phone and Bart Jackson Conan, a.k.a. Bart, came in from the living room where he was watching professional wrestling on TV.

An angry voice was on the other end of the line. "What did you use? A baseball bat?"

"Uh, yeah. A metal bat," Mike said defensively.

"Maybe you should have tried a wooden one. Have you ever heard of a gun with a silencer? A bullet to the head?"

"Hey, we wanted it to look like a hit-and-run accident. We don't want another murder investigation breathing down our necks."

"It was an accident all right. A stupid, messed-up accident. You have $55,000 of my money, and I want to know what you're going to do about it."

"Finish the job."

"When?"

"As soon as the heat dies down."

"I don't have time for that. I'll finish this myself. If you want the other $55,000, do number three."

"That will cost $100,000." Mike looked at Bart, who nodded.

"No it won't. Do it for $55,000 or forget it."

"We'll think about it."

"That's a good idea. Use your head for something besides a baseball cap. I'll call back in a couple of days. No payment until number three is in the morgue. Understood?"

"Yeah."

The phone clicked off.

"Let's split," Bart said. "It's not worth it for $55,000."

"I don't know. I was saving my best plan for last. Simple, fast, impossible to trace."

"What if he doesn't pay?"

Mike shrugged. "We move to number four. I'd do that for nothing."

FORTY-FOUR

Make the truth known.
YEATS

HER EYES BLOODSHOT and rimmed in dark circles, Sarah was sitting beside the hospital bed when Alex moaned and opened his eyes for the first time in three days. He turned his head and gazed at Sarah, trying to focus for a few seconds then lapsing back into unconsciousness. It would be another twelve hours before he made another effort to climb out of the depths of the chasm where his attacker's blows had sent him.

—

Celeste began the meeting of the Mable Ray Circle by reading the journal entry of Laura McClain's prayer for Mac and then told about Mac's response to Archie's sermon.

"Praise the Lord," Naomi said, her eyes beaming. "We need to pray for the right follow-up. He'll need encouragement and help."

"That's not all," Celeste said. She told them about Anna Wilkes. "I think the Lord may be drawing them together."

"Awesome," Kelli said. "The idea of romance at his age."

Naomi looked at Celeste and smiled.

"We should also pray for Alexander Hightower," Kathy Howell said. "He needs a kidney transplant."

"I saw the article in the paper," Naomi said. "What about his younger brother as a donor?"

"I don't know," Celeste said, "But we need to pray for him as well. Naomi, will you begin?'"

There followed a time of thanksgiving for Mac and prayer for God's involvement in every aspect of his future. Celeste almost laughed out loud at the excitement in Kelli's voice when she prayed for Mac's relationship with Anna.

Then they prayed for the Hightower family. When someone mentioned Spencer, Kathy Howell saw a mental picture of four small clouds that were absorbed into a massive thunderhead. Not knowing what it meant, she didn't say anything, deciding not to mention it to the group until she had an opportunity to pray about it herself.

Early Tuesday morning, Mac and David met with Pete at the jail. There was a dignity in the young man's countenance—like a soldier who has survived a major battle. The flat, lifeless look that had greeted Mac the first few times they met no longer remained. Now Pete seemed confident and mature.

"Tell me more about Mr. Hightower's situation," Pete asked when Mac finished.

Mac outlined the injuries mentioned in the paper. "So he'll knit pretty well except for the loss of his kidneys. He'll need a transplant at some point in the future. That best donors are family members."

"Spencer is the only brother?" Pete asked.

"Yes. If it weren't so tragic there would be a sense of irony to the situation," Mac said. "The man most able to help Alex is the man trying to kill him."

"Why would he want to wipe out his brother's family?" Pete asked.

Earlier, Mac and David had been discussing Spencer's motivation. David answered. "With Angela's murder, we thought Spencer acted out of anger and sick retribution, but now there may be a much simpler explanation. Money. With Alex, Sarah, and Angela gone, Spencer would be the sole heir to the Hightower fortune."

"The police may consider Spencer a suspect in the attack on Alex," Mac continued, "but he was out of the country when the assault took place. If something happens to Sarah, it would greatly increase the focus on Spencer."

"How does this affect me?" Pete asked.

Mac shook his head. "None, yet. We need solid proof, not theories."

Pete tapped his fingers on the metal table in the interview room. "I'd like to help Mr. Hightower if I can," he said.

"Help? How would you do that?" Mac asked.

"I could give him one of my kidneys," Pete said in a matter-of-fact tone.

Mac was speechless for several seconds. When he found his voice, he said, "A few days ago Alex Hightower asked a jury to send you to the electric chair!"

Mac looked at David for support, but the younger lawyer had a big grin on his face.

"What are you grinning about?"

"I can't help it. I think it's a great idea."

"I can't agree," Mac sputtered. "I mean—"

"Look," Pete said. "Could you arrange for the doctors to test me and find out if I'm a suitable donor? That would be the first step, wouldn't it?"

"The judge would have to approve the donor suitability testing."

"When can you ask him?" Pete asked.

"This is insane," Mac stood up and walked back and forth across the narrow confines of the room. "You need to think it over a few days."

"I can think it over while they do the test. You said they're asking ordinary people in the community to consider donating a kidney. Why should I be excluded?"

Mac looked hard at Pete. "This won't get you out of prison."

"I understand. It's not a question of brownie points; it's helping save someone's life. It's making my life count for something even though I'm in jail."

"I've heard that before." David smiled.

Mac threw up his hands. "Okay. I'll talk to the judge."

Sarah Hightower took her desperate appeal to the only man with a proven ability to influence Spencer's behavior, Dr. Louis Newburn. The psychiatrist ushered her into his office.

"Have a seat, Sarah. How can I help?"

Sarah sat in a large chair across the desk from the doctor and took a letter out of her pocketbook. Her hand trembling, she handed it to him. "Here's a note asking Spencer to forgive us for the way we've treated him over the past few weeks. But after what he put Angela through . . ."

"I understand," Dr. Newburn said gently. "You don't have to explain. As long as I've known your husband's family, I've always tried to help in any way I could. I'll talk to Spencer as soon as possible."

"Thank you," Sarah sniffled.

"And I'm available as a professional resource for you."

Sarah nodded. "I need to talk with you, but I can't think about anything now except getting help for Alex."

"Of course. Has he been conscious today?"

"For a couple of hours this morning. He said a few words and answered a couple of questions, but he still doesn't know all that's happened to him."

"I'll try to come by the hospital and see him. Hopefully, I'll have good news for both of you."

Dr. Newburn escorted her out of the office and walked with her to the elevator.

"Let me share some of this burden with your family," he offered.

"Thanks, I need that," Sarah responded with a tired smile.

After he absorbed Pete's proposal, Mac enjoyed the consternation his client's offer caused Judge Danielson. David went along for the show.

"I've never," the judge started and stopped. "What about security at the hospital? Thomason has a life sentence."

"Judge, that sort of thing is handled every time a prisoner needs medical attention," Mac said. "And chances are small that Thomason is a donor match. I wouldn't go behind your back and make a public appeal, but what if a newspaper or TV reporter found out you denied Thomason's request?"

"Huh," the judge grunted. "Would Alex Hightower accept a kidney from the man who killed his daughter?"

"If it was his best chance of survival, I hope he would. But we're not asking you to order Alex Hightower to accept the offer."

"I'm not sure."

"That's not all," Mac leaned forward. "I had a tidbit of jailhouse news you might be interested in. One of the officers at the jail told me Cal Musgrave is a changed man."

"Cal? I was about to send him to the criminal detention wing of the mental hospital in Milledgeville."

"Thomason has been in the cell next to Cal talking to him. Now they say Cal has the manners of a choir boy, and the officer credits Thomason with causing the change."

"How did he do that?"

"Prayer."

The judge took off his glasses and rubbed his eyes. "Okay, Mac. I'll allow the tests. Draft an order and I'll sign it."

—

Wednesday morning, Pete shuffled along in leg irons and handcuffs through the front door of Gregory Memorial Hospital. The first hurdle was blood type. Both Pete and Alex were A-negative. The next step involved tissue typing, a test that identified the genetic characteristics of an individual's white blood cells. The most important aspect of a successful kidney transplant was not the surgical removal and attachment of a new kidney but the acceptance of the donated kidney by the recipient of the transplant.

Because white blood cells fight intruders, compatibility of white blood cells between donor and donee would be critically important to the success of a transplant for Alex Hightower. Tissue typing would isolate the key genetic markers in Alex and Pete called Human Leukocyte Antigens, or HLA, on their white blood cells. Because there are many different combinations of HLAs, even siblings can have different combinations that make transplants unfeasible. Each type of HLA has been assigned a number, and the different types identified and labeled through tissue typing.

Piedmont Hospital in Atlanta sent the data on Alex to the pathology lab in Dennison Springs. Six blood samples were drawn from Pete and analyzed. Alex's HLA profile was 1, 8, 10, 2, 7, 11, and Pete's was 4, 7, 12, 2, 7, 11—sufficient similarity to characterize Alex and Pete as a "one-haplotype match," because they shared a common group of three HLAs in their white blood count "pedigree."

The results in his hand, Dr. Matthew Watson, the doctor who performed the test, walked from the lab to the room where Pete was sitting on an examination table. A short man in his midforties with thick brown hair and dark brown eyes, Dr. Watson explained his findings to Pete.

"What next?" Pete asked.

"It's up to you," the doctor replied. "If you're sure you want to go forward, there are more tests and the doctors taking care of Mr. Hightower need to be informed."

"I'm sure. I've had plenty of time to think about it in my cell at the jail."

"Okay. We have a sample of Mr. Hightower's blood that was delivered early this morning by medical courier from Atlanta. We'll mix some serum from his blood with a very small amount of your white blood cells to determine if there is a protein antibody in Mr. Hightower's serum that would attack your HLAs. If his antibodies attack your blood cells, it will let us know that your kidney would not be able to survive in Mr. Hightower's body."

"Do I wait here?"

Dr. Watson looked at the two deputies sitting by the door. "I would think so."

Later, when he finished his analysis, Dr. Watson pushed his chair back from the microscope and wrote on the bottom of his report, "Good donor candidate—recommend acceptance."

Spencer slouched down in the big leather chair in Dr. Newburn's office. The psychiatrist peered over his glasses and blinked.

"I checked to see if you could be the kidney donor for Alex," the doctor began.

"You did what!" Spencer sat up straight. "I didn't give you permission—"

"Hold on," the doctor said. "Because your blood type is O-positive and Alex's blood is A-negative, there is no way you could donate a kidney anyway."

Spencer sat back in his chair. "That's a relief. It should get Sarah off my back."

Dr. Newburn opened a drawer in his credenza, took Sarah's letter, and handed it to Spencer. "Sarah wrote you a letter and asked me to give it to you." Spencer opened it and quickly read the two handwritten pages.

"She wants me to visit Alex in the hospital," he said with a short laugh. "Says she's sorry."

"She's under enormous stress, and a visit from you might help both of them."

Spencer's voice grew louder. "You think I should go? After what Alex did to me? I mean, he kicked me off the board of every family business and said he didn't want to see me again."

Dr. Newburn folded his hands. "Of course, I can't make you do anything, but I think you should go. An apology from Sarah and Alex would make you feel better."

"I'd rather have Alex grovel a little."

"I understand how you feel."

"Did you tell Sarah I couldn't be a donor?"

"Not yet, but I'll handle it," the doctor said.

Spencer stared at the edge of Dr. Newburn's desk for several seconds. "I'd be willing to visit Alex in the hospital, but there are practical things related to the family businesses that have to be worked out."

"Of course. Why don't I try to clear the way for a visit?"

Mac called David Moreland and read Dr. Watson's report to him over the telephone. He then faxed it to Joe Whetstone with a request on the cover sheet: "Please call after you review the attached."

Two minutes after the fax went through, Mindy buzzed Mac, who spoke first. "It's Joe Whetstone on the phone, isn't it?"

"How did you know?" Mindy asked.

"Practice. You'll be able to do it every time if you stay here long enough." Mac punched the phone button.

"Hello."

"If this is your idea of a joke, it's not funny!" Joe said sharply.

"Who said anything about a joke?"

"This report. Thomason as a kidney donor. It's ludicrous."

"Call the pathologist at the hospital yourself."

"Why would Thomason do this?" Joe continued. "It won't change his sentence."

"He knows that," Mac replied. "All I can tell you is that he has volunteered to donate a kidney to Alex Hightower, if he will accept it. The judge approved a series of donor suitability tests, and the doctor turned up the information in your hand."

There was silence on the line. "So this is on the level?"

"Alex Hightower's doctors may want to run their own tests, but for his sake I hope they turn out the same. I thought you might want to be the one to make the offer to the Hightower family."

"Me?"

"Yes."

"There's no way to know how they will react to this."

"So what?"

"This thing could be a big blowup. I'm not sure—" Joe stopped.

"That this is going to be good for you?" Mac finished Joe's thought.

Joe bristled. "Hey, it's a touchy situation. What if Thomason backs out?"

"I don't think he will," Mac answered. "But if you don't want to talk to the Hightowers, I'll ask the local doctor who did the testing to work through the medical channels."

"I think that would be the best. I don't want to be in the loop on this one."

"Okay. I'll handle it from this end."

"Spencer can't be a kidney donor for Alex," Dr. Newburn told Sarah when she answered the phone. "The blood types are different, so it's medically unfeasible."

"Do you think he wanted to help?" Sarah asked.

"I think I could have brought him around. I gave him the letter you wrote, and he seemed receptive to a reconciliation."

Sarah sighed. "I guess we need to do that soon, but Alex isn't up to it yet."

"How is he doing?" the psychiatrist asked.

"Weak. He's been asleep most of the day, and I'm exhausted myself."

"Why don't you go home for a few hours and rest?"

"Good idea. Thanks for talking with Spencer."

"You're very welcome. Everything will work out if we're patient."

Dr. Newburn hung up the phone then immediately called Spencer.

"Can you meet me at the hospital in forty-five minutes?"

"Why?"

"I talked to Sarah. Alex is alert and ready to talk to you."

"I hope he's humble enough."

"She said he's in tears."

"Crying? This I have to see."

"I'll meet you in the lobby."

Dr. Newburn put on his white medical jacket and picked up an old leather satchel he carried when making his rounds at the hospital. Carefully positioned between several sheets of paper in the satchel was a small hypodermic needle and syringe. In the syringe was a 50 cc dose of Cardiotoxin CTXI, a potent snake poison that causes severe constriction of the heart muscle and mimics with remarkable accuracy the symptoms of cardiac arrest. Given Alex Hightower's weakened condition, the dosage would finish the job botched by Mike and Bart.

Spencer would be there as an alibi, or at least an alternate object of blame. In the right time, Spencer could become the focus of a criminal investigation. But not yet.

FORTY-FIVE

Out of the jaws of death.
TWELFTH NIGHT, ACT 3, SCENE 4

SINCE EARLY IN the morning, Ray and Harry had been visiting car dealers who sold Lincolns.

"They sell more cars in Atlanta than I thought," Harry said, as they pulled out of a lot in East Point.

"At five o'clock on I-285 you'd believe it," Ray responded. "Ten lanes solid for miles. It's like pictures of L.A."

The next stop on their tour was a dealership in Peachtree City, a planned community patterned after Columbia, Maryland. Both Ray and Harry spotted the big vehicle at the same time.

"There it is!" Harry shouted.

In the front row of the used-car section was a dark-colored Lincoln sedan. Ray parked beside it.

"Here's where they scraped Mr. McFarland's truck." Ray said, running his finger along a section above the front left tire. "It's been repaired, but there is a slight indention."

Harry was writing down the serial number from the number plate on the dashboard when a hefty, dark-headed salesman walked up.

"It's a beauty. Just took it in a couple of days ago."

"What can you tell me about it?" Ray asked.

"One owner. Low miles. Never a scratch on it."

"Did you handle the trade-in?"

"Yeah. I'd sold it new to a guy who kept it in a garage for a few months then decided he wanted something he could take off-road and bought a Nissan SUV." Patting the big car, he said, "This baby is built to be king of the highway, not slog through a mudhole."

"Could I give the previous owner a call and find out if he had any problems with it?"

"I don't know," the salesman hesitated. "That depends how serious you are about buying it. Why don't you take it out for a drive and then we can talk? You'll be amazed how few pennies it will take to put you in this beauty."

"Okay. Get the key."

While the salesman went inside, Harry asked, "You're not going to buy it, are you?"

Ray grinned. "I didn't hear Mac put a dollar limit on us."

Harry drove while Ray opened the glove box and ran his hand under the seats.

"Here's a French fry." He held up a yellow stick which had once been edible.

Glancing over, Harry said, "Burger King."

"How do you know?"

"French fries are like fingerprints. Every one is different to an experienced eye like mine."

Ray retrieved a lottery ticket with the choices rubbed off and an unopened straw in a white wrapper.

"Hardee's," Harry said after a quick look at the straw.

"Speaking of fingerprints, there may be one or two on this lottery ticket." Ray carefully slipped the ticket in his pocket.

They pulled back into the lot. "Let's take this deal to the next level," Ray said.

Sitting in the salesman's cubicle, Ray asked, "What color is the paint on the car? My buddy thinks it's burgundy. I think it's more of a midnight purple."

"Midnight purple? Let me look at the specifications."

The salesman flipped over his information sheet about the car.

"You're right. Midnight purple."

Ray sat back satisfied. "I told you, Harry."

Ready to close the sale, the salesman took out several sheets of paper. "If you're ready to deal, I'm ready to put you behind the wheel."

"I still need to talk to the prior owner," Ray persisted. "I never buy a car without checking out its history."

"Okay, okay." The salesman opened a file drawer and pulled out a manila folder. "Here it is. I remember the guy. Came in with his brother."

Ray held his breath.

"Sorry, there's no phone number listed. We didn't do any financing on the car and didn't require a phone number."

Ray stood up. "I'm not interested. Thanks for your time."

"Wait a minute, sit down and don't be in such a hurry. I have the name and address—Mike Conan, 4873B Palomino Apartments. I'll check the phone book."

While the salesman flipped the pages of the big white book, Ray and Harry silently repeated the address until they had it memorized.

"Must be a nonpublished number. But you don't need to talk to anyone. You can see the condition of the car. It's a cream puff. Never been scratched."

Ray shook his head. "Sorry. There was a bad odor in the car."

"Odor? We had the car cleaned by our detail shop." The salesman huffed, not ready to give up the fight. "We don't put anything on the lot until it's better than new."

"Maybe, but to me, it smelled like death."

—

Dr. Newburn was waiting in the hospital lobby. "Thanks for coming," he said when Spencer came through the main entrance. "Ready?" he asked.

"I'm ready to see big brother eat crow. Is Sarah still here?"

"No. She's gone home to rest. We'll have Alex to ourselves for a few minutes."

They rode up the elevator together. Alex had been moved from intensive care to a room on the orthopedic wing of the hospital. They passed two patients in wheelchairs and a young boy moving slowly on crutches.

Dr. Newburn stopped at the nurse's station.

"I'm here to see Alex Hightower in room 3892. Could I review his chart for a moment?"

The nurse glanced at the doctor's name on his jacket and handed him the chart. He quickly checked the nurse's schedule for monitoring Alex's temperature and blood pressure. Just completed. There would be no interruptions. IV in place.

"Thank you."

They walked down the hall and pushed open the door. Spencer was not prepared for what he saw. On the drive over to the hospital, he had imagined Alex channel-surfing the TV while he ordering underlings to do his bidding. He couldn't have been more wrong.

A pale, weak-looking image of his brother lay completely immobile on the bed. It wasn't even apparent that Alex was breathing. The entire left side of his head was discolored from the bruising and swelling caused by the crushing blow. His right leg was suspended in a knee-high cast and his left arm was immobilized by his side. Tubes were everywhere.

Spencer stopped in his tracks. "Alex," he said softly.

Dr. Newburn brushed by him into the room.

"Looks like he's gone back to sleep for a minute. Spencer, please go to the nurse's station and get a refill on the ice bucket. We'll wake him up and give him a drink of water so you two can talk."

Shaken, Spencer backed out of the room.

As soon as the door clicked shut, Dr. Newburn took the needle and syringe out of his satchel. The best way to administer the drug would be into the IV tube access port where Alex received pain and antibiotic medication. That would eliminate the remote possibility of a needle prick awakening Alex or leaving any evidence of an injection on his skin. Newburn would inject the poison, leave the room, and let Spencer try to awaken his brother. By the time Alex's heart succumbed to the poison and constricted for the last time, the psychiatrist would be in his car driving away from the hospital. He inserted the needle into the port and put his thumb on the end of the syringe. It would all be over in the next fifteen seconds.

The door opened.

"Dr. Newburn!" Sarah came in. "I didn't know you were coming by."

In his haste to withdraw the needle, Newburn almost dropped it on the floor. Coughing, he bent over and transferred the still-full syringe to the right front pocket of his white jacket.

"Good to see you, Sarah," he managed as he straightened up. "I thought you were going home to rest." Newburn fought off an urge to run out of the room.

"The hospital called as soon as I walked through the door. They may have located a donor for Alex and asked me to meet with the kidney specialist. He should be here any minute."

"Excellent." The psychiatrist smiled crookedly.

"Do you want to wait until the doctor arrives?"

"No, uh, I need to get back to the office." Dr. Newburn made a hasty retreat.

Spencer came into the room with the ice bucket. He saw Sarah and stopped.

"I'm sorry," he said, "I had no idea how bad—"

"He's better than he was," Sarah said. "It's been horrible."

"Can I stay for a few minutes?" he asked, still visibly unnerved by the sight of his brother swathed in bandages and casts.

"Yes."

Sarah and Spencer sat beside Alex on opposite sides of the bed. Neither spoke for several minutes. Alexander's chest slightly rose and fell in a steady rhythm.

"I'm really sorry," Spencer said, glancing up at Sarah's face.

"He's going to make it," Sarah said. "The worst part was the head injury, and if he gets a new kidney, there's hope for a good recovery. "

"No. I'm sorry for harassing Angela."

Sarah quickly looked away.

Spencer spoke slowly, "There was nothing to it except meanness on my part. I treated it as a game, but it was wrong to tease her. I guess it was a way to get back at Alex."

Sarah reached over and laid her hand on her husband's motionless arm, "Spencer, it's going to take time for Alex and me—"

The door opened and one of the floor nurses ushered in a group of physicians. A robust, dark-skinned man with a narrow mustache and gold-rimmed glasses stepped forward.

"Mrs. Hightower?"

"Yes." Sarah stood up.

"I'm Dr. Godfrey Banforth, head of the kidney transplant team," he said with an accent that combined the sounds of London and Kinshasa. "Could you come down the hall to the consultation room so we can discuss your husband's case?"

As they filed out of the room, Spencer held back. Turning, Sarah said, "You, too, Spencer. You need to be in on this. You're his brother."

FORTY-SIX

We thought it was Judgment Day.
THOMAS HARDY

SPENCER WAS SPEECHLESS, and Sarah felt lightheaded and faint when Dr. Banforth finished telling them about Peter Thomason's offer. She sat in a chair and someone brought her a glass of water.

"But he murdered my daughter," she said. "The idea that part of him would be in my husband—"

"Can the decision wait until we discuss this with Alex?" Spencer interrupted.

"Of course. We can't schedule the surgery until Mr. Hightower's medical condition is more stable."

"And he's a drug user," Sarah mumbled.

"What?" Dr. Banforth asked.

"Thomason is a drug user. I don't want my husband to receive a kidney that has been damaged by drugs."

"Of course, more tests need to be performed to make sure the donor kidney is healthy. But regardless of the personal issues, the chances of finding a similar donor are a thousand to one. The long-term success of the transplant is directly related to the compatibility of donor and recipient."

"I don't know," Sarah closed her eyes and shook her head.

When she opened them, Dr. Banforth looked down at her and smiled. "Mrs. Hightower, when I was a little boy, I saw many people die in my country because there was no medical help available for them. I decided to become a doctor to save lives that might otherwise be lost. Life is a precious gift and we must preserve it. A transplant is much better than depending on a dialysis machine. Whatever this man has done in the past, he is making a remarkable offer in the present, an offer that could add many years to your husband's life."

The room was silent. Sarah nodded. "We'll give it serious consideration. Thank you."

"Let me know your decision as soon as possible," the doctor said. He and his entourage left the room.

Sarah and Spencer returned to Alex's bedside. Afternoon shadows came into the room.

Spencer lifted his head and broke the silence, "Today, I realized I care about my brother. When I saw Alex lying here, so pale, so hurt, so weak . . ." he paused. "I don't know. Something happened. And when the doctor talked about someone giving a kidney to Alex, I wished I could do it instead."

"If only Alex could hear you say that."

"He will," Spencer said. "I have several things I need to say to him."

Ray and Harry had been parked under a tree at the Palomino Apartments all afternoon. There was no sign of Mike or Bart. Harry nodded off and began to snore, and Ray's eyelids were drooping lower and lower when the white Nissan SUV came into view. Ray was instantly awake. He nudged Harry with his foot.

"Uh," Harry grunted.

"Wake up."

Each carrying a twelve-pack of beer, the two blond-haired men got out and went into a ground-floor apartment.

Telephoto lens in place on his camera, Ray rapidly took six pictures of the brothers walking up the sidewalk.

"They're big boys, aren't they?" Harry said. "With poor taste in beer, I might add."

"Really? I thought you drank anything that didn't run away."

"Almost, but even I had standards."

Ray wrote down the license plate number of the Nissan on a slip of paper.

"What do we do now?" Harry asked.

"You seemed pretty comfortable a few minutes ago. Why don't we camp out together under this tree? Now that we've found our prey, I'd hate to go back and start over."

"Is this what they call a stakeout?"

"I guess so. We'll watch them tonight and tomorrow morning. If nothing happens, we'll go home."

"What do you think they're going to do?"

Ray turned toward Harry. "How long have I been training you?

"Four days."

"I knew it was a long time. Haven't I trained you better than to ask a question like that? Think. What would you say if I asked you that question?"

Harry looked out the window of the car for a moment. "They're going to drink beer."

"Brilliant. What are we going to do?"

"That's easy. Go back to the Chinese restaurant we passed down the road and order takeout."

"Good. You had me worried. I need a partner I can trust."

When Alex regained full consciousness, he opened his eyes and saw Sarah and Spencer sitting on opposite sides of his bed. For several seconds, he wasn't sure if he was hallucinating or awake.

"Sarah," he said hoarsely.

She quickly moved her chair near his head. "Do you want a sip of water?" she asked.

"I'll get it." Spencer handed a glass and straw to Sarah, who held it for Alex to take a drink. "How are you, Alex?" Spencer asked.

"I've been better. What are you doing here?"

"I want him here," Sarah said. "A lot has happened since you were attacked."

"What do you mean?"

Sarah told him what they knew about the attack, his medical condition, and finished with the call from Joe Whetstone about her own safety. Alex grimaced in pain several times, but when she asked if he wanted her to call a nurse, he said, "No, go on."

She finished and Alex asked, "Do you have someone protecting you?"

"Yes. Several."

"But Thomason is in jail now." Alex shut his eyes and tried to think. "Who is working with him and why?"

Sarah put her hand on Alex's shoulder. "Alex, there is something I need to tell you about Peter Thomason."

When she finished, Alex asked weakly, "Why would he want to give me one of his kidneys?"

"I wish I could do it," Spencer said quietly.

"You do?" Alex looked over at his younger brother.

Spencer repeated his earlier plea for forgiveness. Alex listened with his eyes shut until Spencer finished. He opened his eyes and met his brother's gaze. "I'm sorry, too. I accused you without hearing you out."

Sarah pulled her chair closer to the bed. "Alex, are you going to accept the kidney?" she asked. "I need to tell the doctors as soon as possible."

Alex looked in her eyes. "What do you think?"

Sarah stroked his cheek. "I've been thinking about it while we waited for you to wake up. I want you well."

Alex grimaced in pain. "I don't know if I can talk to the boy."

"If you don't want to see him, I'm sure it can be arranged."

"Okay. Tell them yes."

"I'm sorry I made you cry earlier," Spencer added.

"Cry?" Alex asked, looking toward Sarah. "Did I cry?"

"No," Sarah said.

"Dr. Newburn told me," Spencer said. "I guess he was mistaken."

Inside the apartment the cell phone rang. Mike answered.

"Well?" Dr. Newburn asked impatiently.

"Show us the money and we'll do it."

"Don't be cute."

"It's going to be tougher than we thought. She hired some bodyguards. Somebody is getting very suspicious."

"When will you finish the job?" Newburn asked. "I'm in a hurry to get this over with."

"Within twenty-four hours of receiving the $100,000. I have a foolproof plan."

"I said $55,000."

"Doc, I don't care what you said. We're not budging for less than $100,000."

"No, $25,000 down and the balance when it's finished."

Mike looked at Bart and held up five fingers. His brother nodded. "Listen," Mike said, "We'll do it for $50,000 down and the balance within twelve hours of the time her heart stops beating."

Newburn didn't respond for several seconds. "You've got a good plan?"

"Airtight."

"All right, all right," the psychiatrist conceded. "You've got it."

"Will I read about number two's death in the paper tomorrow?" Mike asked.

"Uh, no. I hit a snag."

"It's harder than it looks, isn't it?"

"Just leave the car door unlocked."

"Usual signal?"

"Yes."

The phone went dead.

Mike put the phone down on the kitchen counter.

"I don't know about this," Bart said.

"Don't worry. This deal has gotten too hot, and we're not going to stick our necks into a noose. As soon as we have the $50,000, we're leaving town and not looking back. How does Vegas sound?"

Bart rubbed a pair of imaginary dice between his hands. "Like heaven."

Ray had saved an egg roll from supper for a midnight snack and was dipping it in duck sauce at 12:32 A.M. Harry seemed able to fall asleep in any location, circumstance, or position. The young man's head was leaned against the window of the truck with his mouth halfway open. A car glided into the parking lot, and Ray slid down a few inches in his seat.

It was a black Mercedes. The driver turned off the headlamps, drove forward in the amber glow of the car's parking lights, and stopped behind the white Nissan. The trunk lid popped open and a short, overweight figure got out, took two briefcases from the trunk, and put them into the backseat of the Nissan. He quietly shut the door of the Nissan and drove away.

Ray shook Harry's shoulder. "Wake up."

"Uh. Why?"

"Wake up."

"Okay, okay."

Ray told him what had happened. "The lights in the apartment have been off for about thirty minutes. I'd like to see what's in those briefcases."

Shaking himself fully awake, Harry said, "I can tell you."

"What?"

"Trouble. It's none of our business. Mac told us to be careful, and I remember you agreeing with him. We can watch and follow, but I don't want to meet those two guys."

Ray opened his door.

"Did you hear what I said?" Harry asked.

"Yes, so don't repeat it. I'll be back in a second."

Ray moved cautiously across the parking lot and crouched beside the rear of the Nissan. He cracked open the back door of the vehicle, causing the dome light to switch on.

Watching from the front window of the darkened apartment, Bart hissed, "Mike, someone is snooping around our truck. Go around back while I watch from here."

There was a sliding glass door in the master bedroom. Grabbing a pistol and a blackjack, Mike unlocked the door, jogged around the building, and hid behind a bush about fifteen feet from the Nissan.

Ray had put one of the briefcases on the asphalt parking lot and was trying to pry it open with his pocketknife. Concentrating on the briefcase, he didn't hear Mike Conan creep up behind him. Mike raised his hand and quickly brought the blackjack down on Ray's head at the base of his skull.

Ray grunted and collapsed on the pavement. Bart came bolting out the door, and the two men dragged Ray's unconscious form into the apartment.

"Get the money while I tie this guy up," Mike said.

"Let's waste him."

"Just get the money. We don't need the cleaning lady finding a dead body after we're gone. Let me think a minute."

Bart returned with the briefcases and put them on the kitchen table. Mike was rifling through Ray's wallet flipping cards onto the glass topped table.

"Ray Morrison. He's from Dennison Springs."

"What's he doing here?"

Mike held up one of Ray's cards. "He's a private detective. Get some rope and duct tape."

Ray was bound hand and foot with rope, and long pieces of duct tape were plastered over his eyes and mouth. As they dragged him into a corner of the living room, he groaned.

"He'll come around in a few minutes. We need to think fast. This is a bad scene," Mike said.

"We don't have a choice," Bart said quickly. "We have to kill him and dump him somewhere."

Mike swore. "Don't be stupid. What if someone already knows he's here?"

"The apartment is in the doc's name. No one can trace us."

The phone rang. Mike and Bart looked at one another.

"Answer it," Bart said.

"Did you get your groceries?" Dr. Newburn asked.

"Yeah, but there was an extra piece of bacon."

"What do you mean?"

"A private detective named Ray Morrison from Dennison Springs is wrapped up in the corner of our living room. We caught him snooping around our vehicle before we could make the pickup."

"Dennison Springs! Did he see me leave the money?"

"Maybe, maybe not. I knocked him out before we could chat, and we don't plan on interviewing him. My plan is to put a bullet through his head and dump him on your doorstep."

"Hold on. I'll call back in five minutes."

"Make that three minutes."

Harry saw Ray fall to the pavement and watched the two men drag his body into the apartment. Reaching under the front seat of the truck, he took out a small black case. Inside was a Smith and Wesson .38 revolver. Holding the gun, he carefully opened the truck's door, ran across the parking lot, and crept behind the apartment building. Only one apartment showed signs of life, and he hoped Ray Morrison was somewhere inside it—alive.

The sliding glass door was still ajar, and Harry quietly opened it enough to squeeze through into the bedroom. His right hand was shaking, and he could hear voices in the next room. He eased along the wall until he was beside the door. Gripping the pistol with both hands to hold it still, he heard Mike's statement about putting a bullet through Ray's head and knew he had only one option.

Spinning around the corner of the door, he aimed the pistol squarely at Mike's chest and pulled the trigger. The gun clicked. Nothing happened. He had forgotten to make sure it was loaded. Bart and Mike lunged across the room. Harry frantically pulled the trigger again, and the gun roared as Mike hit his right arm. The shot missed Mike but passed through Bart's low back, paralyzing his legs and sending a lightning bolt of pain through his body.

Unaware that his brother was hit, Mike knocked Harry to the floor in the bedroom. The gun went skidding under the edge of the bed. The two men rolled over and over, exchanging blows with Harry ending up on top. The larger man threw Harry off and slammed his face into the wall. Both men staggered to their feet and Mike yelled, "Bart, get him!"

Harry spun around just as Mike punched him in the stomach. A second blow missed and Harry grabbed Mike's arm, pulling him down so he could slam his knee into the side of Mike's head. At that point the superiority of Marine Corps hand-to-hand combat training over the undisciplined ways of a street brawler took over. Harry chopped the back of Mike's head just below the skull and followed him to the floor where he pinned him, face to the floor with his arm behind his back. Blood from a cut on Harry's face dripped onto the back of Mike's head.

Mike wailed, "Bart! Where are you?"

Harry anxiously craned his neck to see in the next room. He could see Bart pulling himself forward across the carpet with his hands and arms toward the bedroom.

"I can't move my legs!" Bart yelled.

The phone rang. One, two, three, four, five, six rings.

Dr. Newburn hung up the phone that rested on the antique cherry secretary in his den and walked upstairs to his bedroom.

Mike swore at Harry. "You're going to pay for this."

Harry didn't answer. Mike continued struggling but was unable to shake Harry's hold. Breathing heavily, Bart moved steadily toward the door. Harry leaned over and saw the pistol under the edge of the bed.

Harry applied pressure to Mike's carotid artery, cutting off the blood supply to the brain. Bart made it through the bedroom door, inching closer to the pistol. Mike went limp, and Harry applied pressure to the artery for a few more seconds, then jumped up and staggered unsteadily on his feet. He dived over the corner of the bed and reached for the gun, but he was too late. Bart had the pistol in his hand. He pointed it at Harry's head and pulled the trigger.

The bullet blew away the top third of Harry's right ear, continued through the ceiling and destroyed the Kramers' new television in the apartment upstairs. Fortunately, Mr. and Mrs. Kramer were out of town.

Blood from Harry's wound squirted from the side of his head as he rolled away from the impact and noise of the shot. When Bart tried to turn his body toward Harry to take another shot, pain knifed through his back and he twisted to the side. Harry reached over the side of the bed, grabbed Bart's wrist and they fought for control of the weapon. In the struggle, Harry fell off the bed and landed on top of Bart, who cursed and tried to gouge Harry in the eye. Harry jerked back his head and slowly twisted Bart's wrist until he released his grip on the gun. It fell out of his hand and onto the floor.

Gasping for breath, Harry put his hand to his head and came away with a handful of blood from the gushing wound. Pushing the pistol hard against Bart's forehead with his bloody hand, he said, "If you move, you're dead."

Eyes wide, Bart didn't twitch.

Leaving a trail of red, Harry went into the living room and saw Ray's motionless form in the corner. Grabbing the cell phone, he resumed his position on Mike's back and dialed 911.

A woman answered, "Emergency 911, how may I help you this evening?"

"I'm on a cell phone," he gasped. "4873B Palomino Apartments. Gunshot wounds. Multiple ambulances and police needed."

FORTY-SEVEN

How pleasant it is for brethren to dwell in unity.
PSALM 133:1 (KJV)

MAC DROVE PEGGY MORRISON to Atlanta, and they rushed together into Ray's hospital room at 4:00 A.M. The big detective was sleeping with his mouth open, snoring rhythmically. Peggy touched his hand.

"Ray?" she said, her voice quivering.

"Huh?" Ray opened his eyes and tried to move his head. "Ouch. Hey, baby."

"How are you?" she asked.

"I have a headache, but I'll be fine."

Peggy burst into tears in a release of tension and worry.

"Aw. I'm sorry," Ray said.

"No, it's that you're okay."

"Yeah. I'll be sore for a few days, but I should be chopping wood in a couple of weeks. Have you seen Harry? He's a mess."

"The police said he was shot," Mac said. "How bad is it?"

"He lost part of his right ear and will need some cosmetic surgery. We were lying next to each other in the hallway of the ER, and he put in a request for the same doctor who did the work on Evander Holyfield's ear." Ray managed a weak smile.

"Where is he now?" Mac asked.

"Down the hall. I'm not sure which room it is, but the nurses can tell you."

Ray held out his hand and Peggy grasped it. "Harry saved my life. It was not a good situation."

"I'll leave you two alone and see if he's awake," Mac said.

Harry's head was swathed in bandages. He opened his eyes when Mac walked in.

"Ray says you're a hero."

"A Marine never leaves a buddy on the field."

"What are the damages?"

Harry touched the bandages covering the right side of his head. "Just a piece of my ear, and I hear a constant ringing sound that the doctors say might go away."

"Do you feel like telling me what happened?"

"Yeah, the police just left. I think they want to talk with you, too. The detective's card is on the cart at the foot of the bed."

Mac slipped the card into his pocket.

Harry told Mac the events of the previous day and night.

"Do the police know our suspicions about Spencer Hightower?" Mac asked.

"Yes, but guess who owned the car that we saw stop in front of the apartment."

"It wasn't Spencer?"

"Nope. The psychiatrist. Dr. Newburn."

"Newburn! Why him? Was he working for Spencer, too?"

"Possibly. The detective told me the apartment was in Newburn's name, too."

Mac called the precinct from Harry's room. Thirty-five minutes later, he was sitting in Detective Lyle's office talking to a slender, brown-haired man who looked more like an associate in a law firm than a third-shift detective with the Atlanta Police Department.

"We're going to bring Spencer Hightower and Dr. Newburn in for questioning. Tell me more about the murder case."

When Mac finished, Detective Lyle said, "I'm going to contact the sheriff's department in Echota County. The Conan brothers should be considered suspects in Angela Hightower's murder."

"Have they given any statements?"

"I can't discuss that, but the scope of our investigation is expanding."

"I have a motion for new trial pending."

"Contact me in a few days, and I'll give you an update."

Ray and Harry were sound asleep when Mac returned to the hospital. Peggy was keeping vigil by Ray's bed.

"Are you going back home?" she asked. It took two and a half hours to drive from Atlanta to Dennison Springs.

Mac checked his watch. It was almost 6:00 A.M. "If I leave, you won't have any way to get around."

"Do you think I'm going anywhere?" Peggy smiled.

"Okay." Mac nodded. "I'll call later."

At 6:36 A.M. two detectives and four uniformed officers from the Atlanta Police Department were in position at Dr. Louis Newburn's residence, a brick home with a beautifully manicured lawn and a cluster of azalea bushes that exploded with color every spring. After ringing the doorbell, knocking, and waiting, they broke through the front door and fanned out quickly through the house. No one was home.

Driving north away from the metropolitan Atlanta area, Mac analyzed the events of the past twenty-four hours. The Conan brothers, Louis Newburn, Spencer Hightower, all seemed to have their place in the equation. But regardless of the actual participants in the crime, a tall, rangy young man sitting in an isolation cell at the Echota county jail no longer belonged under judgment for murder. The realization of Pete's innocence swept over Mac and he shouted, "Yes!"

Arriving home, he shaved, showered, and went into the office. Everyone, including David, was waiting for him.

"Good morning, all," he said when he saw the group in the reception area and began walking toward his office.

"Just a minute," Judy said. "We want to talk with you."

Mac stopped and turned around. "Don't get upset. I was going to check my desk for a second."

"Your desk hasn't moved in years," Judy responded. "I heard on the radio this morning that Ray Morrison was in the hospital in Atlanta. What's going on?"

"And don't drag it out," Mindy added. "You need to return a call from Sarah Hightower."

"Okay. Do you want the truth, the whole truth, or nothing but the truth?"

"All of the above," David piped in.

Mac told them about the purple car, Dr. Newburn's unfolding involvement with the murder as Spencer's bag man, and the attempt on Ray's and Harry's lives.

When he finished, David said, "I knew Newburn was not truthful on the stand."

"Maybe more untruthful than we suspected," Mac said. "Somehow Spencer drew him into this thing and ordered him around like a household servant."

"Don't forget to call Mrs. Hightower," Mindy reminded.

"We'll wait here while you talk to her," Vicki said.

"Are any of you going to work today?" he asked.

"No," they said in unison.

Mac dialed the number on the slip of paper.

"Mrs. Hightower?"

"Yes."

"Mac McClain."

"Uh, yes. Thanks for calling. I was wondering if you could give a message to your client."

"What is it?"

"Tell him thank you. The doctors say Alex will be able to have the transplant within the next seven to ten days."

"All right."

"Also," she paused, "Alex wants to meet Peter and thank him in person."

"That will be up to the law enforcement authorities."

"Of course. But it can probably be arranged. We had a long meeting with the detectives about an hour ago. I'll let my husband tell you about it."

Mac covered the receiver with his hand. "Alex Hightower wants to talk to me."

Another voice came on the line. It was Alex. "Mr. McClain," he said weakly. "The police believe Dr. Newburn is the one who had Angela murdered and tried to kill me, too."

Mac was shocked. "But I thought it was Spencer."

"No, no. We found out this morning that Dr. Newburn has been embezzling money from Spencer's trust for years. I have a testamentary trust that provides if my family is dead all my money goes into Spencer's trust. With us gone, Newburn would control everything as surviving trustee."

"Have the police arrested Newburn?"

"They went to his house, but he wasn't there."

Dr. Louis Newburn transferred planes in Miami. Wearing a black hairpiece and carrying a forged passport, he would be in Belize, a small English-speaking country in Central America, by 11:00 A.M. EST. He chose Belize because he had opened a bank account there shortly after

Cecil Hightower's death. Currently, the amount on deposit totaled $17,894,253—all of it money methodically siphoned from the Spencer Hightower Trust. He had hoped to multiply the balance tenfold with funds from Alexander Hightower's family, but he was resigned to his fate. He would travel around the Caribbean for a few years before returning to the U.S. for temporary visits. Things could have been a lot worse.

Friday morning a deputy slid open the door to Pete's cell with a clang. It was time for him to go to the courthouse for the hearing on the motion for a new trial.

"Maybe I'll see you later," Cal said. "If I don't, thanks for everything."

"Whatever happens, I'll be back."

Pete's heart began beating faster as soon as he walked through the doorway into the familiar room. He stared for a moment at the empty jury box, flashed back to the moment when Lyman Bakersfield solemnly announced the guilty verdict, and shuddered.

Mac and David sat in their usual seats at the defense table. Joe Whetstone and his staff didn't bother to make the trip from Atlanta, so Bert Langley was alone at the prosecution table. A few other courthouse employees slipped in the back door. Everyone stood when Judge Danielson came out of his office.

"Please be seated," the judge said.

Bert stepped forward. "Call *State versus Thomason,* Case number 76932. Defendant's Motion for New Trial."

"Proceed, Mr. McClain."

Reports from the Atlanta Police Department in hand, Mac outlined the events since Pete's conviction.

The judge turned to Bert. "What is the State's position?"

Pete held his breath. The next moment would be the difference between freedom and years of appeals while he sat locked up in a prison cell.

"We do not oppose the motion," Bert said. "The State is aware of additional investigative information that supports Mr. McClain's position and does not intend to retry Mr. Thomason on these charges if the motion is granted."

The judge motioned toward the men seated at the defense table. "Mr. Thomason, come forward."

Mac and David flanked Pete in front of the bench.

The judge said, "Having reviewed the information attached to the motion and considered the argument of counsel for the defendant, the court finds that significant new evidence indicates Mr. Thomason did not commit the crime for which he was tried and convicted. I therefore grant defendant's motion and order him released from custody upon his own recognizance."

That was it. Pete was free. Tears welled in his eyes in contradiction to the smile that burst forth on his face. Tears of joy and relief. Mac patted him on the shoulder, and Pete wiped his eyes with the back of his hand.

On the way back to the office, Mac turned to David.

"Are you sorry about the judge's ruling?" he asked.

David stopped in the middle of the sidewalk. "What did you say?"

"Are you sorry the judge set Pete free? It means I won't be paying you five thousand dollars to handle the appeal."

David laughed. "I'll eat out less often."

"I have a better idea," Mac said. "In fact, it's an offer you can't refuse."

"You'll buy my lunch at Josie's every week?"

"No. You know the back room at the office?"

"The one you use for closed-file storage?"

"Yes. I'm going to rent a miniwarehouse and move out the filing cabinets. With a fresh coat of paint and new carpet, the room could be a nice law office. It has a window that gives a good view of the pecan tree on the west side of the building. I think you would enjoy it. I'll even throw in a new desk."

David's grin broadened. "Two conditions."

"What?"

"Spring water in the refrigerator and Josie's once a week."

Mac stepped off the curb. "I think I can handle that, even if I have to work a little harder myself."

Judy, Vicki, and Mindy had prepared brunch at Mac's office. After his release from jail, Pete was sitting in the library eating his third waffle topped with fresh strawberries when Anna Wilkes arrived. She was followed by Ray Morrison, who looked no worse for his experiences in Atlanta, and Harry O'Ryan, who offered to show his "bionic ear" to anyone willing to give him a quarter. He had no takers, and the bandage covering the right side of his head stayed in place.

After everyone had eaten and the conversation in the room died down, Pete spoke up. "I'd like to thank everyone," he said, and then stopped at the collective sight of the faces of the people who had given so much to help him—Mac, David, Anna, Ray, Harry, and Mac's office staff who labored behind the scenes. Pent-up emotions flowed from almost every pair of eyes in the room. Even Ray allowed himself a sniffle. When he could continue, Pete said, "Thank you, thank you." Turning to Mac, he said, "What can I say? "

Mac took two steps forward and gave him a bear hug. "You don't have to say anything."

FORTY-EIGHT

There are three things that are too amazing for me, four that I do not understand: the way of an eagle in the sky, the way of a snake on a rock, the way of a ship on the high seas, and the way of a man with a maiden.
PROVERBS 30:18–19 (NIV)

TEN DAYS LATER, David drove Pete to Atlanta for admission to Piedmont Hospital. Based on results from an MRI, CAT scan, and angiogram, Dr. Banforth had selected Pete's left kidney for the operation. After he was settled in a room, Pete heard a tentative knock on the door.

"Come in," he said.

It was Sarah Hightower.

Pete spoke first. "Before you say anything, you know how sorry I am about Angela."

Sarah nodded sadly. "We know that. And somehow Alex and I will have to find the strength to go on without her. I've cried until there are no tears left."

Pete started to respond but stopped. There would be another time.

Sarah said in a soft voice, "We want to ask your forgiveness for what we've put you through."

"You didn't—"

"No," Sarah stopped him. "We weren't right. And you offered to help Alex before you knew you would be set free."

"I want to do it," Pete said simply.

Sarah looked up into his face. "And we thank you."

—

The Saturday morning air had not seemed so pure and clean to Mac in years. He played with Flo and Sue and did a few household chores until it was time to go to Chattanooga. He picked up Anna for an afternoon drive in the mountains east of Dennison Springs.

"Would you like to see my house?" he asked. "It's just a few miles out of our way. I picked up my dirty clothes and washed the dishes this morning."

"Okay," she smiled at him. "Especially if it's neat."

"We'll only stay for a few minutes."

He stopped the car at the bottom of the driveway so she could get a clear view of the whole house. "I like the way it's positioned above everything around it," she said.

Mac opened the front door and ushered her into the great room with its fireplace. Anna gazed out the tall, clear windows that served as the canvas for the beauty of the mountain scene in the distance.

"It's beautiful," she said.

"Would you like a cup of coffee?' Mac asked. "We could sit on the deck. There's a nice view from the rear of the house as well."

Anna followed him into the kitchen and leaned against the counter while he measured the coffee into the basket. Mac glanced over, saw her, and quickly looked away.

They walked out to the deck, and Mac released Flo and Sue so they could run unfettered for a few minutes. Anna laughed as the excited dogs bayed and chased one another out of sight, but not out of hearing.

"This is a perfect place for them, isn't it?"

"They don't bother anyone, and they're free."

They sat and sipped their coffee in comfortable silence. Mac could not get the image of Anna leaning against the kitchen counter out of his mind. So like Laura, yet wonderfully different in her own unique way.

"Anna," he said, savoring the sound of her name, "you'll never know the influence you have on me. Even today, I feel more alive than I have in years."

"I'm glad."

Mac took a breath. He felt awkward and bumbling. But determined.

"I've also enjoyed getting to know Hunter. He's a great kid. You've done well with him."

"Thanks."

They sat in silence for a few more moments.

"Do you know I'm falling in love with you?" he asked.

Anna faced him and returned his love with her eyes. "Yes, I do."

EPILOGUE

I have made you known to them, and will continue to make you known in order that the love you have for me may be in them and that I myself may be in them.

JOHN 17:26 (NIV)

JANUARY 30

The night before the wedding, Mac put on a warm jacket and went out on the deck. He'd returned home an hour earlier from a wonderful evening, a banquet where he and Anna were surrounded by friends and loved ones. Leaning against the railing and staring at the stars, he thought about the following day. He was happy, mostly.

He went inside and climbed into bed. He fell asleep and dreamed. It was the usual nightmare. Tonight, it started in peace on a beautiful winter afternoon. Snow was on the ground, and Mac, Laura, and the boys were walking around the lake. The boys ran ahead and Mac looked down at Laura. Each time she breathed, a small puff of water vapor appeared in front of her face. Fascinated, he couldn't stop watching the tiny clouds that formed out of nothing—each breath a separate proof of the miracle of life. She glanced up at him and smiled.

His attention turned to his boys, and he remembered another day, years before, when they had made a snowman in the front yard of their home. It had taken all three of them to roll the largest ball the last few feet. Then, they worked together to lift the second ball and place it on top of the first. Finally, each of them contributed something from his personal belongings to the snowman's head. Ben provided a pair of broken sunglasses with one lens missing. Zach donated a faded baseball cap. Mac added an old pipe that he'd never smoked.

The scene shifted. Mac was in a hurry to take his family home from the snowy lake. They were all in the four-wheel-drive vehicle. Even asleep, he knew what was coming, but in his unconscious state he could not stop the projector from flashing the scenes that came before his eyes. He looked at the boys sitting in the backseat. They were watching falling flakes out the windows. Laura reached out and laid her hand on his shoulder. His heart beat faster, and he tried to turn his head away from the pictures that started coming faster and faster. The line between dream and reality blurred. Mac gripped the steering wheel, slammed his foot down on the brake pedal, and prepared to yell a silent scream.

But instead of the familiar abyss of blood and blackness, Mac crashed into a realm of blinding light. As his eyes slowly grew accustomed to the brightness, he saw two figures walking steadily toward him. They stepped out of the light and stood before him.

It was Ben and Zach.

Without a doubt they were his sons. Mac devoured the vision of the only two people on earth who ever mirrored an image of himself. They were strong and handsome, with a maturity unknown even in those who aged many years on earth. They bore no hint of disappointment or regret that their days on earth had ended so early and abruptly. Their eyes reflected perfect peace. They were satisfied and complete.

But how?

Mac knew they heard his unspoken question, and the answer came without words directly to his own spirit. *Ultimate fulfillment and happiness are not based on length of days on earth or achievements recognized by flesh and blood but through relationship with the One who has redeemed us for eternal communion with himself.* His sons had entered into a different realm. They could not be marred by earth; they had been formed anew in heaven. They looked like him, but now, Mac wanted to look like them, to be transformed by the power of Jesus Christ.

They lifted their hands in blessing and washed away Mac's last reservations about the goodness of God. The impossible became possible. The incomprehensible became easy to understand. God causes all things to work together for good for those who love him, who are called according to his purpose. Ultimately, he would dry every tear, heal every hurt, restore everything that had been lost. Forever. His sons faded from view.

Laura's face took their place. She took his breath away. Even the minor imperfections of her natural appearance, though still present, were transformed into a graceful beauty. Her hair, her skin, her features, her eyes. Especially her eyes. She looked at him, and Mac saw the same love he'd seen in Anna's eyes, only richer, deeper, stronger. Laura loved him. More now than when they were together on earth. And he had to ask the question; he had to know the truth. He could not betray the love in her eyes for someone else.

Is it okay?

Her steady gaze never wavered as she received his request into her heart. She smiled and gave a slight nod of her head. Peace and affirmation swept over his soul. But he remained puzzled. How could one who loved him so absolutely release him to love another without jealousy or reservation? Something wasn't right. Once again, the answer came directly to his spirit. *The closest relationships on earth, the best friendships, the most intimate marriages are dim reflections of the love that all the Father's children have for one another in his kingdom.*

Mac was stunned. Someday he, Laura, and Anna would stand together with a vast host of God's children and share a mutual, unhindered love that transcended imagination and time. He would love them, they would love him, they would love one another—completely, and for all eternity.

He woke up and lay in bed replaying the vision again and again. He looked within the depths of his soul and knew that all was well. He was ready for tomorrow. Ready to live, ready to love.